GATTY'S TALE

By the same author

Gatty's Journey to Jerusalem

Hemesh Alles

Kevin Crossley-Holland's depiction of the medieval setting is meticulous, but ultimately this is a novel about heart and song, with the capacity to lift the spirits and move to tears.   *Bookseller*

'Crossley Holland's writing is superlative, bringing the medieval world sharply into focus. This really is a historical novel of distinction.'
       Publishing News

'This is an epic, sweeping book, perfectly realised. Crossley-Holland doesn't put a foot wrong. The language is spare and direct, never flamboyant, and yet it is energetic, vivid and always dynamic . . . in Gatty we find a heroine we really could follow to the end of time and back again.'   *Thebookbag.co.uk*

'skilfully wrought and compelling . . .'   *Inis*

'The heroine of this novel belongs to a medieval world as luminously coloured, as closely linked to nature and as drenched in spirituality as the illuminations in a book of hours . . . The medieval perception that the pattern of Christ's life is deeply imprinted on time and human life comes across beautifully.'   *The Tablet*

'It can't be long before the name Kevin Crossley-Holland is uttered in the same sentence as 'national institution'. His writing is evocative, lively and sharp; he brings history to life on the page so well that readers barely realise they are learning as well as enjoying fiction . . . There are moments when your eyes will brim with tears and when you feel inspired by such an audacious exercise to praise God. Throughout, you will be swept away.'   *Birmingham Post*

'Readers will be enchanted by this rich and fascinating book. It will gladden their hearts, test their compassion, fuel their thinking and challenge their assumptions about faith, life and humanity.'
       Write Away

GATTY'S TALE

KEVIN CROSSLEY-HOLLAND

Orion
Children's Books

First published in Great Britain in 2006
by Orion Children's Books
This paperback edition first published 2007
by Orion Children's Books
a division of the Orion Publishing Group Ltd
Orion House
5 Upper St Martin's Lane
London WC2H 9EA
An Hachette Livre UK Company

1 3 5 7 9 8 6 4 2

A catalogue record for this book
is available from the British Library.

ISBN 978 1 84255 570 5

Printed and bound in Great Britain by
Clays Ltd, St Ives plc

The Orion Publishing Group's policy is to use papers that
are natural, renewable and recyclable products and made
from wood grown in sustainable forests. The logging and
manufacturing processes are expected to conform to the
environmental regulations of the country of origin.

www.orionbooks.co.uk

for Linda – with love

THE CHARACTERS

THE PILGRIMS

Lady Gwyneth de Ewloe
Austin, *her priest*
Nest, *aged 17, her first chamber-servant*
Gatty, *aged 15, her second chamber-servant*
Snout, *the cook*
Emrys, *the stableman*
Tilda, *his wife, a wise-woman*
Nakin, *a Chester merchant*
Everard, *Chester cathedral choirmaster*

AT EWLOE

Crok, *an armed man*
Sir Robert de Montalt, *Lady Gwyneth's husband*
Llewelyn ap Iorwerth, *a Welsh warlord*
Griffith ap Robert, *Lady Gwyneth's baby son*

Armin, *a day-worker*
Simon, *the blacksmith*
Gruffydd, *the shoemaker*
Mansel, *his son*
Hew, *Snout's son, aged 5*

ON THE ROAD

Sayer, *a livery stablemaster in London*
Solomon, *his partner*
Syndod, *Gatty's Welsh cob*
Saviour, *Austin's horse*
John and Geoff, *two hired pilgrims*
A German envoy

A Norwegian merchant
A French nun
A monk *at Vézelay*
Sister Hilda, *a nun at Vézelay*
Aenor, *a novice at Vézelay*
The doctor's accomplices
An Alpine guide

THE CHARACTERS

Brother Benedict

The stablemaster at Treviso and his two daughters

Simona, *a translator*

Cinque and Sei, *her brothers*

Gianni Nurico, *a dentist*

Gobbo, *captain of a pilgrim ship*

Tiny, *an elephant*

A hospice nun in Venice

Alessandra Lupo, *a surgeon*

Three Saracen traders in Venice

Osman, *a Turkish astronomer*

Constance, *a sneak-thief*

Michael Scot, *a scholar*

Sir Umberto del Malaxa, *a Venetian landowner in Crete*

Mansur, *his Egyptian slave*

A justice in Cyprus

Babolo, *a Cypriot baby*

Brother Antony, *a monk at*

Saint Mary of the Mountain

A Saracen fisherman and his two sons

A snake-charmer in Acre

A conjuror in Acre

A wise man in Acre

Brother Gabriel, *a Knight Hospitaller*

Sir Faramond, *a Norman crusader*

Lady Saffiya, *his Saracen wife*

The Bedouin horsemen

Gregory, *a helper at the Hospital of Saint John*

Janet, *his wife*

A blind Jewish singer

Pilgrims, Saracens, traders, and a thief in the Church of the Holy Sepulchre

A young Saracen boy

Kit the Trader

Raven, *his brother*

THE CHARACTERS

AT CALDICOT

Sir John and Lady Helen de Caldicot

Sian, *their daughter, aged 12*
Oliver, *the priest*
Slim, *the cook*
Tanwen, *a chamber-servant*
Joan, *a village woman*
Macsen, *a day-worker*
Storm and Tempest, *two beagles*
Hopeless, *Gatty's cow*

Sir Walter and Lady Anne de Verdon
Winnie de Verdon, *aged 15*
Lord Stephen and Lady Judith de Holt
Lady Alice de Gortanore
Tom de Gortanore, *aged 18*
Merlin

Arthur de Caldicot (now Sir Arthur de Catmole)

AUTHOR'S NOTE AND ACKNOWLEDGEMENTS

Many people have helped Gatty on her long journey.

Hemesh Alles has mapped it with great charm and Christian Birmingham gave me a Venice anthology that has become an elbow-companion; David Cobb thoughtfully offered me his cottage as a retreat; Imogen Cooper introduced me to Saint Mary of the Mountain (Béllapais) and imagined Gatty seeking sanctuary there; John and David Crombie furnished me with medieval reading matter; Gillian Crossley-Holland made useful editorial suggestions and helped me to navigate the night sky, and she and my four children, Ellie and Oenone, Dominic and Kieran, have all buoyed me with the most lively interest and encouragement. Neil Curry sent me his memorable pilgrimage poems (now in print again) while Bruce Hunter, also an old Compostela hand, suggested valuable reading about pilgrimage; Nia Wyn Jones helped me with the Welsh language and ferreted out papers about the early history of the Manor of Ewloe; Leila al Karmy sent me Mary Fairclough's utterly magical *The Blue Tree*, set in medieval Persia; Saber Khan alerted me to books on the cultural history of walking; and with Edward Lucie-Smith I discussed medieval land ownership and social position. Janet Molyneux sent me Clare Leighton's wood-engraving, 'A Lapful of Windfalls' (1935), an image of Gatty so close to my own; kind Hew and Frances Purchas provided me with a light, quiet studio in which to write; Sam Roylance imaginatively gave me two books, both now well-thumbed, about medieval life; Isis Sturtewagen enquired into Gatty's daily activities at Ewloe; and Michelle Superle sent me Jamieson Findlay's horse-wise *The Blue Roan Child*. If I have anywhere unconsciously remembered and quoted (or misquoted!) a phrase from this or any other source, I trust its author will forgive me and regard it as a compliment.

Always rigorous in his thinking, always generous in his latitude to novelists and poets who make use of history, Richard Barber put a dose of wind in Gatty's sails, and lent me marvellous books on the medieval Muslim world. Jennifer Hamilton gave me inspiring tutorials on the singing voice and the teaching of singing. And Ann Jones has again generously helped me with matters Welsh – Gatty's cob is named after the beautiful animal that belonged to her family. To this list, already long, let me add the children and adults who wrote to me about Gatty after meeting her in my *Arthur* trilogy. Their curiosity fired and fed my own.

For me, a first draft is just that. In deciphering my manuscript, taking aboard wave upon wave of corrections and making shrewd editorial interventions – all with great good humour, accuracy and speed – Twiggy Bigwood has been a wonderful ally. I'm so grateful to her.

In Judith Elliott, I have a remarkable editor with an unfailing grasp of sweep and intention, and an eagle-eye for minutiae. We have worked together for thirty-three years, and her incisive, warm guidance has helped me to shape this story. I'm indebted to her, and to my spirited publisher Fiona Kennedy, as well as to Jane Hughes and so many of her colleagues at Orion, all of whom have given this book their most attentive and enthusiastic support.

This book bears my name but, truly, my wife Linda and I have undertaken Gatty's pilgrimage together. Often provocative, always persistent, she first suggested many of its twists and turns, and has made a quite exceptional contribution to its planning, psychology and revision. And more even than all this, she has empowered its author with her belief and love.

Chalk Hill, Burnham Market
May 2006

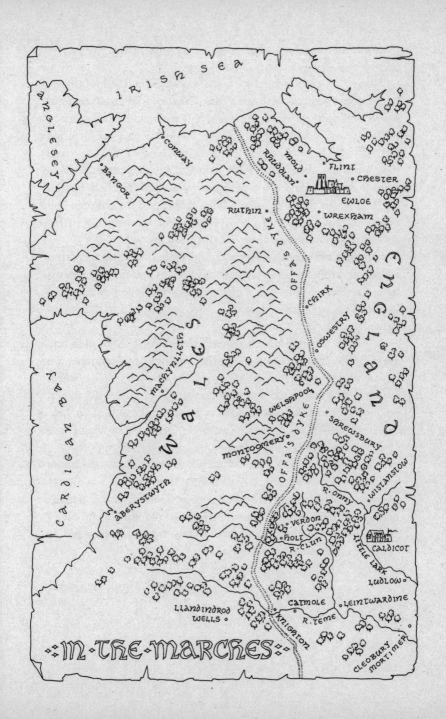

I

'Light of light! Oh, flight! Oh, flight!' trilled the early birds.

In one corner of the cow-stall, the heap of dirty sacking shifted. Something buried beneath it made a sound that began as a gentle murmur and ended as a grouse.

Then the cock crowed and that loosed the tongues of his disciples. Half the neighers and brayers and bleaters and grunters in the manor of Caldicot welcomed the day's dawning, chill and misty as it was.

As soon as Hopeless joined in and mooed, the heap of sacking shrugged and then tossed. In one fluid movement, Gatty stood up, crossed herself, reached for her russet woollen tunic lying on a bale of hay, and pulled it on over her undershirt and baggy drawers. Loudly she yawned. She opened her mouth so wide she could hear all her little head-bones cricking and cracking. Then she stepped round to the next stall.

'Greetings in God!' she said politely to her cow. She gave Hopeless a handful of grain, pulled up her three-legged stool, and began to milk her.

The air in the cow-shed somehow smelt thick and fresh at the same time. Rank with gluey dung and musty straw, but also rinsed with the cool, clean breath of late September, that time of year when the weather begins to sharpen its teeth.

Gatty had chosen to sleep there since her father and then her grandmother had died. After all, Hopeless was company of a sort, and Gatty preferred it to sleeping in her little two-roomed cottage on her own.

So Gatty was alone in this middle-world. There was no one to look after her, and no one for her to look after. And since Arthur de Caldicot had left the Marches to join the great crusade, for two years at least, he said, for two years and maybe three, there was no one whom Gatty could really talk to and laugh with, no one to whom she could open her heart.

But soon after her father died, Gatty had begun to sing. She sang to herself the songs she heard villagers singing as they worked in the fields, love songs sung by travelling musicians, carols for dancing, charms. Not only those! She listened to the choirs of birds and the harping wind and made up her own green songs.

As Gatty filled her pail with bubbling milk, she crooned a milking-song. She could feel how Hopeless liked it. Then, before carrying the pail up to Slim, the cook, in the manor kitchen, she went back into her sleeping-stall, yawning and rubbing her eyes, scrubbing her gold-and-silver curls with her rough fingertips. Gatty stepped over to the water-trough, and made a stoup of her hands – and at this moment she heard the sound of running footsteps.

Almost at once, Sian de Caldicot hurtled through the door of the cow-shed, yelling, 'Gatty! Gatty! Where are you?'

Gatty smiled to herself. She waited a little, and then mooed loudly.

Sian put her head into the stall. 'Here you are!' she exclaimed. 'Gatty! I've been looking for you everywhere.'

'And all!' said Gatty, cheerfully.

Sian stared at the mess of sacking. 'You don't sleep in here?'

Gatty sniffed.

'Do you?'

'What's it look like?' asked Gatty.

'Yuch!' said Sian. 'It's horrible.'

'It's not,' said Gatty. 'Not with Hopeless.'

'And mice and beetles and spiders and . . .' Sian stood on her left foot and tried to twirl round and lost her balance and fell against Gatty, laughing. 'Sir John wants to see you,' she announced. 'After you've taken the milk up to Slim.'

Gatty stiffened. 'Me?'

'I don't know why,' Sian went on. 'He never tells me anything.'

Why does Sir John want to see me, Gatty wondered. What have I done or got to do? Gatty shook her head. I can't do no more, I can't. Not unless God makes each day longer.

'I haven't told my father about us,' said Sian, 'if that's what you're thinking.'

'What about us?' Gatty asked.

'Snaring that rabbit in Pike Forest,' said Sian, 'or about tying the dogs' tails together.'

Gatty half-smiled and compressed her pretty lips – the lower one was quite puffy, as if it were bee-stung.

'You're the best, Gatty!' said Sian with some force. 'You are, now that Arthur's gone. Come on!'

2

Sir John de Caldicot inspected his field-girl. 'So, Gatty, are you always hard-working?'

'I'd starve if I weren't,' said Gatty.

'Except when you're off on some wild goose chase.'

Gatty stared at her chapped knuckles, her earth-stained fingertips. Inside her sackcloth, she began to feel smaller than she really was, and she gave Sir John a doleful look.

'What have I done, sir?' she asked.

Sir John waved at Gatty to sit down on the bench opposite him. 'You're fifteen, aren't you? When's your birthday?'

'Just after the harvest, sir. That's what my father said.'

'Yes, and you're alone now. No one to care for. No one to feed.'

'Hopeless,' said Gatty.

'What?'

'Hopeless,' she said. 'And my seven chickens.'

Gatty glared into the fire.

'We each have our place in this middle-world,' said Sir John. 'Children have duties to their parents, field-men and field-women have duties to their lord. Isn't that so?'

'Yes, sir.'

'And I have duties to the king,' Sir John said. 'Now this is most unusual, I know. But what with you being only fifteen, and Arthur's friend . . . well, for one reason and another I've decided to help you.'

Gatty knitted her brows.

'I want you to work here, in the manor house. In the kitchen with Slim.'

Gatty blinked and swallowed. Her mouth suddenly felt dry.

'Well?'

'I don't know how.'

'Don't know how?'

'I don't know almost nothing.'

'You've got wits, haven't you?' said Sir John. 'You can learn.'

'I can learn you about earth,' Gatty said, 'and the weather-clouds, and hares boxing, and high nests, and why them pigs . . .'

'No doubt,' said Sir John.

'. . . why they won't eat mast some days, and what . . .'

'Will you listen!' Sir John insisted. 'I'm not talking about that.'

Gatty lowered her eyes and her long eyelashes trembled.

'I'm talking,' said Sir John, 'about you working here in the manor kitchen. Working with Slim. That's what you're going to do, and you should think yourself blessed.'

So Gatty learned to slice and dice and knead and spice and seethe and baste and roast and all the other kitchen-skills, and it was much easier work than out in the heavy fields. It's warm in here half the time, she thought. And it's dry. I don't get soaked, and my back doesn't ache. But what about when it's spring and all the shoots and blades are pushing up again? What about when all the birds are whistling?

Gatty often sang to herself as she worked. She did feel blessed. But all the same, she chose not to sleep in the hall – she didn't feel she belonged there. Each evening, still singing to herself, she went back to her own cottage to check whether the chickens had laid any eggs, and then slept with Hopeless in the cow-shed.

'That girl!' said Oliver the priest a couple of weeks later, blinking and shaking his bald head. 'You've heard her sing?'

'Half the time,' said Sir John.

'Like a Welsh girl,' Lady Helen said.

'Even better!' said the priest. He drew himself up to his full height, such as it was, and laced his pudgy fingers over his stomach. 'She's untrained, of course, but she has the voice of an angel. An apprentice angel.'

Sir John rubbed his nose thoughtfully. 'I wouldn't know,' he said.

'In fact,' said Oliver, 'I'm beginning to think she should enter a nunnery.'

'Dear Lord!' said Sir John.

'Sister Gatty!' exclaimed Lady Helen.

'She should enter a nunnery,' said Oliver, who never said a thing once when he could say it twice, 'where she can be taught and give her voice back to God.' The priest took a deep breath and permitted himself a small smile. 'Yes!' he said. 'Yes! A little March miracle!'

'They're grasping, those harridans,' Sir John objected. 'Avaricious, that's what they are. They'd want me to pay outright for board, lodging, clothing, reading lessons, singing lessons, I don't know what. They'd charge you for the sunlight if they could figure out how.'

'Like all you English!' said Lady Helen.

'Anyhow,' said Sir John, 'they wouldn't be in the least keen to have Gatty, seeing as she's a field-girl. A scullion.'

'What about her voice, then?' asked Lady Helen.

Sir John sniffed. 'Brides of Christ! They're old crows. Rapacious crows.'

In early November, Lady Helen rode north with Tanwen, her chamber-servant, to visit her widowed cousin, Lady Gwyneth de Ewloe, and when she came home after three weeks she reported that Lady Gwyneth was in search of a second chamber-servant.

'Well?' said Sir John. 'What am I meant to do about it? Find one under a hedgerow?'

'What about Gatty!' said Lady Helen. 'I promised I'd ask you. Gwyneth's leaving on a pilgrimage, and she needs a second girl.'

'Poor Gatty!' said Sir John. 'Not the shrine of another dismal Welsh saint. Not another mossy, dripping well.'

Lady Helen shook her head.

'Where then?' asked Sir John.

'Je-ru-sa-lem,' said Lady Helen, articulating each syllable.

'God in heaven!' shouted Sir John. 'Jerusalem! What's got into the woman?'

'And she says Gatty's voice should help to keep everyone safe,' Lady Helen added.

'Keep them safe!' exclaimed Sir John. 'Armed men keep people safe – not singing.'

'Gwyneth said she could do with her at once.'

'She'll have to wait,' said Sir John. 'We need Gatty's help here over Yuletide. Macsen can ride north with her the morning after Epiphany.'

When Lady Helen told Gatty about going north to Ewloe, Gatty said, 'I don't know nothing about chamber-servants and all that.'

'You can learn, then.'

Gatty looked doubtfully at Lady Helen under her long lashes.

What daunted Gatty was not so much her duties as a chamber-servant as the thought of leaving Caldicot. Leaving her lifelong friends. Leaving Hopeless who always mooed to tell Gatty to feed her. Leaving her strip of land in Nine Elms, the one she and her father had worked side by side for as long as she could remember. Leaving the glinting clods and the high rookery, the way the cool dawn air fingered her hairline, the way the setting sun bled over Wales. Gatty had never travelled further than Ludlow in her whole life, where she went to the fair with Arthur.

'Lady Gwyneth is going on a pilgrimage,' Lady Helen told Gatty, 'and she means to take you.'

'Where?' asked Gatty.

'Jerusalem!'

'Jerusalem!' Gatty exclaimed. 'Where Jesus was?'

'The Holy Land,' said Lady Helen.

'Will I see Arthur, then?' she asked eagerly.

'That girl!' Sir John said later to Lady Helen. 'So raw! She has no idea whatsoever of all the dangers and terrors awaiting her.'

Lady Helen shook her head. 'Just as well, maybe!' she said in her sing-song voice.

'Jerusalem!' Sir John exclaimed. 'She'll be lucky to get there alive, let alone back home again.'

3

Yuletide.
It came in at a trot, broke into a canter, and left at a gallop.

It was different for Gatty this year, though. For the first time in her life, her father was not blowing the pipe and banging the tabor, leading Slim into the hall; Arthur was far away; and in twelve days' time, she herself would be leaving Caldicot.

Standing in the kitchen with both hands inside a Christmas duck, trying to grasp its slimy gizzards, Gatty suddenly wondered where she would be on the next Christmas Eve:

> Will I be standing in the manger?
> Will I be kneeling at His crib?
> I got no gift I can bring,
> But I can sing . . . I'll bring songs!

'Gatty!' roared Slim. 'What's wrong with you? Standing there like a headless . . .'

Gatty shook her head.

'Get a move on!' barked the cook. 'Jesus is waiting!'

As usual, the priest Oliver treated everyone to a particularly lengthy sermon. He reminded his flock that their hearts were like cradles, waiting for Jesus to be born. 'And if it's God's will,' he went on, 'one of our flock, one of our own Caldicot flock, will reach the Golden Gate. She will stand inside the Church of the Holy Sepulchre, the most holy place in holy Jerusalem.'

Gatty listened, and she felt that Oliver wasn't really talking about her at all but about some stranger.

'Let us pray for Gatty and her great pilgrimage,' Oliver said. 'May she pray for each one of us at each of the holy places.'

On Saint Stephen's day, Caldicot had visitors, Winnie de Verdon and her father, Sir Walter.

They arrived early, in time to join the games, and when they stepped into the hall, the first thing Gatty noticed was Winnie's half of her and Arthur's betrothal penny, strung on a cord around her neck.

The first thing Sian noticed, though, was Winnie's exquisite white fur mittens.

'Where did you get them?' she exclaimed. 'They look like Spitfire did. My cat!'

Winnie turned pink, and shook the mittens off. 'I don't like them, anyhow,' she said. 'They're too tight. Like my betrothal ring.'

'I love Arthur,' Sian declared. 'I wish I could marry him.'

'Well, you can't!' said Winnie. 'I'm not going to wait for ever, though.'

'You can marry my cousin Tom,' Sian went on. 'He said he'd be glad to marry you if Arthur doesn't come back.'

Winnie smiled.

'Winnie!' said Sir Walter. 'Have you even greeted Sir John and Lady Helen?'

Winnie curtsied, she clasped hands, she smiled, she said the right words, but she didn't so much as incline her head to Gatty.

She didn't even notice her.

Gatty was breathless. Her mouth was dry and there was such a knot in her throat.

She had heard all about the betrothal from Sian, of course, but this was the first time she had ever seen Winnie, face to face.

'Arthur told me about the games,' Winnie said blithely. 'He said . . . I . . . he said I . . .'

Gatty's heart ached so. She pressed her right hand against it. She turned away and, as she hurried into the kitchen, her eyes filled with tears.

Gatty was usually the first girl home when everyone chased three times round the Yard but this year she only came fourth. With Sian as her partner, though, she did win the three-legged race. And she was the only girl to lift the great mottled stone and, with her wrist bent right back, balance it on her right hand.

'I been watching you,' Joan the village-woman said. 'Your heart's only half in it.'

'I know,' acknowledged Gatty.

'Do what you do with your whole heart, girl,' Joan told her. 'It's not worth nothing otherwise.'

But Gatty kept thinking about Arthur and going away. Away from everyone, away from everything she had known since the day she was born.

All day Gatty kept her distance from Winnie, her sharp words and flashing betrothal ring, her flame of hair, her wide-sleeved gown and grass-green shoes.

In her stained sackcloth, and untanned boots, Gatty felt as if her own friendship with Arthur didn't really exist. She felt so worthless.

Yuletide! Yes, there was the time to snuggle down under the skins, to doze and dawdle and stretch and yawn; time to listen to the sound of one's own slow breathing. But how soon the twelve days were over.

On the last morning, Gatty carried her squawking

chickens one by one to Sir John's run, and drove Hopeless up to Sir John's byre. She put her arms right round her cow's neck, and felt her calm warmth; then Gatty gave a long moo, soft as the bottom-most notes of a flute and, with an aching heart, walked away.

In the afternoon, Gatty found Oliver in the church vestry. He was sitting at his sloping desk, his feet on a footstool, writing on a piece of parchment.

'There you are!' said Gatty.

'In the service of the Lord,' Oliver replied.

'Oliver, can you write a message for me? Please.'

'Can I or will I?'

'Will you?'

Oliver looked dimly at Gatty. 'To whom?'

'Arthur!'

Oliver smiled. 'There's a surprise,' he said. 'Well, you're in luck. I've one small piece of parchment left over from my labours. My morning labours.'

'Who are you writing to?' asked Gatty.

'Lady Gwyneth's priest.'

'Why? What about?'

Oliver completed the character and then the word he was writing. Then he rolled up the little scroll and gave it to Gatty.

'Keep it safe and dry,' he told her. 'This letter could make all the difference.'

'To what?'

'You'll find out,' said Oliver. 'Now! What's your message?'

'Ready?' asked Gatty. '*Where are you today I keep wondering. I often talk to you and see you easy.*'

'Easily,' said Oliver.

'No,' said Gatty. 'Easy.'

'Easy is wrong,' said Oliver.

'Not for me,' Gatty replied. 'Please Oliver! Write what I say. Then Arthur will hear me.'

12

Oliver pressed his lips together. 'Go on, then,' he said.

'*You got the sky on your shoulders,*' Gatty dictated. '*You remember when I said let's go to Jerusalem? I can't explain but somehow I thought it, I believed it, and now I'm going. You and your singing will keep us all safe, Lady Gwyneth says. Arthur, when are you coming back? I haven't forgot . . .*'

'Forgotten,' said Oliver.

Gatty gently shook her head and then, very boldly, she laid the flat of her right hand on Oliver's back.

Oliver sniffed.

'*. . . I haven't forgot going upstream. You promised. Or you can ride to Ewloe. Them bulls, and me wearing Sir John's armour and rescuing Sian from the fish-pond and going to Ludlow Fair, and everything . . . It's true! It is. Best things don't never get lost.*'

Oliver looked up at Gatty, so eager, her eyes shining. He knitted his brows. 'Just what are you to Arthur?' he enquired.

'Me? To Arthur? What do you mean?' And then, with a smile and a little shrug, Gatty said, 'True.'

'Yes,' said Oliver. 'True.' He wrote four more words, and voiced them as he wrote.

'*By your true Gatty . . .*'

'There you are!' said Oliver. 'That's your letter.'

'Will you keep it and give it to him?' Gatty asked. 'When he gets home.'

'If he gets home,' the priest replied.

'He will,' said Gatty.

'Some do,' the priest said. 'Most don't.'

'I know what,' said Gatty. Then she untied the violet ribbon she wore day and night round her waist, the one Arthur had bought for her with his last farthing at Ludlow Fair. She doubled it, tore at it with her teeth and bit it in half.

'Really!' said Oliver, wrinkling his nose.

'Half for him, half for me,' said Gatty.

So Oliver rolled up the little piece of parchment and Gatty secured it with the violet ribbon.

Gatty took a deep breath, and noisily blew out her pink, freckled cheeks. 'There!' she exclaimed. 'Writing and all!'

She smiled brightly at Oliver and then she wound her half of the violet ribbon round and round her left wrist.

4

Oliver was ringing the church bell as Gatty rode out of Caldicot and she wondered why. Steady and unhurried, neither eager nor forlorn, the bell rang and rang, and it never once occurred to her that Oliver was ringing it especially for her.

For a long while, Gatty and Macsen rode side by side in silence and then Gatty gave a heartfelt sigh.

'You all right, girl?' Macsen asked.

Gatty was not all right. Her strength was bleeding out of her as she left the only place she knew. She couldn't get the strange idea out of her head that the Marches and her body were one: this earth was her mother, and she was mother-earth.

When at noon they reached the Great Dyke, Gatty and Macsen entered a no-man's land. A hovering grey mist blotted out the sun, turned trees into roaming spirits and one-legged giants brandishing clubs, and lay on the earth on either side of the Great Dyke like a vast wraith-ocean.

For three days they rode north, and late the first afternoon they reached Montgomery just before the dark rose up out of England and clamped down over Wales. There they stayed in the damp castle guesthouse. The second day was little brighter than the first. They passed paddock and stream and twitchel, cefn, rhyd and pandy, each with its own name and unsung story. When the rain came on, Gatty checked that Oliver's parchment letter was dry in her saddlebag. Then

Macsen's horse lost a shoe, and Gatty got the squits, and they were unable to reach Chirk before dark. So they slept in a shepherd's little crouching hut, and instead of the herring and bread and beer Macsen had promised, he and Gatty had to fill their wooden mugs with stream water, and suck and chew bacon rind, and eat their last gobbets of stale ewe's cheese, crumb by crumb, as if they were the greatest delicacy in the world.

'What's she like, then?' Gatty asked. 'Lady Gwyneth?'

Macsen stared at Gatty through the gloom, and then pinched his nose.

'What? She stinks?'

Macsen shook his head.

'Perfumed, you mean.'

'High and mighty, like they all are. She's got a sharp tongue. She's Welsh.'

This was the most Macsen had said during the entire journey, but then he relapsed into his usual silence, and Gatty was unable to tempt him further.

After coming down from the Great Dyke at noon on the third day, Gatty and Macsen turned east again, and for the first time in three days the hazy sun blessed them. Down they rode from the high fields and farms, with their huge flocks of sheep and yapping sheepdogs, down into a sopping forest, and somehow their two horses sensed the journey was almost over. They raised their tucked heads; they whisked their tails.

Gatty stared ahead. Nothing but trunks, some silver, some grey-green, some ivied, some carbuncled, nothing but a prison of tree-trunks stretching to the end of the world. But then there was something.

A handsome high wall, brown as an eggshell and speckled, with teeth along the top. Five peephole windows, four of them slits but one round as the full moon.

*

Side by side, Gatty and Macsen rode across the drawbridge. They dismounted and walked up to the huge ribbed oak door.

Macsen jabbed at it twice with his staff.

'Should have warned you,' he said.

'What?'

A metal nose poked through a small opening in the door; then teeth grated in the lock and the door creaked half-open. Two large men blocked the entrance.

'Arms out!' one man shouted. 'Legs apart!'

Then a third man barged out and searched Macsen.

'Go on, girl!' the first man said. 'Arms out!'

The other man put his hands on Gatty's shoulders, and slid them straight down over her body.

'Hands off!' protested Gatty.

'Ooh-oh! Who do you think you are? Queen of Sheba?'

Gatty kicked the man in the shins, and he yelped.

'Waargh! You little shrew!'

The first man just laughed. 'Serve you right!' he said.

'I'm Macsen,' said Macsen. 'Remember? From Lady Helen.'

'Orders is orders,' the first man replied. 'No one enters this hall without he's searched.'

Gatty stepped into the hall, and she caught her breath.

She saw Lady Gwyneth at once, standing at the far end of the hall, very tall and slender and fair, with a girl on her right and a big man on her left, but in that same first long moment she saw the kind tapestries hanging on the walls and the soft honey-light of dozens and dozens of candles, she smelt scents sweeter and thicker than Fallow Field in June, she heard a cascade of notes, more notes than a climbing lark sings in May, and saw another man plucking an instrument with a forest of strings.

Then Gatty let go of her breath again, and Lady Gwyneth

turned to her, took two steps towards her, and inclined her head.

Had Gatty been able to look at herself through Lady Gwyneth's eyes, what would she have seen?

A grubby parcel of sackcloth and, sticking out of the top, a freckled and dirt-streaked face; large river eyes, set quite wide apart; and a storm of curls, now in the candlelight more silver than gold.

Gatty shuffled towards Lady Gwyneth, and grinned.

'God's bones!' she exclaimed. 'I never knew there was no place like this.'

Lady Gwyneth looked, unblinking, at this creature standing before her.

'Gatty!' she said. 'It is Gatty, isn't it?'

'That's me,' Gatty agreed, and as she nodded each of her curls seemed to have a life of its own.

Lady Gwyneth de Ewloe tilted her head slightly to the right. 'Yes,' she said. 'I rather thought so. You and . . .' she hesitated, and her pale brow creased. 'You and . . .'

'Macsen,' Gatty said in a loud voice. 'Saxon, I call him!'

'Welcome back,' Lady Gwyneth told Macsen.

'We was searched,' Gatty complained, raising her mittened hands and running them down her front.

Lady Gwyneth pursed her shapely lips. 'Precautions!' she said. 'Those *Sais*!'

'Sais?' asked Gatty.

'Saxons. You can't be too careful'.

Gatty wagged her finger at Macsen. 'Hear that, you?' she said.

A smile hovered around the corners of Lady Gwyneth's mouth. 'You do both look rather the worse for wear,' she said.

'Mucky!' said the pretty girl standing behind Lady Gwyneth.

Gatty frowned. 'No,' she said. 'I'm Gatty.'

'I said mucky. *Baw isa'r domen*! That's what you are.'

'That's enough, Nest,' Lady Gwyneth said sharply. 'How do you think you'd look after three days travelling?'

'In January,' sniffed Macsen.

'Quite so,' said Lady Gwyneth.

All at once, Gatty felt most terribly tired. She opened her mouth so wide she could have swallowed half the hall, and gave a noisy yawn.

Lady Gwyneth lowered her eyes. 'Up here, Gatty, we cover our mouths when we yawn.'

Gatty looked quite mystified. 'What for?' she asked.

Lady Gwyneth smiled. 'This is Nest,' she said, 'my first chamber-servant. And this is Snout, my cook.'

Snout nodded in a friendly way and raised his right paw. He was a large man with a mop of copper-coloured hair, and eyes to match. But the most striking thing about him was the way his upper lip was split halfway up to his flaring nostrils.

'We were just about to kneel for my retiring prayer,' Lady Gwyneth said. 'Will you join us? We will say it in English.'

Around the fire they all knelt, and in her clean, light voice, that seemed to sharpen each syllable, Lady Gwyneth prayed:

'May groaning Sword Wood and Wepre Wood praise you,
May the speckled quarries praise you,
May the hills of Clwyd rise and praise you,
Clod, grain, bough, bud, may each one praise you,
May each one of your children praise you
As, Shining Lord, we greet you in this hall.'

Lady Gwyneth got to her feet and, wearily, Gatty and Macsen followed her.

'Now,' said Lady Gwyneth. 'First things first. Warm fingers. Warm toes. And you, Snout, find our guests some food and ale.'

'I certainly will, my lady,' said Snout, and when he spoke he sounded as if he had a cold.

Gatty rubbed her red eyelids, and wiped her dripping nose on her sleeve.

'Yes,' said Lady Gwyneth. 'Well, we'll talk in the morning.'

5

Nest screwed up her pretty face. 'Lady Gwyneth says you're to have a bath first,' she told Gatty. 'Then you should go up and talk to her.'

Gatty burst into laughter. 'A bath!' she exclaimed. 'Me!'

So before noon, Snout the cook warmed vats of water in the castle kitchen. Then he and the kitchen-boy carried them into the hall and Gatty had a bath, the first one in her life.

What warmth! What heat! It made Gatty stretch each limb, like a cat. Before long it made her yawn and yawn again. It seemed to make her stronger and weaker, both at the same time.

While Gatty was lying in the tub, naked as a needle, Snout and the kitchen-boy arrived with another vat of seething water, and they tried to walk right in. Nest shouted at them, and blocked the way, so they put it down and retreated, laughing. Then Nest told Gatty to pull up her legs, and she tipped it into the tub herself.

'Here,' she said, giving Gatty a small pot. 'Mutton fat soap. I made it with my own fair hands. Now scrub yourself all over.'

Ruefully, Gatty inspected her own chapped red knuckles and the grime under her nails. It's true, she thought drowsily, Nest's hands are fair.

Nest picked up a pair of tongs from the hearth. 'Your clothes are filthy,' she said. 'How could you have slept in them?'

'What are you doing?' asked Gatty, alarmed.

'Burning them.'

'No!' cried Gatty.

'They're disgusting.'

'I haven't got none others.'

'Ugh!' exclaimed Nest, and she grabbed Gatty's clothes and threw them into the fire anyway. 'Lady Gwyneth says I'm to lend you a gown,' she said. 'Look at you! I've never seen such revolting, scummy water.'

Gatty rose from the tub, pink and white and shiny, like a nymph from a pool. 'I'm as clean as a cat's tongue,' she carolled. 'No, as clean as a conker. You know, when it's just split out of its mucky old shell.'

'This is my solar,' Lady Gwyneth told Gatty. 'It's where I sit when I want to be alone, or to talk to someone without being interrupted.'

'I never been up to Lady Helen's and Sir John's,' Gatty remarked.

'It's quite small,' said Lady Gwyneth. 'Well, everything at Caldicot is quite small, really.'

Gatty looked around. 'It's secret in here,' she observed. 'You know, like petals and dust have settled for years and no one hasn't disturbed them.'

Lady Gwyneth looked at Gatty with interest. 'You're right,' she agreed. 'Petals and dust, and thoughts and feelings. Now, then. Let's begin at the beginning.'

'What's that?'

'Your mother. Tell me about her.'

'Can't,' said Gatty. 'She died birthing Dusty. And he died when he started laughing and choked himself, and he was born two years after me, he was.'

'I see,' said Lady Gwyneth. 'And your father?'

Gatty lowered her eyes. 'He died last spring, with pains in

his stomach. He said it was like an army of elves was jabbing their spears inside him.' Gatty swallowed noisily. 'Sir John's reeve, he was.'

'Oh Gatty!' said Lady Gwyneth. 'What was he like?'

And so, piece by piece, Lady Gwyneth began to put together the jigsaw of Gatty's life: her parents, her brother, her field-work at Caldicot, her duties in the manor kitchen. But not the piece about her friendship with Arthur. Gatty hugged that to herself.

'I got something for your priest,' said Gatty, fishing into the swinging, outsize woollen gown Nest had lent her, and pulling out a little roll of parchment. 'Oliver wrote it.'

'And who is Oliver?'

'Our priest.'

Lady Gwyneth unrolled the parchment, and as she read she moved her lips without voicing the words. 'Yes,' she said, 'your Oliver would like my priest, Austin, to teach you to read.'

'Read!'

'Yes, Gatty.'

'I couldn't never do that.'

'Why not?'

'Not me. I'm only a field-girl. Well, I was!'

'Oliver says here that Lady Helen wants you to learn . . .'

'No one at Caldicot can,' said Gatty. 'Except for Oliver and Arthur.'

'. . . and so does Sir John,' Lady Gwyneth added.

Gatty jammed her right forefinger against her temple and shook her head. 'I don't know almost nothing,' she said, grinning.

'As it happens,' Lady Gwyneth said, 'Austin is already teaching Nest to read, so maybe he can teach you at the same time.'

'God's gristle!' exclaimed Gatty, and she leaped to her feet and laughed for sheer joy. 'Me! Learning to read!'

'My chamber-servants need to be able to read,' Lady Gwyneth said.

'But you can read yourself,' said Gatty.

'Not for long,' Lady Gwyneth replied. 'The words begin to hop around, and stars and little black shapes float across them.'

'Like clouds, you mean?'

'Anyhow,' Lady Gwyneth said, 'there are few joys greater than being read to.'

Gatty sat down again, then bounced on the bench. 'I'll read to you,' she said. 'I'll read to you for ever.'

Lady Gwyneth smiled. 'Very good,' she said.

Gatty looked around the solar, wide-eyed. She gazed at Lady Gwyneth.

'What is it, Gatty?'

Gatty sniffed at her wrist and the sleeve of her gown. 'I'm that clean I don't even smell like me,' she said. 'I don't look like me. I don't feel like me, up here with you.'

'I understand,' Lady Gwyneth replied. 'But you'll get used to it. You'll grow into it. Now, who is going to teach you to sit right and breathe right and tighten your stomach and relax your throat?'

Gatty frowned. 'I know how to breathe right,' she said.

'Yes,' said Lady Gwyneth. 'I've heard all about your voice, and I know who can teach you to sing.'

'Lady Helen told me what you said,' Gatty said.

'What was that?' asked Lady Gwyneth. 'What did I say?'

'About helping to keep us all safe.'

'Helping to keep us all safe,' Lady Gwyneth slowly repeated.

'You didn't say that?' Gatty faltered. 'Did you?'

Lady Gwyneth smiled. 'I told Helen your singing would be like a charm. Like a spell.'

Gatty puffed her cheeks and blew out all the air. 'Why are we going to Jerusalem, anyway?' she asked.

'My lady,' said Lady Gwyneth.

'What?'

'When you speak to me, that's what you must say, to show respect. My lady.'

'I keep forgetting,' Gatty said. 'I can't help it. My lady.'

'Do you know what a pilgrimage is?' Lady Gwyneth asked.

'A journey,' said Gatty.

'It is,' Lady Gwyneth said.

'My lady!'

'What, Gatty?'

'A journey, my lady,' said Gatty, her eyes as wide as draught-pieces.

'And great pilgrimages are long journeys. To England's own Nazareth, the shrine of Our Lady of Walsingham. Over the mountains, to Rome. To the grave of Saint James, in Spain. And by far the longest and greatest of all, the pilgrimage to Jerusalem.'

'It's dangerous, isn't it?' Gatty said. 'Robbers and Saracens and beasts, and that.'

'It is,' Lady Gwyneth said. 'Any pilgrim who wishes to travel to Jerusalem must be prepared to carry Jesus's cross. But I tell you, Gatty, the more dangerous the way, the more likely God is to forgive our sins. Our terrible wrongdoing. The more likely He is to heal our grief.'

Gatty could hear the quaver in Lady Gwyneth's voice and was quite startled.

'Yes, Gatty,' said Lady Gwyneth. 'I've seen death too. Griffith! Griffith ap Robert. My own little baby.'

'My lady,' said Gatty, so tender and sorrowful.

Lady Gwyneth gazed at the little horn-window, and the two of them listened to the January wind bumping into it and something outside the window, tapping and scratching.

Lady Gwyneth took Gatty's warm right hand and led her to the window. 'That's where he's buried,' she said. 'Down there, near the lych-gate, so I can watch over him. He was only eleven weeks old.'

Gatty shook her head. 'Little Luke,' she said, 'Lady Helen's son, he was only ten months.'

'To kiss the earth of Jerusalem!' Lady Gwyneth said. 'To see with my own eyes all the holy places. To see where He walked and died and rose again. I believe my pilgrimage will bring me forgiveness so that, one day, in heaven, I'll hold Griffith in my arms.'

'My lady,' said Gatty, 'if a mother can see her child again, do you think a child can see her mother again?'

'What do you mean, Gatty?'

'I mean, if God forgives me too, can I see my mother again?'

For a moment, Lady Gwyneth was silent. 'Pray for that,' she said quietly. The lines of her face softened, and in that moment Gatty saw how she and Lady Helen looked like beans from the same pod.

Gatty sighed a little, and then smiled. 'You won't be sorry,' she said. 'Taking me. I'll make sure of that.'

'My lady.'

'My lady,' Gatty repeated. 'Nest don't like me, though. Not from the first. I can tell.'

'First impressions are not always true impressions,' Lady Gwyneth replied.

'I'll rub along with her. I'll learn to.'

'You must,' said Lady Gwyneth. 'You have more in common with her than you realise.'

Gatty frowned.

'Neither of you has a mother or father. Nest's seventeen – two years older than you. Her father was the steward at Rhuddlan.'

'What's a steward?' asked Gatty.

'In charge of the household and all the servants,' Lady Gwyneth explained. 'When Nest was only eleven, he and Nest's mother were both burned to death when part of the castle caught fire.'

'Oh!' gasped Gatty.

'That was when I agreed to take on Nest as my young servant, and to care for her and educate her. And like her, Gatty, you must learn manners and obedience.'

'And all!' cried Gatty, enthusiastically. 'Is it just you and Nest and me, then?'

'Three people? No, of course not! There'll be nine.'

'Nine!' exclaimed Gatty, and she quickly counted the number on her fingers.

'You and Nest and Snout and me . . . Soon enough, you'll know everyone.'

'Nothing's not soon enough!' Gatty said.

'Now,' said Lady Gwyneth, 'go and find Nest in the hall. Ask her to tell you your dressing duties.'

After Gatty had left the solar, Lady Gwyneth remained sitting on her padded bench, thinking.

So eager, so staunch and somehow gay: Lady Gwyneth recognised all these qualities in Gatty, and she liked them. But so simple. So very ignorant. And so earthy. True, she thought, Gatty can learn. But she's impulsive, too. She's wilful. Lady Gwyneth bit her left cheek, concerned that Gatty might upset the other pilgrims in the party.

6

All night the north-west wind barged and bumped into Ewloe Castle. It slipped its icy fingers into the hall – one through the keyhole, another through a crack in one of the oak beams and another through a split in the daub. It found Gatty, lying beside the fire-pit, and just touched her forehead and pinched her nose.

Gatty tucked her knees into her chest. But it was no good. She couldn't get warm, and she couldn't get to sleep. She drowsed, only to be woken by the manor timbers groaning, or Nest coughing, or by an eerie whistling from somewhere up in the roof. Once, Gatty sat bolt upright, terrified that a grinning dark elf had let down a hook from the rafters, and caught her by the stomach, and was going to draw out her entrails.

Gatty wrapped her gown more tightly round her shoulders. Clasping her hands across her stomach, she rolled over again and tried to sleep.

It was one of those days that almost decided not to dawn. The reluctant light came seeping from the east. When Gatty made her way down to the church with Lady Gwyneth and Nest, they were surrounded by little swirls of skittish white dancers.

Most of Ewloe's field-women and field-men were already waiting for them, glad on a bone-cold morning not to have to haul fallen branches home from the forest, dress blocks of sandstone, and to do all those other back-breaking jobs that have to be done while the fields lie low at the end of the year. All the members of Lady Gwyneth's household were there too. Snout put Hew, five years old now, on his broad shoulders. He had lovingly looked after his little son from the day his young wife had died three years before.

With her right hand, Lady Gwyneth cupped Gatty's left elbow, and then, for just a moment, she put her arm round Gatty. Quite why, Gatty had no idea, but she found herself thinking of Hopeless and how, early each morning, her cow always took her first mouthful of grain out of Gatty's own hand before dropping her nose into the bucket. Who's feeding her and talking to her now, she wondered? Her eyeballs grew hot with the tears behind them.

Lady Gwyneth, Gatty and Nest made their way up to the rood-screen, and when Austin the priest had banged the pulpit with his knuckles and in his deep voice called everyone to order – well, order of a kind – Lady Gwyneth stepped up into the choir. She turned to face her villagers and raised her right hand.

Seeing her there, so willowy, so fair, Gatty thought Lady Gwyneth looked like some saint come alive again. Mary Magdalen, maybe. She was tall, and had light skin.

Yes, and Nest belongs next to her, Gatty thought. With her swept-back hair and pretty hair-clips and her fresh apron. Standing so still!

'Dear creatures!' said Lady Gwyneth in her clear voice. 'God the Father has at long last granted me my greatest wish. Well! God the Father . . . and the Bishop-of-Asaph-and-the-Prior-of-Spon-and-the-Earl-of-Chester!' Lady Gwyneth smiled and shook her head. 'My wish to go on the great pilgrimage to Jerusalem for the forgiveness of my sins. We will very soon be leaving Ewloe and all our hands will be full between now and then. We need your help. Each one of you. Your help in making everything we need – our boots, our stockings, staffs, everything! I promise you, whether or not you're travelling with us, you will travel with us. We're going on this pilgrimage in the name of each and every soul here at Ewloe.'

'Amen! Amen!' The little grey church at Ewloe rang with bright hopes and blessings. 'Amen!'

'We'll leave on Saint David's feast day,' Lady Gwyneth called out. 'He went on a pilgrimage to Jerusalem, and he will guide our footsteps.'

Gatty drew in her breath, sharp as a sob. Saint David's feast day was Arthur's birthday.

Lady Gwyneth smiled. 'Our priest Austin,' she announced, 'and Gatty and Nest, and Emrys to look after our horses, and Tilda to mix our medicines and keep us well. And Snout to feed us. We will be your pilgrims. Two men from Chester will travel with us. Now if any of you here, if anyone here in this church has a dispute with any of us, you must say so now.'

A woman waved a hand. 'What are you taking that Gatty for?' she called out. 'She's not one of us.'

Gatty's heart began to beat at twice its usual speed.

Several people murmured in agreement.

'Because I need two chamber-servants,' Lady Gwyneth replied. 'And Gatty is travelling on behalf of all God's people in the manor of Caldicot.'

An old man, Simon the blacksmith, waved a hand in the air. 'Me,' he said. 'I got a bone to pick with Emrys. He owes me for twelve horseshoes.'

'I don't,' said Emrys.

Emrys was a big, broad-chested man. He stood at ease, but as soon as he spoke he thrust his head forward as if he were ready for an argument.

'He does,' the old blacksmith said, 'and he knows it. Awkward, that's what you are, Emrys.'

'Well, Emrys?' asked Lady Gwyneth.

'Not twelve,' said Emrys. '*Deg*, Simon. Ten. Two was cracked.'

Gatty liked Emrys's stubbornness and straight talking.

'All right,' said Lady Gwyneth. 'Ten! Do you agree, Simon?'

'Eleven,' the old blacksmith barked.

'Ten,' said Emrys, and he slowly signed himself with the cross, 'unless Simon would like me to pay him in prayers.'

'Save them for yourself,' the blacksmith called out. 'And your old bag!'

'Hear that?' asked Emrys's wife, Tilda. 'Did you?' She scooped her straggly brown hair away from her face, and stared at Simon.

'Witch eyes!' the blacksmith added.

'Aren't you going to say anything?' Tilda complained to her husband.

But before he could, the wind opened its mouth, swept open the church door, and whisked in a little man with fine cheekbones, smooth pink skin, and not a great deal of hair.

'Everard!' exclaimed Lady Gwyneth.

Everyone in Ewloe church turned round to look at him.

'Oh dear!' said Everard in his light voice. 'Dear me!' He patted himself all over, and then looked around with a sweet smile. 'I've been blown all the way from Chester cathedral.'

Simon the blacksmith stared at him. 'You'll be blown all the way to Jerusalem!' he remarked.

Everard, the cathedral choirmaster, smiled and tilted his head to one side, like a long-tailed tit. Then he reached out with both hands towards Lady Gwyneth. 'I'm late,' he called out.

'You are,' said Austin.

The little man advanced through the field of villagers.

'I apologise, my lady.'

'Always the same,' Austin said, and his bushy black eye-brows twitched as if they had a life of their own. 'When I was a priest in the cathedral, Everard always had a ready excuse.'

'Please, Austin,' said Lady Gwyneth, mild but reproving.

'Be a man!' boomed Austin. 'Blame yourself.'

'I am a man,' Everard replied in a haughty voice. 'And I do blame myself – for waiting for Nakin. It's not the first time he's broken his word.'

Once more the wind bellowed and, even though they were standing next to one another, the group of pilgrims had to raise their voices.

'Seems to me,' Emrys said loudly, 'that if you and Nakin can't get yourselves here from Chester, there's not much chance of your reaching Jerusalem.'

'None of us will reach it,' Lady Gwyneth called out over the wind, 'unless we discover Christ in each other. We need Everard. He can read and write, like Austin, and speak French and Italian. He can sing. He knows about music.'

Hearing this, Gatty looked at Everard with new eyes.

'Yes, Gatty,' Lady Gwyneth said. 'These are your teachers. Austin and Everard, the cathedral choirmaster. I told you I knew who could teach you to sing.'

Lady Gwyneth turned to all her people again. 'We need Nakin. He's a merchant. He's travelled to Venice. He uses money. We pilgrims bring ourselves as offerings to God, but we also bring our own skills to each other. Don't we, Nest?'

Nest smiled and kept on smiling, and Gatty thought how at ease she looked and how much Lady Gwyneth valued her.

The wind disagreed, though. It began to wail.

'Oh!' cried Lady Gwyneth. 'This is hopeless.' She made a circle of her arms. 'Pilgrims,' she said, 'we'll meet in the hall at this time tomorrow and, God willing, the wind will have settled by then. And you, Everard, please return to Chester and bring Nakin back with you.'

As the pilgrims eased their way through the press of villagers, the choirmaster asked Gatty, 'What did Lady Gwyneth say? What's your name?'

'Gatty.'

'Gatty!' repeated Everard. 'Gatty! A low register! Most promising.' The little man touched Gatty's wrist with two light fingers, and then hurried away up the churchyard path after Lady Gwyneth and Nest.

Gatty dawdled. She kicked through two molehills. She picked a white berry, she picked a scarlet berry.

'Bring?' she said out loud. 'Me? What skills could I ever bring? I haven't got none.'

Between the east wall and the old yew-tree, right next to the lych-gate, there was a little gravestone, a new one, Gatty could see that. It had gathered no moss, and the lettering was young and sharp. Gatty squatted beside it. With her right forefinger she traced the characters, shook her head and sighed.

Down on her knees Gatty dropped, wet as the grass was, and wet as the grave-soil beneath it. What can I offer God, she thought. What can I offer anyone? She closed her eyes, and after a while she began to intone in a low, steady voice:

'Jesus of the Marches,
Spring in my heart
And speak in my head.

Little Jesus,
Sharpen my eyes
And sing in my ears.

Jesus of everywhere,
Dance in my heart
And teach my thick tongue.'

Where such words came from, Gatty had no idea, though sometimes, when she sang, she was aware of how her mother had sung to her when she was a baby.

Then Nest and Snout came back through the lych-gate and Gatty scrambled to her feet.

'Whatever are you doing?' Nest demanded.

'This grave – whose is it?' asked Gatty.

'Griffith's.'

'I thought so.'

'Lady Gwyneth says you're to come at once.'

'She told me about him dying,' said Gatty. 'What was it?'

Nest shrugged. 'It was very sudden.'

'She tends his grave each day,' Snout said thickly. 'I don't know what I'd do if I lost Hew.'

'She loved him so, she almost devoured him,' said Nest. 'She didn't even give him to a wet nurse, and she always brought him to sleep in her own bed.'

'When Griffith died, Lady Gwyneth stopped eating,' Snout told Gatty. 'I made her favourite delicacies, but she wouldn't touch them.'

'Worse!' said Nest. 'She wouldn't get out of bed. For weeks she didn't even wash. Still, that would scarcely bother you.'

'She looked like a mouldy skeleton,' said Snout.

'What about her husband?' asked Gatty.

'Sir Robert,' said Snout. 'He died three months before Griffith. He was fifty, twice as old as Lady Gwyneth, and had scabs and weeping sores all over his body.'

'So she's a widow,' Gatty said, almost to herself. 'She's all alone.'

'And she owns Ewloe,' said Snout, 'every stick and stone of it.'

'I didn't know a woman could own a castle and land and that,' said Gatty.

'Her overlord is the Earl of Chester,' Nest told Gatty. 'She has to swear fealty to him, even though he's English.'

'I'm English,' said Gatty.

Nest made a face as if she'd just eaten something rotten.

'Well,' said Snout, 'me and Nest and Lady Gwyneth, we're all Welsh. *I Dduw y bo'r diolch*.'

'What?' exclaimed Gatty.

'God be praised!' Snout translated.

'Austin saved Lady Gwyneth,' Nest continued. 'He told her it was natural to grieve for the death of her baby, but not to go on as if there's no life after this life. He said she should make Ewloe shine, shine in memory of Griffith, and shine to the glory of God.'

'That's when it all began,' said Snout.

'It was,' Nest agreed. 'You know those tapestries in the hall? Lady Gwyneth shipped them from Arras.'

'What's Arras?' asked Gatty.

'A town in France. Harpists and bards came to Ewloe. And a schoolman from Oxford. And an astronomer who could read the map of the skies . . .'

'You mean the stars and that?' Gatty asked.

'He came from Malvern,' said Nest. 'And he said compared to what the Saracens know, the English and Welsh are like babbling babies.'

'And a priest came and read to us about our own place,' Snout told Gatty. 'Lady Gwyneth had everyone up to the hall to hear him. About the young man plagued in his cottage by hundreds and hundreds of toads. They got into his bed. His friends put him in a bag and hoisted him to the top of a tree – but even that was no good. The toads scrambled up the tree, and tore at the bag, and killed the man and ate him.'

'Yes,' said Nest, 'and he read about our beast – he's still here, in the cow pasture. He's got long shaggy hair and looks like a deer from in front but a cow from behind, hooves and all.'

'I want to see him, I do,' said Gatty.

Snout sucked his cheeks. 'You say it was Austin saved Lady Gwyneth,' he told Nest, 'but I say it was you. Partly you. The way you cut and sewed dresses for her, and braided her hair, and got her to work with you on that tapestry. For season after season, while she waited for all the permissions to go on this pilgrimage, you were at her side and helped her.'

Nest gave Snout a half-curtsy.

'Yes, it was Nest brought Lady Gwyneth back to life,' he told Gatty.

'You know what a Book of Hours is?' asked Nest.

Gatty shook her head dismally. Somehow, the more Snout went on about Nest and Lady Gwyneth, the smaller she felt.

'No, well, you wouldn't,' said Nest. 'It's a kind of prayer book and some of them have lovely decorations on each page. All I can say is that we decorated this place as no man could. With care and love. People are happy when they come to Ewloe and sad when they go away.'

7

'So, Gatty!' said Austin, the priest, in his booming voice, as if she were in another room. 'You're ready, are you?'

Gatty nodded, not by lowering her chin as most people do, but by upending it.

'Where's Nest, then?'

'Frog in her throat,' said Gatty. 'She's complaining about nothing.'

The priest smiled a kind of fleeting inward smile. 'A strange name,' he said. 'Gatty.'

'Short for Gertrude,' Gatty told him.

'Ah yes! May God's light shine on her.'

'Amen,' said Gatty politely.

'You know who she was?'

Gatty shook her head.

Austin considered Gatty. 'No,' he said. 'What about Amen?'

Gatty frowned. 'What about it?'

'Amen. Amen. Amen. That's what we all say. But what does it mean?'

Gatty pushed out her lower lip.

'Amen,' said Austin. 'It's Hebrew. You know what Hebrew is?'

'No.'

'The language of the Jews. Amen means truth. It means certainty. When you say *amen*, you're saying yes, truly, yes certainly. You're agreeing with your priest's prayer.'

Gatty smiled. 'Amen!' she said.

Austin motioned to Gatty to sit down on the bench facing him, and Gatty found herself thinking he was as unlike Oliver as chalk was unlike cheese. Oliver was fat; Austin was thin. Oliver had poor eyesight and blinked a lot; Austin had keen eyes and bushy eyebrows. Oliver loved the sound of his own voice; Austin never used two words where one would do.

'Your priest has asked me to teach you to read,' said Austin, 'and Lady Gwyneth has given her consent. Quite why, I can't imagine. Turning Ewloe into a monkey-house.' Austin sharpened his eyes. 'You know what that is?'

Gatty frowned. 'Where monks . . . where they read.'

'Dear God!' exclaimed the priest. 'All right. Let's make a start.'

'What about Nest?'

'Coming and going as it suits her,' said Austin, with a flash of anger. 'Anyhow, she already knows her alphabet.'

Out of the vestry chest the priest pulled a little flat piece of parchment, and then a rough-edged square of silvery slate and a lump of chalk. He laid the piece of parchment in front of Gatty.

A.a.b.c.d.e.f.g.h.i.k.
l.m.n.o.p.q.r.s.t.
v.u.x.y.z. amen.

'Letters,' said Gatty. 'Characters, that's what Oliver calls them.'

'Letters,' Austin replied. 'That's good enough.'

'What's this at the end?'

'Begin at the beginning,' Austin said. Then, using a pointer, he advanced from letter to letter, naming it, sounding it, and having Gatty copy him. 'Ai . . . a. Bee . . . b. See . . . c. Dee . . . d. Ee . . . eh.'

'There you are!' said Austin. 'The letters we use to make words. Now copy each letter on to the slate.'

'I will!' cried Gatty, eagerly.

Some while later, after a fair deal of sighing and spittle and slate-wiping, Gatty looked up at Austin, alight.

'I got it,' she announced. 'I have!'

'Well?'

'At the end. Amen! Isn't it!'

Austin gave Gatty a sharp little smile. 'Amen,' he said. He walked round behind Gatty's back and stared down at the slate.

'My hand don't do what my head says,' Gatty said ruefully.

'Not bad, not good,' said Austin. He reached out and, with his flapping black sleeve, wiped the slate.

'What you do that for?' Gatty demanded.

'So you can do it again.'

8

Lady Gwyneth stood up. 'Nakin!' she exclaimed. 'At last! And Everard!' Then she turned to all the other pilgrims. 'At last!' she said again.

The merchant bundled over to Lady Gwyneth. He got down on one knee and kissed her right hand, and Lady Gwyneth lowered her eyes and almost smiled.

'My lady!' said Nakin. 'My most sincere apologies!'

'I should think so,' said Lady Gwyneth.

'I mixed up my Thursdays and Fridays,' the merchant said. Gatty saw that his brow was damp, and the whites of his eyes were slightly pink.

Lady Gwyneth gazed at Nakin. 'You lost count,' she said.

The smile that slowly spread across the merchant's fleshy face was rather like oil spreading across ruffled water.

'You can count on me,' he said in an unguent voice. And he levered himself to his feet.

'Now come and sit down,' said Lady Gwyneth. 'And you, Everard.'

'The worst part of the journey was getting past those two wolves outside the door,' Nakin complained.

'I'm glad to hear it,' said Lady Gwyneth. 'That's their duty. You're *Sais*, aren't you?'

'As English as you're Welsh,' the merchant replied. He plumped himself down on the bench across the fire from Gatty, and immediately pointed at her. 'Who's she?'

'My new chamber-servant,' Lady Gwyneth said.

'Chamber-servant!' exclaimed Nakin, looking very surprised. 'She's not coming with us.'

'I need to talk to you, Nakin.'

'The sums don't add up,' Nakin said at once. 'They don't begin to. We need three armed men, not chamber-servants.'

Lady Gwyneth's long neck turned slightly pink. 'I need two chamber-servants,' she said in a level voice. 'Nest and Gatty.'

'Whatty?' asked Nakin.

'Gatty,' said Gatty.

'Strange,' said Nakin, wrinkling his nose.

'So's Nakin!' Gatty retorted.

Lady Gwyneth took a deep breath, and sat down in her fire-chair. She looked fondly at the eight women and men sitting on the log-benches on the other three sides of the fire. Around them, candles burned.

All my life, thought Gatty, I've risen at dawn and worked myself to the bone. But now? Now I'm warm. And Lady Gwyneth says she needs me. Behind Nakin's head, she could see Lady Gwyneth's and Nest's great tapestry hanging on the wall. The silver thread in it kept winking at her.

Lady Gwyneth crossed herself, not on the chest but on her right shoulder. 'This is where we'll wear our crosses,' she said. 'Here and on our hats.'

Gatty gazed up at her. Yes, she thought. She looks like Saint Mary Magdalen.

And then, all on two low notes, she began to sing-and-say:

> 'Saint Mary, you save us from the cold.
> You feed us and clothe us
> From cradle to mould.
> Guide your pilgrims to Jerusalem. Amen.'

The silence that followed was broken when Nakin harrumphed. 'What was that, exactly?' he asked.

Lady Gwyneth looked at Gatty. 'From your heart,' she said.

'What?' asked Gatty. The back of her neck began to prickle.

'That prayer.'

Gatty frowned. 'You could hear me?'

'Well, of course. We all did.'

Gatty's cheeks flamed. And then her ears.

'What is it, Gatty?' asked Lady Gwyneth. She looked at Nest, puzzled, and Nest rolled her eyes and shook her head.

Gatty lowered her eyes. 'I thought,' she began in a low voice. 'I thought . . .' She looked up, and her eyes were blazing. 'I thought as when I pray – when I pray – no one can't hear – except for Jesus and Saint Mary.'

Nest pointed her forefinger at Gatty and laughed, and then several other pilgrims laughed too.

'I understand,' said Lady Gwyneth.

Everard smiled at Gatty. 'Only Saint Mary heard your true meaning,' he said gently.

Austin licked his thin lips. 'According to Saint Everard,' he said.

Lady Gwyneth leaned forward. 'Gatty,' she said, 'when you pray, you must speak the words inside your heart, inside your head, if you don't want anyone else to hear them.'

Gatty lowered her eyes again, and looked at her lap.

'Now then,' said Lady Gwyneth, and she edged right forward. 'I've waited many months for this moment when we pilgrims would all meet for the first time. Three years, in fact. I was twenty-six when I began to plan this pilgrimage. Now, we might not have chosen each other as travelling companions. We're all different.'

'Indeed we are,' Nakin said. 'Four of you are women!'

'And four are not Welsh,' Lady Gwyneth added. 'You, Nakin. And Everard and Tilda and Gatty.'

'You're not Welsh,' Tilda said to Austin.

'Half Welsh,' Austin replied. 'My mother.'

'Yes,' said Lady Gwyneth, 'we're all different, but here

42

around this fire are the people God has given to us as our partners. Our sisters and brothers.'

'The list, my lady,' said Austin.

'I was coming to that,' Lady Gwyneth said. 'Yesterday, we had thirty-five days left. Today, thirty-four. Those days will fly, they'll fly like . . .'

'Geese,' Gatty said at once. 'Wild geese.'

'*I'r dim*,' said Lady Gwyneth. 'Exactly! So Austin has written a list of everything we need.'

Austin held up a piece of folded leather. He opened it with a flourish and inside was a slate tile – the same one he had given Gatty to write on.

'Austin,' said Tilda, shaking her head. 'The conjuror.'

Austin held up the slate. 'A cooking-pot,' he said.

'It's not!' exclaimed Gatty. 'It's a slate.'

Everyone laughed.

'A cooking-pot,' repeated Lady Gwyneth. 'Snout, you must ask Simon to make us one.'

'Only if you want a cracked one,' grumbled Emrys.

Austin laid the slate across his knees. *Snout,* he wrote, after the first item on his list.

'Next?' asked Lady Gwyneth.

'Cloaks,' said Austin.

'Yes,' said Lady Gwyneth. 'We each need a cloak of strong, grey cloth.'

'Not grey!' said Nest.

'Jerusalem pilgrims wear grey,' Lady Gwyneth said, 'with a red cross sewn on to the right shoulder. Nest, I want you to ensure that each pilgrim has a cloak. A long one. Below the knee. A strong one.'

Nest, wrote Austin. 'And a broad-brimmed hat with a scarf sewn to it.'

'I want you to be responsible for the hats as well, Nest,' said Lady Gwyneth, 'and they must also have a red cross sewn on to the front of them. You're a good needle-woman. You can get Gatty to help you with cutting the felt and the loose stitching.'

'I can do it myself, my lady,' said Nest.

'No,' Lady Gwyneth said. 'I'd like you to work on the hats and scarves together.'

Nest narrowed her eyes at Gatty.

'What's next, Austin?' asked Lady Gwyneth.

'Flasks,' replied Austin. 'Leather flasks . . . Stockings . . . Knives . . .' One by one he named each of the items and noted the name of the pilgrim responsible for them.

'Next?' asked Lady Gwyneth.

'Scrips.'

'What's a scrip?' Gatty asked.

'A leather pouch,' Austin explained.

Gatty looked mystified.

'For your bits and pieces.'

Tilda laughed.

'A coin or two. I don't know! A charm. An apple. We must carry our own passes and letters of commendation.'

'I just may be able to help,' Everard said. 'I know a young man . . .'

'Eek!' squealed Nest. 'A rat! Look!' She grabbed Lady Gwyneth's arm.

'Give me that!' Gatty told Nakin. 'Your stick.'

'No!' barked Nakin. 'The knob's silver!'

'Yours, then,' said Gatty, and she picked up Emrys's staff.

'You won't get it,' Emrys said.

'I will and all,' Gatty called out.

She chased the rat into the kitchen, cornered it, thumped it, and broke its back, and then she finished it off with a second blow.

When Gatty reappeared at the door, all the pilgrims were standing up.

'Well?' Lady Gwyneth called out.

Gatty nodded, with that quick upward tilt of her chin.

Emrys gave her a thoughtful, warm look.

'We don't want a rat in here,' Lady Gwyneth said.

'Unless it was warning us,' said Tilda. 'The soul of my father got into a rat and warned me my mother was going to die.'

Lady Gwyneth clicked her tongue. 'Come on. Let's finish this list. Where were we?'

'Pouches,' said Everard.

Then Everard volunteered to supply soft leather for the pouches from the cathedral tannery. Emrys said that he would cut willow staffs about five feet long and, sighing, agreed to ask Simon to tip each of them with a double-pronged iron point. And his wife Tilda undertook to fill one scrip with the most essential medicines – powdered geranium to quieten headaches, masterwort to reduce fever, horehound for soup to ease blocked noses, and the like.

'Nakin will carry our gold and silver coin,' Lady Gwyneth said. 'Many abbeys and monasteries will give us alms and lodging in the name of God, but we'll need money in taverns and pilgrim hostels, and we'll have to pay for our places on the boats from Venice.'

'And the Venetians,' added Nakin, 'drive hard bargains. Some weeks ago Lady Gwyneth and I agreed that I should place a large amount of silver coin in the hands of a Venetian company with a trading-house in London – I've traded with them for seven years now – on the understanding we'll be able to collect the same amount when we reach Venice.'

'What's the point of that?' Nest asked. 'Why not just take the money with us?'

Nakin fixed Nest with his beady little eyes. 'If you're not carrying money, there's no danger of losing it,' he said. 'Armed bands of robbers. Sneak-thieves! Sharp-eyed pickpockets. Holes in your pockets. Sweet-tongued stallholders. There are all kinds of ways of losing your money.'

'Why are you paying for us, then?' asked Nest. 'So you can sell us as slaves or something?'

'I'm not paying for you,' Nakin replied, and he nodded to Lady Gwyneth.

'I'm not wealthy,' Lady Gwyneth said, 'but I can afford to pay for each of my people. And in return, each of you is bringing a skill to our pilgrimage.'

I'm not, thought Gatty. I haven't got no skills these people need.

'So far as I can see,' Nakin said, 'no one here has the skill we need most. Skill with sword and dagger and shield. Skill to defend and protect us.'

'Is the journey dangerous?' asked Everard.

Nakin parted his puffy lips and gave a vulpine smile. 'Yes,' he said. 'It is. Look at you all! Cooking and needlework and praying and singing: what are they worth when a bandit's holding a knife across your throat?'

'What are we to do, then?' Lady Gwyneth asked. 'If I pay for more men . . .'

'No!' said Nakin sharply. 'This party's large enough already. We don't need more people. We need different people.'

'We don't need Gatty,' Nest said. 'My lady, I can easily look after you.'

'Or I could stay here,' said Snout. 'I mean, I could teach Tilda to cook . . .'

'I've got a better idea,' Lady Gwyneth said. 'Let's do it the other way round. Snout, let's get Armin and Crok to teach you swordplay.'

Emrys guffawed and all the other pilgrims laughed and slapped their knees at the thought of Snout becoming a swordsman.

'Sir Snout!' exclaimed Emrys. 'Sir Snout of the Spit.'

'You, too, Emrys,' Lady Gwyneth said. 'You can learn to thrust and parry.'

'God help us!' said Tilda. 'He couldn't even shield his wife from a sniping blacksmith.'

'I'll talk to Armin and Crok,' Lady Gwyneth said.

Nakin shook his head, unconvinced. 'I'll have to see,' he said. 'Above all, we have to be well defended.'

'You can begin your lessons tomorrow morning,' Lady Gwyneth told Snout and Emrys. 'Now, then! Is that everything?'

'Flints!' said Austin. 'For the fire.'

'Me!' cried Gatty. 'I done that all my life.'

Nest looked down her nose at Gatty.

'Very good!' said Lady Gwyneth. 'Gatty will strike sparks for us. And she'll sing for us! Won't you, Gatty?'

Gatty nodded eagerly.

'Gatty's voice is a gift from God,' Lady Gwyneth told them. 'Like charms, her songs will help to keep us all safe. And you, Everard, you're going to teach Gatty all your singing skills, aren't you?'

So while Gatty looked from one pilgrim to another, bright-eyed, Austin added the words *Songs* and *Gatty* next to *Flints* on his silvery slate.

'That's it, then,' said Lady Gwyneth.

'An altar,' said Austin in a dry voice.

'*Neno'r holl Saint,*' said Lady Gwyneth, and she crossed herself. 'In the name of all the saints, how can I have forgotten our Lord's own table?'

'I will bring it,' said Austin.

'Nature herself will show us altars along the way,' Tilda added.

'And there's another thing,' Lady Gwyneth said, banging her forehead with her little white fist. 'Boots! I've told

Gruffydd each of us will need stout new boots. Look at yours, Gatty. They're falling apart.'

Gatty shrugged. 'All I got,' she said.

'My lady,' Lady Gwyneth said. 'Go and have Gruffydd measure your feet.'

'I'm sure Mansel will,' Nest said quickly. 'He kept looking at Gatty. In church.'

Lady Gwyneth smiled. 'You're spoilt for choice then, Gatty.'

Gatty lowered her eyes.

'Remember,' said Nakin, 'we've got to walk all the way to London.'

'That's all, then,' said Lady Gwyneth. 'Isn't it, Austin?'

'The wills, my lady,' said the priest.

'Oh yes! Yes!' said Lady Gwyneth. 'Each of you must make your will with Austin. Name each item of your property, and name your heirs, and he will write them down for you.'

Without even knowing why, Gatty thought of words from the Bible, and said them inside her head: 'Naked I came into this world, naked from the womb, and naked I will leave it.'

'Come one by one, and in the afternoon,' Austin told the pilgrims. 'I will prepare a good supply of parchment and ink.'

'Austin!' said Lady Gwyneth. 'Will you say a prayer?'

Everyone got up and bowed their heads.

'Saint Mary,' the priest began,

'Saint Mary, you save us from the cold.
You feed us and clothe us
From cradle to mould.
Guide your pilgrims to Jerusalem.'

'Amen,' chimed all the pilgrims.

Austin smiled at Gatty.

'Amen,' he said in his firm, warm voice.

9

Gatty led Everard up the circular stone steps to the small room with the full-moon window.

'Lady Gwyneth says we should use this room because it's quiet in here.'

'And we,' said Everard, 'will fill it with sound.' He slipped off the woollen bag sitting on his right shoulder.

'What you got?' Gatty asked eagerly.

Out of the bag, the choirmaster drew a little stringed instrument. Its frame gleamed in the gloom. 'Maple,' said Everard. 'But the pegs are willow. Willow doesn't snap.'

'Go on, then!' said Gatty.

'It's a psaltery,' said Everard, savouring the sound of it. 'That's what it is. And what angels play.'

'Really?' exclaimed Gatty. She reached out her little finger, blunt and rough, and carefully stroked the frame.

'And you, I hear,' said Everard in a smooth, measured voice, 'have the voice of an angel. An apprentice angel.'

'I don't know nothing about that,' Gatty said. 'Me and my voice are friends. It keeps me company.'

'When did you start to sing?' Everard asked.

'When my father died. He never liked me to sing, he didn't. He said it just reminded him of my mother.'

'And what do you sing?' asked Everard.

'Everything,' said Gatty. 'Prayers and field-songs. Carols. You know, dancing-songs.'

'Where did you learn them?'

'In church,' said Gatty. 'In the fields. From them musicians who come to Caldicot. I'll sing you one.'

'All in good time,' Everard replied.

'Listening to the birds,' Gatty went on. 'Some of them I just make up.'

'Sing me a scale.'

'A what?'

Everard plucked one string of the psaltery and, making an open purse of his lips, sang 'Uuuuu-t . . .' Then, waving his delicate white hands, he signalled to Gatty to join in.

'Uuuuu-t,' sang Gatty, a whole octave lower than Everard.

Everard plucked the next string and half-opened his mouth. 'Re,' he sang.

'Re,' sang Gatty.

Now Everard covered his upper teeth with his top lip, like a horse. 'Mi,' he sang.

'Mi,' sang Gatty.

'Good,' sang Everard. 'Very good. Very rich,' he sang, all on the same note. 'Keep it steady.' And then, plucking the next strings. 'Fa . . . Sol . . . La . . .'

'La-a-a-a-a . . .' sang Gatty.

'Go on,' sang Everard, 'and on and on and on and on . . .'

'a-a-a-a-a-a.'

'On!'

Gatty coughed. 'Can't,' she said. Her eyes were bright with excitement. 'I haven't got no more breath.'

'When my boys get breathy,' the clerk said, 'I chastise them.'

'You're not beating me, you're not,' said Gatty.

'You must learn to breathe, then,' said Everard.

'How?'

'I'll teach you. Though, in heaven's name, I've never heard of such a thing.'

'What?'

'Teaching a girl to sing. What next!'

'Learning to read,' said Gatty. 'Austin's teaching me.'

Everard sighed. 'Most irregular. But then, that's what Lady Gwyneth's like. She has a mind of her own, and does as she chooses.'

'Close your eyes!' Gatty said unexpectedly.

Everard did as he was told.

'Listen now!' whispered Gatty.

The clerk thought he could hear the wind kissing the horn-windows, and gently hissing. He heard the soft cu-ic, cu-ic of the nightjar. Then the bird clapped its wings. Everard leaned forward, eager not to miss a note. P'weet, sang the lapwing, p'weet, p'weet.

Everard smiled. He looked quite blissful. Wind, more wind! And then, right behind him, Everard heard a mare, loudly neighing. He giggled and opened his eyes.

'Well, Gatty!' said Everard. 'I see . . . or, rather, I hear I've something to learn from you.' He plucked a few notes on his psaltery, and in his light voice began to sing:

> 'Summer's here, and so is love!
> That's what meadows and birds prove
> With sweet blossom, with sweet singing . . .'

'More!' cried Gatty. Her fingertips were tingling.

Without taking his eyes off Gatty, Everard rustled the strings of his psaltery and they murmured like all the sounds in Pike Forest on a May morning. Then he laid his long white fingers across the strings.

'Everything,' he said, 'as that slimy Nakin tells us, has its own price. Learn to breathe before our next lesson, and I'll sing you the next verse.'

'How?'

'Light a candle, and sit beside it, with your mouth quite close to the flame. Take a deep breath, and sing uuuuu-t.

Sing it so slowly, so steadily that the tip of the flame never flickers.'

'I will,' said Gatty, wide-eyed.

'I will,' the clerk repeated, in the same low pitch Gatty had just said it. 'That's the note for you to begin on. Your normal pitch. Then go up one note, and sing re for as long as you can, then mi, fa, sol, la . . . And always so steadily the flame never once flickers.'

'Then what?' asked Gatty.

'That's all. I must ride back to Chester.'

'Already!'

'And Austin said that as soon as we'd finished, you're to go and find him in the vestry, and make your will.'

10

'The will,' said Austin. 'And high time too.'

Gatty nodded. 'Lady Gwyneth says I must.'

'I say you must,' said Austin, busying himself at the chest, taking out parchment, weights, quill, ink, and setting them on his writing-desk. 'Everyone else has made theirs already.'

'I haven't got nothing,' Gatty said.

'*In the name of Almighty God*,' Austin wrote, enunciating each syllable as he did so. '*I, Gertrude . . .*'

'Gatty,' said Gatty.

'I, Gertrude,' Austin repeated, '*on the eve of my pilgrimage to Jerusalem, do in this document declare all my property and all my possessions, and I acknowledge they will be handed to my heirs if I fail to return to Ewloe within one year and one day, First . . .*' wrote Austin, and then he looked up. 'Well? What's first?'

'Nothing,' said Gatty. 'I told you. I haven't got nothing.'

'But before. When you lived . . . where was it?'

'At Caldicot?'

'Caldicot, yes. Your cottage there?'

Gatty shook her head. 'That's Sir John's.'

Austin knitted his thick eyebrows. 'Well, what about . . . I don't know. A cooking-pot?'

'No one won't thank me for that,' said Gatty.

'A saddle? A bridle?'

Gatty clucked. 'Sir John borrowed them to me.'

'I see,' said Austin. 'What about animals, then?'

53

'Hopeless!' cried Gatty. 'How could I have forgot her? Hopeless and my seven chickens. I borrowed them to Sir John.'

'Hopeless?'

'My cow. She's a good milker, and all.'

'I'm sure she is,' said Austin. 'There, then. A cow and seven chickens. Now who are your heirs?'

Gatty sighed. 'I haven't got none,' she said.

'Your father's dead and your mother's dead?'

Slowly, very slowly, Gatty drew in her breath. 'I know!' she said in a low voice.

'Who?' asked Austin.

The priest stared at Gatty. She had looked quite lost, but now she looked found!

'Who, then?' Austin asked.

'Write this,' Gatty instructed him.

'*I grant my cow Hopeless . . .*' the priest wrote, '*and my seven chickens . . .*'

'Well?' asked Austin. 'To whom?'

'Arthur!' cried Gatty. 'I grant them to Arthur de Caldicot.'

Gatty watched as Austin wrote down her words. 'You written them all?' she asked suspiciously.

'You can trust me,' said the priest. 'Now, you must write your name.'

'And all!' said Gatty eagerly. 'I haven't wrote with a quill before.'

'Gee . . . g,' Austin began. 'Ai . . . a.'

'I know how,' said Gatty.

'Lightly,' said Austin. 'Lightly now, or you'll splay it.'

II

The moment the first crowing cockerel woke her, Gatty was awake. She unlocked the hall door, and long-legged it to the rainwater barrel; she drove her fist through thin ice and, gasping, dashed-and-splashed the freezing water over her face and head; she shook herself like a terrier, and then fleet-footed back into the hall with little rivulets running down her chest and her back.

Nest was still cocooned and yawning, so Gatty quickly dressed herself and went to wake Lady Gwyneth in her chamber, and help her to dress.

'You're very bright-eyed,' said Lady Gwyneth, smiling.

'It's a pilgrim morning!' Gatty replied.

'It is!' said Lady Gwyneth.

'A once-in-a-life morning.'

'That's how we should treat each morning,' said Lady Gwyneth.

'And now your smock, my lady . . . your sandals . . . Here's your hat-and-scarf. And here's . . .' Gatty opened Lady Gwyneth's new grey cloak with the scarlet cross stitched to the right shoulder.

'Gatty!' said Lady Gwyneth, shaking her head. 'You're in too much of a hurry. You're doing everything in the wrong order. At this rate I'll get to Jerusalem before I leave Ewloe, with a sandal on each hand and my socks hanging over my ears!'

Gatty grinned. 'You wear so many things, my lady,' she

55

said. 'It muddles me up.'

'Yes, very bright-eyed!' Lady Gwyneth repeated. 'Bright eyes are signs of life and health. Do you know what Abbess Hildegard says about blue eyes, like mine?'

'No, my lady.'

'Thoughtless and wilful! I'm not, am I? Wilful? Well, I'm determined. Still, Hildegard says a person with blue eyes makes sure everything turns out well.'

'And here's your staff, my lady.'

'Come on, then!' said Lady Gwyneth. 'It's high time Nest stirred her lazy bones.'

Away they went to pray in church, and before long they were joined by the other pilgrims, even Nest, and by everyone living at Ewloe.

The church was full of whispering and coughing, sniffing and scratching, foot-scraping, laughing, until Austin rose up before God's people and quelled them with a stony stare.

The priest blessed the pilgrims, and named and blessed each and every thing they were taking with them. Even Gatty's grey-and-green fire-flints. Then he commended the manor of Ewloe and each soul who lived there to the mercy of God.

And that was that. Everyone shuffled out of church, and stood around in the churchyard.

Lady Gwyneth gathered her pilgrims around her. 'Nest,' she said. 'Gatty. Stand on either side of me. We'll lead the way.'

For a moment the three of them gazed up at the speckled walls, the four little slit-windows, the moon-shaped window. Then they turned away. They raised their eyes to a bright star, still shining in the east.

Snout hoisted Hew on to his shoulders. Tilda carried her baby granddaughter. Emrys walked arm in arm with his shaky father. Everyone in Ewloe accompanied the pilgrims through Wepre Wood, and into Sword Wood. It wasn't very long before they all grew quiet, sobered by thoughts of the separation ahead. The pilgrims knew that some of them might reach the end of their lives before they returned to Ewloe, and the villagers knew some of them would not live to see the pilgrims return. One by one, those who were leaving embraced parents, children, friends, everyone who was staying behind.

Not Gatty, though. There was no one at Ewloe who particularly cared whether she was going or staying.

Don't matter, Gatty thought. The people I care about are at Caldicot. Them and Arthur. Yes, and Lady Gwyneth and Snout and Everard and all.

But then, at the very last moment, Mansel, the shoemaker's son, stepped up to Gatty. He put one hand into each pocket of his breeches and pulled out two soft felt shoes, yellow as finches, their toes and heels patched with russet leather.

'For me?' said Gatty.

Lady Gwyneth and Nest walked on, and Gatty and Mansel were left together. His eyes were so bright.

'You made them?' asked Gatty.

'When you're tired, see. When your feet are aching. You can wear them in the evenings.'

Gatty felt her eyes pricking. 'I will,' she said huskily. She grabbed Mansel and hugged him. Then she took a few steps, turned back and waved, and walked briskly away.

Snout sank his buck teeth into his wedge of bread, bit off a lump, and chewed it for almost as long as a cow chews her cud. Lady Gwyneth nibbled the edge of her wedge, quick and keen as an Armenian mouse.

'Well?' she asked. 'Why are we here? Why are we making this pilgrimage?'

The pilgrims looked glumly at one another, uneasily shifted their buttocks, rubbed their chins, and raised their eyes to heaven for guidance. Each of them knew how Lady Gwyneth liked plans and explanations, but no one had expected to have to speak up this soon.

'Lord Jesus,' Emrys began, 'He rode into Jerusalem on a colt. If I can ride in after Him, I'll be happy. Anyhow you asked me to come, my lady, and look after all our horses.' The stableman looked round the group, and suddenly drew his dagger and waved it menacingly. 'Anyhow,' he said, 'where would you be without me and Snout?'

Everyone laughed and Lady Gwyneth rewarded Emrys with a warm smile. 'What about you, Tilda?'

'To beg Lord Jesus to purify my body and loosen my stiff limbs,' Tilda replied. 'Especially my poor hands. And then I'm going to beg Jesus for a better husband.'

'Better than Emrys?' asked Nakin.

'You devil!' said Tilda. 'I mean I want Emrys to treat me better. I'm not a big . . . big . . . what is it?'

'Bigamist,' said Lady Gwyneth.

'Like you said the Saracens are.'

'No!' said Lady Gwyneth. 'No, I didn't say that. Nakin! What about you?'

'I'm most at home away from home,' the merchant replied, 'and for me travel means trade.' Nakin cheerfully rubbed his hands. 'And while I'm in Jerusalem, I'll ask for forgiveness! Forgiveness for all my past sins and,' said Nakin with a sly smile, 'any little new ones I commit on the way.'

Nakin's words, thought Gatty, they're slick as snot.

Snout made a squelching sound and unglued his mouth. 'I'm going to get on my knees and rub my nose against Jesus' grave and . . . and . . .'

'Snort!' exclaimed Nest.

'Nest!' protested Lady Gwyneth.

'. . . and cry out, I am. Cry out to Lord Jesus to cure it.' Snout looked at his fellow pilgrims. 'To tell you the truth,' he confided, 'I doubt it will make any difference.'

'Believe that it will,' Austin told him.

'Yes, and I'll come home with a sackful of herbs and spices,' Snout added.

'Very good,' said Lady Gwyneth.

'I'm eager to learn more about the singing skills of the Saracens,' volunteered Everard, 'and their famous singing teachers. Who has not heard of Ziryab?'

No one had heard of Ziryab, not even Lady Gwyneth.

'And Lady Gwyneth has charged me with a duty,' Everard said in a solemn voice. 'To teach Gatty how to sing.'

'Indeed I have!' Lady Gwyneth said.

'Is that all?' demanded Austin. 'Is that all you're coming for?'

Lady Gwyneth ignored her priest. 'Now, Nest! What about you?'

Nest put her forefingers to her temples and slowly shook her head. 'I have such a terrible headache, my lady.'

'You must tell us later then,' Lady Gwyneth said, kindly. 'Who is left? Austin?'

'By enduring this pilgrimage, with all its slings and arrows, we commend ourselves to God,' said the priest gravely. 'I, too, long to see the places and touch the walls and walk the ways I've heard about and read about and preached about.'

'Amen,' said Lady Gwyneth 'Well now, Gatty, what about you?'

Gatty heard Lady Gwyneth's question in her gut.

'Well?' asked Lady Gwyneth.

Gatty took a deep breath and combed her golden curls with her fingers. 'I want to see where Jesus was born,' she sang out, ' and . . . and I'm going to strike sparks for you.'

Lady Gwyneth smiled. 'I'm sure you will, Gatty,' she said.

'I didn't use to think Jerusalem was any further than Chester.'

Nakin shook his head at how anyone could know so little. His dewlaps wobbled.

'I didn't know it was across the sea,' Gatty said.

After finishing their bread and dried fish, and drinking water from their leather flasks, the pilgrims continued their journey, and their first exhilaration was shadowed by uncertainty, then by tiredness. Only Gatty, on her way north to Ewloe, and Emrys and Nakin, had travelled such a distance in one day before. And after months working in the kitchen at Caldicot, and weeks sewing and serving and reading and writing at Ewloe, Gatty was glad to be in the open again.

'The way to think of the journey,' Nakin told them, 'is in parts. This first part from Ewloe to London is on foot, and that'll take nine days.'

'Nine days!' exclaimed Nest.

'With a following wind!' said Nakin.

'And after that we'll have our horses,' Lady Gwyneth said. 'Nakin, how long with horses from London to the coast at Sandwich?'

'Three days,' replied Nakin.

'You see, Nest?' said Lady Gwyneth. 'A journey in parts. And remember, each mile brings us a little nearer to Jerusalem, and to Paradise too.'

'How many calves' tails do you need to climb from earth to heaven?' Gatty asked.

'Calves' tails,' Lady Gwyneth repeated. 'I don't know!'

'One,' said Gatty. 'One if it's long enough. That was a Christmas riddle at Caldicot.'

By the end of the afternoon, everyone was quite giddy with exhaustion. Half the time they laughed at riddles as simple as Gatty's, and horsed about, and half they didn't really want to talk at all.

Not long before dark, the pilgrims reached the hostelry at Whitchurch, as Nakin had predicted. Its earth-walls were grey; the thatch was grey. Its shoulders were lop-sided and it kept its head well down.

'Please go in and check there are no fleas,' Lady Gwyneth told Nakin.

'There's nowhere else to stay,' Nakin replied sharply. Still, he ducked his head and went in, and before long reported, 'No fleas. Only rats and mice!'

To begin with, each day was less easy than the previous one. Nest had pinching boots and a raw left heel and Tilda had to mix an ointment each morning, and rub it into Nest's feet.

'At this rate,' Tilda complained, 'we'll be out of ointment before we're out of England!'

On the fourth day, Nest's heel was so painful that, after the pilgrims had stopped at noon in the middle of a wood to eat bread and dried fish, she refused to stand up and continue the journey.

'You must,' said Lady Gwyneth.

'I can't, my lady,' said Nest. 'You've seen how I was limping.'

'Well, you can't stay here,' said Lady Gwyneth. 'We're not even halfway to London and we're in trouble already – because of one raw heel. What are we going to do?'

'Come on!' Gatty said impatiently. 'Get up, Nest!'

'No,' said Nest.

Gatty clicked her teeth and looked to heaven; Snout and Emrys looked at each other.

'We'll have to carry you,' said Snout.

'Piggyback!' exclaimed Gatty. 'I often carried piglets like that!'

So that's what Snout and Emrys did. Taking turns, they carried Nest piggyback all afternoon.

That evening, Gatty asked Nest whether she would like to wear Mansel's soft felt slippers.

Nest shook her head.

'You can,' said Gatty.

'No,' said Nest impatiently. 'They're only made of scraps anyway.'

On the fifth morning, the pilgrims kept arguing, and Everard clutched his throat and complained his glands felt as large as pigs' bladders, and Tilda's arthritis in her left hand hurt so badly she carried her arm in a sling. Of all the pilgrims, Gatty was least affected by small aches and pains. After all, she had spent almost every day of her life ploughing, stone-picking, sowing, haymaking, reaping, stooking, hauling.

So when they all trooped into another shabby hostelry shortly before noon, Lady Gwyneth decided to call a halt for the remainder of the day.

'The afternoon needn't be wasted,' she said. 'Austin, will you please give Nest and Gatty their lessons?'

Nest closed her eyes and sighed noisily.

'And you,' Lady Gwyneth went on, turning to Emrys and Snout, 'you two can practise your fighting skills. Heaven knows, you need to!'

'Sir Snout!' exclaimed Gatty.

'It's no laughing matter,' Lady Gwyneth said. 'There may not be too much to fear crossing England. But after that? Nakin's absolutely right. It's crucial that we're properly protected.'

True, Lady Gwyneth's armed men, Crok and Armin, had tried to teach Snout and Emrys how to thrust and parry with their double-pronged willow-staffs that were as long as quarterstaffs, and how to circle an opponent with a drawn dagger, and use a scrip as a kind of leather shield. But although Emrys and Snout were not fearful or unwilling, they were still very poor material.

Egged on by the other pilgrims, they lunged and stumbled and swiped clean air and sweated and swore until it was all Gatty could do to stop herself from joining in. Then they tripped over each other, and got their arms and legs into a tangle, and Nest completely forgot her raw heel and rolled over on her back, laughing.

'We both know what to do,' Snout gasped, 'but we can't persuade our bodies to do it.'

'So I see!' Lady Gwyneth said, smiling.

'Snout's too clumsy,' Emrys panted, 'and I'm too slow.'

'Well,' said Lady Gwyneth. 'We're depending on you. You must practise whenever you can.'

The next morning, Gatty and Nakin led the group south.

'What's London like, then?' Gatty asked him.

'London!' Nakin said. 'Where can I begin?'

'It is as large as Ludlow?' Gatty demanded.

Nakin gave a short, scornful laugh. 'It's larger than all the Marcher towns rolled together!'

'Is it as large as France?' Gatty asked.

Lady Gwyneth overheard her and smiled, then quickly tucked her chin into her cloak.

'You can't compare London to France,' laughed Nakin.

'Why not?'

'One is a city and the other's a country.'

'I didn't know that,' Gatty said.

'London's like a monster with one hundred arms,' Nakin said. 'It's like the monsters in the sea beyond Venice.'

Gatty opened her eyes sky-wide.

'Yes, there are. And there's a huge fish, more than one mile long.'

Gatty gasped.

'But London's even longer than that,' Nakin told her. 'And as wide as it's long. It's noisy. It's dirty. It's everything. You'll see.'

12

As they walked on, Gatty thought of the largest, noisiest and dirtiest things she had ever seen or heard, but nothing began to prepare her for the shock of stepping through the wide arched gate in the towering wall, and into the city of London.

The first thing was: a burly man pushed right between Gatty and Lady Gwyneth, in a hurry to get out through the gate as they were coming in.

The second thing was: Lady Gwyneth was smacked on the left shoulder by a flying cabbage.

'Yach!' bawled a woman at the burly man. 'Next time I'll give you cabbage ears.'

Lady Gwyneth took Gatty's arm and held it tightly. She walked on as if nothing had happened.

Ugh! The stink! Sewage pits. Putrid fruit. Fish so rotten they glowed green in the gloom. Scrapheaps of heaven knows what. Mud. Under the sky's leaden lid, all London's foul odours swarmed and stewed around them. The smell was so thick Gatty could taste it! She grinned and screwed up her face like a pickled walnut.

There was no stopping. The pilgrims were part of a seething throng. Two men rolling a cart loaded with samples of wool. Another man carrying an oblong brass plate on his head! Another wearing harness. Three women clutching awkward hens to their breasts, and another cradling the horn of a cow. Dozens and dozens, hundreds, hundreds of men and women and children side-stepping, jostling, striding, barging, talking, bargaining, laughing, arguing, playing, skipping, tripping, yelling, wailing – or, like some people, slumped against walls, somehow sunken into themselves, with nothing left in this world to hope for.

'Where are we going?' Gatty called out.

'The Three Archers,' Nakin shouted. 'Down by the river. Follow me.'

At the far end of the long street leading away from the city walls, there was a market-place with three lanes spoking out of it.

Some people took the left lane, some the right, and some, like the pilgrims, chose the middle one. For the first time since entering the city, they had a little space to pause, and draw breath.

At this moment, two boys came running up behind Nest at the back of the group.

The younger one brushed past her left arm; the other whisked the leather strap off her right shoulder and ripped away her pouch.

Nest shrieked; the pilgrims turned round to see what had happened; the two young boys just kept running.

'I'll get them!' yelled Gatty.

'No, Gatty!' shouted Emrys.

'Gatty!' Lady Gwyneth called after her. 'No!'

But Gatty took no notice. She tore down the street after the two boys.

When the boys saw Gatty was following them, they separated and Gatty chased after the bigger one, the one carrying the purse.

The boy led her through another market-place and down a narrow passage where Gatty could hear her own footsteps echoing. She followed him through a kind of tunnel, all dripping and dark, where hands reached up and tried to clutch her. Then left, then right, then right again – or was it left? Then across a courtyard. That's where the boy tripped and, before he could get up, Gatty threw herself onto him.

'You rat!' she gasped. She reached for her knife.

The moment the boy saw it, shining, he didn't struggle at all. He went quite limp, and meekly allowed Gatty to take back Nest's pouch.

Gatty glared at him. 'You,' she said, panting, 'you should lose your left hand!' She got up, and at once the boy scrambled to his feet and ran off. Gatty opened her own pouch and tucked Nest's inside it. Still panting, and excited at catching the boy, Gatty started to retrace her steps. Left . . . then right . . . then left again, was it? People kept getting in her way and after a while Gatty realised she had actually walked right round in a circle. She began to tremble. She had come back to the courtyard where she had pinioned the sneak-thief.

What about the gate then, Gatty said to herself. They'll have gone back to the gate, won't they? They'll wait for me there.

Several people told Gatty how to get back to the city wall but, when she did so, there was no gate. Gatty felt scared. She didn't know which way to go.

First she hurried east along the track following the inside of the wall, then she retraced her steps and set off west.

Stands to reason, she said to herself. We came in from the west, we did.

At last Gatty did come to a city gate, but it wasn't the right one, and no one was able to help her.

Gatty began to shake then. Her heart hammered in her chest. It was almost dark as she gathered up her cloak and hastened along the towering wall.

What if I can't find it, she thought. What if I can't find them?

God took pity on Gatty. In the dark, she stumbled upon

the gate through which she and all the others had entered the city. Panting and trembling, she pressed her back against its ribs and sucked her red knuckles. She stared up at the wide arch . . . and that was when she remembered.

The Three Arches. No! The Three Archers. That was it, wasn't it? Down by the river.

Gatty gulped. For the second time, she set off down the long street leading away from the city walls, and took the middle lane spoking out of the market-place.

When at last, after asking the way dozens of times, Gatty stumbled into the low-slung, candlelit tavern, Nest and Tilda saw her at once, and wrapped their arms around her; Nest began to sob. When Gatty extracted herself, she saw the corners of Lady Gwyneth's eyes were moist too.

'God forgive you!' she said, shaking her head.

'We thought . . .' sobbed Nest.

'I was!' exclaimed Gatty. 'Lost like the Tribes of Israel!'

'No!' sobbed Nest. 'We thought you were taken.'

'Or murdered,' said Tilda.

Gatty ran her hands through her hair. 'There was a kind of tunnel,' she said, 'and hands . . . and I swatted them!'

'Gatty!' cried Nest.

'I seen half of London. Where are the men?'

'There's Nakin!' said Tilda, pointing with her toe at the man lying with his face to the wall, snoring. 'The others have gone right back to the gate.'

'I did that,' said Gatty. 'A long way, that is.'

'You didn't catch them, then,' Tilda said. 'The boys.'

Gatty's eyes brightened. 'And all,' she said. She opened her pouch, and pulled Nest's out of it.

Nest began to snivel all over again.

'What's in it, then?' Gatty asked.

'My hairpins.'

'Hairpins!' exclaimed Gatty. 'Is that all?'

'They're beautiful,' said Nest, opening her pouch. 'My best ones.'

'What's in those pots, then?' Gatty asked her.

'My lotions,' replied Nest. 'My eye-blacking.'

'I don't remember Austin blessing those,' Lady Gwyneth said. 'Who said you could bring them?' And then she turned to Gatty. 'Rushing off on your own like that was foolhardy,' she said.

'After hairpins and lotions and all!' said Gatty, slapping her forehead.

'And you put us all at risk,' Lady Gwyneth continued. 'You put our whole pilgrimage at risk. Are you listening?'

Gatty lowered her eyes.

'You heard me calling after you,' Lady Gwyneth said angrily. 'There's no place whatsoever for disobedience on this pilgrimage. If you're going to disobey me, I'd rather make do with one chamber-servant. And I will.'

'I'm sorry, my lady.'

'Now!' said Lady Gwyneth. 'Tilda! Order food and ale for Gatty.'

But Gatty couldn't eat. She felt too chastened and upset by Lady Gwyneth's reprimand, too exhausted. She felt as she used to feel when field-work had worn her to the bone, or Hum had beaten all her energy out of her. She just wanted to curl up like a woodlouse. Gatty slipped down onto a wall-bench, and Nest and Lady Gwyneth sat on either side of her.

After a while, Nest put her mouth close to Gatty's left ear. 'I know I'm sometimes unkind,' she whispered. 'Forgive me, Gatty.'

Before they tried to sleep, Lady Gwyneth said prayers for the men, and asked God to guide them safely through the night to The Three Archers.

Tilda couldn't stop weeping. 'I know I said I wanted a

better husband,' she snivelled. 'But I'll be a better wife. Bring Emrys back and I will.'

Lady Gwyneth put one arm round Tilda and the other round Nest. 'It's in God's hands now,' she said.

That night, lying on a straw pallet, Gatty couldn't get to sleep for a long time because she kept thinking about how angry Lady Gwyneth had been, and kept worrying about the men. When she did fall asleep she dreamed about the two young boys who had run off with Nest's pouch. They stole into The Three Archers and sat her down in front of a pot of steaming stew, even though it was forbidden to eat meat during Lent. But Gatty had nothing to eat with except her fingers, and the stew was bubbling and boiling. The young boys laughed. Each of them drew a shining knife. First they speared and stabbed pieces of meat, and gulped them down, and scraped the gravy from their chins. Then they grinned and began to prick Gatty.

Gatty sat up in the dark. She reached out, and then she realised: the straw on the pallet had been prickling her neck and her arms.

The four men didn't reach The Three Archers that night. And they didn't get there in time to break their fast.

So Nakin couldn't visit the Venetian trading house where he had deposited gold and silver coin to check that a credit note had been sent ahead of them to Venice.

'There's no point,' he said. 'For all I know we're going to have to turn back.'

'How long should we wait, do you think?' Lady Gwyneth asked him.

Gatty knew it was all her fault. She gnawed her knuckles, and said nothing.

When Snout and Emrys, Austin and Everard did at last troop in late that morning, they were footsore, weary, hungry and frustrated. And when they saw Gatty sitting with the other women and Nakin, their first reaction was not so much one of relief as indignation and reproach.

'Where have you been?' Everard demanded.

'We walked halfway round the city walls,' said Snout. 'Four gates.'

'And said prayers at each of them,' Austin added.

'We've been halfway to Jerusalem already,' said Snout.

'Gatty knows she's done wrong,' said Lady Gwyneth. 'She knows she almost wrecked this pilgrimage for us all. Now where did you men sleep?'

'Sleep!' exclaimed Austin. 'We didn't.'

'We bought flares,' said Everard, 'and kept searching.'

Snout looked at Gatty. He saw how downcast she was. Like a sodden, shivering terrier. Without saying anything, he took both Gatty's hands between his huge warm paws and cradled them.

Gatty sniffed and swallowed. Then she gave a loud hiccup and began to sob.

'Nakin,' said Lady Gwyneth. 'You can go to the bank now.'

Tears were streaming down Gatty's freckled cheeks.

Lady Gwyneth nodded to Snout, reached out and put both arms round Gatty.

'We all admire your bravery,' she said in a quiet, warm voice. 'And I forgive you, Gatty. But from now on, don't just jump in – stop and think first. Yes?'

Gatty rubbed her forehead against Lady Gwyneth's left shoulder.

'You men,' said Lady Gwyneth. 'You need bowls of fish-stew. You need to drink and sleep. We'll have to wait until tomorrow morning to hire our horses.'

13

As the pilgrims picked their way along the muddy bank, there were more gulls about than people. Fast and low they flew over the greasy river, beating the bounds, reasserting their fishing rights with screeches and little yelps.

It was so early that the livery stables looked deserted. The hire-horses were still dozing in their stalls, the fire-pits had burned out, and when at last Emrys found Sayer, the stablemaster, sleeping in an empty stall, he had the devil of a job waking him up.

'It's too early for man or beast,' Sayer yawned. 'You'll have to wait.'

'Wait for what?' asked Emrys.

'Solomon,' said the stablemaster. 'I don't do deals without him, and he can't do deals without me.'

Emrys sighed and reported back to Lady Gwyneth.

'We're in your hands now, Emrys,' Lady Gwyneth said immediately.

'Nine horses, that's what we want,' Emrys told the stablemaster.

'Are you deaf?' Sayer demanded. 'I've told you already. You'll have to wait.'

'Nine horses,' Emrys repeated doggedly. 'To go to Venice.'

'You can't go to Venice, anyhow,' Sayer said yawning. 'You can't ride on water. Treviso, you mean. Treviso and back again.'

'That depends,' said Emrys.

'Depends?'

'How sound your horses are,' Emrys said carefully.

'You good-for-nothing!' the stablemaster exclaimed. 'All my horses are sound.'

'We'll see about that,' Emrys said.

'And Solomon and me will see about you,' Sayer retorted. 'You wait here. I'm having my bread and ale, I am.' And with that, he turned his back on the pilgrims and clumped across the other side of the stable.

'Did you have to be so . . . so gruff?' Everard asked.

'I met like with like,' Emrys replied. 'To let him know what's what.'

'We don't want to have to walk to Venice,' Everard said.

'I'm not walking for one more day,' Nest complained.

The stableman's breakfast put him in a more emollient mood. Smiling to himself, he led into the yard a huge roly-poly horse, standing at least seventeen hands. Its shining chestnut body was like a massive barrel.

'In the name of heaven!' exclaimed Emrys. 'No one here is going to ride a draughthorse.'

The pilgrims pointed at the horse's heavy quarters and stubby legs, but although some more refined horses might have been offended, the draughthorse just gave the pilgrims a dim look and flicked his short ears.

'This,' said Sayer, his voice rising in pitch, 'is Solomon. Aren't you, boy?'

By way of reply, the draughthorse raised his large head, dropped it, and then raised it again.

'You mean Solomon's a horse?' said Nest.

'What a clever girl!' Sayer said. 'Isn't she? Isn't she, boy?'

Emrys heard the way in which, this time, the stablemaster's voice lowered in pitch.

'Isn't she, boy?' the stablemaster repeated, and Solomon obliged by shaking his broad head from side to side.

The pilgrims laughed, all except Emrys, who was standing on his own. He put his hands around his mouth, and neighed like a mare.

At once Solomon lumbered towards him, and Emrys patted his nose. 'You know what's what, don't you boy?' he said with a rising pitch. And, sure enough, the draughthorse gave a cumbersome nod.

The stablemaster, now in altogether better humour, asked Emrys to help him lead twenty horses, ponies and mules out of their stables so the pilgrims could inspect them.

'Come and help us, girl,' Emrys told Gatty. 'You've got good horse sense.'

'Yes, Gatty, you have,' Lady Gwyneth said warmly.

For the first time that morning, Gatty's heart lightened. She sighed in relief, and then she smiled.

From the moment she saw the Welsh cob, Gatty knew she was the pony for her.

What was it? The way she arched her neck? Her silken feathering? Her foursquare, slightly bloodshot gaze? Or was it that she reminded Gatty so strongly of Pip, Arthur's cob? Her bright bay coat. Her white stockings.

Gatty stepped towards her, and the cob held her ground. She inclined her head to the pony's muzzle and picked up her breath: slightly sweet, like new grass; delicate, like violets.

Sayer walked up and slapped the cob's withers. 'Lovely, isn't she?'

Gatty nodded, wide-eyed.

'She'll be a good friend,' the stablemaster told her.

'A friend is what I need,' Gatty replied.

'And she's tough. She'll go day and night.'

'What's her name?' asked Gatty.

'Syndod.'

'Welsh!' Lady Gwyneth said. 'Wonder! Marvel! Show her to Emrys.'

73

Lady Gwyneth made a fine choice, too: a beautiful Arab, a stallion with gentle, wide-apart eyes and a silken mane.

'The best horse I've had in years,' the stablemaster said. He combed the Arab's mane with his fingers. 'Jerusalem,' he said. 'Arabia. Those parts. That's where he comes from.'

Emrys approved of Lady Gwyneth's choice. 'He'll have a temper on him,' he warned her. 'Arabs do.'

'But his eyes!' said Lady Gwyneth.

'I know,' said Emrys. 'He'll have a temper but he's gentle, he is.'

One by one, as the lemon sun swung up into the sky, Emrys helped each pilgrim to choose a horse or a pony. Austin was the last to decide, and he picked a fine white Andalusian horse.

'Saviour,' the priest announced. 'Saviour!'

Lady Gwyneth clapped her hands.

'Is that everyone?' asked Emrys. And by the time he and Sayer had sorted out sweat-pads, saddles, bridles, bits, and all the other tack, and checked that each animal was well-shod, it was already noon.

The pilgrims walked their mounts round the yard, getting to know them a little, getting the feel of being up in the saddle, and Nakin pulled coin after coin out of the stiff leather pouch stitched to his belt, and gave them to the stablemaster.

'All right, then,' Sayer told them. 'You can sell these horses, any of them, to the livery stable at Treviso. Or you can leave them there while you sail to Jerusalem, and collect them on your way back home without further payment. That's right, isn't it, boy?'

Sagely, Solomon nodded his heavy head.

14

A boy skinning a white cat. Two bearded men tipping a cartload of filthy straw into the river. A funeral procession led by a priest, following the corpse of a dead girl, dressed in white and strapped to a pallet.

Armed men, buffoons, cornmongers, dung-men, eagle-eyed stallholders, friars, fortune-tellers, fish-merchants, guards, hook-nosed Romans, ironmongers, Jewish money-lenders: a whole alphabet of people swarmed round Gatty and the other pilgrims as they picked their way out of London.

At dawn, Gatty had thought the city was too empty, too quiet, but now it seemed too crowded and noisy. She was glad to cross London Bridge, and to feel the wind fingering her scalp, pawing her left cheek. She was glad to leave seething, thieving London.

On the far side of the bridge, a group of children, twenty at least, were sitting on the ground, and a man with a tricorn hat was talking to them. The boys cheered, the girls jeered and then they all began to prod and push one another. The other pilgrims ignored them, but Gatty reined in.

'Not only that,' the man called out. 'Your tummies often rumble! You often fart!'

Again the boys cheered and the girls jeered.

'And as soon as you've been washed,' the man went on, 'you make yourselves ab-so-lute-ly filthy!'

More cheers, more jeers. But before Gatty could find out

why the man should choose to talk to children, and deliberately make them laugh, something she'd never once come across before, Everard rode up.

'Are you trying to get lost again?' he demanded in his dulcet voice.

'Sshh!' said Gatty. 'He's telling jokes.'

'Lady Gwyneth says you're to come at once.'

For some while after that, Gatty, Lady Gwyneth and Nest rode three abreast: Lady Gwyneth silently mouthing words as she told her rosary, Nest sometimes sighing and rearranging her cloak, Gatty still wondering about the man and the group of children, and rather indignant she had no chance to find out what was going on.

'My lady,' said Gatty after a while, 'I don't know how to say it exactly, but is our pilgrimage a kind of story?'

Lady Gwyneth reached up and played with a strand of her fair hair that had escaped her wimple. 'Yes,' she said hesitantly. 'In a way it is. An unfinished story.'

'And inside our story,' said Gatty, 'there are bits and pieces of all kinds of other stories. I mean, how did the stablemaster train Solomon? And why was that woman throwing the cabbage at that man? All those children on London Bridge? What were they laughing at?'

'I don't know,' said Lady Gwyneth.

'That's it,' said Gatty. 'We never will.'

Lady Gwyneth nodded. 'That's how the story of a pilgrimage is,' she said. 'Because we have to move on each day. But all the stories we step into become part of our own story. Our pilgrimage.'

'The parts we know do,' said Gatty.

Once again, Gatty and Syndod began to drift, to fall back, until they were at least a stone's throw behind the other pilgrims. Then two young men mounted on rather mangy ponies trotted up and fell into step with her.

'I'm John,' said one of them. 'He's Geoff. Going to Canterbury, are we?'

Thinking about John later, all Gatty could remember distinctly were his sharp, dark eyes. That, and the way his tunic was open at the neck. The blades of his shoulders.

'Where?' said Gatty.

'Canterbury.'

'What's Canterbury?'

John grinned. 'You having us on or something?'

'Either that,' said Geoff, 'or . . .' He tapped his temple with his right forefinger.

'I'm not,' said Gatty loudly. 'I'm with Lady Gwyneth. I'm her chamber-servant.'

'What about Becket?' John asked her. 'Heard of Becket?'

Gatty shook her head.

'You've got a scarlet cross on your shoulder and a staff in your hand,' said Geoff, 'and you're on the highway to Canterbury, but you've never heard of Canterbury or Becket. It doesn't add up.'

'She's just a pretty face,' said John.

Then the two young men told Gatty how Thomas Becket, Archbishop of Canterbury, had been hacked down by four knights in his own cathedral on a dark day in December thirty-two years before; and how, after touching his tomb, a dumb boy was able to speak for the first time in his life, and an old cripple threw away her crutches and skipped like a lamb.

'Since then,' said Geoff, 'there's been a miracle each week.'

'What you going to Canterbury for?' Gatty asked them.

Then John and Geoff told Gatty they were pilgrims, hired by rich people too old or too sick to travel themselves, or hired by the dead.

'How can the dead hire you?' Gatty asked.

'In their wills,' said John. 'To pray for their souls at the

Shrine of Saint Thomas or Our Lady of Walsingham. To pave their way to heaven with prayers. We're praying for the soul of a salty old sea captain – he died last week.'

'You don't know much, do you,' said Geoff.

Gatty lowered her head and squeezed Syndod's mane. 'Nobody told me,' she said, reproachfully.

'Here! Have a look at this,' said John. He tugged at the thong around his neck, and pulled out of his tunic a little lead flask. He took it off, and passed it to Gatty, making sure he brushed her fingers with his as he did so.

Gatty shook it. 'What's in it, then?'

'Blood,' said John. 'Blood and water from the Well of Saint Thomas. Tell you what! You keep it.'

'Me?'

'She can, can't she, Geoff?'

'It's yours,' said Geoff. 'One kiss each and it's yours.'

'Never!' exclaimed Gatty. Her face and neck began to burn.

The two young men laughed.

When Gatty raised her eyes again, she saw Nest trotting back towards her.

'Who's this?' asked Geoff, cheerfully.

'One girl each!' said John.

Waving their arms, the two of them sang out together:

> 'My sunlight, I desire you.
> My moonlight, shall I sleep with you?
> My starlight, I am in your bed already!'

Then Geoff and John threw back their heads and brayed like donkeys, and Gatty couldn't help herself: she laughed as well.

Nest pulled up in front of the three of them. 'Lady Gwyneth says . . .'

'This is Nest,' said Gatty. 'Me and her are Lady Gwyneth's chamber-servants.'

'. . . she says you're to come at once,' said Nest.

'What a beauty!' said John. 'Eh, Geoff?'

'She certainly is!' Geoff agreed.

'Come on!' said Nest.

Gatty laughed. Nest, she just kissed her fingertips twice, and then she dug in her heels and cantered back to Lady Gwyneth, with Gatty alongside her.

'Twice in one afternoon!' Lady Gwyneth said very sharply. 'I'm warning you, Gatty. I require you to be obedient, not to harum-scarum off whenever the fancy takes you. Do you understand?'

'They was telling me about Becket,' said Gatty, wide-eyed, and then she burst out laughing.

Lady Gwyneth gave Gatty a long, cool look. 'That poor man! Murdered. And you, shameless.'

Gatty shook her head, and her curls danced.

'We must pray for his protection,' Lady Gwyneth said. She looked over her shoulder and called out, 'Austin, we must pray to Saint Thomas, mustn't we?'

'Why is that, my lady?' Austin replied.

'To throw his cloak around us.'

Austin rode up. 'The saints who travel with us,' he said, 'are Saint David, who was a pilgrim to Jerusalem, and the blessed Christopher who carried the whole world . . .'

'I know that story,' said Gatty eagerly. 'Oliver told it us. He carries a small boy on his back across a river, and the boy gets heavier and heavier, and the boy is Jesus, and Jesus is the whole world.'

'Exactly,' said Austin. 'Saint Christopher, and Saint David, and also Michael the Archangel.'

'I know that story, too,' Gatty said.

'All right, Gatty,' said Lady Gwyneth. 'You're to ride beside me, and pray silently to those saints. That's your

79

penance, and you're not to speak one word until I say you can.'

Gatty did ride close to Lady Gwyneth, but she didn't pray to Saint Christopher or Michael the Archangel or anyone else. She thought about Geoff telling her she didn't know much, and about how much she did not know. Inside her head she kept singing-and-saying:

> I didn't know I didn't know.
> Nobody told me so.
> All I know is Hopeless lowing,
> Scythe and rake, spade and plough.
> I didn't know I didn't know,
> I never been beyond Ludlow.
> Nobody told me so.
> What and when and where and how?
> I didn't know I didn't know.
> Nobody told me so.

Gatty's reverie was interrupted by Nakin. 'Look!' he called out. 'Hares boxing!'

Just ahead, two hares were standing up on their back legs, and pummelling each other. Then they broke off, hared away, stood up and began to box again.

'Strange beasts!' said Everard. 'Boxers, little buskers. No rhyme or reason.'

'There is!' said Gatty. 'They box before they mate.'

'Gatty!' Lady Gwyneth exclaimed. 'Who said you could speak?'

'Oh!'

'I'll box your ears if you don't listen to what I say.'

'I'll keep quiet,' said Gatty. 'I will.'

'My lady,' said Lady Gwyneth.

'There are tiles in the cathedral with hares on them,' Everard said. 'I don't know why.'

On they went, the pilgrims, along the king's highway, over kindly hills, through scruffy, huddled villages, under bending naves of trees, on they went through pale sunlight and gusts of wind, rainstorms and sleet, arriving before daylight failed at noisy, jostling hostels.

On the third morning they drew near to Canterbury, and the road was seething with travellers. But then the way divided. To the right was a broad track leading to Canterbury, and to the left a track no less broad leading to Sandwich, and the sea.

Gatty's cob, Syndod, was greatly surprised not to take the way to Canterbury, and for quite some while she tugged at the reins and kept looking over her right shoulder, as if she were convinced Gatty had made a mistake.

That afternoon, Gatty ambled beside Everard, and the choirmaster began to tell her about Abbess Hildegard.

'I know about her,' said Gatty. 'What she said about blue eyes. Lady Gwyneth told me.'

'Do you know what she called herself?' Everard asked.

'How would I?'

'A feather on the breath of God.'

'Oh! Does Lady Gwyneth know that?' Gatty asked. 'That makes me tremble.'

'Because it's so submissive,' Everard told her. 'And do you know how a tongue of flame came down from heaven and settled on her head? And how after that she made up many beautiful songs?'

Gatty listened wide-eyed.

'And how she sang about Jerusalem? The gold-and-purple city? *Fenestre tue Ierusalem*,' sang Everard in his airy, light voice, '*cum tapazio et saphiro . . .*'

Everard was interrupted by a scream.

'Tilda!' exclaimed Emrys.

'You never speak up for me! You don't care a jot for me.'

'Please, Tilda!'

'I've told you!' Tilda yelled. 'You can go on your own!'

Then Tilda wheeled away. And spurring her rather stout pony, she cantered back the way they had come.

'What is it?' asked Gatty.

'We'll round her up!' shouted Snout.

'*Aros*!' Lady Gwyneth called out, raising her right hand. 'Wait!'

Emrys trotted up to Lady Gwyneth, and gave her a knowing look. 'One of her states,' he said. 'It'll pass.'

'You're a patient man, Emrys,' said Lady Gwyneth admiringly.

'An unclean woman!' said Nakin loudly.

'She won't get far,' said Emrys.

'Neither will we,' Lady Gwyneth said. 'Not without you, Emrys.'

'That's not the first time, is it?' Emrys said. 'You ride on, my lady, or you won't reach Sandwich before dark. We'll catch you up.'

'Do you want anyone . . .'

'I will,' said Gatty. 'I'll go.'

Emrys shook his head. 'You ride on, all of you. I'll round her up.'

The pilgrims reached Sandwich in the blue hour. And standing, without knowing it, where Arthur had first stood eighteen months before, Gatty tasted the salt-sharp air. Nest dismounted and came and huddled close to her. So did Snout. Then all the others. Except for Nakin, not one of them had ever seen the sea before. Wave-dance; water-music. The whole world of it!

Gatty opened up her arms and reached out, and hurrahed. Followed by the others, she ran down across the beach to the many-tongued sea.

15

Gatty couldn't find her footing. She couldn't even stand still. She lurched; she took one step forward and had to take several more to regain her balance; she tripped over her own feet.

The air – it was seething and so bright. Piercing saltspray! The wind bellowing and neighing! Gatty couldn't bring herself to climb down the ladder into the dark hold, where most of the pilgrims and other passengers were sheltering.

The boat bucked and bucketed and Gatty half-ran, half-slid right across the deck. To save herself from smacking into the port railing and, who knows, being catapulted into the boiling sea, she grabbed hold of the keel of the little skiff lying on its side, lashed to the deck. Then she saw two people were sitting on the other side of it, completely protected from the wind and the spray, and when Gatty pressed her ear against the boards, she could hear them talking.

'. . . Gatty.'

'I know!'

'Gatty! That's what she is. Cattish!'

'I know!'

'So spiteful.'

Gatty squeezed the keel. She tried to crush it between her fingers. Why, she thought. What have I done? I'm not spiteful.

'She's always complaining.' That was Nakin. Gatty was

sure it was. 'How many times have you told her?'

'I know!' wailed the other voice for the third time, and Gatty knew it was Lady Gwyneth's.

'I told you! You shouldn't have brought her.' Then Nakin lowered his voice and, although Gatty flattened one ear against the wooden boards, she couldn't make out what he was saying.

Gatty thought her fingertips were going to burst. She thought her heart was going to burst. She sat down and pulled herself backwards across the weeping deck, away from the skiff, away from the hateful words.

Spiteful . . . How can they say that? Gatty gnawed her lower lip until it bled. I don't belong with the likes of Lady Gwyneth and Nakin, she thought. I never will.

During the afternoon, the wind eased, and Nakin rounded everyone up, and told them Lady Gwyneth wanted to talk to them.

'Where's Gatty?' asked Lady Gwyneth.

'Has no one seen her?' asked Nakin.

'I did,' said Nest.

'Where?'

'Sobbing. And slobbering.'

'Where?'

'Down with her horse.'

'Go and get her, Nest,' Lady Gwyneth said sharply. 'She's keeping us waiting,'

Gatty looked piteous. Her hair was matted; her clothes were drenched, and had bits of straw sticking in them; her eyelids were rosy and puffy.

'God's kneecaps!' exclaimed Lady Gwyneth. She sighed deeply. 'Can you all hear me?'

'No,' said Austin.

'Then draw closer, man,' Lady Gwyneth ordered him. 'I want you all to listen.'

Gatty didn't want to hear what Lady Gwyneth was going to say.

'I've told you before that we must all think for each other and find Christ in each other. Unless we do that, our pilgrimage will be . . .'

'Wrecked,' said Nakin.

'Yes,' said Lady Gwyneth. 'Wrecked! Winds and waves beat at our boat, there are dangers all around us. We may be many, but unless we are one . . .'

'We'll all be drowned,' said Nakin.

Lady Gwyneth waved away the merchant's words. 'Gatty!' she cried. 'You chased those boys. What if we'd been unable to find you? And the next day you were disobedient. Twice. Have you no regard for me, or our pilgrimage?'

Gatty said nothing. Two large tears slipped down her cheeks.

'And you keep on answering back,' Lady Gwyneth added. 'As for you, Tilda! You cost us two days, running away like that.'

'I don't know what comes into me, my lady,' Tilda said. 'I see things that frighten me, and then I do things I don't mean. Not afterwards.'

Nest sighed noisily. 'If we were all like Gatty and Tilda . . .' she began, and she closed her eyes and shook her head.

Lady Gwyneth gave Nest a disdainful look. 'Keep your spiteful words to yourself,' she snapped. 'We've heard quite enough of them, and enough of your moaning and complaining as well.'

Tilda gulped and gave a great sob.

'Not again!' said Nakin.

'*Wyt ti'n deall?*' Lady Gwyneth demanded. 'Do you understand? Think for each other and act for each other. I will not put up with disobedience, and I will not tolerate so much arguing and complaining. Did our Lord complain when He suffered for us?'

Tilda moaned. A desolate moan that seemed as if it would never end.

Nest clamped her hands over her ears and rounded on Emrys. 'Stop her!' she cried. 'Can't you?'

'Let me make myself clear,' Lady Gwyneth said in a steely voice. 'Now we've left England, things can only get more difficult. If you fear you'll fail yourself, any of you, turn back here and now. You can go back on this boat, and I'll pay your passage.'

Lady Gwyneth paused and looked each pilgrim in the eye.

'If any of you lets yourself down,' she warned them, 'you let us all down, and I will not hesitate to leave you behind when we reach Venice. You will never reach Jerusalem.'

Gatty had set out on this great pilgrimage with such pride. Such high hopes. But now she knew her lady didn't think her worthy, and she bitterly regretted being so disobedient.

She lurched round and round the deck, and then flopped down by a coil of thick rope. But as soon as she did so, she realised she had sat in a pool of pitch. Her hands stuck to it; the heels of her sandals stuck to it; the seat of her cloak was glued to it.

Miserably, Gatty levered herself on to her feet and bunched up her cloak and screwed round to look at it.

At this moment, arm in arm to stop themselves from slipping and sliding, Nest and Austin staggered towards her.

'What are you doing?' Nest called out. 'Admiring your buttocks?'

Gatty dropped her cloak and splayed her hands like a cat. They were black and shining.

'Yuch!' yelled Nest.

Austin smiled grimly. 'Half-pink, half-black,' he observed.

'You're a devil-in-the-making.'

'As black as Mansel's bitch!' added Nest.

Gatty stared at her hands; then she inspected her sandals.

'Look at your gown!' said Nest. 'It won't wash out, you know.'

'You must cut the pitch out,' Austin told her. 'Like a heretic's tongue.'

Hearing this, the sea opened its mouth and vomited over the deck. Austin and Nest were swept back beyond the wheel-house; Gatty was thrown into the pool of pitch again.

There she lay, her head pillowed on the coarse coil of rope. But then it was as if God had looked down on poor Gatty, and crept into her heart. Gatty began to smile at her own misfortune, and then to hum. And before long, she was matching words to her hum:

> 'You look ratty.
> Spotty. Sticky.
> You look shitty.
>
> Gatty, Gatty!
> Don't spit. Don't curse.
> You known even worse.
>
> Cow-bloat. Burrow-lice.
> And what's worst is
> Ghastly rotting ghostses!'

After Gatty had prised herself apart from the pitch for the second time, she went below deck. She rubbed her chapped hands against the rough timbers; she lay on her back like a cat and wriggled until she'd rubbed off the worst of the pitch; then she took off her gown and sandals, and scrubbed them against the ship's timbers too.

Back on deck, Gatty saw Snout leaning over the gunwale,

and then she heard him sobbing. Quietly, she walked up behind him. Without saying a word, she simply slipped her hands round his waist.

For a while, Snout went on gulping and swallowing.

Gatty locked her sticky fingers together, as if they were the clasp to Snout's belt, and gently laid her head against Snout's back.

'I dropped it!'

Gatty waited.

'I dropped it,' Snout said again. His whole body jolted.

Gatty had no idea what he had dropped. 'Oh Snout!' she said, sweetly.

The sound of Gatty's sympathy unlocked Snout's word-tide.

'Hew gave it me,' he said. 'His stone. He found it and there was a flower in it, and he said, he said . . .' Snout's heavy body shook with another great sob. '. . . he said it kept him safe from demons and he gave it to me . . . and I dropped it. I dropped it!'

'Oh Snout!' said Gatty again. 'You and Hew. You're such a father! Not like mine.' With her head still lying against the cook's back, Gatty began very slightly to rock, as if she were singing a silent song.

The short March day began to fail, and although the pilgrims could see the French coast, it was plain they wouldn't be able to reach it before nightfall but would have to stand offshore until morning.

'Well, Gatty,' Lady Gwyneth said wearily. 'Will you sit and sup with me?'

Gatty backed away a step.

'It's all right,' Lady Gwyneth said. 'You're filthy and soaked, I know, but I'm well protected.'

Then she put her arm round Gatty's shoulders, and led her

over to the skiff lashed to the deck. 'We can sit here,' she said, 'out of the wind. Nakin and I did this morning.'

Gatty felt so confused. She lumped down beside Lady Gwyneth and gnawed at her crust of bread. Exhausted by the wind and the waves, and the storm of her own feelings, she closed her salty eyelids.

After a while, Lady Gwyneth drew Gatty's head down onto her lap. She laid her warm right hand on Gatty's shoulder, and closed her own eyes too.

When she woke, Gatty knew she had slept for a long time because the eastern skyline had turned pale. She gazed up at Lady Gwyneth and, beneath her, the boat swayed, and shuddered a little. Nothing was certain. She was at sea.

After a while, Lady Gwyneth opened her eyes. 'Gatty!' she said, and she yawned. 'I was dreaming.' She looked down at Gatty, gauzy-eyed. 'Dreaming . . .' she repeated, and she yawned again.

'I was on a dark ocean in a skiff like this one. The tide was taking me away, away from Ewloe, and I knew I could never come back. But I could see everything . . .' Lady Gwyneth paused. 'Snout was a boar, with tusks. Nest was a spitting cat. Green-eyed and spitting. And you, Gatty . . . Can you believe it? You were the new Lady of Ewloe.' Lady Gwyneth smiled and shook her head.

Lying and listening, Gatty wondered why Lady Gwyneth was talking to her like this. Why she was telling her these things when she thought Gatty was spiteful, and wished she hadn't brought her?

'Come on!' said Lady Gwyneth. 'All this nonsense! Let's walk round the deck.'

Gatty sat up. 'My lady,' she began, without stopping to think whether it was the right moment.

'What is it, Gatty?'

'I heard you.'

'Heard me?'

'You and Nakin. Sitting here.'

'Ohh!'

'Cattish! And spiteful. My lady, I'm not spiteful.'

'Gatty!'

'I'm not. I got a big mouth, I know, but I can keep it shut.'

Lady Gwyneth ran the tips of her fingers through Gatty's salt-sticky hair. 'Gatty!' she said. 'Listen!'

'I can!' insisted Gatty.

'Gatty, will you listen? How can you have thought . . . how can you think . . . Oh! Don't you know how much?'

Only as Lady Gwyneth fumbled for words did she realise quite how much she already depended on Gatty's quick wit, warm heart and plain sense.

Gatty stared at Lady Gwyneth, wide-eyed. 'Honest?' she asked.

Lady Gwyneth took hold of both Gatty's ears. 'This comes of eavesdropping,' she said. 'Nakin and I weren't talking about you at all.'

'You weren't?'

'No.'

'Who, then?'

'I need you, Gatty,' Lady Gwyneth said warmly and firmly. 'Our pilgrimage needs you. Don't you know that?'

When, before long, the boat docked, Gatty felt unconscionably joyous. With Lady Gwyneth's words still ringing in her ears, she ran down the gangway and the French earth rose up to meet her. It swayed and lurched beneath her, and for a while, amazed, Gatty was unable to stand upright and foursquare on her pink-and-black feet.

16

Which way; what weather; water and bread and Lenten stew and fish; caring for their horses; nursing their sores; the punctuation of prayers: after the pilgrims had landed in France, the ingredients of each day were the same, and yet their colour, detail and mood kept changing. On the first day, they heard the music of French spoken by Normans, fresh and pretty as a meadow of spring cowslips and forget-me-nots; on the second, Simon's cooking-pot sprung a leak, stirring Emrys to anger and delaying the hungry pilgrims while a blacksmith hammered out a new one; on the third day, Gatty wore her soft yellow felt shoes for the first time and, like a tender April shower arrived a little too early, she wept sweet, warm tears when she thought about Mansel, the shoemaker's son; on the fourth day, a red-faced pardoner accosted the pilgrims at a town gate and, as soon as he discovered Lady Gwyneth was Welsh, tried to persuade her to buy Saint David's little toe.

'A little toe but a very large price!' Lady Gwyneth said, shaking her head. '*Dim peryg!* Not a chance!'

'Go away!' said Nakin. 'You pest!'

The pardoner spoke only broken English but not so broken that he was unable to insult the Welsh. He angrily called them sorcerers, and fickle, and even bestial.

Lady Gwyneth was terribly upset. 'Scabrous!' she exclaimed. 'I'll have your name dropped to the bottom of each cursing-well in Wales. There was a Welsh pope, I hope you know. Kyric! The Welsh pope!'

On the fifth day, late March sunlight warmed the pilgrims' backs, and on the sixth a yapping dog attached himself to them for most of the morning, and exasperated them even more than Tilda's endless sniffing and sobbing, but Nakin said that difficult as their pilgrimage was becoming, it was still preferable to being at home with his quarrelsome wife.

'He's a strong man, is Emrys, taking on both,' Nakin observed. 'This pilgrimage, and his wife as well.'

'Are you insulting Tilda?' demanded Emrys.

'Still, Everard,' Nakin went on. 'Better a bad wife than no wife at all, wouldn't you say?

> 'By all the silken hairs on my chin-chin-chin,
> I wish I had a wife at home-home-home . . .'

Which way; what weather; water and bread and Lenten stew and fish: so, like a cartwheel the slow week turned, and on the evening of the seventh day, unable to reach the pilgrim hostel at Reims before dark, the pilgrims rode into the scruffy yard of a tavern.

In the courtyard, a crowd of people were watching two pigs stumbling and tumbling around as if they were drunk.

'That's just what they are,' a French nun shrieked, almost helpless with laughter. 'They're drunk!'

'How come?' asked Emrys.

'They knocked over a beer barrel,' explained a young man with a little forked black beard, 'and drank some of the grounds.'

One sow advanced towards Gatty, snuffling.

'Come here, then,' said Gatty.

But as soon as Gatty tickled her right ear, the sow's front legs gave way beneath her. She rolled right over onto her back.

'I never seen that before,' Gatty laughed. 'She won't be sober this side of morning.'

'Disgraceful!' said Austin.

'Desirable!' said Nakin.

That evening, the tavern served hot herring, and it didn't taste too good. In fact, it tasted bad and no amount of beer could disguise it.

Lady Gwyneth spat hers straight out into the mouldy straw covering the floor.

Everard chewed, and chewed some more, and screwed up his face, and swallowed his.

'Got the stomach for it, have you?' Nakin taunted him. Then he gulped down his portion as if it were the most tasty wild rabbit, or gosling fattened with groats and oatmeal.

Snout shook his head and pushed his portion to one side. 'Lent!' he said in disgust.

'Yes,' agreed Austin. 'March is the cruellest month.'

'No meat,' Snout went on. 'No eggs. No cheese. Rotten food.' He turned to Gatty. 'I wouldn't, if I were you.'

Gatty smelt the herring and wrinkled up her nose, and then she ate it. 'Known worse,' she declared.

After the pilgrims had gone out to the piss-buckets or the trenches, they retreated to the dormitory where all the women slept on straw at the far end of the room, and all the men slept at the near end. Emrys, Snout and Nakin played dice, and Lady Gwyneth told Gatty about her childhood in Clwyd and how her father used to call her his 'pearl'. Then they and Everard gossiped with some of the other travellers: the young man with the forked beard who was on his way to the University of Paris to study; a self-important German envoy whose mouth was stuffed with platitudes, and who refused to tell them whence he had come or whither he was going – 'Walls have ears!' he kept saying. These two, and a friendly merchant from Norway with shining pale blue eyes, who was on his way south with amber, seal-skins and walrus tusks, and in clipped, clean English told them how in his country summer nights were days and winter days were nights.

'That's nothing!' said the German envoy. 'I've sailed to an island in the Red Sea, and in the night sky there are no constellations. No Little Bear. No Great Bear.'

'Great Bear?' repeated Gatty.

'The Plough,' murmured Everard.

'No,' said the envoy, pumping his elbows so that his cloak flapped and he looked like a stork settling on its nest. 'Not even the hunter, Orion. There's just one star and the people there call it Canapos. The hills on the island are made of gold. I've seen them. They're guarded by pismires.'

'I've seen the Merry Dancers,' the Norwegian merchant told them. 'Streams ice-blue, violet curtains, streaks and bands, gold-and-silver – all of them swelling, trembling in the northern night sky.'

'A miracle!' said Lady Gwyneth.

'Probably not,' said the student with the forked beard.

'Who are we to say?' asked Lady Gwyneth, smiling an inward smile and gently shaking her head.

'What I say is that understanding explains many things we think of as miracles,' the student replied. 'The tip of a black twig unfurling, soft as a baby's fingertips. Is that a miracle?'

'And a boy's voice breaking,' added Everard. 'The same boy, the same body, but a different voice.'

'What I mean,' Lady Gwyneth replied, 'is that these things are God's plan, and we should wonder at them.'

'Ah!' said the student. '*Mirare*. Yes, *miraculum*.'

At that moment, the French nun bustled into the dormitory, and plumped herself down on the straw beside them.

'What are you talking about?' she asked, and she giggled.

And then, without waiting for a reply: 'Would you like to hear a story?'

'I'm sure we would,' said Lady Gwyneth.

'Well,' began the nun, 'this came from the Caliphate of Baghdad.'

'The what of what?' Gatty exclaimed.

'Beyond Jerusalem,' Everard told her.

'What's a Caliphate?' demanded Gatty.

'Sshh!' said Lady Gwyneth. 'A Caliph is a leader.'

'A successor,' the student corrected her. '*Khalifa*. A successor to the Prophet Muhammad.'

'A pagan,' said Everard. 'An enemy of God.'

'Will you all be quiet!' Lady Gwyneth insisted.

'Yes,' said the nun, 'this is a Saracen story, but it doesn't matter. Now! There was this merchant. He lived in a street lined with palm-trees and at the bottom of the garden there was a white fountain.'

Gatty didn't know what palm-trees or a fountain were, but she saw Lady Gwyneth look at her out of the corners of her eyes, and kept her mouth shut.

'He was a poor man, though,' said the nun, 'and it was his own fault. He wasted his money, gambling and dicing. Now one night this merchant had a dream. A man in scarlet clothing stood beside him and told him to go and find his fortune in Cairo in Egypt.'

Gatty was sure she had heard the name Egypt before, but she couldn't think where.

'It took the merchant weeks and weeks to walk there – he couldn't afford a horse, you know – and when he got there, he couldn't afford to stay in the tavern. He lay down in the courtyard of the mosque.'

'Where Saracens pray,' Lady Gwyneth whispered to Gatty.

'That night, robbers rushed through the courtyard into the house next to it,' the nun continued. 'When the constables arrived, they thought the merchant was one of the robbers and beat him until he turned purple. Then they locked him in a prison cell and, three days later, they dragged him before the Chief Constable.

'"Where do you come from?" the Constable asked him.

'"Baghdad," said the merchant. "I had a dream. A man in scarlet clothing stood beside me and told me to come. He said I'd find my fortune if I came to Cairo."

'"You fool!" the Constable exclaimed. "You came all this way because of a dream? Why, I had a dream last night about going to Baghdad and finding gold in a garden, right under a white fountain. You see? Nonsense. Take my advice and go back home."

'"I will," said the merchant.

'As soon as the merchant got home,' the nun went on, 'he started to dig up his fountain, and under it he found a pot full of gold coins. He found his fortune.'

The nun giggled happily, and Lady Gwyneth sighed. 'A very good story,' she said. 'Even the Saracens have good stories. Thank you for telling it.'

'*De rien*,' the nun replied.

'Dreams,' mused Lady Gwyneth. 'Partly true, partly untrue. Such a strange mixture.'

Everard coughed and swallowed noisily. He swallowed again.

'Everard!' said Lady Gwyneth. 'Are you all right?'

Ashen-faced, Everard stood up and without another word hurried out into the courtyard, and was at once violently sick.

That night, at one time or another, surrounded by a circle of indifferent pigs, Emrys and Snout and Nakin and almost everyone else who had eaten the herring was sick as well.

Not Gatty, though.

All night Lady Gwyneth's chamber-girl lay innocent, with her hands flung back above her head, palms up.

'So you slept?' Lady Gwyneth asked her.

Gatty gave a prodigious yawn, and then clamped her right hand to her mouth.

Lady Gwyneth gingerly placed her hands over her stomach.

'I known worse, my lady!' said Gatty, grimacing.

17

'No!' said Lady Gwyneth. 'Not today and not tomorrow. And not the next day either.'

'Why not?' whined Nest.

'How many more times do I have to tell you?' Lady Gwyneth demanded. 'We've already forfeited five days. Gatty cost us one in London, and we lost three in Sandwich . . .'

'So it's because of Gatty and Tilda,' said Nest cattily.

'. . . and then the day after we ate that rotten herring,' Lady Gwyneth continued.

'Austin could give us another reading lesson,' Nest said slyly.

'We've no idea what risks and delays lie ahead of us. We have to cross high mountains, and Nakin says there'll still be snow and ice on the high passes.'

Nest sighed noisily.

'How difficult you make life for yourself,' Lady Gwyneth said, 'and for us all. Complaining. Whining. Have you forgotten my warning? Don't you want to see Jerusalem? You must just accept your bruised knee, your hoarse voice, your . . . your neck. I don't know. What else?'

'My buttocks,' said Nest. 'All this riding. Jolting.'

'On Palm Sunday,' Lady Gwyneth said loudly, 'on this very day, Jesus meekly rode on the colt of an ass from the Mount of Olives into Jerusalem. All His uncomplaining! He chose to suffer, Nest, He chose to die, and you complain to me about your buttocks!'

This tirade shamed Nest into silence.

It wasn't very long before Emrys rode up alongside Lady Gwyneth. 'My lady,' he said. 'Our horses could do with a rest-day.'

'They'll get one,' Lady Gwyneth snapped. 'They'll get three. Good Friday and Easter Eve and Easter Day. But first we have to reach the great monastery at Vézelay.'

Lady Gwyneth's grey wheezed.

'Hear that?' asked Emrys.

Lady Gwyneth leaned forward and patted her Arab's neck. 'I've told her Good Friday,' she said brightly. 'Our aches and pains – all our small sufferings – they're part of our pilgrimage. We must learn to welcome them.'

'You've told the horses that, have you, my lady?' Emrys asked.

'Emrys!' exclaimed Lady Gwyneth.

'As with humans, so with horses,' Emrys warned her. 'Ignore a small complaint and you risk a greater one.'

'We'll rest over Easter at Vézelay,' Lady Gwyneth assured him. 'We really have no choice but to ride on. We mustn't run the least risk of missing the last sailing from Venice.'

So while Jesus rode on a colt into Jerusalem, and overturned the stalls of all the traders in the temple, while He gave a blind man back his seeing eyes, and infuriated the chief priests, while He was betrayed by Judas Iscariot – while all these things came to pass, the pilgrims rode south.

Emrys had pockets of pus all over his face; Tilda had such pain in one arm, the left one, that she kept it strapped up the whole time; Snout's throat glands were swollen; Nakin had too much evil-smelling gas in his body; the pilgrims were all aching, limb-weary, bone-weary.

The next morning, it began to rain. Not a clean, sweet early April shower but a persistent drizzle that worked its way through the pilgrims' hats and cloaks and inside their boots, until they were all drenched and bone-cold and miserable.

For a while, they ploughed on because there was nowhere to shelter. But when they came to a small wooded cliff, and saw through the mist a shallow cave, Lady Gwyneth agreed to call a halt, worried though she was about the slow progress they were making.

When they got there, she and Everard were both so stiff in their saddles that they needed help to dismount.

'My fingers won't work,' Lady Gwyneth said.

'Now you know what mine are like,' Tilda told her. 'And my toes. The whole time.'

While Nest helped Lady Gwyneth to undress, and the other pilgrims squelched around and peeled off their sodden clothes and pulled on whatever dry clothing they had in their saddlebags, Gatty found in the back of the cave the remains of a fire – charcoal, a few sticks and branches, ashes – and settled herself beside it.

She burrowed into her scrip. 'My fire-starter,' she said to herself. 'Where is it?'

Gatty pulled out a little wooden box. Inside it, and mercifully still dry, were little strips of char-cloth, a mouse-nest of fibres, the thinnest strips of birch bark. Those and Gatty's lumps of grey-green flint and steel, with which to strike sparks.

Holding them close to the box, Gatty clashed the flint against the steel over and again. But when at last she did strike a spark, it flew in the wrong direction. Patiently, Gatty kept trying until a spark landed on the mouse-nest and at once she cupped it between her hands and very gently, very steadily blew on it.

As soon as the first flame flickered, Gatty tipped the nest onto the floor of the cave, added little sticks to it, and asked all the others to hunt for wood.

'Anything lying around in the cave,' she called out. 'And fallen branches outside. It doesn't matter if they're damp. Anything!'

After this, Snout set up a tripod, and filled the cooking-pot with water from the pool at the entrance to the cave, and put meaty soup-bones into it; Emrys, meanwhile, built a frame behind the fire so the pilgrims could at least dry their stockings.

'Very good, Gatty!' said Lady Gwyneth. 'Not at all easy on a day like this.'

Snout's soup slowly warmed the pilgrims. Sitting close to one another around the fire, they began to steam. To talk. Even to laugh again.

Grey mist stood outside the smoky cave. Inside, the nine pilgrims coughed and huddled together for warmth, they drowsed and fell asleep.

When the pilgrims woke, all the rain-clouds had blown away.

South they rode, under the sun's primrose eye, and before reaching Auxerre they came to the banks of the River Yonne. There they boarded a flat-bottomed ferry, but the ferry began to rock from side to side and Lady Gwyneth's stallion whinnied and kicked out at the passengers standing behind him. Then he leaped right out of the boat. He swam ahead of it to the river-bank, shook himself until he whirred, and then stood quite quietly, waiting for Lady Gwyneth to disembark.

'The distance from success to disaster,' Lady Gwyneth told Emrys, 'is no wider than this milky French river.'

Now the pilgrims saw the Morvan hills rising up ahead of them, and before long they breasted the first of them. They picked their way down into sloping valleys past little hillside vineyards, they padded through whispering pinewoods.

After three more days, they crossed the great pilgrim road leading west all the way to Saint James of Compostela in

Spain. And, as Lady Gwyneth had predicted, they rode into the great monastery of Saint Mary Magdalen in Vézelay in good time to die with Jesus, and lie with Him in the cold rock tomb, and on the third morning rise with Him again.

While all the others hurried straight to the stables, Gatty stared about her in absolute amazement. A giant courtyard! Walls so white and bright they half-blinded her. Chapels and colonnades and pointed towers and granaries. The monastery was a town in itself. Nuns and monks, hundreds and hundreds of them, all wearing black habits, were striding and streaming and criss-crossing and huddling, busy as ants. And up in the high belfry bells chorused with rich, shining voices, the fruit not only of their tongues and throats but their whole bodies.

'*Pays de dieu!*' a monk called out. '*Pays de la Madeleine!*'

Gatty frowned.

'*D'ou venez-vous? D'Espagne? D'Angleterre?* English?'

'English,' said Gatty.

'Ahh!' said the monk, and he spread his arms. 'This is Vézelay! God's own country! Home of *la Madeleine.*'

'What's Madeleine?' asked Gatty.

The monk looked at Gatty strangely. 'Sainte Marie,' he exclaimed.

'Oh! Saint Mary Magdalen, you mean,' Gatty said.

'*Enorme!*' said the monk. 'Big in Europe.'

'What's Europe?' Gatty asked.

The monk opened and closed his mouth like a fish. 'Europe,' he repeated. 'Europe! *Nom de dieu!*' Then he showed the palms of his hands to heaven, and walked away.

Inside the guesthouse reserved for pilgrims, women and men went two different ways – even those who were married, like Tilda and Emrys.

In the refectory, Gatty found herself sitting at one of three long tables between Lady Gwyneth and Sister Hilda, a dumpling of a nun whose jowls rested on her breasts and breasts rested on the table.

Opposite Gatty sat Aenor, a pale girl who was much the same age as she was, and still a novice.

Both of them spoke English.

'Jerusalem, you say?' Sister Hilda demanded.

'God willing,' said Lady Gwyneth.

'Why?'

'Why?' exclaimed Lady Gwyneth. 'Let me finish this excellent trout, and I'll explain.'

'From everything I've heard,' the stout nun announced, 'it's quite obvious you're likely to fall by the wayside on pilgrimage. Reeling drunkards, swearing gamblers, whoremongers! Foul songs in the taverns!'

'It's not like that at all,' said Nest. 'You can't imagine the hardship. Each day's a penance.'

'I should have liked to go on a pilgrimage,' said Aenor, the young novice.

Sister Hilda snorted. 'You wouldn't get as far as Autun,' she said. 'Not with your weakness. Your place is here, my girl.'

The novice laid a white hand over her chest, and coughed delicately. But her sepia eyes! Gatty saw how they were burning.

'Your English is strong, though,' Lady Gwyneth said kindly.

'She was brought up in England,' Sister Hilda said. 'Bury Saint Edmunds.'

'I know that saint,' said Gatty. 'He's in our church at Caldicot.' She smiled at Aenor, and the novice nervously smiled back.

'Aenor's half-English and half-Italian,' Sister Hilda said stiffly. 'Now, you've finished that trout, haven't you?'

Lady Gwyneth licked the tip of her right forefinger and dabbed the corners of her mouth. 'Yes! Well, I can tell you I've brought three sacks with me on this pilgrimage. One sack is full of patience, one contains as much money as we will need, and the third sack's brimming with my belief, my faith.'

At this moment, the nun sitting at the head of the middle table vigorously shook a handbell. All the nuns at once stood up, and the pilgrims followed them.

'*Benedicamus benedicantur,*' intoned the nun at the head of the table. '*Per Jesum Christum Dominum nostrum.*'

'Amen,' everyone responded.

'That's it!' Sister Hilda said in a hoarse voice. 'Silence now until morning – after we've broken our fast.' Briskly, she made the sign of the cross over her place at table, picked up her wooden trencher and mug and, with a purposeful nod to pale Aenor, stumped out of the refectory.

As Gatty followed Lady Gwyneth, she felt a hand on her elbow. The hand guided her to the left, at once to the right, and away into a dark cloister.

'What is it?' asked Gatty.

Aenor led Gatty through the cloister garden ashen in the moonlight, and over to a lime-tree.

'*Tandaradei!*' she sang in a low voice. 'We got away!'

'I'll be in trouble,' Gatty said.

The pale novice gazed at Gatty. 'Sshh! Whisper! Your mother . . .'

'My mother?'

'She loves you.'

'What do you mean?'

'Lady Gwyneth. I can see how she does.'

Gatty guffawed, then clasped a hand over her mouth. 'I'm not Lady Gwyneth's daughter!'

'You're not?'

'I'm a field-girl. Well, I was.'

'You mean . . . low-born?' The pale girl considered Gatty.

'I got to go,' whispered Gatty. 'I'll be in trouble. We can talk tomorrow.'

The pale girl grasped Gatty's right wrist.

'What?'

'Please! I must ask you.'

'What?'

'Can I come with you?'

'Where?'

'To Jerusalem?'

Gatty drew in her breath. She had no idea how to reply.

'I can't stay here. I can't. Not one day longer.' Aenor's breath quickened. 'Not with what she does to me. God doesn't want me to. I can walk and ride. I can.'

Gatty stared at the girl. She could hear her desperation.

'Will you ask Lady Gwyneth?' she asked, standing in the moonlight like a wraith.

Gatty reached out. She wrapped her arms around the pale girl. Fiercely she hugged her frail, flat-chested body.

'I'm afraid,' Aenor whispered.

Dog-tired as she was, Gatty couldn't sleep for a long time that night because of all the thoughts and questions giddying round inside her head.

Why can't she stay one day longer? Why's she so afraid? What does that lump, Sister Hilda, do to her? I must help her, but how? It did just cross Gatty's mind that Lady Gwyneth could leave Nest and all her complaining behind at the monastery and take poor Aenor with her instead. Gatty sighed in the darkness, and smiled. No, she thought. She'd never agree to that.

In the roof of the women's dormitory, the beams cricked and creaked; and in her sleep, Tilda was talking nonsense in a completely reasonable voice. Someone sighed. Someone sniffed. And then, somewhere up on the pantiles, a monastery dove cooed promises. Gatty fell asleep.

Gatty's Welsh cob, Syndod, needed fitting out with a new set of shoes, and she needed a poultice for the weeping sore on her girth. She needed grooming. And seasoned and hardy as she was, Gatty's own body needed repairs and remedies: for her constipation, fennel tea; and for her bleeding gums, the bitter smoke of aloe and myrrh heated over beechwood and sucked through a straw.

What with time to see Saint Mary Magdalen's bones and marvel at the shining basilica, time to drowse and rise again as the monks and nuns sang the six offices (pilgrims were excused the two o'clock Matins on the grounds that God required them to rest and recuperate), time to see the cross where Saint Bernard stood and preached the second great crusade, and time to hear how Coeur-de-Lion and Thomas Becket, Archbishop of Canterbury, had both come to pray at Vézelay, time to resume reading and singing lessons while Emrys and Snout practised their fighting skills, time to eat, time to sleep, Gatty had no time at all to talk to moon-pale Aenor during the next two days, and she wasn't altogether sorry about it.

The novice's shadow at the stable door; her thin arm pressing against Gatty's arm on their way into Vespers; her unblinking gaze across the refectory table: these moments left a stone in Gatty's heart. She didn't know what to do.

At the Easter feast, the nuns and pilgrims ended their long Lenten fast. First they ate cheese and eggs.

'Be wary how much you eat,' Lady Gwyneth counselled Gatty, Nest and Tilda. 'Forty-six days! It's a long time since your stomachs welcomed such a feast.'

'Mine didn't last year,' Gatty said, and she pretended to throw up.

'Please Gatty!' said Lady Gwyneth.

'And now hare!' said Sister Hilda. 'Caught three weeks ago. Right here, in the cloister.'

'How do you preserve it?' Lady Gwyneth asked.

'I'll spare you that,' the stout one said.

'Go on, then!' Gatty urged her.

Sister Hilda gave a grim smile. 'Scalp it. Dig out its brains. Then fill its brain-box with salt. Sew the skin back on again, and hang it by the ears.'

'Ugh!' cried Nest, clutching her throat.

'It's the only way to do it if you catch the beast during Lent,' Sister Hilda said.

'At Caldicot,' began Gatty, 'where I used to live, there's an Easter Hare in the manor house.'

'What do you mean?' Sister Hilda asked.

'Not like this,' said Gatty. 'No one never sees him. He lays a nest of eggs . . .'

'Hares don't lay eggs,' said Sister Hilda.

'What are you talking about?' Lady Gwyneth asked.

'And before that, we all go to Mass, and tell the story.'

'What story?' asked Aenor.

'The Easter story, of course,' Gatty replied. 'The three Marys and the angel and the soldiers and the stone. Everyone in the manor house has a part. Arthur – you don't know him – he was a Roman soldier and on Easter morning he found out Jesus' body had disappeared!

> What? Gone? Not a sign? Not a trace?
> Where's the corpse that lay in this place?
> . . . Er! . . . Um! . . . We'll be in disgrace.'

Gatty frowned and clicked her tongue. 'Er! Beast? Behest? No! I can't remember the rest!'

'Thank you, Gatty,' Lady Gwyneth said coolly. And then she burst into laughter.

Gatty's face was shining. She was more at Caldicot than Vézelay. More living than reliving.

'I can see it!' said Aenor.

'And all!' Gatty cried joyfully.

On Easter afternoon, Gatty decided she must tell Lady Gwyneth about Aenor.

'So that's where you were,' Lady Gwyneth said. 'I looked for you.'

'It's no good, it isn't,' Gatty said. 'My heart says help her, help her, help her, but my head says we can't.'

'Your head's right,' Lady Gwyneth replied. 'We can't always help other people, much as we'd like to. I can see the poor girl's very unhappy, but this is not our business. Not yours, not mine.'

'I think it's to do with Sister Hilda,' Gatty said.

'Meaning well, we might give terrible offence,' Lady Gwyneth said. 'We might make bad things worse.'

'She thought . . .' Gatty began.

'What?'

Gatty shook her head. 'Don't matter!'

'What, Gatty?'

'She thought I was your daughter.'

Lady Gwyneth looked startled for a moment. Then she reached up, and laid her hands on Gatty's cheeks. 'Think of this, Gatty,' Lady Gwyneth said after a while. 'What if I say yes? What if we do take this girl with us? Have you thought what Austin and Nakin and everyone will say?'

'I know, my lady,' Gatty said.

'We're facing enough difficulties as it is,' Lady Gwyneth went on. 'Days when we go to bed hungry, or eat rotten food. Days when we're soaked. All the arguments!'

'I know, my lady,' Gatty said again. 'But that doesn't mean I was wrong to ask you.'

'You were right, Gatty,' replied Lady Gwyneth. 'Right to

hear your heart and your head, right to ask me.'

After supper, Gatty meant to lead Aenor out in the darkness and the silence. To explain. To try to, at least. But the novice sadly shook her head. She mouthed two words.

'I understand.' That's what Gatty thought she said. Before she turned away, she gazed at Gatty. Her sepia eyes were brimming, and she stretched her mouth wide to stop herself from sobbing.

Gatty stared at her in consternation. Easter evening. Jesus risen. Everywhere, new life springing. Gatty knew she would never lose sight of that girl's eyes for as long as she lived.

18

' I can't explain it,' Gatty said.

'Try!' said Everard.

'When I listened to them monks hidden and singing behind that screen, it was like . . . well . . . overhearing voices in heaven.'

Everard smiled sweetly. '*In velamento clamabant Sancti tui alleluia, alleluia,*' he intoned.

'Like that!' cried Gatty. 'What does it mean?'

'Hidden in the cloud, thy saints cry alleluia, alleluia. Now you sing it. So that the flame never even flickers. Remember?'

'We'll be hidden in the cloud when we climb the mountains,' Gatty observed.

'Who says so?'

'Nakin.'

'Saint Nakin Know-all,' said Everard in a mocking voice.

Gatty waved her right hand. 'You and Nakin,' she said. 'You're always across each other.'

Gatty and Everard were ambling along the valley at least two bowshots behind the other pilgrims. On either side of them, high hills reached for the sky, and bright, oyster clouds hovered over them.

'Look!' exclaimed Everard. 'See them?'

Two horsemen came slithering down the slope to their left. They galloped up to Gatty and Everard and reined in, blocking the way. A man with a black beard. Small, with keen eyes set close together. A young woman with only one arm.

'English?' the girl demanded.

'What is it?' asked Everard.

Without letting go of her own, the girl grabbed Everard's reins.

'What do you want?' Gatty said in alarm.

'The doctor,' said the girl. 'Come with us. The doctor wants to see you.'

'What doctor?' asked Everard.

The man's eyes glittered like mica and when, for a moment, the girl's eyes met Gatty's, Gatty saw how fearful and how desperate they were.

The man reached inside his cloak and pulled out a knife with a blade as long and pointed as a heron's beak. Gatty felt the tip of a freezing finger slip up her spine, right up to the nape of her neck. She began to tremble.

Everard pointed up the valley. 'They're our friends,' he piped.

'We'll look after them!' the girl said. 'Nico will look after them.'

The man bared his teeth and touched the point of the blade to his tongue.

All instinct, Gatty filled her lungs and gave a violent scream.

At once the man's horse reared up. Gatty dug in her heels and Syndod sprang forward. She barged into the girl's horse.

Gatty's cry pierced the valley. Somehow, and only heaven knows how, it arrowed all the way across the waste acres to the other pilgrims. Five hundred paces at the least, wild and more desolate than a rabbit with a stoat at its neck.

Then Emrys and Snout wheeled round and came barrelling back down the valley, shouting and waving their weapons. As soon as she heard them, the girl let go of Everard's reins; she and the bearded man galloped away over the scree, between huge boulders, up, away, and into the cover of the pinewoods.

'What did they want?' Emrys bellowed. 'Who were they?'

'Are you all right?' asked Snout.

Gatty closed her eyes, and tried to steady her jerky breath. Then she nudged Syndod sideways so she could reach out to Everard. The two of them dropped their reins, turned in their saddles to face each other, and clasped hands; they inclined their heads until their foreheads met.

'What did they want?' Emrys asked again.

'To take us to the doctor,' Everard said.

'What doctor?'

'Did you see his knife?' said Everard.

'His eyes glittered,' Gatty said. 'But the girl – she was terrified.'

'God saved us!' said Everard.

'No!' said Gatty. 'You two, you saved us!'

'You know the rule,' Emrys said. 'At least three in a group together.'

'I know,' said Gatty unhappily.

'Your scream!' exclaimed Snout. 'I've never heard anything like it.'

'It didn't come from her throat,' Everard explained. 'It came from her whole body.'

'I just did it,' Gatty said.

'Exactly,' said Everard.

Then the four of them slowly rode up the track towards their companions.

The April afternoon sobered from oyster to ash, ash to pewter. Well before the pilgrims had reached their destination, a tavern halfway between Bourg-en-Bresse and Chambery, the world had begun to blur.

That evening, the pilgrims learned more about the doctor and about his accomplices.

'He cut off the girl's arm,' the taverner told them. 'Sawed it off.'

'Why?' asked Gatty.

'To sell,' said the taverner's wife. 'He sells body parts.'

'Revolting!' shrieked Nest.

Nakin put his right arm around Nest's shoulder.

'Don't!' cried Nest. 'You keep your hands away from me.'

Lady Gwyneth's teeth began to chatter.

'There's a hospital here . . .' the taverner began.

'Where?' gasped Nest.

Gatty quickly looked round, as if the hospital were somehow hiding inside the tavern.

'. . . near Lyon,' the taverner went on, 'and another over the mountains, in Italy. The doctor packs body parts in snow and ice to preserve them. Hands. Legs. Heads. There's always a good market for parts.'

'Why?' asked Gatty.

'To dissect,' said the taverner.

'What's that?'

'To cut up and examine.'

Now Lady Gwyneth trembled, and Nest comforted her.

Gatty knew better than to say anything. She would have preferred Lady Gwyneth's anger to her distress.

'Well,' said the taverner's wife. 'That one-armed girl, she's lucky. When she came to her senses the doctor gave her a choice: to procure other . . . patients for him; or to lose another limb.'

Gatty shuddered.

'How do you know all this?' Austin asked in his deep voice.

The taverner shrugged. 'Just from what we've heard,' he replied. 'From putting pieces together, you might say.'

'First he robs travellers,' the taverner's wife told them. 'Coins, ornaments, stones. Spices. Anything of value . . .'

'And then,' added the taverner, 'he robs them of their own bodies.'

'The last group here lost a lad,' the taverner's wife said. 'He was a squire and all.'

That evening, nothing really revived the pilgrims' spirits, not even the spicy sausage and bean dumplings and black ale with which the taverner and his wife plied them. Before they all lay down, Gatty and Everard hugged one another, and Lady Gwyneth praised Snout and Emrys.

'My cook!' she said. 'My stableman! You two defended and protected us.'

And that night she, Gatty and Nest huddled together.

'You do understand,' Lady Gwyneth whispered. 'You do understand why we made the rule that at least three of us should travel in a group together.'

Gatty pressed her forehead into Lady Gwyneth's right shoulder and nodded.

'One part of me . . .'

'My lady!' yelped Nest.

'What?'

'Don't talk about parts! Please!'

'. . . one part,' Lady Gwyneth continued, 'was so angry with you and Everard for falling behind, but another was so upset. I was asking myself what I'd do if I'd lost you. I'd never, never forgive myself.'

Gatty burrowed into Lady Gwyneth's shoulder again to signify that she understood.

Lady Gwyneth sighed. 'God has been merciful,' she said. 'But unless we learn from this, we betray Him.'

Lying quiet, Gatty was conscious of the shape and weight and warmth of her own body. She scrunched up her toes, and one of them, the little one on her right foot, cracked. She tightened her kneecaps.

Before long, Lady Gwyneth gave a small sigh. Then her

breathing lengthened, her right shoulder loosened, and Gatty knew she had fallen asleep. Slowly Gatty eased away and placed her hands on her firm hips; then she laid them gently over her breasts. She bit her lower lip. In the darkness, she opened her eyes as wide as she could; then she screwed them up, tight as cockle-shells.

'Gatty!' whispered Nest. 'Are you awake?'

Gatty pretended to be asleep. She wanted to be alone with her own precious, growing body – each part of it.

19

Gatty made a ball of her fist. 'How many fingers?' she asked.

'None,' said Nest.

Gatty gave a wicked grin and shook her head. 'No,' she said. 'Nothing can be nothing. Everything's something.'

'What do you mean?'

'Everything's something,' Gatty repeated, 'otherwise you're saying God created nothing. Are you saying that?'

'Go away!' said Nest. 'You're making my head ache.'

Gatty did go away. She urged Syndod up the steep slope, until she caught up with Nakin, Austin and Tilda.

As the four of them breasted the hill, they all felt the chill breath of the hidden mountains ahead of them.

'I wish those clouds would hurry up and lift!' Gatty said impatiently. 'I want to see a mountain.'

'We were talking about our fixed world and the spheres of gold and silver stars revolving around us,' Austin told her. 'As I was saying, there can be no doubt, no argument, about the sky's curvature.'

'What's curvature?' asked Gatty.

Nakin reined in. 'Let's wait here,' he said. 'The others are falling a long way behind.'

'Curvature,' Gatty repeated.

'I'd have thought that was obvious,' Nakin said.

'Curvature,' said Austin. 'It's . . . being curved. Being round.'

'Like buttocks, you mean,' said Gatty.

Tilda laughed.

'They're round,' said Gatty.

'Like an apple,' Austin said.

'And like the sphere of the world,' added Nakin.

'The world's not round,' Gatty said.

'It is, Gatty,' said Tilda, 'and the stars and the planets dance round it.'

'It's not,' said Gatty, 'otherwise we'd all drop off it.'

'The world is like the yolk of an egg,' Austin explained. 'It has three lands with water all around them, like the white of an egg.'

'Who says so?' Gatty demanded.

Austin sighed.

'I'm only asking.'

'Astronomers say so. Mathematicians say so,' Austin replied. 'Philosophers say so.'

'The Bible doesn't,' said Gatty.

Nakin clicked his tongue against his teeth and swatted the air. 'You're as tiresome as a horsefly,' he said.

Gatty stuck out her chin. 'The Bible says God is the Creator of the ends of the earth. If the world's round like you say, it wouldn't have ends, would it?'

Austin smiled. 'That's very clever of you, Gatty, but the prophet Isaiah was writing thousands of years ago . . .'

'And the earth was flat then?' said Gatty.

'People thought the earth was flat then,' Austin corrected her.

Gatty tossed her head. 'It was flat then and it's flat now!' she said. 'And that's flat!'

'Ignore her!' said Nakin.

'Gatty,' said Austin. 'If you stop talking, I'll give you all the answers.'

'That's what the devil does!' Gatty exclaimed. 'He prom-

117

ises people he'll tell them whatever they need to know if only they'll stop pestering him.'

'Who told you that?'

'Oliver! The devil silences people and then they're in his power. I don't want anyone to stop me asking whatever I want to ask.'

'What's got into you today?' Austin asked. 'Ah! Here come the stragglers. See them down there?'

'I wanted to talk about the world's lands,' Nakin said. 'You say three but I say four.'

'And I wanted to talk about the stars,' Tilda said, 'how they control our lives.'

'There are miles and time enough between here and Jerusalem,' said Austin.

'As soon as I see the first star,' Gatty said, 'I wish a wish.'

'So do I,' said Tilda, and she began to sing:

> 'I wish this wish, this is my wish.
> Star at dusk! Star of wonder!'

Gatty joined in, singing those same words while Tilda continued:

> 'While you shine, while you wander,
> I wish the wish I wish comes true.'

Then Tilda went back to the beginning again, and Austin joined in after the first line, Nakin after the third line. So there they stood, the four of them, little lower than the angels, singing a round, high on a green hill halfway between earth and heaven.

Lady Gwyneth looked up and listened to them and it did her heart good.

'The music of the spheres,' she said.

'No,' said Gatty.

Lady Gwyneth stared at Gatty.

'My lady,' added Gatty. 'Everard says . . .'

'Later, Gatty!' Lady Gwyneth said.

Still standing on the hilltop, Austin and his fellow pilgrims gazed back over the land they had all just crossed: the attentive dark pinewoods, the cup of the valley, the bones of pink rock that had broken through the green skin, the close stitchwork of fields around a hamlet, the length of the horizon hemmed by white light.

The priest opened his arms. 'What do you see?' he asked in a lofty voice.

Everyone heard the question but no one knew quite how to answer.

'Ah!' exclaimed Nakin. 'Yes! Curvature!'

'Amen!' pronounced Austin.

Points and needles of light danced in Gatty's gold curls. She inspected her blunt, calloused fingertips, and shook her head. 'Not if you got your eyes to the ground,' she said in a quiet, flat voice. 'Not if you'd worked the earth like I have.'

20

The guide's eyes were bloodshot and his voice was a bark. He had led travellers across the rough, gruff mountains for so many years he had almost become a wildman.

Ah! But when he gave tongue to the musical necklace of towns in Italy, on the other side of the mountains, it was a different matter.

'Susa,' he intoned. 'Torino, Tortona. Piacenza and Cremona. Vicenza. Treviso.'

Gatty had never heard of places made of such sounds. 'Tre-vis-o,' she sang, fluttering her tongue, then laying it flat and pushing out her bottom lip, then rounding both lips.

'Treviso,' said Lady Gwyneth. 'Yes, that's where we have to leave our horses.'

The guide's face was criss-crossed with as many cracks and crinkles as an unstretched parchment. 'Mountains first,' he barked. 'Mountain music! *Si?*'

'We're ready,' Lady Gwyneth said.

But the pilgrims were not ready. Only Nakin had crossed the Alps before, and the pilgrims had somehow skated and slid over his warnings.

'Your skin will burn,' he'd warned them. 'Even your eyes will burn . . . And you, Everard, with your bald pate, you'd better keep your hat on, or the sun will scalp you . . . You'll sweat like pigs . . . And when you stop to recover your breath, you'll begin to freeze . . . The cold will make your teeth ache.'

The guide insisted the pilgrims should wear every stitch of

clothing they had brought with them. But when they saw him stepping into a fleece and hauling on oiled leather breeches and wrapping a bandage of felt round his head, when they watched him stepping into high boots with iron spikes in their soles, they began to feel uneasy.

No, the pilgrims were not ready when their horses dug in their newly-shod hooves, and they had to dismount and lead them. They were not ready for the string-thin path that kept doubling back on itself, climbing the left side of a narrow valley, nor for the steep ascent that stretched their calves and thighs, the sudden short drops that jarred their kneecaps and lost them ground so hard won. And they were certainly not prepared for their first sight of a high peak, dazzling and crystalline, so high in the sky that it was nearer to heaven than to earth. The mountain's icy breath caught them by the throat; their own breathlessness caught them by surprise.

Mountain music! In the misty pastures on the floor of the valley, it was the tinny clanking and tonking of cow-bells so large they wouldn't have disgraced wayside chapels, interspersed with the pretty chinking of smaller bells. Then it was the light shisshh-shisshh of firs and pinetrees; the rushing of a lacy horsetail of a waterfall always shape-changing, always keeping its shape.

Gatty felt as if she were hearing with her eyes and seeing with her ears. The music of the bells and the trees and the water. Her own voice bouncing back from a rockface, huge and hollow, like the voice of a giantess. This, and then the sudden grim roar of the mountain ahead of them, followed by bottomless silence.

'We have mountain called Ogre,' the guide growled, baring his teeth at Gatty. 'It always has a black face but in summer its body is made of flowers.'

Gatty knew what the guide meant. In May and June, Pikeside and the cow pasture and even the headlands were made

121

of flowers. As she led Syndod upward through muddy shale, through mushy patches of snow, she kept trying to remember the story about the Welshman who made a woman out of flowers. Then she heard someone shouting.

It was Tilda and she was pointing at something high up, almost above their heads. The whole train of humans and horses came to a halt.

'Did you see them?' Tilda cried. 'Did you?'

The pilgrims shielded their eyes, frowned, and stared up at the angry, simmering clouds hugging the huge rock wall to their left.

'Angels!' cried Tilda. 'Angels!'

The guide looked at Tilda with a knowing eye. In his time he had accompanied many a pilgrim who had seen angels or saints descending from heaven.

Tilda raised her right arm, as knobbly as the exposed roots of fir trees in the forest below them. Then she slumped onto her knees and began to sob.

Gatty stared at the misty rock wall, and the patches of snow on the pasture leading across to it.

Nakin had all the answers as usual. 'It was just a window in the clouds,' he explained. 'A glimpse of snow.'

'Wings!' cried Tilda.

'A dazzling peak.'

'Shining wings! Three angels.'

'Angels!' said Nakin, grinning. 'Tilda! Really!'

Gatty wasn't so sure. She sucked her cheeks, and gazed at the rock wall, the pasture around them . . . She blinked, she screwed up her eyes. The white patches on the pasture were no longer snow. They'd turned into flowers. Little tiny flakes of flowers, hundreds, thousands of white crocuses, sprung up in the winking of an eye.

The pilgrims had to walk in single file, silent and wary of each step, imprisoned inside their own heads, and except for

Gatty and Tilda, they did not see the mountains as the home of angels or made of flowers. They were in the wilderness; waves of chill mist clung to them; the taste in their mouths was sour.

In mid-afternoon the guide called a halt.

'One hour!' he called out, and he pulled off a mitten and wagged his right forefinger. 'Hospice of Saint Peter! Top of this pass. Beef stew on brown beer mush with corn.'

'I could eat a horse,' said Austin.

'You will,' said Nakin, with a grim smile. 'In Italy.'

Lady Gwyneth gave Gatty a wan look.

'Are you all right, my lady?'

'I think so,' said Lady Gwyneth. 'I keep feeling faint. That's all.'

Gatty dropped Syndod's reins, and edged past her. Then she opened her arms and Lady Gwyneth stumbled into them.

'Oh! Gatty,' sighed Lady Gwyneth, eyes closed. 'Worthwhile is hard-won. Isn't it? We'll rise through this . . . this cloud of unknowing. We'll see God's shining truth.'

As the train plodded on, picking its way across a recent rockfall, the mist at last began to lift. Gatty could see how the ground on their right sheered clean away, plunging into the depths of the valley. After a while the path opened onto a wide, flat ledge between the rock wall and the precipice, where all the pilgrims could stand in a circle and catch their breath.

Gatty gave Emrys Syndod's reins, and pulled herself forward on her stomach so she could look over.

'Don't!' gulped Nest.

Gatty took no notice.

'Gatty!' screeched Nest. 'You're making me giddy.'

'Don't look, then,' said Gatty. 'Just look at the clouds.'

Nest whimpered. 'When I do,' she said, 'the rock wall looks like it's toppling over me.'

Then a buzzing devil-insect, bigger than a hornet, disappeared into the left ear of Austin's horse and stung him with a hellish sting. Later some of the pilgrims swore they had seen it, just as Tilda swore she had seen three angels.

The Andalusian reared up on his hind legs, snorting, and the priest was pulled and jerked behind him with the horse's reins wound round his right wrist and hand. Then a loose rock gave way under Saviour's left foreleg. His shank twisted and cracked – everybody said they heard that too – and he crashed to the ground, only to rise again, twisting and whinnying in pain.

On three legs, Saviour waltzed towards the precipice, and Austin was unable to restrain him, unable to disengage himself.

With a fearful whinny, the white horse launched himself over a boulder and landed on a much smaller, sloping shelf overhanging the huge drop. The priest was pulled right off his feet and slammed straight into the rock, face first. His left shoulder was crushed and the boulder was the only thing saving him from being flung over the precipice.

Saviour yelped. He kept straining at his reins, dragging Austin's arm further and further down towards him, cutting through the flesh of his right wrist, and almost pulling his shoulder out of its socket.

Gatty and Emrys both advanced to the boulder, one of either side of it, but neither could reach down as far as Austin's wrist and the reins, let alone haul him back up again.

'Nakin!' yelled Emrys, without turning round. 'Everard! Grab Austin's ankles. Hang onto them! We've got to be quick.'

Gatty drew her knife. 'Hold my left hand,' she told Emrys. 'I'll go down.'

'No!' shrieked Tilda.

Lady Gwyneth and Nest couldn't even bring themselves to look.

'Don't cut it!' cried Tilda.

'Saviour's dead already,' Gatty said under her breath.

Emrys heard her. 'You're right, girl,' he replied.

'Please!' barked the guide. 'Please!' He stepped up to Gatty with a coil of rope. 'Yes,' he said, 'you are the lightest. You go!' He tied one end round Gatty's waist and then looped the rope behind Emrys' back.

'Sit!' he told Emrys. Then the guide grasped Emrys' belt and sat down behind him. 'I hold the holder,' he said in his gruff voice. 'And you,' he said, pointing to Snout, 'you hold me. Gatty, go now! Brave girl!'

Slowly Gatty climbed down onto the sloping ledge. When she looked down over the drop into the sage-green valley far, far beneath, her stomach turned over inside her. Stay calm, she told herself. Don't look down.

But then Gatty slipped on loose pebbles, and just for a moment her feet were dangling over the drop. She cried out in terror. She grabbed at the rope and her knife slipped out of her sweaty right hand, bounced on the shelf and fell over the precipice.

Gatty gasped for air; her legs were shaking.

'It's all right!' Gatty could hear Emrys's voice above her. 'I've got you, girl! I've got you!'

'God save her! God save her!' Gatty could hear Lady Gwyneth's voice crying.

Nest and Tilda both got down onto their knee-bones, whimpering.

'I'll pull you up!' Emrys panted.

'Wait!' Gatty called up to him. She wanted so much to come back up, but she couldn't abandon Austin. Her eyes were streaming; tears were rolling down her cheeks. 'I got an idea.'

Then Gatty squatted on her haunches. She leaned forward until her heels and her calves were stretched tight, she gently rocked forward and with her fingertips touched Saviour's withers.

Saviour was sweating. He was blowing steam out of his nostrils. Gatty laid both her palms against him, and spread herself alongside the horse's quivering body. Crooning and saying words so softly it was impossible to hear what they were, she unbuckled Saviour's bridle, and pulled off his headpiece, his browband, his noseband. Saviour had taken hold of his bit but Gatty gently coaxed him to let go of it.

At once the reins slackened, and Austin was no longer trapped. The priest was lying on his stomach and his forehead and nose and chin were gashed and bleeding; his right hand and wrist were mangled.

'Merciful God!' he said, and that was all he said before he fainted. Then Nakin and Everard dragged him back from the precipice by the legs, and with lumps of snow Tilda began to clean Austin's wounds.

'I'm pulling you up, girl,' Emrys called down.

'Austin's saddlebags,' Gatty said. 'Wait!'

'Be careful!' Emrys warned her. 'I've got you.'

As Gatty put one hand on Saviour's girth, he twisted back his head. Gatty looked right into his eyes, and they were rolling with terror. Then the horse sobbed and gulped, and tried to get to his feet, and in doing so he lost his balance.

Still carrying the saddlebags, Saviour slid off the little shelf and over the precipice; he slid and fell, writhing and screaming, onto the scree far beneath.

21

In the infirmary, Brother Benedict mashed the concoction in his mortar, and added a little more pig's fat and wine. Then he pounded it again and stared at Austin who was lying on his back on a trestle table, eyes closed.

Lifting the lid from a little stone box, the monk took a pinch of muddy gold powder and sprinkled it into the mortar. 'Cumin from India,' he informed Lady Gwyneth and Nakin. 'Very expensive. Saint Peter in heaven! You two look in as much need of treatment as he does! Slumped there like that.'

Lady Gwyneth straightened her back and pressed her shoulders against the rough stone wall. The bench squeaked.

Brother Benedict shook his head. 'Coming up the last pitch,' he said, 'not one of you was standing upright except the guide. One girl was crawling on her hands and knees, and so was the woman. One man was crouching lower than his staff and one had both hands on the shoulders of the man in front of him. And you, Nakin, you were supporting this priest.'

'And Gatty was supporting me, that's the truth of it,' Lady Gwyneth said meekly. 'We all pulled together. We were all sisters and brothers.'

'It won't be long before everyone's accusing and blaming each other again,' Nakin predicted.

'A very brave girl,' said Brother Benedict. 'Your Gatty.'

'She is,' agreed Lady Gwyneth. 'She was afraid, all right. We all were. But despite her fear . . .'

Austin moaned. His whole body shuddered. Then he opened his eyes.

'Quite so,' said Brother Benedict, punching his concoction with the pestle. 'You need this poultice, not all these fine words.'

Now the monk busied himself with the tinder-box. In one corner of the room he struck sparks and teased a little nest of moss into flame, and added shavings and twigs to it. Then he positioned a four-legged tray over the fire and poured his concoction onto it.

Austin groaned. 'How bad?' he asked.

'Mangled,' the monk replied in a matter-of-fact voice. 'Four fingers broken. Not your thumb, though. Four knuckle-bones bared.'

'Oh! Austin,' said Lady Gwyneth tenderly.

'You, Nakin,' Brother Benedict said. 'Come here and hold Austin's elbow. You talk to him, my lady, while I just try this.'

'Austin,' Lady Gwyneth said in a low voice, 'can you hear me?'

Austin opened his eyes.

'Your saddlebags. What was in them?'

'Everything,' said the priest. 'My altar. The silver crucifix. The linen cloth.'

Lady Gwyneth sadly shook her head. 'And Gatty so nearly saved them.'

'My Bible,' said Austin.

'You're holding his elbow?' the monk asked Nakin.

'Your Bible,' repeated Lady Gwyneth.

All at once, Brother Benedict grasped Austin's right fore-finger and tugged it and Austin shrieked and jerked his elbow back into Nakin's stomach.

'Very good!' said the monk. 'That's straightened it.' He smiled down at poor Austin. 'The other three fingers should mend fairly straight. I'll heat the poultice and bandage you now. This won't hurt much.'

Brother Benedict removed the bubbling poultice from the fire and, as soon as it had cooled just a little, he smeared it all over Austin's right hand and wrist with a wooden ladle. 'Chickweed and smallage and groundsel,' he told Lady Gwyneth and Nakin, 'if you're interested. Pound them together with pig's fat and sheep's fat. Yes, and a little cumin. Boil them in clear wine. Then add the dregs from a barrel of wine and wheat-bran, and bring it back to the boil again.'

Before the monk had finished bandaging his hand, Austin had drifted into sleep again, exhausted by the pain.

'Wait here!' the monk instructed Lady Gwyneth and Nakin, and he strode out of the room.

Lady Gwyneth looked at Nakin. 'He's very . . . imperious,' she said.

'High-handed,' said Nakin, and his dewlaps shook a little. 'I don't know who he thinks he is. Well! God has spared Austin.'

'And Gatty and Emrys saved him,' Lady Gwyneth added.

'They did,' said Nakin, rather reluctantly.

'What have you got against Gatty?'

'Nothing,' said Nakin in a measured voice. 'A peasant girl. I wouldn't have thought she'd be up to it.'

'Do you know what she said when I praised her?' asked Lady Gwyneth.

'What?' asked Nakin.

'Poor Saviour!' Lady Gwyneth replied. 'That girl never asks for praise or thanks.'

Nakin gave Lady Gwyneth a glum look. 'She ran away in London,' he said, 'and argued her way across France, and never a day passes without your reproving her.'

'I know, I know,' Lady Gwyneth said. 'But she's learning fast.'

'She needs to,' said Nakin. 'She knows next to nothing. She even thinks the earth is flat!'

'Nakin,' said Lady Gwyneth in a serious voice, 'this pilgrimage depends on each one of us. Where would we be without you and your knowledge of money?'

Nakin slightly parted his fleshy lips.

'Gatty's like a diamond before it's cut and polished. Her manners are rough, and, yes, she may think the earth's flat, but she's bold.'

Nakin made a sucking sound.

'I tell you, Nakin,' Lady Gwyneth said, 'you can teach someone a skill but you can't teach them spirit.'

At this moment, Brother Benedict walked back into the infirmary. In his left hand he was holding a linen cloth, white as a field of snow, and in his right a small silver crucifix.

Lady Gwyneth and Nakin bowed their heads.

Then the monk stepped over to sleeping Austin. He spread the cloth over the priest's chest and stomach, and on the cloth he laid, lightly, the glistening crucifix.

22

Absurd, really! Gatty knew it wasn't really like that, but from the moment she turned her back on the high mountains until she reached the stables at Treviso, fourteen days later, she felt as if she were travelling downhill.

To begin with, it was literally and steeply true, of course. Roping themselves together for safety, and leaving their horses to make their own choices, the pilgrims gingerly prodded and picked their way across a blinding field of snow strewn with boulders and slithered down precipitous, slushy paths.

Austin was white-faced with pain, and Nest and Tilda found the way down was even less comfortable than the way up. They couldn't bear to look over the edges. So the guide called a halt, and pulled a cowhide out of one of his mule's packs.

'Look at that!' marvelled Gatty. 'A mule carrying a cow!'

Snout guffawed. 'The wrong way round!' he chortled.

'There's a riddle like that . . .' Gatty began.

'Gatty!' warned Lady Gwyneth.

The guide spread out the hide, and attached it to his mule's girth.

'Now sit on it!' he told Nest and Tilda. 'And keep hold of it.'

So that's what they did. They clutched the hide for dear life, and the mule dragged them down the mountain, bumped and bruised, down and away from the snow and slush and sheer rock faces.

131

It all happened so fast. One moment, the pilgrims were picking their way through a cropped wilderness of clattering rockfalls and rushing waterfalls, home of the winds. The next they were crossing a meadow of sopping grass where cowslips and bright blue eyes looked up and winked at them. Small birds raced around them, scissoring the pale blue sky. In this way, they left behind danger and disaster, and came down out of the mountains into Italy.

This was when the pilgrims met a young man shouting his four cows home. Gatty inspected them and one looked so like Hopeless that she caught her breath, and paused, and thought fondly of her cow.

The cowherd had long black hair that flopped over his forehead and fingered his collar, and when he saw Gatty, he just stood in her way, gazing at her and grinning. He gave a low whistle.

Gatty smiled back. She wasn't sure quite what to do.

Then the cowherd stooped, scooped up a cowslip, slipped it between Gatty's bruised and blistered fingers, and kissed the back of her hand – all in one breath.

And that was almost all there was to it. Gatty looked into the young man's eyes; she stared down at the flower, pale and shining. The young man stepped off the path, allowed the pilgrims to pass, shouted to his cows. And Gatty stumbled on.

'A spotted cowherd!' said Nest, wrinkling her pretty nose. 'I saw how he looked at you.' But the envy in her voice was there for all to hear.

'And how Gatty looked at him,' Nakin added.

'Not a cowslip!' said Tilda. 'When that fades and shrivels, you'll fade and shrivel. That's true as death.'

Gatty heard them, but she didn't care. Smiling to herself, she mounted Syndod and once (well twice, actually) she turned round and looked over her shoulder. Only later, when she lent her cob to Austin, and rode pillion behind Nest, did she realise she was still holding the cowslip, hot and crushed, in her right hand.

'A shaft of sunlight!' said Lady Gwyneth.

'What, my lady?'

'A shaft of sunlight for your thoughts. Are you still back up there in the mountains?'

Gatty gave Lady Gwyneth a slow, rather wistful smile.

'You're not still thinking about that boy?'

'She is,' said Nest.

'I didn't even hear his voice,' Gatty said. 'Well, only his shouting! Not what he sounded like inside his body.'

Lady Gwyneth smiled gently. And after a while, she said, 'Nothing goes to waste, even when we think it does. It's all part of God's plan.'

Gatty stuck out her lower lip.

'I was a faithful wife,' Lady Gwyneth told her. 'I was a mother. Nothing goes to waste, Gatty.'

Once the pilgrims had passed through the old Roman gate at Susa, their road headed east to Torino; and throughout those lovely last days of April and first days of May, the mountains were always sitting, as it were, on their left shoulders.

A ring of children holding hands and singing high and even higher, like larks climbing, and then bursting into peals and squeals of laughter; green barley blades, all shotsilk and shiver; a slender belltower with humming bells; two talkative Italian pepper merchants on their way home to Milan from Bruges; a stand of mysterious dark cypresses, utterly still, furled as tight as winding-sheets; a party of French pilgrims drinking wine and singing under a walnut tree, solitary and as beautiful as the trees that grew in Eden; and at last the fork in the road they'd followed for so long – one way leading south to Rome, the other to Venice and Jerusalem: each fresh and scented day brought its own marker, and no day seemed arduous compared to those preceding it.

The pilgrims had not enjoyed such warm sunlight since they left Ewloe, and one afternoon, while they were picking their way across a stony, sparkling stream, Gatty and Nest dismounted and just threw themselves into the waiting water.

Tilda followed them, gasping and laughing, and before long all nine of them were splashing around. First they gambolled and stumbled; then they washed themselves; and then they scrubbed their tunics and gowns before they rode on, steaming, under the sun.

Daydreaming, almost asleep in the saddle, Gatty sometimes felt as if she were alone, completely alone on this middle-earth, but at other times she sensed she was part of an immense human procession – one with all the quick, all the dead who had ever made the pilgrimage to Jerusalem, ploughing along gouged and muddy tracks, lifting their eyes to fierce mountains, quickstepping across Lombardy to Venice.

'I'm both, aren't I?' Gatty said to herself. 'Always in company yet always alone. One is one and all alone and evermore shall be so.'

Three days later, exactly ten weeks after leaving Ewloe, Lady Gwyneth and her companions at last rode into the livery stables at Treviso, where the elderly stablemaster and his daughters welcomed them. The pilgrims relieved the beasts of their burdens, and then the two women spread out a sky-blue cloth on the ground and covered it with food and wine.

'Morterel!' Gatty exclaimed.

'What?' asked Nest.

'Bread. You boil it in milk.'

Nakin took Nest's right arm. 'Peasants' food!' he sniffed.

'Leave me alone!' said Nest.

But Nakin changed his tune as soon as he'd tasted a mouthful. This Italian morterel, if that's what it was, was made of boiled cake, not bread, and the cake was laced with wine and spotted with currants and diced almonds.

'I'll make this when we get home, my lady,' the cook promised Lady Gwyneth. 'I can get almonds in Chester. Or else I'll use hazelnuts. They'll taste just as good.'

While their horses and ponies wandered round the livery courtyard, now and then pausing to slurp a mouthful of water or chew a mouthful of hay, the pilgrims sat with the old stablemaster and his daughters; and weary as they were, but still quite clean from their splash in the stream only three days before, they felt the early evening sun on their backs and gave thanks to God.

'You can sell your horses to us,' one of the women said in good English, 'or stable them here while you sail to Jerusalem, and collect them on your way home. The choice is yours.'

'And either way,' said Nakin, 'the profit is yours.'

'We've already decided,' Emrys said. 'Lady Gwyneth will keep her Arab.'

'Forever and a day,' Lady Gwyneth sang out. 'I'll ride him back to London and then I'll buy him from the stables there.'

'If Solomon says so,' cautioned Snout.

'I'll buy him and bring him to Ewloe,' Lady Gwyneth said.

'And Gatty here,' Emrys continued, 'she'll keep her Welsh cob.'

Gatty nodded vigorously.

'She's valiant!' said Austin.

'What's that?' asked Gatty.

'Brave.'

'She is and all,' Gatty exclaimed.

'So that's two,' said Emrys, 'and . . . I'll keep my Frisian.

He's alert. He's kindly.'

'He's got an ugly mug,' said Snout.

'So have you!' Emrys retorted. 'Yes, I'll keep him. He's strong. He'll last.'

The old stablemaster looked puzzled. He counted the pilgrims on his fingers, then counted the horses.

'Yes!' said Emrys. 'Eight horses. Nine pilgrims.'

He pointed to Austin's heavily bandaged right hand, and told the stablemaster and his daughters about the disaster in the mountains, and his description was punctuated by much tooth-clicking, many exclamations and little cries.

One of the young women laid her hand on the priest's left arm. 'But God saved you!' she said.

'How does your hand feel now?' Lady Gwyneth asked Austin.

'Hot,' replied the priest. 'Throbbing.'

'So, then,' Emrys told the stablemaster, 'we must pay you for Austin's horse . . .'

'. . . and you must pay us for five horses,' Nakin said quickly. 'The other three we'll keep and collect on the way home.'

The stablemaster laughed and said something to his two daughters, and they both put their hands to their cheeks.

'He say,' one daughter translated, 'he say you take us instead.'

'Really!' murmured Nakin in an oily voice.

'Not really!' said the daughter.

'It's all decided, then,' said Emrys.

'Thank you,' Lady Gwyneth said. 'We all have good reason to thank you, Emrys. And so do our horses!'

Then Gatty led Syndod to her stall. She checked that her manger and trough were well-stocked, and then she rubbed her cob's poll and nose.

'You're so strong,' she told her in her rich, low voice. 'My marvel!'

Syndod stood foursquare and, with her slightly bloodshot eyes, gave Gatty an alert look.

'I'm going to Jerusalem,' Gatty told her. 'Then I'll come back to you.'

And with that, she kissed Syndod on the side of her nose.

That night, the pilgrims ate and slept in the tavern at Treviso and, close at last to Venice, they had every reason to sleep content.

But when Snout went out to the latrines for 'deliverance', as he put it, he saw a corpse-candle and lumbered back into the tavern still clutching his breeches.

'It came out of the churchyard,' he panted. 'Straight at me.'

'A flame,' said Tilda.

'A small flame, yes. A ball. It passed right by me.'

'Then it wasn't for you,' Tilda reassured him. 'What colour was it?'

'Blue. Ghost-blue.'

Tilda nodded. 'It was on its way to collect a child's soul,' she said.

'Not Hew?' Snout said anxiously.

'Of course not,' said Tilda. 'There'll be a dead child here in Treviso before daybreak.'

As if the corpse-candle weren't enough, Lady Gwyneth three times heard something whistling in the dark. Lying on her pallet of bristling straw, she thought of all the things she'd heard about whistlers, and none of them were good. How many times had her father warned her that any kind of whistling after dark meant danger? Was the whistler a witch raising a wind, and would dark waves drown them on their way across the water to Venice? Or was it a night-bird? Not one of the Seven Whistlers! No, surely not. It couldn't have flown all the way from Ewloe to Treviso . . . This is when

137

Lady Gwyneth fell asleep.

As soon as day dawned, Lady Gwyneth told her companions about the night-whistling, and Tilda wore a funeral face.

'We must wait here then,' she said, 'wait for a day and the danger will pass.'

'We can't!' cried Lady Gwyneth. 'We've got to get to Venice as soon as we can!'

'My lady,' said Nakin. 'The last pilgrim ship doesn't leave until the first day of June. We do have time.'

'And I can sleep,' yawned Nest, 'and then sleep.'

Lady Gwyneth wrung her hands. 'We've faced so many dangers already,' she said. 'Losing Saviour, and rockfalls, and that revolting butcher, and food that made us ill! Those thieves in London!'

'I'm not going one step further,' Tilda said firmly.

Lady Gwyneth locked her fingers and twisted them. 'What do you think, Austin?' she asked.

'I think,' Austin said slowly, 'I think you're fortunate to be able to twist your fingers!' He looked solemnly at the dirty parcel of cloth covering his own right hand. 'Let us put our faith in God and continue on our way.'

Tilda looked at the priest angrily.

Austin raised his right paw and carefully made the sign of the cross over the bowed heads of the pilgrims.

Lady Gwyneth looked up; the light of Venice was dancing in her eyes.

23

Without their horses, for so long their travel-companions, the pilgrims felt vulnerable. And maybe because the first stage of their journey was almost at an end, and they now had to carry everything for themselves, they developed all kinds of aches and pains.

The warm sunlight eased Tilda's stiff fingers but she sprouted ugly boils on both her arms; Snout kept spitting green phlegm; and Lady Gwyneth complained of stabbing pains in her head. And Gatty herself: all her lower teeth somehow pounded, and no amount of rubbing them with garlic and rocksalt, or cleaning them with a hazel sprig, made any difference.

But then! Early in the afternoon, the pilgrims realised the shimmer ahead of them was not a mirage. It opened wide; gold-and-silver it dazzled them; it seemed to come forward to meet them, and the pilgrims reached out to it, the cradle of the great lagoon and Venice floating upon it. They all got down on their knee-bones. Then Tilda began to sob, and that set off Nest and Snout, and Everard sang alleluia upon alleluia.

After a while, Austin began to pray and, with one voice, all the pilgrims responded and gave thanks to God.

'This place is where our pilgrimage, the greatest journey in our lives, truly begins,' Lady Gwyneth told them. She had no idea, none at all, that for one of the companions kneeling there, Venice was where life's pilgrimage would soon end.

At the landing-stage, there were many boatmen eager to row the pilgrims across to Venice. At a cost.

'We can all fit in one boat,' said Lady Gwyneth.

The boatmen shook their heads. 'Five in a boat most,' one of them said. 'Venice rules.'

'I told you,' Nakin warned Lady Gwyneth. 'Venetians are grasping. Everything costs double here, if not three times as much.'

To Gatty, sitting in the gently rocking bow, listening to the sip-and-rush of water, the passage seemed like crossing from waking into the most delicious dream, one that might last for ever.

'Hands!' shouted the boatmen. 'Mind hands!'

Like a cat, Gatty was instantly awake. And the next moment, the two boats bearing Lady Gwyneth and her companions swung sideways, then bumped into a staked landing-stage.

'Engleesh!' the boatmen yelled. 'Pilgrims! Engleesh!'

As the boatmen handed them ashore, Gatty noticed a young woman step out of the crowd waiting on the jetty. She was quite small and smiling and round. Her skin was sandy-pink and slightly furry, like an apricot.

She smiled at Gatty, and Gatty returned her smile.

The young woman opened her arms to include them all. 'I am for the English,' she announced.

Lady Gwyneth nodded. 'And for the Welsh, I hope.'

'*Si, si!*' the young woman replied. 'I am translator for merchants and pilgrims. I am here to help and guide you.'

Again she smiled straight at Gatty. Then she took Gatty's left hand and squeezed it.

'My name is Simona,' she said.

140

24

'Can you jump?' Simona asked.

'Can I jump!' said Gatty. She bunched up her cloak with both hands, ran forward and leaped over the stinking stream. 'Mind you,' she said, 'I know a man what jumped forty-seven feet.'

'Forty-seven!' Simona exclaimed.

'He can do magic,' said Gatty. 'Where are we going?'

'I'll show you the Arsenale.'

'The what?'

'You'll see. We needn't hurry. That merchant bank is always busy, and Nakin will have to wait for at least an hour.'

What Gatty saw were soaring stone walls, two proud stone lions roaring on either side of the massive gateway, and inside . . .

'Foreigners aren't allowed,' Simona said. She took Gatty's rough right hand with her much smaller pink hand. 'Neither are Venetians without the password.'

A guard was standing under the gate, blocking their way, but as soon as he saw Simona he called out and then kissed her on both cheeks. A small bow towards Gatty, a click of heels, another kiss for good luck, and Gatty and Simona were inside, standing on the edge of an absolutely enormous courtyard, brimming with water.

'He worked for my father,' Simona explained.

Gatty looked around, amazed. To her left and right were stacks of tree trunks, piles of planks, coils of hawser, masts;

anchors; ironmongery; barrels of caulk; and stretching down each side of the yard dozens of half-made galiotes, saetta, busses, and all kinds of other boats, lying in huge wooden cradles under open-fronted, high-roofed buildings.

'Biggest shipyard in the world,' Simona told Gatty. 'Two miles round walls. Come!'

As Gatty and Simona walked through the shipyard, they were greeted with friendly shouts, waves and whistles.

Simona looked at Gatty and raised her eyebrows. 'Men!' she said.

'Your father worked here?' Gatty asked.

Simona took hold of Gatty's right arm and plumped herself down. Then she kicked off her sandals and dabbled her feet in the water.

'He was the Master Shipwright,' Simona said. She slowly opened her arms. 'The Master Shipwright of this whole Arsenale.'

Gatty heard the pain as well as the pride behind Simona's words. 'What happened?'

'He's dead,' said Simona. 'He was drowned. I was, nearly.'

'My father's dead too.'

'When?'

'Last summer. Dark elves got inside him and doubled him up.'

'Did he serve Lady Gwyneth too?' Simona asked.

Gatty shook her head. 'We didn't live at Ewloe. My father was reeve of a whole manor. He wore the maroon jacket.'

'What's that?'

'The one the reeve wears. He used to beat me lots.' Gatty stared at the water. 'Don't matter.'

'It does,' said Simona. She leaned towards Gatty so that they touched shoulders.

'I'm not saying he wasn't fair,' Gatty replied hotly. 'He was fair to me, he was . . .'

'But not to everyone?'

'. . . except he wouldn't let me sing. He said it just reminded him of my mother. Gatty felt close to tears. 'Don't matter,' she said. 'He was what he was. I just . . . wish . . .'

Simona waited quietly.

'Well! I wish he said I mattered. To him.'

'Oh, Gatty!'

'I might have been that much pigswill!'

'No.'

Gatty tossed her head fiercely. 'He did care,' she said. 'He just didn't say it.'

'He cared,' said Simona. 'Each daughter needs her father. And each father loves his daughter, even when he doesn't say it.'

Gatty put one hand over her right cheek. 'My tooth's aching again,' she said.

'I know a man who'll pull it out,' Simona told her.

'He blew the pipe better than everyone,' Gatty said, 'everyone at Caldicot. He blew the pipe and banged the tabor. What is it? What you looking at me like that for?'

Simona was sitting bolt upright, though she still looked far more like an apricot than a cucumber. 'Where did you say?' she croaked. 'Better than everyone where?'

'Caldicot.'

Simona gave a little scream. She clapped her hand over her mouth.

'What is it?'

'Arthur! Serle!'

Now it was Gatty's turn. She cried out in amazement and then burst into tears, hot salty tears.

'Arthur!' gulped Simona. 'He came back here only eight weeks ago.'

'Eight weeks ago!' exclaimed Gatty. 'Arthur did?'

'Lord Stephen was injured . . .'

'Never!' said Gatty.

143

'He was wounded and Arthur was taking him home.'

'You mean . . .' said Gatty. Her face was burning; she put both hands to her cheeks.

'To the ostrich's head!' said Simona, smiling.

'What?'

'England! That's what England looks like on a map.'

Gatty shook her head. 'He's not . . . not in Jerusalem, then?'

'Oh, no! No, Gatty!'

'But that was his . . . quest. His quest! That's what he told me.'

Tenderly, Simona unlaced Gatty's boots. She put them side by side. 'Bathe your feet,' she said. 'It will cool your whole body.'

And then, sitting there in the sweet May sunlight, Gatty and Simona talked and talked, they talked hungrily as if, however much they said, it could never be enough.

Simona began at the end and worked backwards. 'Arthur told me I looked like an apricot,' she said.

'What's that?'

'*Albicoccho.*'

Gatty shook her head.

'Fruit. It's small and orange-pink. He said we must think of each other when there's a full moon.'

'Why?'

'And send a blessing.'

Gatty felt a pain in her heart.

'He told me about you. I know about Winnie, but he said you . . . Well, Arthur smiles when he talks about you. He said you and he have the best times. You share the best things, and talk about everything.'

Gatty stared at Simona, amazed. 'He said that?' She felt her face and neck begin to glow, and the glow spreading out to her whole body.

Then Simona told Gatty about how she came to love Arthur's brother, Serle. 'Arthur said I made Serle happy.'

'Happy?' said Gatty. 'Serle?'

'Arthur said the crusades made him different. More understanding.'

'He must have changed,' said Gatty.

The longer they talked, the faster Simona spoke. She told Gatty how Arthur had been knighted and was the youngest while his father Sir William was the oldest knight in the whole crusader army, and told her the whole story of Sir William's death and Lord Stephen's injury, and how Arthur had saved her life, and how a boy was trussed like a chicken and thrown over the city walls in a giant catapult, and how Arthur sobbed when he had to leave his horse Bonamy in Croatia . . .

Gatty looked at Simona, wide-eyed. Her poor head! Her poor heart! They were reeling and pumping with everything Simona had told her.

'You're not listening!' Simona accused her.

'I am.'

'What are you thinking?'

Gatty shook her head. She was still marvelling at what Arthur had said about her, and wondering whether he had reached Caldicot and read her message. How strange, she thought. Arthur, a squire, a young knight, he dreamed of reaching Jerusalem but has had to go home, while I, a landgirl, am on my way to the Holy Land.

'When Arthur and Lord Stephen reached here last June,' said Simona, waving toward the gateway, 'they stayed on *San Niccolo*.'

'What's that?'

'Saint Nicholas. An island. All the crusaders did. I'll take you there if there's time.'

'Yes,' Gatty said at once. 'Did Arthur teach you English, then?'

'No, I told you, I'm a translator.' Simona looked down and scrubbed the tips of her fingers against the gritty ground. 'I was betrothed to an Englishman from Norfolk.'

Gatty drew in her breath; she could hear the ache in Simona's voice.

'He was killed.'

'No!' cried Gatty.

'By bandits!' Simona threw her arms round Gatty's shoulders, and squeezed her fiercely. 'Aylmer,' she said huskily. 'Aylmer de Burnham. I loved him.'

'What was he like?'

'Nakin!' cried Simona.

'Nakin?' exclaimed Gatty, shocked.

'No! No!' said Simona, scrambling to her feet. 'I mean, we've been talking and talking. Nakin's waiting!'

Gatty whistled. 'I clean forgot him.'

'Get your boots on. I'll help you.'

'Won't harm him,' said Gatty. 'He thinks he's so high and mighty and top of the ladder. This'll bring him down a rung or two.'

25

All next day, the pilgrims felt like sea-creatures washed in by the tide and stranded on the foreshore. Like a jelly-fish, moon-faced and blue-veined, Nest feebly blobbed around the pilgrims' hospice, complaining of a headache and somehow sinking deeper and deeper into herself; Lady Gwyneth's head-pains had gone, but she told Gatty there were crabs walking sideways inside her stomach and nipping her with their claws; Snout kept wheezing and bubbling like a bloated cockle; Everard was as pink as a boiled shrimp, but not as whiskered. As for poor Austin, he was feverish and his throbbing right hand, swathed in its slimy, discoloured bandage, looked like a giant cuttlefish.

'It feels so tight it could burst,' he said.

'Better if it does,' Tilda told him.

Nakin wiped his damp upper lip. 'Well, Austin,' he said. 'Which would you prefer? To live with one hand or die with two?'

Austin was not amused.

The clammy heat put its hands round each of the pilgrims' heads. Mosquitoes whined around them, and tiny little sand-flies hip-hopped in and out of their clothing and were much tempted by Snout's hairy nostrils.

'It's too hot to wear our cloaks,' Lady Gwyneth told her companions. 'Nest, will you please stitch red crosses to the right shoulders of the men's tunics and our gowns?'

'My head!' moaned Nest. 'It's hammering.'

But Gatty, too felt ill. The ache in her mouth sharpened to a wicked point inside one of her lower molars.

Simona came to the pilgrims' hospice at noon, and Lady Gwyneth immediately asked her, 'Can you find a dentist who will look at Gatty's tooth? Nakin will give you money to pay him.'

Simona led Gatty through a maze of dark, narrow lanes to the dog-end of the city. 'Gianni. Gianni Nurico,' she said. 'Good man! My father's brother.'

Doctor Nurico peered inside Gatty's mouth, and scraped her lower molar with one of his fingernails, and then poked it with a metal probe.

Gatty yelped.

'Worms!' said Doctor Nurico. 'Worms have been eating it.'

'Can you get them out?'

Doctor Nurico shook his head. 'Not with all the aloe and myrrh in Venice,' he said in excellent English. 'Not even that would smoke them out.'

'Dig them out,' said Gatty. 'Like worms in a turnip. I'll hold firm. I will.'

Doctor Nurico put his hand on Gatty's shoulder, and looked down at her rather admiringly. 'I'm sorry,' he said. 'It'll have to come out. You'll feel better afterwards.'

Doctor Nurico picked up a saddler's hook lying on the floor. He nodded at Simona, and Simona, standing behind Gatty, clamped her hands over both Gatty's ears.

'Open!' said Doctor Nurico. 'Open wide!'

At once he drove the hook down into Gatty's red gum around the molar.

'Where are the pliers?' he said.

Simona kicked at them with her left foot.

'Right!' exclaimed her uncle. 'I'm always losing them.' Then the dentist grabbed Gatty's molar with the pliers, and half-pulled, half-twisted the tooth out.

Gatty howled, and her mouth filled with warm blood. She choked; she spat onto the floor.

Doctor Nurico held up Gatty's tooth. 'Very good!' he pronounced. 'Both roots!'

Gatty was blinded by her own tears. Standing behind her, Simona lightly laid her forearms on Gatty's shoulders, and linked her fingers.

'So that's a piece of luck,' the dentist said with a knowing smile, 'unless you prefer to call it experience.'

Gatty had no idea what Doctor Nurico was talking about, and anyway his voice came from far off, separated from her by a curtain of pain. Then the dentist told Gatty to open her mouth again, and he gently smeared some grease onto her bleeding gum.

'The brain of a hen,' he said. 'Diluted, of course.'

Inside Gatty's brain, there floated the thought that hens don't have brains, but she couldn't dress it in words. She closed her eyes.

'Let the blood form a scab,' Doctor Nurico told her, 'and don't be in any hurry to eat. The ointment will help to reduce the swelling.'

Gatty nodded.

'Tomorrow,' said Simona's uncle, 'eat lettuce and chervil. Chop them, mash them, add some wine, and chew them. A lovely young woman like you must look after her teeth.'

It wasn't until the third day after their arrival in Venice that the pilgrims felt well enough to leave the hospice and give thanks for their safe journey in the basilica of Saint Mark's.

Gatty's gums were still very sore and her jaw was swollen, and Lady Gwyneth still had crabs edging around inside her, but the fresh wind sweeping in from the sea gave them all new energy, and their energy gave them hope.

As soon as Gatty, Nest and Everard stepped out of the

hospice into the May sunlight they heard music. One young man was playing the flute and his companion was plucking a string instrument with a rounded back, like a pear cut in half.

'What is it?' asked Gatty.

'A lute,' said Everard.

'Lute,' repeated Gatty. 'I like that word.'

The flautist gave Nest a lingering smile and began to play a light-hearted song, a tune somehow on the tips of its toes; and his companion began to sing:

> *'Li noviaus tens et mais et violete*
> *Et rosignols me semont de chanter . . .'*

What the words meant, Gatty had no idea. She closed her eyes, and listened to the liquid way the flute picked up from the voice and the voice from the flute so that the whole song was seamless – or seemed so, anyhow!

Gatty gently swayed from side to side, like a baby being rocked in its cradle.

'Cinque and Sei,' said a voice right behind her.

Gatty, Nest and Everard turned round, and it was Simona, pink and pretty, with painted lips and painted nails.

'My brothers!' she announced. 'Cinque and Sei. Five and six. My fifth and sixth brothers.'

'You got six brothers?' exclaimed Gatty.

'Sei likes the look of you, Nest!'

'I like the look of him,' Nest replied, smiling. 'What do the words mean?'

'Love,' said Simona. 'And love!' Her eyes simmered.

'Say them to me,' Everard instructed them. 'Slowly.'

Then Sei recited the words, and Everard translated, 'This new season, this month of May . . . er, the violets and the nightingales make me sing. At first, he – no, she – she was so loving to me, her smiling mouth . . . and I never believed, er, I never believed she'd give me such pain. Dear God in Heaven!

150

Let me hold her just once . . .' Everard paused. He turned pink.

'What, Everard?' Gatty demanded.

'. . . just once in my arms . . .' said Everard.

'What's so strange about that?' asked Gatty. 'You wouldn't hold someone with your legs, would you?'

'Well,' said Everard, 'well, er . . . naked!'

'Naked!' exclaimed Gatty, and she and Nest hopped around, laughing, while Everard stood rooted to the spot, pink and shamefaced.

Cinque laid his hands across the choirmaster's slim shoulders. '*Ainz,*' he sang, '*ainz que voise outre mer.*'

'Just once before I go to the Holy Land,' Everard translated.

Simona put an arm round Gatty's waist. 'Your mouth?' she asked, and she winked.

'It's getting better,' Gatty said. 'It is.'

Then for some reason, quite why she had no idea, Gatty remembered lying on wheatstraw and sacking in a cart, lying blue and bruised and feverish, and looking up at Arthur standing on the back of the cart. She heard herself telling him, 'You got the sky on your shoulders,' and Arthur smiling, and replying, 'Well, you've got stars back in your eyes . . .'

'Come on, now,' said Simona. 'Lady Gwyneth's waiting to go to Mass. Then we're going to see the two pilgrim ships.'

Sei winked at Nest, and she blew him a kiss.

Then, sheepishly, Gatty looked under her long eyelashes at his brother. But Cinque, he was smiling at Everard.

'Come on!' Simona repeated. 'You'll see them again when Venice marries the sea.'

26

During Mass in the basilica of Saint Mark's, Gatty kept gazing up at the burnt gold cupola, and staring at the thousands of tiny coloured stone circles and triangles and squares covering the floor, and tracing out their pictures and patterns with her right forefinger.

Two birds with breasts as blue as Lady Gwyneth's sapphire ring, their rusty tail-fans spotted with sapphire-and-saffron eyes . . .

Simona saw Gatty gazing at the mosaic peacocks. 'They never, never die,' she whispered.

'I seen them before,' said Gatty. 'Lord Stephen's got them. I heard them screaming.' She opened her mouth as wide as she could and pretended to scream.

'Gatty!' croaked Lady Gwyneth. 'What do you think you're doing? Behaving like a jackdaw!'

As soon as Mass was over, Simona led the pilgrims straight across the huge orchard in front of Saint Mark's, then she dived down a long narrow passage and delivered them to the waterfront.

Two ships were moored there, heel to toe, one with two masts, the other with three; and on the quay in front of each was a white banner with a large scarlet cross sewn onto it.

'God has been good to us,' Lady Gwyneth exclaimed. 'Yes, God has guided our footsteps.'

'Except for Saviour's,' said Nest.

Just a wisp of a sad smile played round the corners of Lady

Gwyneth's lips. 'This part of our journey will be easier for you, Emrys,' she said.

'I don't feel myself, my lady,' Emrys said. 'Not without horses.'

Lady Gwyneth nodded. 'I understand,' she replied warmly. 'Still, yours will be waiting for you. And mine. And Syndod.'

'Syndod,' said Austin. 'Syndod. Have you ever heard of Sindbad, Gatty?'

'Who?'

'Sindbad. He was a Saracen sailor. He came from Baghdad.'

'Like that merchant!' Gatty exclaimed. 'In the story that nun told us.'

'Like us,' the priest said, 'Sindbad went on a voyage. Seven voyages, in fact. His boat was attacked by little savages with yellow eyes, their bodies were covered in black fur, and they swarmed up the masts and gnawed all the ropes. Then Sindbad met a giant . . .'

'Tell us later, Austin,' said Lady Gwyneth. 'We have to choose our ship now.'

Austin deferred to Lady Gwyneth. He lifted his paw to his mouth and sucked it, as if he were a savage himself, draining the last drop of marrow from the bone.

'I hope we're not going to meet savages or giants,' said Snout.

'Or knotted serpents,' Austin said, 'or seashell-birds, or cannibals who roast their captives, or Diamond Mountains.'

'Austin!' Lady Gwyneth exclaimed.

'I wouldn't count on it,' said Nakin. 'There's no profit without peril.'

'Marvel!' Lady Gwyneth said. 'That's what we must all do. Marvel at the wonders ahead of us, and thank God for them.'

Then Lady Gwyneth gasped, and clutched the right side of her stomach.

'My lady!' cried Nest, and the pilgrims gathered round Lady Gwyneth.

'It's all right,' sobbed Lady Gwyneth. 'I think it is. Just a . . . sudden stab. A shooting-star.'

Gatty looked at Lady Gwyneth. No, she's not a shooting-star, she thought. Lady Gwyneth's our mother moon, leading us through the dark with her grace and her bright words. And we're the stars, trailing and traipsing along after her. Nest, she's the Swan, and Everard's the Lyre, and Emrys, what's he? He's the Charioteer, no, Orion the Hunter, and Tilda, I don't know what she is.

Simona took Gatty's left elbow. 'Over there,' she said. 'That's Saint Nicholas.'

The moment she was aboard, Simona was as much at home as an ant in its hill. Busy and bright-eyed, she handed the pilgrims down from the gangplank to the deck, and led them to the stern, up a short flight of wooden steps into the tower, and out onto a platform.

The ship's captain was awaiting them, and so was a low table laden with jugs and little mugs and a large wooden platter piled with small, brightly-coloured cakes. Gatty could scarcely take her eyes off them.

'I told him you were coming,' Simona told the pilgrims, and she kissed the captain on both his stubbly cheeks.

'Ah!' said Nakin, with the air of one moneymaker recognising two more.

'Gobbo,' said the captain. 'I am Gobbo.'

He stood with his legs slightly apart, knees flexed. His blue eyes bored into Gatty.

'My father's friend,' Simona explained, nodding and smiling.

After the captain had poured sweet wine, he offered each

pilgrim a little square of cake – robin's egg blue and vetch yellow, thrift pink, willow.

'Marzipan,' said Gobbo, smiling. 'Saint Mark's bread. Venice bread.'

'Very good,' said Snout, reaching out for another piece.

'Almonds and sugar,' Simona added.

Then Gobbo began to tell the pilgrims about the voyage in what he called his 'goodbad English.' He said it would take five weeks to sail to Jaffa, and that in Jaffa he would secure and pay for asses and mules to carry the pilgrims to Jerusalem. Gobbo promised the pilgrims seven full days in Jerusalem. He undertook to feed them with two hot meals each day, and to bring them safely back to Venice no later than the first day of September so that they could cross the mountains before winter.

'Other ship . . .' said Gobbo. He shrugged and burst into laughter.

'What?' asked Lady Gwyneth.

'You see,' said Gobbo.

'We will,' said Nakin, smiling and leaving his mouth slightly open, as if he hoped to trap something inside it. 'We'll have a look for ourselves.'

Like any good salesman, Gobbo knew the advantage of belittling his rival but also knew it was more important to show off the advantages of what he had to offer, and to spoil his clients. He led the pilgrims on a tour of his ship, built in the Arsenale only two years before, and then he led them back up to the bridge where he regaled them with more sweet wine and marzipan.

'What's the price for each pilgrim?' Nakin asked.

The moment Gobbo named a figure, Nakin frowned. He mopped his brow; he kept tutting and shaking his head.

Gobbo drained his mug of wine and looked at Lady Gwyneth earnestly. 'In God's name, my lady,' he said, 'I hope you sail with me. I will . . . I will service you.'

'Serve you,' said Simona.

'I will serve you. You will never forget it.'

'Too expensive,' said Nakin.

The second ship, a filthy old galley, was altogether cheaper. Her barnacled bottom needed scraping, and so did her slimy insides, and she looked as if she might only be held together by layers of caulk.

'Gobbo has sails,' the captain said. 'We have sails and oarsmen. High wind or flat calm, we are ready.' But he was nothing like as welcoming as Gobbo, and looked like a man soured by disappointment. His manner was charmless.

The pilgrims were of one mind. They wanted to sail with Gobbo. So, with a heavy tread, Nakin went back up the gangway to talk to him again.

The pilgrims waited quite some while until at last Nakin and Gobbo appeared at the end of the gangplank, smiling broad smiles. They beckoned the pilgrims aboard.

'*Deo gratias*!' Gobbo exclaimed, opening his arms wide. 'You are wise pilgrims.'

'Poor pilgrims,' Lady Gwyneth replied thoughtfully. And then, as soon as she was on her own with Nakin, 'Did he lower the cost?'

Nakin nodded. 'I told him the other captain was charging fifty silver groats for each pilgrim.'

'Nakin!' she exclaimed. 'That's shameless. You know very well it was forty-five.'

'It's business!' said Nakin. 'With truths and lies you buy and sell merchandise. Anyhow, I told Gobbo we couldn't begin to pay his price.'

'And so?'

'Forty groats,' said Nakin. 'I've paid him the first half.'

'Disgraceful!' Lady Gwyneth said, smiling despite herself.

First Gobbo led the way back to the bridge, where those

pilgrims who were able to write entered their names in a large black book, and then Gobbo added the names of Nakin, Snout, Emrys and Tilda.

After this, the captain swarmed down the steps to the main deck and from there to the lower deck, altogether more purposeful than before. He spoke rapidly to Simona.

'This deck,' she said, 'is where all the travellers have their quarters – pilgrims, envoys, Jews, Saracens, traders, everyone.'

'Saracens!' exclaimed Gatty.

Nakin stepped over to the port side. 'We'll settle ourselves here,' he announced. 'Better air. And fewer passengers tripping over us.'

'No,' said Gobbo.

'Why not?'

'This is for traders. Traders on port and starboard. Pilgrims in middle. Germans, Hungarians, French, English . . .'

'Welsh,' said Lady Gwyneth.

Nakin grunted and kneaded his dewlaps. But the deal was already done; the contract was signed and the first part of the payment handed over. There was nothing he could do about it.

The captain picked up a hunk of chalk lying beside the bilge-pump. He drew a line on the deck about a head longer than Snout, the tallest man in the party, and another line parallel to it and three feet away from it. Then he squared it off into a coffin-shaped box.

'Name?' he said. 'You?'

'Snout.'

Gobbo wrote a large S inside the box, and proceeded to draw another line, another box the same size, and to label it, and so he continued until all the pilgrims were accounted for.

'I'm not sleeping next to Nakin,' Everard said in a prickly voice.

'And I'm not sleeping next to my husband,' Tilda complained, 'and I should be.'

'Of course, Tilda,' Lady Gwyneth reassured her, 'and I must have Nest and Gatty on either side of me. We can sort out who has which berth when we come aboard.'

'Last night of May,' Gobbo told them. 'We sail at dawn on the first day of June.'

'First,' said Simona, 'festival in Venice! Venice marries the sea! Elephant in Venice! Murano glass! Music!' The pitch of her voice was rising higher and higher, in tune with her excitement.

'And time for us to get over our aches and pains,' Lady Gwyneth said. 'It's only when you stop that you realise how exhausted you are.'

'You buy pilgrim badges,' Gobbo told them. 'You buy bones.'

'Bones?' asked Gatty.

'In Venice,' remarked Lady Gwyneth, 'everyone seems to be buying, selling, making contracts, banking, extending credit, securing loans, charging interest. Even the nuns in our hospice. They wanted to charge us double for our hot meal yesterday because it was a holy day.'

'And almost every day's a holy day,' Everard added.

'So!' said Gobbo. 'Archangel Raphael and Saint Martha . . .'

'. . . and Saint Christopher and Michael the Archangel,' said Simona.

'They all protect pilgrims,' said Gobbo. 'Each day we arrange you go to one shrine?'

'I will take you,' said Simona, but none of the pilgrims looked particularly enthusiastic.

While the pilgrims filed down the gangplank, Simona dawdled for a moment with Gobbo. Looking over her shoulder, Gatty saw Simona scrape his cheek with one painted fingernail and kiss him, and then the captain counted out a number of shining silver coins and Simona slipped them into her breast pocket.

A seagull left its perch – a tall spear with one of the pilgrim banners tied to it – and flew away, screaming. Dark wavelets swallowed themselves, and turned silver. Gobbo's ship groaned. Gatty could smell seaweed, salt and, from some-where, burning bread. Out of a high window appeared two naked arms, and then someone leaned out – wearing an ugly mask!

Gatty frowned. In Venice, nothing was quite as it seemed to be, and everything kept changing. One moment the city was candid; the next secretive. One moment cradle-safe, the next coffin-threatening. One moment beautiful, the next hideous.

27

Gatty woke from a confused dream, but the words in her head were clean and clear:

> On your two shoulders you carry the skies.
> Head-in-the-clouds! You got stars in your eyes.
>
> But the I that I am is made of these *Is*:
> An earth-fingered girl whose thick tongue ties,
> Stumbling and slow for all that I tries.
> Yet I got a true heart that never lies.
> I seen despair and know what hope buys.
>
> On your two shoulders you carry the skies.
> Head-in-the-clouds! You got stars in your eyes.

Lying between Lady Gwyneth and Tilda, Gatty opened her eyes wide to the darkness, and listened.

A bat looping the loop . . . the double-thump of her heart . . . the sound of hair growing on the back of the dog in the corner of the room . . . the faint hissing of the moon's misty halo . . .

Lady Gwyneth gave a start, and moaned. Gatty gently nuzzled her, and Lady Gwyneth sank into deeper sleep again.

At first light, though, Lady Gwyneth sat bolt upright, clutching her stomach, and Gatty sat up beside her.

'It's worse,' she said.

'Must be that eel,' Gatty said quietly. 'That's when it began. It's the only thing you had what we didn't.'

Lady Gwyneth breathed in deeply, and let out her breath bit by juddering bit.

'All over?' Gatty asked.

Lady Gwyneth licked her lips. 'No,' she whispered. 'Here. My right side.'

'I wish Johanna was here,' Gatty said. 'She's got a temper on her, and a moustache and whiskers, but she knows the best medicines.'

'So does Tilda,' whispered Lady Gwyneth.

'I'll wake her, my lady.'

'Not yet,' said Lady Gwyneth. 'Look at her! All those boils.'

'Everyone at Caldicot got boils once,' Gatty said. 'Not even Johanna could cure them.'

Lady Gwyneth took a deep breath. 'I want you to go to the festival today,' she said in a low voice.

'What do you mean, my lady?'

'Without me.'

'No, my lady!'

'I'll rest here today.'

'I'll stay with you.'

'No, Gatty. I know how you and Nest have been looking forward to it. Out on the water with Simona and her brothers.'

Gatty shook her head until her curls danced.

'You're my chamber-servant,' Lady Gwyneth said, 'and you will do as I say. I want you and Nest to go. I want everyone to go.'

'Yes, my lady.'

Lady Gwyneth gave Gatty a wan smile. 'How strong-willed you are,' she said.

Gatty stuck out her chin. 'I wouldn't be here if I wasn't.'

'Weren't,' Lady Gwyneth corrected her.

161

'Weren't,' said Gatty. 'All these weren'ts and wasn'ts and wouldn'ts!'

'You're always playing with words,' Lady Gwyneth said.

'I never thought about them before I came to Ewloe,' Gatty replied.

Lady Gwyneth gingerly removed her hands from her stomach. 'And talking to you like this has eased my pain a little,' she said.

'I'll stay here with you, my lady.'

'That you won't,' said Lady Gwyneth. 'Dear God! I'm perfectly all right. I'm not about to die.'

On Lady Gwyneth's other side, Nest stirred, and stretched.

'May God's light shine upon you, Nest!' Lady Gwyneth said.

'And upon you, my lady,' murmured Nest.

Before Simona collected the pilgrims from the hospice at noon, one of the nuns opened a gourd and very carefully poured out a spoonful of brown treacle that looked exactly like the foul stream Gatty and Simona had jumped on their way to the Arsenale.

'Teriaca!' the nun exclaimed. '*Tout!*'

'It's called teriaca,' Everard translated, 'and it cures everything. Everything except for the plague, I suppose. You can't cure death!'

'If you catch the plague, you're dead before you're dead,' said Tilda.

'The best medicine in the world,' Everard translated. 'Stomach, intestines, liver, kidney, worms.'

'What's it made of?' Tilda asked.

'*Ambre . . .*' the nun began.

'Amber,' said Everard. 'Rose petals. Opium. Pepper. Sixty different herbs.'

162

'Sixty!' exclaimed Nest.

The effect of the teriaca on Lady Gwyneth was almost immediate. She lay back, and closed her eyes, and began to snore.

The nun gave the pilgrims a knowing smile. '*Le sommeil*,' she said. 'Panacea.'

'Sleep,' said Everard. 'The best medicine.'

Nest yawned.

The nun said she would keep an eye on Lady Gwyneth throughout the afternoon, but when Nest asked her whether there was any more comfortable bedding in the hospice, she replied that everyone – nuns and pilgrims alike – slept on straw mattresses.

'I can see she's a fine lady,' Everard translated, as the nun pointed at Lady Gwyneth with a charmingly arched little finger, no less delicate than the quills of her plucked eyebrows. 'So she must be used to fine clothes and fine bedding.'

'We're all the worse for wear,' Austin said. 'This long journey has worn her out.'

Everard translated his words, and the nun smiled.

'Well,' she said, 'my advice to you is to buy Lady Gwyneth a feather bed and pillows and sheets. She'll need them between Venice and Jaffa, unless she wants to sleep on bare boards.'

'Where can we buy them?' asked Nest.

'Out of my pockets!' Nakin said with a loud sigh.

'I do know a man who can let you have them cheap,' Everard translated, 'and you can sell them back to him when you return to Venice.'

Gatty eyed the nun, and recalled what Lady Gwyneth had said about everyone in Venice buying and selling. Here was this charming, finely-boned nun, who had taken vows of chastity, obedience and poverty, excited by making a profit.

When Simona arrived, the pilgrims were glad to get out of the hospice into the misty sunshine of San Marco.

Inside a ring of people was an enormous grey animal, at least four times as large as Syndod, waving its long, thick nose in the air.

'Our elephant,' said Simona. 'Venice elephant. Tiny.'

'Tiny?' exclaimed Gatty.

'That's his name! He comes from a floating island – an island that dances when it hears music.'

The pilgrims stared at this creature, amazed. He looked bald; he had little piggy eyes and pointed tusks and huge ear-flaps hanging down on either side of his head.

'Young elephant,' Simona told them. 'Only three years old.'

'Look how he can stretch his nose!' Gatty cried in delight.

Tiny's owner picked up a handful of hay and laid it on the flat of Gatty's outstretched hand. Then Tiny curved and lowered his nose, delicately removed the hay and twisted it up to his mouth.

'You do it,' Gatty told Nest.

'No,' Nest said at once.

'Elephants are gentle,' Simona reassured her. 'Their enemies are bulls and dragons. Dragons lasso them with their tails, and when they fall over they can't stand up again.'

'How do you know?' Nest demanded.

'Only one beast frightens an elephant,' Simona continued. She said something to Tiny's owner, and he took a little box out of a pocket. When he opened it, a mouse scuttled out of it, right between the elephant's legs.

Tiny lurched backwards, waved his trunk and roared. He trumpeted to high heaven, and showered everyone with spittle and saliva.

The mouse didn't know which way to turn and, before it had made up its mind, Tiny's owner pounced on it and put it back into the box.

Simona winked at Nest. 'You know how to make babies?' she asked.

Nest put her hand over her mouth.

'Don't encourage her!' Snout told Simona.

'When elephants make babies,' Simona told them, 'they stand back to back!'

And with that, she saluted Tiny's owner and led the pilgrims down to the waterfront.

The Grand Canal and the lagoon were seething with hundreds and hundreds of little boats, flapping sails, flashing oars, men and women and children, shouting and singing.

Simona made her way through the mass of milling people to three small boats lying side by side, each of them manned by two of Simona's brothers.

Then Uno and Due, who was a monk, handed Austin, Everard and Snout aboard the first boat, and Emrys, Tilda and Nakin stepped onto the middle boat.

'*Si*,' said Sei, reaching out for Nest. '*Si*.'

Nest gave him her fingertips, and Sei bent over them and kissed them, and then reached out for Gatty. '*Si*,' he said.

Gatty gave him a knowing look. She grasped the swept-up bow and swung herself aboard.

'*Bravo*!' laughed Simona.

And with that, they were off – three boats in a fleet of almost three hundred, arching their necks and advancing across the dazzling lagoon.

'Where are we going?' asked Nest.

'Look at those people!' Gatty exclaimed, pointing at a small group standing on a pale mudflat, waving giant spades. 'What's going on?'

'Saltpans,' said Simona. 'Salt-gatherers.'

'It wouldn't surprise me,' Nest declared, 'if Venetians were half-human and half-fish.'

'Like mermaids and mermen, you mean?' asked Gatty.

'Sei's a merman,' Simona exclaimed, and she said something to her brother.

Then Sei rested his oar and held up his hands and splayed his fingers. They were webbed.

Nest and Gatty gasped.

'His feet are webbed too,' Simona told them.

Sei laughed and reached out towards Nest with both hands.

'He says you're a mermaid with your beautiful long gold hair,' Simona translated.

'I haven't got scales,' Nest protested. She showed Sei her pale arms and stroked them.

'Sei says life is a boat,' Simona translated. 'He says love is a sea.'

Nest giggled, and then fluttered her eyelids at Sei.

As the armada of little boats drew close to the sea-gate, Cinque and Sei kept showing off their skills, shipping their oars, resting them, backpaddling, avoiding the other boats, working their way closer and closer to a much larger ship, painted gold all over, with scarlet and azure banners draped over her gunwales.

'Ship of the Doge,' Simona said.

'God in Heaven!' exclaimed Gatty.

Almost at once, four trumpeters raised their trumpets and four drummers raised their drumsticks.

'Ohh!' breathed Gatty. 'I wish . . . I wish Lady Gwyneth . . .'

Nest put her forefinger to her lips. '*Hisht*!' she whispered.

Gatty glared at Nest. 'I WISH SHE WAS HERE!' she said loudly.

'*Sei*! *Pronto*!' Simona told her brother. 'Ready!'

Sei stood up and pulled his loose white cloth shirt over his head. Then he peeled off his tight breeches so that he was wearing nothing but his braies. Nest could scarcely bring herself to look, but, looking, she was relieved to see that Sei had no scales at all.

Then Simona pointed out a man standing at the gunwale high above them, dressed in crimson velvet and wearing a thick gold chain. 'It is the Doge's son,' she said. 'Ranier.'

'What's he doing?' asked Gatty. 'What's he got in his hand?'

'A gold-and-diamond ring,' Simona replied. 'He drops it into the water.'

'Why?' demanded Gatty.

'To show the sea belongs to Venice, and must serve us all as a wife serves her husband. Venice gives a ring to the sea each year, and many, many people dive after it.'

Around them, everyone began to shout and whistle and stamp – the boards and planks of all their little boats boomed.

How long did Ranier stand there? How long did he show the ring to the people of Venice?

All at once, there was a howling and scuffling as Sei and a host of young men and young girls, more modestly clad, dove into the water.

'No one has ever saved a ring,' said Simona, smiling.

'What if you do?' Gatty asked. 'What if you do save it?'

'It's yours to keep,' Simona replied.

At this moment, Sei resurfaced like a cork popping out of a bottle. He gasped, took a deep breath and plunged straight back into the water again.

Cinque smiled and drew his lute from its leather bag. He plucked it and began to sing.

'The years wheel us round,' Simona translated,

'The years wheel us round,
Our whole life's a quest,
And Death in his black mask
Is no more than a jest.

All times are good times
But first times are best:
For mermaids with mermen,
And for Sei with Nest!'

'Sing it again!' said Nest.

Sei surfaced for a second time, and grabbed the side of the little boat. He reached out – to Nest – and Nest gave him her hand. Sei clambered in, spluttering and dripping.

'Next year, Sei!' said Simona cheerfully. 'Gatty, you sit in the bow.'

'I'll row!' said Gatty.

Simona shook her head. 'It's not as easy as it looks,' she said.

Then she and Cinque each took one oar, and Sei and Nest sat close together in the stern and, as the thick knot of boats around the Doge's ship began to loosen, the two boats bearing their companions mysteriously appeared on either side of them. Together the three of them eased through the water.

From time to time the six brothers called out to one another. As dusk crept in from the sea, and shreds of gauzy mist drifted across the face of the water, many of the returning boats lit lanterns in their prows.

Now and then, Cinque plucked his lute; now and then he sang.

You can't arrange to be happy, Gatty thought, and you can't make happiness last. It just sneaks up on you, and then before long it disappears again.

Sei reached under the bench in the stern and pulled out a flask.

'What is it?' asked Nest.

'Love potion,' said Simona.

'Love potion!'

'The essence of love, *si*. He bought it from a witch.'

Sei poured a drop of the liquid onto his little finger, and touched it to Nest's lips.

Sei thinks life's for laughing, thought Gatty. He thinks love's just a game.

Sei took a gulp of the potion and then watched with satisfaction as Nest did the same.

'It doesn't taste like love,' said Nest, grimacing.

'Horn of unicorn,' said Simona. 'Very rare. Unicorn and rose petals and wine.'

At this moment Gatty realised with a start that she hadn't even thought about Lady Gwyneth and her stomach pains since before the Doge's son dropped the ring into the water. There and then her happiness faded.

Darkness lowered its lid over Venice, the chill mist rose up to meet it; and Gatty, a creature as much of instinct as reason, felt within her an unconscionable, dark foreboding.

Cinque and Sei and their brothers brushed sea-snails off the slimy stanchions on the landing-stage; they tethered their little boats to them, and handed the pilgrims ashore.

Nest grasped Gatty's forearm. 'Gatty,' she whispered. 'Sei and I are going walking together.'

'Where?'

'Just the two of us, I mean. He asked me.'

Gatty felt a pang. Sei had asked Nest, but Cinque hadn't asked her.

'He'll bring me back to the hospice later,' Nest whispered, her eyes shining in the gloom. 'I'll see you there.'

28

Gatty was right.

The hospice nun who had promised to keep an eye on Lady Gwyneth opened the door to the pilgrims and at once called out, 'Alessandra! Alessandra!'

A woman carrying a second lantern advanced down the gloomy passage towards them. Gatty saw she was wearing a white linen gown.

'Alessandra Lupo,' the nun told the pilgrims. '*Chirurga.*'

'A surgeon,' Everard translated.

The doctor, a small, intent woman with deepset, dark eyes and scars on both arms, as if she had experimented by operating on her own body, led the pilgrims to their room but Lady Gwyneth wasn't there.

'Where is she?' demanded Gatty.

Doctor Lupo nodded and softly patted the air, and one by one the pilgrims sat down in a row on two of the straw mattresses. Then she got onto her knees in front of them.

'Lady Gwyneth's stomach has burst inside her,' she said gently, in good English.

The pilgrims looked as if they had been turned to stone. Their blood chilled.

The nun came and squatted beside Doctor Lupo. 'She vomited all afternoon,' she said, and Everard translated. 'I pressed my hand against her stomach, and when I lifted it, she yelped. That's when I sent for Alessandra.'

The doctor looked at the row of stricken pilgrims, and

170

shook her head. 'She cannot live,' she said in a quiet voice.

In the falling air, the nun made the sign of the cross, and said something.

'Lady Gwyneth is a precious dove of God,' Everard translated. 'She will fly to paradise.'

'Can't you . . .' began Gatty in a strangled voice.

'You're a surgeon,' said Tilda.

'She cannot live,' Doctor Lupo repeated, in a quiet, deliberate voice.

'We've carried her to another room,' the nun told them. 'A quiet room!'

'She wants to see you all,' the doctor said.

'Nest!' exclaimed Gatty. 'She's not even here.'

'She'd be afraid,' said Nakin. 'I'm afraid.'

'Think of Lady Gwyneth's needs,' Doctor Lupo said, 'and you will not be.'

Gatty stood up. 'I'll go to her,' she said.

'No,' said the surgeon, unfolding herself and getting to her feet. 'I'll go first.'

'I'm coming with you,' Gatty insisted.

Leaving the others still sitting on the mattresses too stunned to speak, Gatty followed the doctor down the passage.

Doctor Lupo paused outside the door of Lady Gwyneth's room. 'She may be asleep,' she said in a low voice.

Gatty nodded. 'How long?' she asked.

'What?'

Gatty looked at her unblinking. 'How long?' she repeated. 'I seen death before.'

The surgeon shook her head. 'For one person, a few hours; for another, a few days. I can't tell.'

'You can't do nothing?'

Again Doctor Lupo shook her head, and she grasped Gatty's forearm. 'I will give her medicine to soften her pain.'

'She knows?' asked Gatty.

Doctor Lupo nodded.

Then Gatty opened the door, somehow expecting Lady Gwyneth to look ghastly and grisly, but there she was, propped up on two pillows, appearing much the same as usual. Flushed, yes, but blue-eyed, fair-haired, willowy.

Lady Gwyneth turned her head a little, and saw Gatty.

And Gatty, she gazed at Lady Gwyneth with such love, such longing. Then she took two strides and launched herself onto her knees.

'It's you,' murmured Lady Gwyneth.

At once Gatty heard how shallow her breathing was. She looked up at Doctor Lupo. 'I'll stay here with my lady for a while,' she said quietly. 'I'll fetch the others.'

Doctor Lupo almost smiled. 'Then we are in your hands,' she said, and she left the room.

'And I,' whispered Lady Gwyneth, 'I'm in God's hands. My blood's boiling. I keep shivering. Oh Gatty!'

Gatty pressed her forehead against Lady Gwyneth's shoulder.

'I may not have long,' Lady Gwyneth said. 'And I have to tell you.'

Gatty lifted her head. 'I am here, my lady.'

'Where's Nest?'

'She's . . . coming back,' faltered Gatty. 'She'll be here soon.'

Lady Gwyneth feebly reached out for one of Gatty's hands. 'Feel my stomach,' she said. 'So hard. So swollen. Oh!' Lady Gwyneth winced with pain and, noiseless, she wept.

Gatty closed her eyes and breathed deeply.

'It was like this before. When I was with child.'

'My lady?'

'Griffith. I loved him so. I sang songs to him. I even fed him myself. And . . . and . . .'

'He died,' whispered Gatty.

Lady Gwyneth hiccupped, then shrugged, as if even the air lay too heavy upon her.

'I seen how you prayed at his tiny grave, and how you tended it,' Gatty said.

'I loved him so,' Lady Gwyneth sobbed, 'and I killed him.'

'No, my lady. You told me. His little heart was weak and it stopped and he was only eleven weeks old.'

'That wasn't true.'

'My lady?'

'While I was asleep I lay over him, and smothered him. I killed him.'

'Oh, my lady!'

'I've never told anyone.'

'Not even Austin?'

Lady Gwyneth miserably shook her head.

'My lady, you must. You must confess it.'

'I woke and Griffith's breath was gone. My darling son! His skin was like skimmed milk. I killed him. That's the reason why I have to make this pilgrimage. To do penance and save my soul.' Lady Gwyneth's breathing became more shallow. 'I cannot,' she said. 'I cannot. I cannot reach Jerusalem. But if I do not . . .'

'My lady,' interrupted Gatty, in a strong, deliberate voice. She took both Lady Gwyneth's hands inside her own. 'I will,' she said.

Lady Gwyneth stared up at Gatty.

'I'll go. I'll go for you.'

Lady Gwyneth swallowed and winced.

'I will do penance for you.'

Now Lady Gwyneth's eyeballs were hot and somehow too large for their sockets.

'Like them young men, remember, on the way to Canterbury. John and Geoff. They were hired by an old stick too shaky to be a pilgrim herself.'

Lady Gwyneth would have smiled but she couldn't make her cheek muscles do what she wanted.

'I'll pray at all them places you told us about,' Gatty said. 'Holy Sepulchre and the Golden Gate and that. Austin will know.'

'To save my soul,' whispered Lady Gwyneth.

'I will and all,' said Gatty. 'You can trust me.'

Lady Gwyneth nodded, or thought she did. 'I believe I can,' she whispered. 'But if you fail to reach Jerusalem, I'll never rise to paradise.' Lady Gwyneth gasped. 'I will never see Griffith again.'

This long conversation exhausted Lady Gwyneth, but it also calmed her. She closed her eyes, and for a while the only sound in the dying-room, that's what the hospice nun later called it, was Lady Gwyneth's rapid, scratchy breathing.

Then the door creaked and, led by the nun with her lantern, the other pilgrims filed into the room. Nest was with them and Gatty saw at once how pink-cheeked and bright-eyed she was.

Nest took hold of Gatty's shoulders and lowered herself onto her knees beside her, and all the other pilgrims shuffled and subsided around the bed.

'The doctor said you were coming for us,' Nest said in a low voice.

'You weren't even here!' Gatty whispered. 'Where have you been?'

After some while, Lady Gwyneth opened her eyes and Gatty noticed at once that they were more misty. To begin with, she scarcely recognised her companions, or knew where she was.

'We are all here,' Austin said in his good, firm voice. 'The four angels of the Lord are standing at each corner of the room.'

The corners of Lady Gwyneth's mouth twitched. 'I cannot see them,' she said. She inspected the semicircle of pilgrims and sighed, then tried to lever herself up on her pillows. At once she yelped, and then gave a long moan.

'My new vocabulary!' she said, and the corners of her mouth twitched again.

Snout mumbled something and crossed himself; Nest began to sniff.

'I told you once,' Lady Gwyneth said, 'that we were partners, and sisters, and brothers.' Her voice may have been weak, but her resolve was unwavering, and so was her concern for her companions. 'Together we planned this pilgrimage, and together we've undertaken it.'

Nest sniffed more loudly.

'When one sister fails,' Lady Gwyneth went on, her voice becoming hoarse, 'the others must not. They must do what she'd have done. I want you to continue with our pilgrimage and reach Jerusalem. I believe each step you take is a step nearer paradise.'

Suddenly Lady Gwyneth arched her back. She cried out and began to writhe.

'*Basta!*' said the hospice nun. 'Enough!' She put a hand under Austin's arm and helped him up, and then all the other pilgrims stood up as well.

'Come on, Gatty,' said Nest, and she pulled at her forearm.

Lady Gwyneth screamed, and her scream died away to a moan.

'I must hear her last confession,' Austin insisted.

'And after that I'll keep watch,' the nun told the pilgrims, 'I will come and call you.'

*

The pilgrims were too shocked to talk very much. They were worn out by their long day on the water. One by one they fell asleep.

Even Gatty dozed for a while, only to sit upright, instantly awake, and wonder how long she had been asleep.

She looked around at her sleeping companions. Then she quietly removed the lantern from the hook and crept back down the passageway.

Lady Gwyneth didn't move, but Gatty saw her eyes were shining.

'I'll keep watch for a while,' she whispered, and the hospice nun nodded gratefully, stifled a yawn and left the room.

Then Gatty leaned over Lady Gwyneth. 'I'm here, my lady,' she said in a warm, calm voice. 'Gatty.'

'My heart,' whispered Lady Gwyneth. 'Like a bird fluttering inside me.'

'A dove,' said Gatty. She got down onto her knees.

'I've been watching you,' Lady Gwyneth whispered, staring at the rafters. 'How you've changed.'

'I have and I haven't,' Gatty replied.

'Some people say field-women are just animals.'

'Nakin does.'

'I've never thought that.' Lady Gwyneth paused; her breathing was jerky. 'Some people say they care only for themselves.'

'That's not true,' said Gatty. 'My lady.'

'I know,' whispered Lady Gwyneth. 'But you were so rough and raw. So wilful.'

'Standing up for myself.'

'Stubborn.'

'I still am.'

'Like a bull glued to mud.'

Gatty smiled. 'I know all about that,' she said. 'Good thing too! I got to reach Jerusalem.'

176

Lady Gwyneth made a supreme effort. She turned her face towards Gatty, panting. 'Your energy gives me energy,' she whispered. 'Gatty, I am so proud of you.'

'Proud?' Gatty repeated. Her eyes began to sting.

'You're very brave. You saved Austin's life. You're learning to read, learning to write. And your voice . . .'

'No, my lady,' said Gatty. She wiped her eyes with the back of her right hand.

'I thought your voice would keep us all safe.'

'I will get there for you. I will,' Gatty said.

'Your singing's a silk ladder – a silk rope ladder – between earth and heaven.'

Gatty shook her head. 'You're thinking of them monks and nuns.'

'I want you to sing at my funeral. I told Austin.'

Gatty gave a low sob. Her face began to crumple.

Lady Gwyneth closed her eyes and paused, summoning up her strength. 'Once,' she said, in a strange, floating voice, 'you dreamed you were the new Lady of Ewloe.'

'No, my lady,' replied Gatty. 'You dreamed that! You told me you did, and you said it was a nonsense-dream.'

'Did I?'

'But that novice, Aenor,' Gatty said softly, 'she thought I was your daughter.' Gatty shuddered, and sobbed again. 'You're my lady, I know, but you been like my mother, almost.'

Lady Gwyneth looked at Gatty with her misty eyes. 'Open my right hand,' she whispered.

'My lady?'

'My right hand.'

Gatty unlocked Lady Gwyneth's tight white fingers, one by one. In the palm of her hand was an almond-shaped silver badge – a seal.

'What is it?'

'*Y ddraig*,' Lady Gwyneth whispered. 'You see the dragon?'

Gatty narrowed her eyes and stared at the dragon etched on the silver.

'Take it!' said Lady Gwyneth.

'What is it?'

'Whatever you do, you must keep it safe. Sew it into the hem of your cloak.'

'What is it, my lady?'

'Safe and secret until you get back to Ewloe.' Lady Gwyneth's breath was stuttering. 'You understand?'

'Yes, my lady.'

'Then show it to Austin. He will explain it.'

'Don't die!' cried Gatty. 'Don't!'

'And when I die,' Lady Gwyneth whispered, 'cut a lock of my hair. Leave half in Jerusalem, Gatty, and take half home. Bury it in Griffith's grave.'

Then, without a complaint, without even a sigh, Lady Gwyneth just faded. Just died back into herself. A little bubble formed between her lips, and shone in the lantern-light, and did not burst.

29

To begin with, the pilgrims behaved almost as if it hadn't happened. Once Simona and the hospice nuns had taken in hand all the arrangements for the funeral, they were relieved to get on with small jobs and to help one another. True, Gatty and Nest and Tilda embraced several times but they didn't say much. Gatty went out to buy lettuce and chervil for her teeth from a market stall, and she came back with a little pot of perfumed grease for Tilda to smear onto the scabs of her boils, and Tilda smeared it on the cooking-pot as well while she was about it; Nest mended a tear in her gown and in Everard's ripped breeches, and then she went out without saying where; Everard hurried off to Mass and Snout trundled along to the hospice kitchen where the nuns soon had him cracking bones, tearing apart joints and chopping up meat; whistling a mournful song under his breath, Emrys set off with a nun to find a blacksmith to sharpen everyone's knives and replace the broken tines on his and Austin's sticks; Austin prayed and then he unwound his clotted bandage; Tilda helped him to scrape away the poultice, inspected the red mangled mess of Austin's hand, and dressed it with ointment given to her by a white-faced nun; Nakin laid out rows of silver coins on a bench and counted and recounted them, and then asked Austin to check the pilgrims' passes and letters of commendation.

'Without them,' he said, 'we can't go on and we can't go back.'

Austin grunted.

Neither man said anything more; both knew how difficult and painful would be the discussion they must all soon have.

Lady Gwyneth's funeral was not like any Gatty had been to at Caldicot. First, there was the funeral of little Luke, Lady Helen's son, who had died in the same year he was born, and then her brother Dusty's funeral. Only the previous June, Gatty's father had died, and very soon after that, Gatty's grandmother had been buried next to her son.

At these funerals, each person living in the manor had followed Oliver to the graveside, and sprinkled a little earth into the grave, and for a long time after that the bereaved had visited the grave each day and kept their dead company.

On the second afternoon after Lady Gwyneth died, Simona led the pilgrims to a canal where two boats were awaiting them. The first was draped in black velvet. Lady Gwyneth's coffin was raised on trestles, and in the bow and stern stood two groups of little children, carrying bunches of wildflowers.

The moment she saw them, Gatty felt the blood in her leaden veins quicken. Blebs of tears swelled in the corners of her eyes, and then rolled down her freckled cheeks.

The pilgrims stepped onto the second boat, and Gatty saw that Simona's six brothers were sitting at the pairs of oars. She wept some more and, through her tears, smiled at them.

'Where are we going?' she asked Simona.

'*Santa Marta*,' said Simona. '*Santa Marta* is best.'

'Saint Martha?' Austin repeated. 'Is that what you said?'

'*Si*,' said Simona.

The priest shook his head. 'Protector of pilgrims,' he said.

'Venice smells bad,' Simona said. 'The dead smell worse.'

Gatty wished she hadn't said that.

'And what sinks to the bottom sometimes pops up again.'

Gatty wished she hadn't said that either.

'One day we will make a burial island,' Simona said. 'Not yet.'

In the first boat, one of Simona's brothers lit a bowl of dried rose petals and herbs and spices. Gatty could smell the sweet smoke drifting back past her. Then, as the two boats rode out into a larger canal, she saw a floating cormorant, funeral-black, shrieking, bending its neck into an upward loop and a downward loop both at the same time, and suddenly disappearing! It seemed to Gatty that the whole of Venice was water, the whole ground of this place was water. Nervous and jumpy. Half of what it swallows it chokes up again, she thought. All the churches and markets and graveyards are afloat and barely anchored. Rotting timbers; rotting wattle; rotting food; rotting bodies.

At Saint Martha's, the six brothers passed straps under Lady Gwyneth's coffin and lowered it into a muddy grave. Austin pronounced the words, absolute yet comforting, and dear because familiar. One by one, the little children dropped their wildflowers on to the coffin, and Gatty saw how a daisy – or a white violet, was it – stuck to one side of the grave.

'Our lady,' Austin said, 'she told me she wanted Gatty to sing at her funeral.'

'It's all Lady Gwyneth's words,' Gatty told them. 'It's all things she said to me, except for "Aiee!" I made that up.'

Nest edged closer to Sei and then, as everyone stood still around the grave, in death and yet in life, about their bowed heads small birds whistling, children somewhere near singing a skipping-song, streetcriers far off shouting their wares, Gatty began to sing:

'I was conceived, and I was born
While waters broke in the red barley corn.
     Aiee! Aiee!

I was a baby, I was a girl,
My father called me his pearl, his shining pearl.
     Aiee! Aiee!

I crossed the years, a misty maiden,
Green and rising, unproved, unladen.
     Aiee! Aiee!

I was a faithful wife, I was a mother
And my son, my son . . .
     Aiee! Aiee!

I was a woman of Clwyd's holy hills,
Magic in her bones, songs in her sweet rills.
     Aiee! Aiee!

Like the waking bell, sound in Ewloe steeple,
I tried to ring true for each one of my people.
     Aiee! Aiee!

I was the pilgrim Death took down for his wife,
And I was a pilgrim all my life.
     Aiee! Aiee!'

How beautifully Gatty sang. The birds stopped to listen to her.

'Amen!' said Austin and 'Amen!' everyone mumbled as Gatty's sweet, clear voice ascended to heaven. But before the pilgrims and Simona and her six brothers had left the graveyard, Nest and Nakin closed in on either side of her.

'She asked you to sing?' said Nest.

'You didn't like it?' asked Gatty.

'No.'

'What right have you to put words into your mistress's mouth?' Nakin asked.

'I told you,' said Gatty. 'It's only things she said when she talked to me.'

'What's "Aiee!" supposed to mean?' Nest demanded.

To their consternation, Gatty lifted her voice in another terrible aching cry of loss and pain. 'Aiee!' Then she looked at Nest and Nakin. 'It means like it sounds,' she said. 'It does to me, anyhow.'

As soon as Simona had guided the pilgrims back to the hospice, she took Austin to see Doctor Lupo about his swollen hand. And no sooner had they left than the other pilgrims began to argue.

'I knew we should never have come,' said Nest. 'I just want to go home.'

'You heard what Lady Gwyneth said,' Nakin told her.

'We can't go on!' wailed Nest.

'It's not up to you,' Nakin retorted. 'If I say we can, we can. Our passage is paid for.'

'With you, Nakin,' Tilda observed, 'it's always about money.'

'Gobbo will have to repay Lady Gwyneth's fare,' Nakin said. 'Everard! What do you think?'

Everard gave a low whistle. 'You must be up against it,' he said, 'asking my opinion.'

'Dear God, man!' exclaimed Emrys. 'Why can't you just answer him?'

'What I think,' Everard replied in a calm voice, 'is that we should respect Lady Gwyneth's wishes, and remember how she said that each step we take is a step nearer paradise.'

'Exactly!' said Nakin.

'And I've got work to do, teaching Gatty. Besides, I want to hear how Saracens sing.'

'We must stick together,' Emrys said. 'That's the important thing.'

'I'm going home!' Tilda proclaimed. But then she burst into noisy, messy tears and, curiously, that set Nakin off too. He sobbed and he dribbled, and Nest put an arm around him.

'Part of me died when she did,' he gulped. 'I mean, everything I'm not.'

'I don't understand,' said Nest.

'Her honour and eagerness, her wholeheartedness. Her . . .'

'You're coming with me, Tilda,' Emrys announced in a forceful voice.

'No!' screamed Tilda.

'What about the horses? How would they manage without me?'

'What about you, Snout?' asked Nest.

Snout shook his head. 'First I think one thing, then I think another.'

'Snout can never make his mind up,' said Nakin. 'Always sniffing and snivelling!'

'I'm going out!' Nest announced. 'Lady Gwyneth's dead, and all you do is argue!'

And with that, she turned her back and flounced out of the room.

'She means all she can do is think about Sei,' said Tilda. 'Did you see her in the graveyard?'

Nest was out all afternoon and only came back to the hospice, her cheeks on fire, her lips puffy, just before Austin and Gatty returned from Doctor Lupo with very bad news.

'She says I may have to lose my hand,' the priest told them.

'No!' shrieked Tilda.

'There's no time for it to heal before our ship sails. She says I must stay in Venice and each day she'll treat it.'

184

The pilgrims were dumb as donkeys.

'Gobbo's ship is the last of the season,' Austin said, shaking his head. 'I'll have to wait for you here.'

'I'll wait with you,' said Nest.

'No, Nest!' said Gatty.

'Emrys said we must all stick together,' Nakin observed.

'He's right,' said Austin.

'Tilda's coming,' said Emrys. 'We've both put our hands to the plough of this pilgrimage.'

'And so have I,' said Everard.

'Yes,' said Nakin, licking his lips. 'Necessity makes strange bedfellows. What about you, Snout? Have you made your mind up yet?'

Snout slowly nodded his big, hairy head. 'I'll do what Gatty does,' he said.

'I'm coming!' said Gatty. 'Of course I am! I promised Lady Gwyneth I would.' But then she stared at Austin in consternation. 'My reading lessons!' she cried.

'Yes,' Austin said in a weighty voice. He turned to Everard and raised his eyebrows.

'I will,' said Everard. 'Indeed I'll teach them.'

Nest clicked her teeth and sighed noisily. 'No!' she said. 'Not without Lady Gwyneth. I couldn't! I'm staying here.'

30

Gatty and Simona stood on the spine of Saint Nicholas. On one side, just a sniff away, lay the lagoon, pink and placid as a well-fed baby. And on the other lurched the fretful, flint-grey Adriatic.

'This is where his camp was,' said Simona.

'Right here?' Gatty demanded.

Simona nodded. 'There were camps all the way down the island. Crusaders from Provins, Italy, Picardy, Germany, Anjou, Normandy, Flanders. You should have seen them.'

'I can,' said Gatty.

'And Navarre and Burgundy and I don't know. More than twenty thousand men, and that's not counting us Venetians! And more than two hundred boats.'

For some while, Gatty stared to left and right, and out to sea. 'Bonamy,' she said. 'Was he here?'

'He was,' Simona replied. 'His eyes!'

'I never seen him,' Gatty told her.

'Damson,' said Simona.

'Arthur was going to ride him over, when we went to Ludlow fair, but he's so strong and handsome someone might have stole him.'

'He is,' said Simona.

'Where is he?'

'I told you, Arthur had to leave him in Zara . . .' Simona waved at the boundless sea. 'Serle said he'd do his best to look after him.'

Simona sensed that Gatty wanted to be on her own. She sat down on a baking, flat stone and, before long, Gatty wandered off down to the beach. In front of her, the ocean's battalions were rolling in, flying their sparkling silver flags, beating their dark drums.

All this water, thought Gatty. It's not just Venice, the whole world's mainly water. Tides of saltwater. What can I do without Lady Gwyneth? Lady Gwyneth and my mother . . . my father . . . Dusty . . . why do the people I love desert me? Why have they all died? Oh, Arthur!

Gatty meandered along the foreshore. She picked up a little shell, pale as a lemon, and then a larger orange one, each of them ribbed and shaped like an open fan. Then she found such a pretty, closed winkle, nipple-pink, and a sliver of sage-green grass, and a tiny glass bead, creamy on the inside, cinnamon on the outside. Gatty stooped and scooped up a handful of the fine, muddy-dark sand, and let it trickle between her fingers.

This is when she saw it.

Gatty gasped. She bent over it. She dropped onto her knees and very carefully reached out for it as if there were some danger she might frighten it away.

The bruised gold ring was warm to her touch, warm on her cheek. Gatty studied it: on the little square seal was a woman with a baby in her arms, and the baby was holding out something to its mother . . .

It's not the ring Ranier dropped into the water, Gatty thought. It can't be. It's not a diamond ring.

Gatty examined the scratched seal again. She tried it on and it fitted her middle finger. Then she rolled it between her thumb and forefinger and looked closely at the inside.

Scuffs and scratches, she thought. Oh, no! No, they're not. Gatty was looking so closely at the ring that it all but touched the tip of her nose. 'A D,' she said out loud. 'Yes, A D E. And the last letter's C. I'm sure it is.'

Gatty splayed her fingers and combed them through her hair; several sandflies hopped down onto her shoulders.

'A D E C,' said Gatty. 'ADEC. DECA. DACE. ECAD. CADE. What does it mean?'

One small dark cloud rushed in from the east. The water quivered.

'Oh!' cried Gatty. 'A DE C. It can't be! It must just be chance. How can it be?'

The dark cloud swept away west. Once more Saint Nicholas basked in hot sunlight, and Gatty stood on the foreshore, shivering.

31

Gatty didn't show it but she was shaking. She knew the crusaders were fighting to recapture Jerusalem from them, and she'd heard Oliver say hell's mouth was wide and waiting for them, but she had never met any Saracens before.

The first thing she noticed was that their skins were even darker than the Venetians', and the second was how gentle their voices were – not just the woman but her husband and brother-in-law as well.

'This is Gatty,' Simona told the three traders. 'Friend of Sir Arthur.'

'Sir Arthur?'

'The English boy,' Simona reminded them.

'Ah!' exclaimed the husband. 'Head-line heart-line.'

'Him, yes.'

'What are you talking about?' Gatty asked.

'Didn't I tell you?' Simona said. 'They read Arthur's palm.'

Both men bowed slightly to Gatty. Their long dark gowns swayed.

'I'm not a lady!' Gatty exclaimed.

Then the Saracen woman, who was wearing a kind of mustard wimple covering her hair and draped under her chin, took both Gatty's big hands between her own and murmured something.

Gatty looked at her, bright-eyed.

'She says Sir Arthur's friend is their friend,' Simona translated. 'Good prices. You want to buy?'

'I haven't got no money,' Gatty replied. 'When we come back to Venice, I want to.'

Gatty scrutinized the table between her and the traders. The little bottles and sponges, the dried herbs and spices.

'What's this?' she asked, pointing to a square tablet the size of a kneecap.

'White soap,' the woman replied. 'From oil of olives.'

Gatty shook her head. 'We make ours from mutton-fat and wood-ash.'

'Yech!' growled her husband, screwing up his face.

'From Castile,' said his wife. 'Very good for your skin.'

'And this?' Gatty enquired, boldly picking up a little conical-shaped loaf.

'Lick it,' said her husband.

Gatty dabbed the loaf with the very tip of her tongue. 'Sweet!' she exclaimed, and she gave it a bigger lick.

The trader reached out for the loaf.

'Sugar,' said his brother. 'From Egypt.'

'Egypt!' repeated Gatty. 'I heard of Egypt.'

'That's where this family comes from,' Simona told her. 'Here in this market there are traders from Morocco and Syria, Andalusia, Chios and Cyprus.'

'I never heard of them,' Gatty said.

Simona smacked her lips. 'Cyprus. Good sugar.'

'Egypt best!' said the husband.

'Why are Saracens allowed to trade here?' Gatty asked. 'They're enemies of God.'

The trader understood her question. He flashed her a smile, and dovetailed his hands.

'You see?' said Simona. 'He is saying we are traders and they are traders. We sell and they buy, they sell and we buy. We need each other.'

190

The Saracen woman took Gatty's hands again and asked her something.

'She asked if you and Sir Arthur are betrothed,' Simona translated.

'Betrothed! Of course we're not!'

'She knows your feelings,' Simona said. 'She sees into your heart.'

'How?' Gatty demanded.

'Through your eyes,' said Simona. 'But they say you're so sad . . .'

'I am,' Gatty said in a low voice, 'and you know why.'

'. . . but you are strong.'

Gatty sighed, 'People always think that.'

'Look!' said Simona.

It was Nakin, advancing on them. 'You two young ladies,' he said. 'I spied you from afar. What have we here?'

Nakin delved into his scrip and produced a small felt bag; it was pinkish grey, like an earthworm. He untied its neck-string, and tipped into the Saracen woman's palm a dozen iron thimbles, each with a little flower incised on its flat top.

'The best iron!' said Nakin. 'From Nuremberg.'

The Saracen sniffed. 'Iron for locks, yes, and spades and nails and knives. But women's thimbles?'

All the Saracens laughed, and the husband slapped his right thigh and said something.

'Good joke!' Simona translated. 'Now! Gold? Silver?'

Nakin wiped his damp brow. 'Tell them I can't carry precious metals right across Europe,' he said. 'Brigands and bandits would soon smell them out. Tell them one-and-a-half pennies for each thimble.'

The husband shook his head, held up all ten fingers, and said something.

'All right! Ten pence for all twelve thimbles,' Simona translated. 'Ten pence for a posy of flowers!'

Nakin's piggy eyes gleamed and his mouth flapped. 'Oil and slime!' he told Gatty. 'They're fishy traders!'

'You're one to talk!' Gatty replied gaily.

The Saracen husband pointed to the red cross stitched to Nakin's right shoulder and said something.

'You believe your God came out of a woman's womb?' Simona translated.

'Of course He did,' Nakin replied earnestly.

All three Saracens shook their heads.

'You Christians are fools!' said the husband.

The brother held up two fingers, and said something to Simona.

'Two pence more,' Simona translated. 'Twelve pence? One for each thimble.'

Nakin grunted.

'To help you, he says, on your way to his city.'

'It's not his,' Nakin objected. 'It's ours, and he knows it.' Then Nakin smiled his open-mouthed, crafty smile, and shook the Saracen's hand. 'Twelve pence,' he said.

The next day was the pilgrims' last in Venice and, solicitous as ever, Simona insisted they should walk halfway across the city to the church of Saint Zanipolo to buy small phials of holy water.

'Why so far?' Nakin complained. 'There's holy water in every church.'

'This water is more holy,' Simona replied. 'It comes from Saint Peter's spring and runs over many relics. Put one drop into Gobbo's water, and it will taste as fresh as a mountain stream.'

'What do you know about mountain streams?' Tilda asked.

Simona waved airily towards the distant spiky peaks. 'I rode north,' she said, but she didn't elaborate.

Gatty glanced at her. Without even asking, she knew that Simona and her Englishman, Aylmer, had ridden to the mountains together, and had been happy there.

'I'll stay here this morning,' said Nest. 'I want to think.'

'You're meeting Sei again,' Gatty said. 'Aren't you.'

Nest sighed. 'I don't know,' she said.

'Nest!' said Gatty. 'Please come! It's our last day.'

But Nest would not change her mind. 'Anyhow,' she complained, 'we've visited relics almost every day we've been here. I've seen more of Saint Martha than she had to begin with, unless she really had twelve fingers and three shin bones.'

'I know!' said Gatty, grinning. 'I been counting. All in all, I've seen seven skulls and five shin-bones and two penises and twenty-one toes!'

Early that evening, Nest took Gatty completely by surprise.

'When you went off to that church, Saint whoever-he-was, I kept wanting to talk to you and you weren't here.'

'I won't be here for weeks and weeks,' Gatty said. 'None of us will, except Austin.'

'That's exactly it!' said Nest, shaking her head. 'I know I've said things about you.'

'And to me!' interrupted Gatty. ' "Mucky!" That's the first thing you said when I came to Ewloe.'

'I know. And sometimes I've thought worse than I've said.'

'Because you were jealous of me and Lady Gwyneth,' Gatty replied.

'I've never told you about what happened,' said Nest. 'But I know Lady Gwyneth did.'

Gatty shook her head. 'Not much,' she said gently. 'I think she wanted you to tell me.'

So Nest told Gatty about how she and her mother and father had lived in the castle at Rhuddlan and had their own sleeping-room because her father was the steward. She told Gatty about all the games she had played with them, and how her father used to jog her up and down on his knees and then suddenly open them so she fell through, screaming and laughing.

Gatty listened and ached. Why didn't my father do that, she thought? He never said nothing. If only my mother had lived a bit longer.

'And after the fire . . .' said Nest. 'You know about the fire?'

'Lady Gwyneth told me.'

'She came to Rhuddlan herself, and brought me back to Ewloe with her. She cared for me. She loved me, and I loved her.' Nest wiped her eyes. 'You're right. I was jealous of you. But it's different now. My feelings are different. I mean, I know what you're like. Running after those boys in London, and saving Austin, and . . . lots of things.'

Gatty shook her head.

'I couldn't do them,' Nest said. 'It's right to go on with our pilgrimage. I know it is. It's just I'm not strong enough.'

'Who says?' asked Gatty.

'Not without Lady Gwyneth. I get so afraid. I can't stop myself.'

'You're strong enough!' Gatty said, smiling. 'I think you are.'

Nest gazed at Gatty, wide-eyed.

'It's just you don't think you are.' Gatty reached out, and pinched the end of Nest's nose.

'Don't!' exclaimed Nest. But then she threw herself into Gatty's arms, and the two of them reeled across the room, clutching each other.

'Can I come?' cried Nest.

Gatty narrowed her eyes. 'Are you sure?'

'I know I'll be afraid. Simona says that on Gobbo's ship

there are giant biting flies, and she told me about harems and Assassins. But it's what I promised Lady Gwyneth.'

'Amen!' said Gatty in a loud voice.

'It's only . . .' Nest began. Her gaze drifted over Gatty's head; her eyes misted.

'What?' asked Gatty. 'Sei, you mean?'

Nest sighed.

'I thought so.'

'I don't know how it's happened, but it's happened. I've never had feelings like this before.'

'Nest!' said Gatty tenderly.

'I know! I know he'll be here when I come back.'

'He will.'

'But after that, Gatty?'

'Wait and see,' Gatty advised her.

'Will the others understand? Me changing my mind?'

'Our priest at Caldicot,' Gatty replied, 'Oliver, he'd say something about it's never too late, and laughter in heaven.'

'But what about Nakin and Everard and everyone?'

'They'll be glad. Emrys will say it's what Lady Gwyneth wanted, and Tilda will be pleased there's another woman. So will Nakin!'

Nest laughed. 'He can't keep his hands off me.'

'And Everard,' Gatty continued, 'he'll say something about women always changing their minds, and Snout . . . well, he'll be glad, and so am I!'

'You are? Really?'

'You remember how Lady Gwyneth said we're all sisters and brothers and each brings something different to this pilgrimage?'

Nest nodded.

'Well, you're a maker. A needle-and-cloth magician! I could never do what you did, making them cloaks and red crosses and hats-and-scarves.'

'You helped me,' said Nest.

'If you come to Jerusalem,' Gatty said, 'you'll mend our clothes, and trim our hair so we still look almost human.'

'Oh, Gatty!'

'And show us colours and patterns and shapes.'

'Oh, Gatty!' Nest exclaimed again. Her eyes filled with tears.

On their way down to the waterfront that night, Gatty gently took Austin's arm. She told him how she'd pray for his hand each day and remind everyone else to do so, and asked him to pray for them.

'There are seven of you,' the priest said, 'and seven's a blessed number.'

'Not the Seven Whistlers,' Gatty replied. 'They drown you.'

'True,' said Austin. 'But the Holy Spirit gives us seven gifts . . .'

'Understanding and good judgement,' Gatty began, 'and being brave . . .'

Austin smiled a wry smile. 'I believe Jesus will watch over you all the way to His city, and will bring you home, sound and safe. But He may need a little help.'

'Jesus doesn't need help.'

'Understanding and good judgement and being brave,' Austin said. 'You must use those gifts for a start. And you must work at your reading and writing with Everard.' Austin wheeled Gatty right round to face him, and put his left hand on her shoulder. 'If you're all to reach the Golden City,' he said, 'and return safe home, a great deal depends on you, Gatty.'

Gatty looked at the priest. A calm, unblinking, grey-green gaze. Then she lowered her eyes, and her eyelashes flickered. 'I know,' she murmured.

196

The waterfront was lit with lanterns and flaming brands, and heaving with priests, pilgrims, pardoners, traders, sailors, quartermasters, suppliers, stallholders, and the merely curious. Simona led the pilgrims to Gobbo's ship, and the captain came halfway down the gangway to meet them.

'Greetings in God!' Gobbo began.

'God's greetings!' Nakin replied.

'Tax,' Gobbo said.

'What tax?' asked Nakin.

'Last ship of the season. Four groats for each pilgrim.'

'You never mentioned this before,' Nakin objected, and he rounded on Simona. 'Why didn't you tell us?'

Simona shrugged. 'You can't tell what you don't know about.'

'No!' Nakin protested. 'I won't pay it.'

Gobbo barred the way. 'No tax, no ship,' he said, and he sounded quite apologetic.

Nakin turned his back on Gobbo, and set off down the gangway and almost immediately the captain landed a heavy hand on his shoulder. 'You are my friends,' he said, smiling. 'Three groats.'

'No,' said Nakin. 'Two silver groats. Take it or leave it.'

'Take,' said Gobbo.

'Dear God!' said Nakin. 'That's a lot of thimbles!'

Out of the dark Sei appeared, holding a lantern. Nest cried out and put her arms right round him, lantern and all, and then Sei put his lantern down on the ground.

'You'll see him in fourteen weeks,' Gatty told her. 'Tell him that.'

'I did!' Nest exclaimed. 'This morning. And yesterday.'

In the warm wind, a hundred flags fluttered like wild birds eager to be unleashed, or imprisoned souls longing to be set free. Then a band of bright shawms and bombards and trombones lifted their loud voices and blew half the clouds away.

Gatty hurled herself at Austin, she grasped him and clasped him. Then Simona took Gatty's right hand and squeezed it.

'Oh Simona!' cried Gatty. 'What was it? Apricot?'

'*Albicoccho*,' Simona said in a low voice. 'When you come back, I'll be waiting for you.'

Gatty ran up the gangway, followed by Nakin and Everard and Emrys and Tilda, by Snout, and last of all by Nest, fresh and flushed from Sei's long embrace.

Gatty spun round and grabbed the gunwale, so eager, so hungry for everything. She gazed at the milling hubbub on the waterfront, the dancing-and-gliding lights, the quiet hulks of houses, maltings and granaries in the almost-dark.

The pilgrims waved, they waved to Austin, and with his left hand Austin waved back.

Then Gatty reached for the dark sky with both hands, as if she were propping it up.

'No,' she said, 'you're not a shooting-star. You're our mother moon, you are.' In her clear, bold voice she carolled, 'For you I will and all!' And louder yet, 'I will!'

32

'Into the wilderness of the sea!' Nakin proclaimed.

He and Gatty and their companions stood next to the forecastle, staring ahead as Gobbo's ship glided right past the place where Ranier had dropped the diamond ring.

At the entrance to the lagoon, the water became quite choppy. But then, almost at once, the ship picked up the north-west wind. Shouting, the sailors hoisted the second and third sails, and the ship sped over the olive-green waves.

'Forty days and forty nights in the wilderness of the sea,' announced Nakin. His lower jaw slackened and his mouth hung open. 'Though not, I fear, with undue temptation.'

'Yah!' yelled a sailor, advancing towards them with a spar levelled straight at them.

The pilgrims dived out of the way.

'God's bodkin!' piped Everard.

'Jousting!' exclaimed Emrys, 'Without a horse.'

'If he'd caught one of us with that,' Nakin said, 'we'd be in kingdom come.' He led the other pilgrims down one side of the maindeck until they were standing opposite the kitchen and immediately above their sleeping berths. 'We're out of the way here. What was I saying?'

'Undue temptation,' said Nest, looking longingly back at Venice. She gave a heartfelt sigh.

'Ow!' yelped Gatty, hopping on one foot. She opened her gown, tugged at her tunic and her undershirt and, unembarrassed, inspected her right hip.

'A flea?' Nest asked.

'The size of a blackbird,' Gatty replied.

Nakin rubbed his chin. 'We're scarcely underway and we've almost had our heads knocked off and Gatty's been bitten.'

'We'll soon get used to everything,' Emrys said.

'We won't get used to the bilge-water,' Nakin said. 'Ugh! Each time you smell it . . .'

'What a Jeremiah you are!' Tilda exclaimed.

'When you're at sea, to begin with you're at sea,' Everard said, smiling at his own little joke.

'At least we've brought our own food with us,' Snout said. 'Our own sausage and cheese. And our chickens.'

'And wine,' said Emrys.

In spite of their grief, the pilgrims were relieved to be on the move again. Except for Nest, that is. Often she sat on her own, and twice Gatty found her in tears. 'I wish I'd stayed,' she told Gatty. 'Sei wanted me to. What if I never see him again?'

Forty days and forty nights, and there were forty passengers aboard Gobbo's ship.

One man came from Scotland. He was completely bald and had terrible breath.

'You wait,' he told Gatty. 'The Adriatic gets riled, she's got a temper.' His mouth was full of *t*s and *c*s and rolling *r*s.

This Scotsman seemed interested only in proving how little Gatty knew and displaying his own knowledge.

'Did you know an Arabic mile is not the same as an Italian mile?'

'No,' said Gatty.

The Scotsman shook his large head. 'I thought not. I'll tell you why . . . You know what happens if the Evening Star rides low, do you? . . . Do bees sleep? . . . What's your opinion of Aristotle? . . . Have you never heard of the Sargasso Sea? . . . What's the cure for pimples?'

Gatty took to avoiding this Scotsman. Lying in her berth at night, she imagined she could hear him, droning like a June bug. And then she remembered Austin telling her, 'It's one thing to know, Gatty, but quite another to understand.' I'll miss my lessons with Austin, she thought. I hope his hand heals.

Another of the passengers wore an orange cotton scarf wound round his head. He had dark eyes, a ready smile, and a carefully-combed beard. On the fourth evening he sat himself down next to Gatty at one of the three dinner tables.

'Where are you going?' she asked.

'Home,' the man replied. 'Turkey.'

'You're a Turk,' exclaimed Gatty. She was aware how large and watchful his eyes were. 'Are Turks Christian?'

The man stiffened. 'By Allah, no!' he said.

'Why not?'

'You Christians are People of the Book, but you are not believers.'

'I do believe!' Gatty protested. 'Of course I do.'

'Not in Allah and the Prophet Muhammad.'

'If you're a Saracen,' Gatty asked, 'how can you speak English?'

'I need to talk to English scholars. English astronomers.'

'Astronomers!' Gatty exclaimed. 'The stars and that?'

The Turk pinched his small black beard and nodded solemnly.

'Lady Gwyneth . . .' Gatty began. 'Well, she was my lady. She died in Venice.'

'Peace be upon her,' said the Turk.

'She said an astronomer came to Ewloe,' Gatty told him.

'Ewloe?' the Turk enquired.

'Her castle. She said he came from Malvern, and told Lady Gwyneth that Saracens are starwise. They're like learned adults and the English are babbling babies!'

The Saracen courteously shook his head but permitted himself a small smile. 'That's not wholly true,' he said. 'Adelard of Bath. Daniel of Morley. Some Englishmen and Scotsmen are perhaps better known to us than in their own countries.'

'If you're an astronomer,' Gatty said, 'you can tell me. The earth's flat, isn't it?'

'Young lady,' the astronomer began.

'I'm not a lady!' Gatty exclaimed.

'Let us go up on deck. Let us look.'

The Saracen led Gatty to one of the small boats strapped to the side of the ship. He hoisted his long gown and lowered himself into it. Then he offered Gatty his hand and she jumped down.

'My observatory,' the astronomer told her. 'Much the best place aboard – or not quite aboard – this benighted ship.'

'Benighted?'

'Foul,' replied the Saracen, showing his teeth. 'And Christian!'

'Amen,' said Gatty solemnly, and she crossed herself. 'The earth, our priest says it's like an egg yolk, and the ocean is like the white.'

'And Bede, your historian . . .'

Gatty had never heard of Bede.

'. . . he wrote that the earth was like a ball.'

'We'd drop off.'

'Young lady,' said the Saracen. 'As you can see, the sun's just setting.'

Gatty and the astronomer viewed the way in which the fiery sun had somehow broken and split along the whole horizon.

'And now look east,' the astronomer told her. 'What do you see?'

'It's getting dark,' said Gatty.

'It is indeed,' the Saracen replied. 'And the nearer the sky drops to the horizon, the darker it becomes. Violet, purple . . .'

'Like a plum,' said Gatty. 'Its blue sheen.'

'Well,' said the astronomer, 'why is the east almost dark while the west is on fire?'

Gatty screwed up her whole face.

'If our earth were flat,' the Saracen said, 'surely we would all share the same daytime and night-time. But as you can see, we do not.'

Gatty slowly nodded.

'Look ahead of us,' the Saracen told her. 'What do you see?'

'I know. It looks curved.'

'This difficult problem,' the astronomer said gently, 'has exercised minds greater than yours and mine for hundreds of years.'

Gatty liked the way the Saracen talked to her, and she was sure Lady Gwyneth would have liked it too. Sitting there in that little boat swaying like a cradle, she felt like telling him how much she did not know, and how very much she longed to know. I wish he could be my teacher, she thought, now that Austin's had to stay behind. Gatty shook her head. But he's a pagan. He's an enemy of God, an enemy of Christians, he may be a warlock or something.

'What is your name please?' the astronomer asked her.

'Gatty.'

'Gatty of . . .'

Gatty shook her head. 'Just Gatty,' she said.

'Yes,' mused the astronomer. 'In Alexandria, one thousand years ago, the astronomer Ptolemy said the earth was round and the sun and planets and fixed stars revolve around the earth in their nine heavens.'

'Is that what you think?' Gatty asked him.

'We must study the work of great scholars but also trust the evidence of our own eyes,' the astronomer replied. 'We must look around us, and question what we see.'

'You believe the earth's round, then?'

'On balance,' said the astronomer, with some sympathy. 'Yes, I do.'

For a while, Gatty was silent. Then she asked, 'How does sunlight sound?'

'Young lady?'

'Sunlight. And how do stars sound?'

'There you have me!' the Saracen replied, flashing a smile at Gatty.

'Sometimes,' Gatty told him, 'my eyes and ears get mixed up. And my nose does as well.' And then she said-and-sang:

'I can touch what I smell
And smell what I hear
And hear what I see.
Mongrel-and-jumbled-and-scrambled-and-tangled.
      That's me!

I'm topsy-turvy and arsy-versy,
Heels in the air,
YZX and BAC.
Mongrel-and-jumbled-and-scrambled-and-tangled.
      That's me!'

The Saracen astronomer laughed.

'Can you hear the stars too?' Gatty asked him.

Before the astronomer could reply, a figure loomed over them in the almost-dark.

'Gatty!' said a voice. 'Is that you, Gatty?'

'No,' said Gatty.

'I've been looking for you everywhere,' the voice said. 'We thought you must have fallen overboard. Help me down.'

Gatty grasped a damp hand, and Nakin plumped into the little boat. He was carrying a leather flask and immediately took a draught from it.

'Better than the watered stuff the sailors are selling,' he said, and he offered the flask to the astronomer.

The Saracen shook his head. 'Alcohol!' he growled. 'The work of the devil.'

'As you please,' said Nakin. 'Who are you, anyhow?'

The Saracen astronomer courteously inclined his head towards Nakin. 'Osman of Trebizond. Now of Byzantium.'

'What names!' cried Gatty. 'Zz-zz-zz!'

'Can you smell them?' the astronomer asked her, smiling.

'Smell them?' exclaimed Nakin, and he gave a loud hiccup. 'Nakin,' he announced, holding out a hand to the Saracen. 'A merchant from Chester.'

'Chester,' Osman repeated. 'Yes! Across the Sea of Darkness.'

'God's own country!' Nakin declared.

'I've heard rumours,' Osman said, 'that there are scholars in Chester. But Allah knows best what goes on at the ends of the earth.'

'Allah!' barked Nakin.

'What do you mean?' asked Gatty. 'Ends of the earth?'

The astronomer smiled and nodded. 'Just in a manner of speaking,' he told Gatty, and then he laid two fingers on Nakin's wrist. 'Let us not argue,' he said. 'What are the words of that psalm? "You made the moon to mark the seasons; the sun knows when it must set. You bring on darkness and night comes." Let us sit together and watch this pale moon climb the slope of the sky. I believe more unites us than separates us.'

Nakin hiccuped again. 'Trade,' he said.

For a little while, sitting there, Gatty could hear the moon: a kind of faint, breathy whistling. But all she could smell was salt and pitch and, now and then, the wad of sandalwood the Turk was chewing.

'I've heard there are tiles in Chester cathedral,' Osman said, 'tiles with leaping and boxing hares on them, and the hare is the creature of the moon.'

'Yes,' said Gatty. 'I remember. When Lady Gwyneth said she was going to box my ears, Everard told us about them.'

'Everard?'

'He's the choirmaster,' said Nakin, 'at the cathedral. The little man with pink cheeks.'

'He's teaching me to sing, and to read and write,' Gatty told him.

'Very good,' said Osman, and he stood up and stretched the dark wings of his gown.

Nakin opened his mouth so wide he could almost have swallowed the sky, and yawned noisily. 'Time to sleep,' he said. 'Come on, Gatty.'

Gatty sensed the astronomer wanted to be alone with the stars, and so she climbed up out of the boat.

Nakin stumbled across to the hatchway. He backed onto the topmost rung of the ladder – but the ladder was not there. With a yell, Nakin fell into the dark hole and landed with a heavy thud on the sacking at the bottom. And there he lay, silent and motionless. Before long, under the light of a single swinging lantern, a crowd of other pilgrims began to gather round Nakin while, up above, Gatty kept calling out to find out if he was all right.

The merchant cautiously moved his left arm, his right arm. He flexed his left leg, his right leg. He explored his whole body and discovered nothing broken.

Emrys pushed his way forward and gave him a hand.

'Ooh!' groaned Nakin. 'My hip!'

Tilda stroked the merchant's right arm. 'It's a good thing you're so well padded,' she said.

Gatty carefully lowered herself through the dark hatchway. She supported herself on her arms. 'I'm coming down,' she called. She lowered herself further, until she was clinging by her fingertips, and then she dropped onto the sacking.

Slowly and dismally, Nakin crawled away on his hands and knees. 'Errch!' he choked. 'Cur-ch!' Then he vomited. He threw up each morsel of food and every gulp of wine he'd swallowed that evening.

Lying in her tight berth between Nest and Everard, Gatty took some time to go to sleep. What if Nakin had broken his head, she thought? Or even his legs? And what about Nest? She's left her heart behind in Venice. Why does she keep going off on her own, and walking around at night? We're all like lost sheep without Lady Gwyneth. How will we ever get to Jerusalem?

At dawn the sea was milky blue, and there wasn't a single lamb-cloud in the blue fold of the sky. The air was quite crisp, and most of the pilgrims were in good spirits, even Nakin, despite his bruised hip and wounded pride.

In the early afternoon, Gobbo's ship sailed into the welcoming little horseshoe harbour on the island of Curzola. Unwelcome news awaited them.

33

'Crusaders!' the harbourmaster told Gobbo. 'We're expecting the main fleet tomorrow. They'll eat your food and rape your women and commandeer your boat.'

'We'll take aboard provisions and water and leave immediately,' Gobbo said.

'There's danger to the south as well,' the harbourmaster warned him. 'A boat came in from Corfu yesterday and the captain said he couldn't get away fast enough. They've caught the plague.'

'We'll have to take our chance on it,' Gobbo replied.

Ashore on Curzola, the passengers stretched and shook themselves and explored the little town. Gatty hadn't walked more than a few hundred yards round the harbour wall before she was accosted by a slight young man, a squire with pale skin and sloping shoulders and close-cropped dark hair. He was wearing a gambeson the same burnt orange as Arthur's, and carrying an azure shield with an angry-looking bird painted on it. His sword-sheath was strapped to his belt.

'*Sprechen Sie Deutsch*?' said the squire in a voice surprising sweet.

'What?' asked Gatty.

'*Parlez-vous Français*?' the young man enquired. 'English. Do you speak English?'

'I am English!' Gatty exclaimed.

'You are English,' said the squire. His eyes began to flood

with tears, and he roughly brushed them away. 'I am English,' he sobbed.

Gatty frowned and grasped the squire by the shoulders. 'You may be English,' she said, 'but you're not a man. Are you?'

Without replying, the squire led Gatty along the harbour wall.

'I can trust you,' said the squire.

Gatty nodded.

'You're right. I'm a woman.'

Gatty gave a low whistle. 'I knew it.'

'We can sit against this wall,' the young woman said. She took Gatty's left hand, and inspected it. 'Field-fingers!'

Gatty nodded with a quick upthrust of her chin.

'I'm Constance,' the young woman told her. 'Who are you?'

'Gatty,' said Gatty.

'Gatty, I need your help. I have to get to Corfu.'

'That's where we're going.'

'You are?' the young woman cried. 'Oh! Merciful God!'

'The captain says there are too many passengers already,' Gatty told her.

'He needn't know,' Constance said quietly.

'But why?' Gatty faltered.

'My husband! He's there! He's a crusader and I couldn't bear to let him go. After he left home I followed him, and for three days I slept in the open. I've had to travel in disguise.'

'Not enough of a disguise,' Gatty said.

'It's too dangerous to travel alone as a woman and crusaders aren't allowed to bring their wives. So I travel as my husband's son.'

Gatty shook her head. 'But if your husband's in Corfu . . .'

'Why am I here, do you mean?' the young woman said. 'He had to go on ahead. I'll explain everything. Can you smuggle me aboard?'

'All right,' said Gatty. 'I will.'

'My husband will reward you. God will reward you. You can sneak me below deck while everyone's ashore, and I'll hide until we're underway. I'm used to all that.'

'I'll go and check no one's about,' Gatty said.

'Don't tell anyone,' Constance warned her.

Gatty shook her head. But when she hurried back up the gangway, she ran straight into Snout.

'Who was that?' he asked.

'No one.'

Snout grasped Gatty's right shoulder. 'I was watching you. What did that man want?'

'Nothing,' said Gatty. 'Please, Snout. Let go!'

Snout sniffed. 'I know you. Go on. What are you up to?'

'You won't tell no one?'

Then Gatty, wide-eyed, told Snout about how the squire was really a young Englishwoman and how her husband was in Corfu.

Snout threw back his head, and snorted. 'You believe that?'

Gatty shivered.

'You listen to me, girl. Stop and think.'

'I got to help her,' Gatty insisted.

'What if Gobbo finds out? What if she hasn't got no husband? What if she isn't who she says she is?'

Gatty didn't reply. She had never heard Snout so impassioned.

'And you're going to leave her below deck, with all our possessions? What if she's a sneak-thief?'

'She's not like that, Snout.'

'You don't know that. It's good to trust, but you trust too easy.'

'All right,' Gatty replied, 'you come and talk to her. You'll see.'

But when Snout followed Gatty down off the ship, and

scanned the harbour wall and the beach, and the road up to the town, the young woman had completely disappeared.

'Your friend saw us talking at the top of the gangway,' said Snout. 'I thought as much.'

Gatty spent hours searching for Constance, at first impatient, then hot and indignant. That evening she was the last passenger back, and when Nest asked her where she had been, Gatty pretended not to hear.

'Gatty keeps disappearing,' Nakin said. 'She's got no regard for the rest of us. If she hadn't disappeared with her astronomer . . .'

'Her Saracen, you mean!' said Tilda, with great distaste.

'. . . we'd never have had to search for her and I would never have fallen down that hatchway.'

As he had planned, Gobbo left Curzola that night, and soon after sunrise next morning, most of the passengers gathered on deck. They shielded their eyes, and marvelled at the huge walls of the city of Ragusa.

'The crusaders could never lay siege to it,' Nakin said. 'Not unless they get right round the back.'

'There are other ways,' Everard sang out.

'I see,' said Nakin nastily. 'And what ways are those?'

'Seven priests,' said Everard, 'blowing rams' horns for six days, remember? Then on the seventh morning all the people shouted and the walls fell down flat.'

'Jericho!' Gatty and Nest exclaimed together.

'Yes!' said Everard. 'Music is mightier than the sword.'

True, a few passengers did their best to sleep by day as well as by night, but most of them passed the day on the maindeck. Some exercised by walking round and round, planting their legs nicely apart like seasoned seafarers; three Germans climbed up and down and up and down a swinging rope ladder. Osman the astronomer sat cross-legged and listened to the voluble Scotsman. Each morning Everard gave Gatty

211

and Nest reading and writing lessons. Snout did his best to talk to a Norman pilgrim who spoke a few words of English and whose lord owned land somewhere in the north of England. Emrys sat on his own, athwart a spar, whittling at a piece of wood. And Tilda spent most of the time leaning over a gunwale, telling her rosary.

'This sea-journey,' she said to Emrys, 'it's a kind of time between times. You're not busy with the horses. I'm not busy mixing medicines or cooking.'

Emrys agreed. 'It's like Yuletide.'

When Gatty and Nest had finished their lessons, Nest ran her fingers through Gatty's hair. Then she took a little comb from her purse, and started to tease out the tangles. 'Come on!' she said. 'We'll have to wash it first. We can use water from one of the barrels.'

'You can't! That's for drinking.'

'For drinking and washing hair,' Nest said firmly. 'The water-sailor lets me.'

Nest not only had a comb but soap as well.

'Where did you get that from?' asked Gatty.

Nest smiled. 'Sei gave it to me.'

'That's not all he gave you, neither,' Gatty said knowingly.

Nest gripped Gatty's wrist. 'Oh, Gatty! I never knew I could feel like this.' She stared at Gatty, in panic almost.

Gatty stroked Nest's forearm.

'You and Arthur?'

'What about us?'

'Do you feel the same?'

Gatty smiled a small sad smile. 'I'm a land-girl,' she said. 'Well, I was. He's a young knight.' Gatty thought for a while. 'I've scarcely seen him for three years. I was only twelve then. Twelve, thirteen . . . Anyhow, he's betrothed to Winnie. For you, Nest, it's here and now. For me, it's just a dream. I know it can't never be.'

'Is that what Arthur thinks?'

'I told you, he's betrothed now.'

But Gatty knew and treasured what Simona had told her. 'Arthur said you and he have the best times. You share the best times, and talk about everything.'

'I should have stayed in Venice,' Nest said. 'I want to go back.'

'Sei will still be there after Jerusalem,' Gatty replied.

'No! I can't wait that long.'

'You can't go back,' Gatty told her.

'Come on!' said Nest. 'Your hair. It's so lovely, much better than mine. All your thick curls. Gold-and-silver. It's just you don't look after it.'

While Nest was rinsing Gatty's hair, two sailors came clattering down the hatchway.

'*Pronto!*' they said loudly. '*Pronto!*' And they pushed both girls up the ladder.

When they stepped out into the bright light, Gatty and Nest saw all the passengers and sailors – more than one hundred people in all – gathered round the mainmast. Gobbo was standing on a hawser and the talkative Scotsman was next to him.

'What is it?' Gatty asked Snout.

But before he could reply, Gobbo called out in good English, 'One of you has stolen this man's scrip. His scrip, and the coins inside it. Five gold coins. Three silver coins.'

'And quills,' the Scotsman added. 'And inks.'

'I will not have it!' Gobbo bellowed. 'Not on my ship!'

Nest threaded her fingers through Gatty's.

'You can be sure,' Gobbo went on, 'no one will disembark until we've found and punished this thief.'

'One of the sailors,' Nakin muttered. 'Must be.'

'What if it wasn't anyone on this ship?' Snout demanded.

'That sneak-thief, you mean?' Gobbo replied. 'At Curzola.

213

I've seen her before, pretending to be a squire! But she never came aboard. I was watching her, watching her talk to . . .' Gobbo pointed straight at Gatty, and Gatty wished the sea would open its jaws and swallow her.

Nest squeezed Gatty's fingers and Snout wedged himself in front of them. 'Are you saying Gatty stole the scrip?' he demanded.

'No!' said Gobbo slowly. 'She's not the only one who goes off on her own, and noses around other people's berths, and walks by night . . .'

'It wasn't you,' said Snout under his breath.

'Of course not!' Gatty retorted.

'Have no doubt!' said Gobbo in a threatening voice. 'I'll find the thief.'

The suspicion hanging over the passengers also came between them. Some people gossiped and pointed fingers, some padded about on their own, gazing over gunwales. Days passed and everyone waited to see what Gobbo would do.

The sun was like a young lion. It roared. It pounced on the passengers, and Gatty wrapped a cloth round and round her head to stop it from burning.

Osman approached her while she was daydreaming in the shadow of the forecastle.

'Oh! You startled me.'

'May I give you some advice? Before I disembark.'

'You're not coming to Jerusalem?'

The astronomer shook his head. 'My friend Michael and I . . .'

'The Scotsman? He's your friend?'

'A friend to all Saracens,' Osman said, 'and to scholarship. He's translating a great book about medicine from Arabic into Latin.'

Gatty slowly shook her head. 'I didn't know,' she said.

'We're on our way to Byzantium,' Osman told her, 'to talk to scholars there.'

'What about his scrip?'

The astronomer shrugged. 'He'll have to live without it. And someone will have to live with the guilt of stealing it. But you, Gatty, you're going to Crete and Cyprus, Jaffa and Jerusalem. You'll meet many Saracens.'

'I'm not afraid,' said Gatty. 'Not now I've met you and them traders in Venice.'

'This is my advice,' Osman said. 'When you meet a Saracen, you shouldn't laugh.'

'Not laugh?' exclaimed Gatty. 'Why not?'

'He'll think you're laughing at him.' The astronomer paused. 'And you shouldn't wear a white turban.'

'What's that?'

'A white cloth, wrapped around your head.'

'Oh!' exclaimed Gatty, and she quickly pulled off her headcloth. 'Mine's white – well, it was!'

'It's what we wear when we mourn our dead,' Osman said.

'I am mourning,' Gatty said quickly. 'I'm mourning Lady Gwyneth.'

'Then your turban is quite proper,' the astronomer said gently. 'When you're in Allah's realm, it's wise to do as Allah's worshippers do.'

'What else?' asked Gatty.

'If you were a man,' Osman said, 'I'd warn you not to stare at Saracen women. And, Gatty, be very careful never to step over a Saracen's grave. You must always respect the dead, otherwise the living will avenge them.'

'I do respect them,' said Gatty, 'and at home we put flowers on graves, and kneel and pray in the graveyard. We keep our dead company.'

'Travellers often give offence without meaning to,' Osman said. 'I've enjoyed talking with you, Gatty. May the moon and stars shine on you. May your mind and heart remain open.'

'I wish you were coming to Jerusalem,' said Gatty.

'Do you think Gobbo knows who it is?' Nest asked Gatty on the day before the ship reached landfall.

'He's watching us,' said Gatty.

'What's the punishment?' Nest said in a small voice.

Gatty pushed out her lower lip. 'One person says it's three duckings. Another says it's a fine. Another says it's your right hand chopped off. That's what happened when Lankin stole the mutton at Caldicot.'

Nest shuddered.

'But Emrys says he thinks it's drowning.'

'Oh!' cried Nest.

'The thief's arms and legs are lashed, and he – or she – is thrown overboard.'

'That's horrible!' whispered Nest. And then, after a while, 'Do you know who did it?'

'Do you, Nest?' asked Gatty.

Nest nodded. Her eyes were as wide as shining coins, and she looked terrified.

'Oh Nest!' cried Gatty, and she seized Nest by the shoulders, and hugged her.

Nest shook. She burrowed into Gatty.

'Why, Nest, why?'

'I need it!' cried Nest.

'Need it?'

'To pay my way back to Venice.'

Gatty shook her head. 'The fare's already paid. We're going back there after Jerusalem.'

'What if I'm pregnant?' Nest began to sob. 'I think I may be. I want to go back.'

Gatty wrapped her arms right round Nest, and Nest trembled and wept.

'Sei and I . . .' she began, 'we mean everything to each other. I was blind. I didn't even look after Lady Gwyneth properly, not when she needed me most. Now she's gone and Sei's gone and I'm alone.'

'No, you're not,' said Gatty.

'I deserve to drown,' Nest said.

Gatty held her tightly. 'If you drown, we'll drown together,' she said. 'Come on! I'm here. We all are.'

Nest gulped.

Gatty pushed Nest a little away from her without letting go. 'Right!' she said. 'First things first.'

'What do you mean?'

'You must put it back. I'll stand guard.'

Nest's and Gatty's luck held. No one noticed when they slipped down to the deserted lower deck, and no one saw how Gatty stood on the lowest rung of the ladder while Nest disappeared into the creaking, stinking gloom.

Nest's heart was pounding when she rejoined Gatty.

'Right!' said Nest. 'No one can prove it.'

When, that evening, the Scotsman discovered his scrip wedged under his mattress, he was perplexed and much relieved.

'I could have survived without gold and silver,' he told Gobbo, 'but I'm very glad to be reunited with my quills and my inks again.'

Gobbo smiled grimly. 'Sometimes inaction is the best action,' he said.

'Very shrewd!' the Scotsman observed. 'And maybe very merciful of you! You know who it was?'

'I have my suspicions,' the captain replied.

When Gatty saw how the landing-boat, unstrapped from the side of the ship, leaped around on the waves, she was glad

Gobbo had instructed everyone to stay aboard because of the plague on Corfu.

First the boat dropped, then it climbed steeply, then dropped again. Osman and Michael stood poised to jump aboard several times, and they got completely soaked. Only with daring, and the good luck that bravery invites, did they at last both throw themselves into the bottom of the boat.

Gatty and Nest watched. They waved, and the astronomer and the Scotsman waved back.

'Do you really think you are?' Gatty asked.

'What?'

'Pregnant.'

'I don't know,' said Nest. 'I feel different.'

'Sea-journeys make us feel different. That's what Nakin says.'

Nest shook her head. 'It's not like that.'

'And the sea makes some of us do things we'd never do on land.'

'This morning I vomited, and the sea wasn't even rough.'

'Well, we can't do nothing, can we?' Gatty said. 'We're going to Jerusalem. That's the first thing.'

'Sei doesn't even know,' said Nest, clasping her stomach, 'but he loves me, I do know that. I've worked it out. If I am, I'll be fifteen weeks by the time I see him.'

'Almost halfway,' said Gatty.

'I wish I was home.' Nest's voice rose to a wail almost. 'I don't know! I wish Lady Gwyneth was here.'

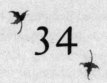

34

On they went; on.

By the time Gobbo's ship eased through lashing rain into the port of Candia in Crete ten days later, there was very little water left in the barrels on the passengers' deck, and that was rancid – good enough to wash salt-sticky hair but foul to drink. Gatty's companions religiously put drops of their holy water into it, but it made no difference.

The food had taken a turn for the worse as well. Worms, some white and some rust-coloured, threaded their way through the store of meat, and although plenty got crushed underfoot or tossed overboard, plenty more were mashed into the kitchen stewpots.

On most mornings, Gatty and Nest did their lessons despite Nest complaining that there was no point now that Lady Gwyneth had died.

'No point!' repeated Everard. 'Everything you say makes you seem more foolish.' He tilted his head and shook it sadly. 'Whereas,' he said, 'the point of words is wisdom.'

'You know what that astronomer told me?' said Gatty. 'He said the quill is a miracle because it drinks darkness and sheds light.'

'Very good!' exclaimed Everard. 'True, and succinct.'

'What's succinct?' asked Gatty.

'To the point,' said Everard. 'When one word does for two.'

219

'It never does for Oliver,' said Gatty, smiling. 'Our priest at Caldicot.'

Gatty had also resumed her singing lessons with Everard. But then her throat was too sore, and for several days her voice was foggy.

'During this pilgrimage,' Everard told her, 'the sound of your voice has grown fuller. Less silver, more gold.'

'Why's that, then?' asked Gatty.

'Less of a girl, more of a woman.'

Gatty shrugged.

'You must learn to hear yourself,' Everard said.

'How?'

'Feel your voice. Feel your whole body. When you sing in one way, you can feel it in your fingertips; in another, you can hear it in your shoulders. We think we hear sound only with our ears but it's not like that.'

'I can smell what I hear,' Gatty said. 'Sometimes, anyhow.'

'You have a beautiful voice,' Everard said. 'I want whoever hears you to feel passion.'

Not only Gatty had a sore throat. As so often, Snout did. He stuck three fingers into each of his nostrils. 'Everything good and everything bad,' he said. 'They let it all in.'

Then Emrys became hoarse too. He could scarcely swallow his supper.

'Everything's horse with Emrys,' said Tilda. 'His voice is hoarse. He thinks horse and talks horse . . .'

'. . . and eats horse,' laughed Nakin.

'Never!' croaked Emrys.

'You just have,' said Nakin, smiling. 'The cook told me.'

Emrys grimaced and delved into his pocket. He fished out something.

'What is it?' Gatty asked.

Emrys opened his hands. 'Yours,' he whispered.

220

Gatty stared at the little lumpen dun pony standing there. Syndod.

'Oh!' cried Gatty. 'Look! The way she arches her neck! Look! Her white stockings.'

'The grain of the wood,' Emrys croaked. 'It came out like that. She's yours, Gatty.'

Then Gatty threw both arms around Emrys's neck. 'I wondered what you were carving,' she said. 'You wouldn't show no one.'

'Best like that,' the stableman said, 'until you're finished.'

One day Gatty and Nest watched big fish leap shining behind the ship; one day they alarmed Tilda by pretending they had knotted their limbs and were unable to untie themselves; and one day Nest busied herself with Gatty's appearance. 'The better you look, the better you feel,' she told her.

First Nest coiled Gatty's curls, so that they were like the golden springs of some marvellous mechanical clock; then she unpicked the scarlet cross on the right shoulder of Gatty's cloak and sewed it back above her right breast.

'You're utterly shameless!' Tilda told them both. 'Drawing attention to what you should hide.'

Next, Nest unstitched the hem of Gatty's cloak. She raised it an inch and slit the sides.

'What's that for?' asked Gatty.

Nest gave her a sidelong smile.

'You're sluts, both of you!' Tilda told them.

'I wish we were at Ewloe,' Nest said. 'Lady Gwyneth's got two chests full of glass necklaces and furs and cuffs and belts and satin skirts and slippers and we could try them on. When we get back . . . Oh, Gatty!'

'What?'

'Will we be able to? Without Lady Gwyneth? What will happen to us?'

'I don't know,' said Gatty. 'I'll go to Caldicot, I suppose.'

'It's not the same for me. You know it's not,' said Nest. 'I've lived at Ewloe since I was eleven, and Lady Gwyneth cared for me.'

'I haven't got no one to go back to neither,' Gatty told her.

'I know,' sighed Nest. 'Lady Gwyneth said I'd got more in common with you than I thought. You can tell me if you want to.'

'I will and all,' said Gatty. 'I will some time. There's not much to tell, though.'

After this, Nest opened her scrip and pulled out a little box of pinkish brown cream. 'Essence of brazil-wood,' she informed Gatty. 'Softened with rosewater.'

'What's it for?'

Nest dipped a fingertip into the cream, touched it to each of Gatty's cheekbones, and lightly worked it in. 'To make you beautiful!' Nest replied.

'I'm not beautiful.'

'You could be,' said Nest, dabbing the remainder onto her own cheeks.

'Did Sei give it to you?'

Nest looked at Gatty with half-closed eyes. 'He did,' she said. With the tip of her little finger, she gently massaged Gatty's lips. 'There!' she said. 'That's a start, anyway.'

Gatty shook her head and smiled.

'You know the saying,' Nest told her. 'Flowers break rocks.'

'What's that supposed to mean?' asked Gatty.

'Work it out!' said Nest.

Nest felt sure her own body was flowering, all right; it told her so when she woke each morning.

Rain or no rain, the passengers crowded on to the maindeck as Gobbo's ship drifted into Candia, greatly relieved at the prospect of going ashore. But no sooner had the sailors thrown ropes to the harbourmen, and let down the gangway, than a handsome man with blond hair strode – in fact, he almost bounced – up the ramp onto the ship.

Gobbo was waiting to meet him. The two men embraced and immediately walked away from the passengers, talking.

'Look at his gown!' Nest marvelled. 'That fur. And the scarlet lining.'

Gatty shook her head, and grinned. 'I'm looking at you,' she said. 'Your face!'

'*Avanti! Avanti!*' the sailors shouted.

Then all the passengers jostled each other, like a flock of sheep penned for too long; they streamed down the gangway, and stepped onto the quay.

Whereas time aboard drifted, time ashore was in a hurry. Arm in arm, Gatty and Nest explored the market and, as the rain blew away and the hot sun glared down, everything smelt as good as it looked: freshly-cut bunches of rosemary and thyme, wooden bowls heaped with rice and cumin, little cones of currants and cloves and cinnamon.

But then Gatty and Nest saw two dark-skinned girls, sitting next to a stall in the sandy mud, wearing manacles and leg-irons.

'What have they done?' Gatty asked.

No one could speak English.

Gatty squatted down beside the girls, and the smaller one momentarily raised her almond eyes, then lowered them again.

The stallholder tapped Gatty on the shoulder and showed her four hands of fingers.

'Ten . . . fifteen . . . twenty,' Gatty worked out. 'They're never twenty. They're younger than us, Nest.'

'That's the cost,' said Nest.

'The cost!' cried Gatty.

'They're for sale,' said Nest uneasily. 'Come on now.'

Still thinking of the girls in chains, Gatty and Nest walked away from the market.

'Look!' said Nest. 'The sky's turning rusty.'

Next moment, the air was full of flying dust and grit. Gatty and Nest pulled up their hoods and covered their faces with their scarves but it still got into their eyes, their noses, their throats, their clothing.

Once the dust storm had passed through, Gatty and Nest shook themselves out and ambled into the town's Venetian quarter. Fluttering pennants were strung across the narrow streets. First they came across a hubbub of Cretans sitting at benches in a kind of open pit, drinking and eating skewers of roasted lamb; and then they realised they were being followed by two dark-haired young men.

'Ignore them!' Nest told Gatty. 'If you take any notice, it will only encourage them.'

When Nest stopped at a stall selling ceramic and glass beads, Gatty walked on – just a dozen paces – and at once the men closed in on her.

At first Gatty did try to ignore them, but then she grew impatient. She shook her head in exasperation and swatted them away as if they were overgrown black flies. The young men laughed, and made vulgar gestures; they hopped and skipped around her.

'Go away!' exclaimed Gatty, and she tried to walk faster.

All at once, one of the men grabbed Gatty's right hand and pulled her off balance. Then the other seized her left hand, and together they dragged her down a dark passage leading out of the narrow street.

'Help!' Gatty yelled. 'Help!'

But there was no one in the passage, and Nest was too far away to hear her.

Gatty wrestled; she tried to bite the men's hands; but she couldn't break free.

At the end of the passage, Gatty found her footing, but the first young man bared his white teeth and put his arms right round her.

'Stop it!' Gatty protested, and she kicked his shins.

Grinning, he slipped both his hands inside Gatty's short shift and slid them up over her breasts.

'No!' shouted Gatty.

But the other man, standing behind Gatty, put his hands round her waist and tried to untie the cord of her breeches.

Gatty would never have been able to break free on her own, but by sheer good fortune Nest ran into Emrys, Snout and Tilda. She told them at once about the two young men, and as soon as Emrys and Snout saw the little passage, they suspected the worst. Hurrying down it, they called out for Gatty; and when they saw what was happening, they raised their long staffs.

They jabbed the two young men with the metal prongs; they whacked them; they drove them off.

Gatty sank to her knees, gasping, and remained there for a while.

'Come on, girl,' said Snout, helping her up.

Gatty felt as if all her strength had drained out of her body.

'Come on!' said Snout. 'Carry your own weight, girl.'

Gatty looked at Snout and Emrys. She was flushed, and dishevelled, and shaky, and outraged.

'I couldn't escape,' she panted.

'We saw,' said Snout.

'Just in time!' Emrys added.

Then each man took one of Gatty's arms, up under her shoulders, and together they made their way back up the passage.

Nest and Tilda were awaiting them, and at once Gatty

stepped into Nest's embrace. She stood completely still, as if carved out of stone, until she could hear her breath steadying.

Gatty took a step back. She puffed out her pink cheeks, then gently blew out all the air.

'What did you say to them?' Tilda demanded.

Gatty shook her head. 'Get off!'

'No,' said Tilda. 'Before that. You must have encouraged them.'

'I didn't!' said Gatty sharply.

'I told you,' said Nest. 'I told you to ignore them.'

'You're one to talk,' Tilda told Nest. 'Gatty, you're fifteen. You're a tender young woman. Can't you see how men are drawn to you?'

'Men!' Gatty exclaimed angrily. 'Animals!'

'Yes,' said Emrys. 'A few men are. You must take more care.'

'You certainly must!' said Tilda. 'And all the more so now we've sailed south. The darker a man's skin, the more hot-blooded he is.'

Walking sedately back to the ship, Gatty felt troubled. She didn't want anyone to know what had just happened – anyone except Nest, perhaps. She felt somehow so ashamed.

Gatty thought of the laughing students, John and Geoff, on the way to Canterbury; the handsome cowherd in the mountains who had so devoutly pressed a cowslip into her hands. She thought of Arthur . . .

'Now, Gatty! You remember what I said,' Tilda told her as they walked along the quay. 'Moths to a flame! Bees to a honeypot!'

Is Tilda right then, Gatty wondered? About men, how they see me? She thought of Nest rubbing cream into her cheeks, and massaging her lips, telling her she could be beautiful.

'I do want to break rocks,' she said under her breath.

'What's that?'

'I do want a boy who's bright-eyed for me,' Gatty said seriously, 'but only if I am for him.'

'That's as may be,' Tilda replied.

When Gatty and Nest came aboard again, Gobbo was waiting for them. He greeted them, smiling, and led them straight up to his cabin in the forecastle.

'Now, young ladies,' he began, pouring each of them a little egg-cup of sticky yellow wine. 'Muscatel. The finest wine made here on this island.'

Gatty sipped it. The wine tasted strong and sweet.

'A gift to you,' said Gobbo.

'Who from?' asked Nest.

'You saw him come aboard, I think.'

'That man!' said Gatty. 'The one with fair hair.'

'The handsome one!' exclaimed Nest. 'Is he a merchant?'

Gobbo smiled. 'Dear God, no! He's a great landowner. Here and on the island of Cyprus.'

'Oh!' said Nest. 'I thought so.'

Gobbo sat well back on his stool, and spread his legs. '*Si!* Signor Umberto del Malaxa. He's a Venetian. His dead sister married my brother. His family, my family: good, good friends.'

Down below, the supper-trumpet sounded three times.

'Young ladies,' said Gobbo. 'I have the pleasing . . . the pleasing . . .'

'The pleasure,' Nest corrected him.

'Signor Umberto will sail with us from Crete to Cyprus,' Gobbo told them.

'Can he speak English?' asked Nest.

Gobbo waved airily. 'Not best, not worst. He saw you when he came aboard, and he will pleasure to know you.'

Gatty lowered her eyes. Nest hugged her knees.

Throughout the pilgrims' second day ashore, Gatty and Nest stuck with their companions, and Gatty was unusually quiet. They watched a donkey turning a wheel, pulling up pots of water from a well; they sat and listened to a woman singing a wild, caterwauling song, 'more like an animal in pain than a human,' Everard observed; they sheltered from another dust storm carried on the back of the hot south wind; they prayed for Lady Gwyneth's soul and for Austin, and they went to Mass, and at the door of the church in the Venetian quarter they were besieged by Cretans trying to sell slivers of saints' bones, phials of holy blood, holy hair, holy nail-clippings, holy saliva, and little crucifixes cut from Cedars of Lebanon.

But just as Gatty had regained her spirits and the seven pilgrims had found their land-legs, they heard the ship's trumpets in the distance. It was time to set sail again.

35

Signor Umberto del Malaxa lost no time.

Next morning, the sun was only halfway up the dome of the sky when one of Gobbo's sailors pointed-and-pushed Gatty and Nest up to the captain's cabin. Gobbo and Signor Umberto were awaiting them.

'Gatty!' said Signor Umberto. 'Nest.' He bowed to each girl. 'Raindrops. Wind in pines. Nest. Gatty. Beautiful names.'

Gatty shook her head. 'Not mine,' she said. 'It's gat-toothed.'

'Sounds pretty,' said Signor Umberto. 'Light on my tongue. You are pilgrims?'

'Our lady died,' Nest explained.

Signor Umberto made the sign of the cross. 'Gobbo told it to me.'

'We were Lady Gwyneth's servants,' Gatty said, and she turned to Nest. 'What would she say, our being here like this?'

'She wouldn't mind,' said Nest. 'It's different on board; everyone talks to everyone.'

Signor Umberto was even more handsome than the girls had supposed. Not only was his hair blond but his watchful blue eyes were set wide apart, and his tanned, olive face was not in the least pitted or pocked; he had a full, almost womanly mouth, and a slow, gathering smile. When he took her right hand, Gatty was amazed.

'Your skin!' she exclaimed. 'It's as smooth as Lady Gwyneth's.'

Signor Umberto smiled. 'I learn from Saracens,' he said.

Signor Umberto's gaze! At first Gatty boldly returned it, but when she lowered her eyes, she felt it still playing, lazily almost, over her cheeks, her brow, her hair, her mouth, her neck. The scarlet cross stitched above her right breast!

Signor Umberto snapped his fingers and at once a dark shadow glided through the door connecting the cabin to an inner room.

'Yes,' he told Gatty and Nest, 'I learn recipes from Saracens. You two English girls, you are beautiful, and I make you more so.'

'Oh!' exclaimed Nest. 'Yes!'

Signor Umberto pointed to the shadow – a man with skin so dark that his teeth looked shockingly white. 'My slave . . .' he began.

'Slave!' cried Gatty.

'*Si*,' said Signor Umberto.

'Beni Sulaym,' said Gobbo.

'Is that his name?'

'No, no. The name of his tribe,' Gobbo explained.

'There were girls in the market,' Gatty said. 'Younger than us.' She clutched her wrists and her ankles.

'Yes, yes,' said Gobbo. 'Slaves from Beni Sulaym. Egypt.'

Saying this, Gobbo left the cabin and Signor Umberto smiled at Gatty and Nest. 'His name is Mansur,' he said. 'He will make you more beautiful.'

Then the rich landowner gave his slave instructions, and snapped his fingers again. Mansur bowed, and soon returned carrying a small tray with little pots and tweezers and files and scalpels on it.

'First is a pomade for your skin,' Signor Umberto told Gatty and Nest. 'Your face, your hands. Sit please.'

'Pomade?' asked Nest.

'Pig's grease,' Signor Umberto replied. 'Sweet apple, bitter almonds. Other things. I do not know their names.'

Mansur gently massaged the pomade into Gatty's and Nest's hands, and then into their faces.

'There's rosewater in this,' Nest told Signor Umberto. 'I can smell it. I'll show you my cream if you like. It's made of rosewater and brazil-wood.'

Mansur coughed and rolled his eyes and said something in a gentle voice to Signor Umberto.

'He says he will make your fresh breath more fresh,' the landowner told them. 'Please to open your mouths.'

Mansur slipped part of a laurel leaf marinated in musk under each girl's tongue, and Gatty spluttered.

'Hold it there under your tongue while Mansur shapes your eyebrows.'

'What do you mean?' gulped Gatty.

'They are too strong,' said Signor Umberto.

With his tweezers, the slave said something and at once began to pluck Gatty's eyebrows. Her eyes stung.

'Mansur says a woman's eyebrows are her scimitars,' Signor Umberto told them. 'Curved and sharp. Now one more recipe for Signorina Gatty.' He laid his fingertips very lightly on her cheeks. 'Spots,' he said.

'What spots?' asked Gatty.

'*Si*,' said Signor Umberto. 'Brown spots. All over.'

'They're freckles,' Gatty protested.

'*Si*,' said the Venetian. 'Freckles. This cream is many, many things: yolk of egg, myrrh, rock sugar, I don't know. You, Gatty. Rub it on your face tonight, and wash in the morning and your spots . . . your . . .'

'Freckles,' said Gatty.

'. . . your freckles will go off!'

'What's wrong with them? I got them all over.'

231

The Venetian smiled. 'You are very beautiful,' he said. He picked up another little phial. 'You and Nest,' he said, 'tonight sprinkle a little powder and you will have rose-pillows.'

'Oh, yes!' said Nest enthusiastically.

Gatty shook her head and laughed.

Then Signor Umberto bowed to each of them, and the two girls left the captain's cabin.

Back on the maindeck, Gatty's feet were still not quite on the ground. She grabbed hold of the rope ladder, next to the mainmast.

'Come on!' urged Nest.

'I'll catch you up,' Gatty told her. And then, with her strong arms and legs, she quickly scaled the ladder. More than twenty feet above the deck, she grasped the rigging, and gazed at the wild silk of the sea, the rugged, dry mountains of Crete.

His smile, she thought. His smooth olive skin. The things he said! His eyes.

First, Gatty rounded her mouth and sang long, low notes. Mysterious notes, dangerous even. Then, as if there were no in-between but only depths and heights, she pursed and almost pointed her lips and sang notes thrillingly high – flying bright arrows. Trills.

When at last Gatty looked down, she saw Everard clasping the bottom of the ladder. Twined round it, face upturned.

'Unlocked!' he cried. 'Oh, Gatty! Your voice! Growing out of you, and growing into you!'

But Gatty's and Nest's companions were less rapturous about Signor Umberto's recipes and the amount of time the girls had spent in the captain's cabin.

'You're pilgrims, not playthings,' Tilda warned them.

'The better you look, the better you feel,' Nest retorted.

Emrys shook his head. 'Lady Gwyneth will be turning in her grave.'

Gatty knew this might well be true. She stared at her feet.

'And sweet's better than sour,' argued Nest.

'In that case,' Tilda said nastily, 'keep well away from Gatty's armpits.'

'You look good as you are,' Snout said. 'You, Gatty, you look like apple-pie. My best one, with raisins in it.'

Gatty smiled at him under her eyelashes.

'If Austin were here . . .' Emrys began.

'Pomades and lotions and powders!' spat Tilda. 'You should be thinking about penance and purgatory.'

Nakin looked at Gatty and Nest with his gleaming little piggy eyes as if the girls were so much tender meat. 'Well, Tilda,' he said in a measured voice, 'at least they're not salty old mutton.'

Tilda yelled at the merchant and Emrys raised his fist.

'Lightly spiced lamb!' Nakin went on. 'There's nothing wrong with that. But as for Signor Umberto . . .'

'Rose-pillows!' protested Tilda. 'What next?'

'Exactly!' said Nakin. 'Just what is that man up to?'

36

'I need your help,' Signor Umberto told Gatty and Nest on the evening before the ship docked in Cyprus. He shook his head mournfully. 'Only you,' he said.

'What?' asked Gatty.

'Love-land!' said Signor Umberto, looking into Gatty's eyes.

Gatty felt a tremor in her heart. 'What do you mean?'

'My father take away my beautiful land in Cyprus and give it all, all of it, to my greedy young brother.'

'That's not right,' protested Gatty.

'Wrong,' agreed Signor Umberto. 'Very wrong. In his will, my father say I cannot have my land because I have no . . . no *bambino*.'

'*Bambino*?' Gatty repeated.

Signor Umberto cradled his arms and made a rocking motion.

'Oh!' chimed the girls. 'A baby!'

'Baby, *si*. A boy baby.' The Venetian sucked his cheeks. 'Wrong. Very wrong. I need your help.'

'How?' asked Gatty.

'You have my baby.'

'What!' exclaimed Gatty.

'Yes,' said the Venetian, looking at her. 'You have my son.'

'Me?'

'Tomorrow,' said Signor Umberto.

'Tomorrow!' repeated Gatty, and she burst out laughing.

'I ride alone with Mansur to village far, far away from port of Larnaca and find a *bambino*.'

Gatty giggled. 'What? Under a bush?'

'A poor woman with a baby son. I pay her and take her baby for one day, two days. I bring him back to Larnaca and you, Gatty, you feed him.' Signor Umberto gently squeezed his chest. 'You can?'

'Neither of us can,' Gatty said, blushing but knowledgeable. 'No one can wet nurse until she's had a baby.'

'I bring mother's milk,' Signor Umberto informed them. 'I have papers,' he said. 'Many papers. Baby's name is Babolo and he is four months old. He was born in Candia on the fifth day of March.'

'I'll help you,' said Gatty, secretly pleased that Signor Umberto was favouring her and not Nest. 'I will!'

'You, Gatty,' the Venetian said, 'you be my beautiful young wife, you be Babolo's mother. We go to the court and prove it. You, Nest, you be Gatty's servant.'

Nest put her nose in the air.

'I have clothes for you,' said Signor Umberto, 'and I reward you. Ten silver groats each.'

At this moment, the captain walked through from the inner room.

'We dock at dawn,' he informed them, almost as if he had been listening to their conversation. 'We rest one day and one night in port of Larnaca.'

'Time enough,' Signor Umberto told the girls.

'What if it's not?' asked Nest.

'No risk,' said Signor Umberto. 'My friend Gobbo knows my business.'

'Important business,' the captain replied. 'No risk. I will wait for you.'

'Come!' said Signor Umberto. 'Let us kiss on it!'

And with that, the handsome Venetian put his hands on

Gatty's shoulders, and drew her to him, and kissed her on each cheek.

'Wine,' said the captain, and he pulled the stopper out of a wooden flask.

'Come!' Signor Umberto said again. 'We say a prayer, yes?

> Lord of justice,
> Shine on your servant, Umberto.

> Lord of love,
> Reward and embrace

> Your sweet Gatty and Nest,
> This night and always.'

'Amen,' said Gobbo loudly.

'Amen,' whispered the girls.

'Both of you, meet me here at noon tomorrow,' Signor Umberto reminded them. 'Wind in pines. Raindrops. You will not regret this.'

37

During that July night, a hot wind sprang up in the south. It made the waves foam and spit. It drove them half-mad. Then the wind discovered a small split, a wind-eye, in the mainsail; it seized the oatmeal sheet between its teeth and shook it and wrestled with it until the huge sail screamed and ripped. Gobbo's ship was badly lamed and, far from reaching Larnaca at dawn, she limped along the north coast of Cyprus and docked at Kyrenia in the late afternoon.

Signor Umberto found Gatty on her own on the maindeck. 'Different port, same plan,' he reassured her. 'Here, every-where, you are my wife! Meet me at noon tomorrow in Gobbo's cabin.'

Early the next morning, the pilgrims rode out of town to watch the builders at work on the new abbey of Saint Mary of the Mountain, and they talked to one of the monks, Brother Antony, who spoke good English. But Gatty's and Nest's hearts weren't really in it. They kept thinking about their meeting with Signor Umberto.

By mid-morning, though, Nest had developed a fever. As soon as they got back to the ship, she flopped onto her mat-tress, and couldn't stop shivering. Her head pounded, her eyes ached.

Then Nest vomited.

'Oh, Gatty!' she croaked. 'Will I lose my baby?'

Gatty's eyes shone. 'There are plenty more in Cyprus!' she

replied. 'Anyhow, we can't let Signor Umberto down. He's already been wronged by his father.'

'I can't come,' said Nest. 'I can't.' First she had a fit of coughing; then she began to weep silently.

'I'll have to go alone, then,' Gatty said.

Nest pressed her face into her pillow and trembled.

When Gatty climbed the hatchway on to the maindeck, she saw her companions standing round the massive spare anchor.

Emrys and Tilda had cracked two of the pullets' eggs they'd bought in the market on their way back, and were frying them on one of the anchor's flanges.

'Feel how hot the sun is,' Snout marvelled. 'Almost hot enough to roast meat on the spit. Where's Nest?'

'She's sick,' said Gatty.

Tilda folded the white flaps of her egg over the yolk. Then with her spoon she carefully lifted it from the flange and, watched by the others, stuffed the lot into her mouth.

'Lord, but this is good!' said Tilda, smacking her lips. 'The best egg I've eaten in my life.'

'She's got a fever,' Gatty said. 'She just vomited.'

'Gatty,' said Everard, 'I want you to come with me this afternoon.'

Gatty immediately lowered her eyes.

'No!' said Tilda. She sucked her eggy cheeks and swallowed. 'I need Gatty's help. I saw a stall . . .'

''Not the one with all those parts?' said Nakin. 'Toad and hare and mole and raven . . .'

'No,' said Tilda. 'The one with dried herbs you can't find in Ewloe.'

'While you were in the market,' said Everard, 'the musicians by that palm tree showed me their instruments. One was an *oud* and one was a flute cut from a reed. That's called a *ney*. And one . . .'

Nakin gave a mirthless laugh. 'Poor Everard, with all your lutes and flutes!'

'The woman sang with a strange rough voice,' Everard went on. 'A wild voice.'

'And you want Gatty to sing like that?'

'No,' said Everard. 'I want her to hear – difference!'

'You just want her to yourself,' Nakin said.

'All you use your voice for is contempt and greed,' Everard retorted.

'High and mighty Everard!' Nakin taunted him. 'So perfect in every way. You come with me, Gatty. I've found a den where women dance. Like wild animals.'

'Revolting!' cried Tilda.

'You all want to go off on your own,' Emrys said, 'but Lady Gwyneth told us we must be companions. Let's all listen to the musicians. Let's all go to the market.'

'And the den,' said Nakin with a lascivious smile.

'No, Nakin,' said Emrys. 'We'll do what our companions can also do – not dance with the devil.'

Gatty jammed the toe of her boot into the deck. 'I can't,' she said.

'Can't?' demanded Tilda. 'Why not?'

Gatty looked troubled.

'Nest, is it?' asked Snout.

Gatty gave Snout a grateful look. 'Nest, yes. I need to look after her.'

Tilda gave Gatty a suspicious look.

'She needs me,' pleaded Gatty, and she dived down the hatchway again.

Nest stared up at Gatty, and coughed feebly.

'Quick!' said Gatty. 'I'm keeping Signor Umberto waiting.' She rubbed some of Mansur's pomade into her face and hands.

'Freckles!' she said to herself. 'What's wrong with freckles?'

Gatty dabbed perfume of cinnamon, sandalwood and musk behind each ear; she daubed her lips with Nest's brazil-wood cream.

'Do I look all right?' she demanded.

Nest looked up at Gatty dimly. 'Come here,' she said.

Nest sat up and patted and massaged Gatty's brow, her chin, her neck. Then she wiped the back of her hand firmly across Gatty's mouth.

'What you do that for?' Gatty protested.

'Give me the cream,' croaked Nest. 'You're not careful enough.'

'Who cares anyhow?' Gatty replied.

'You do,' said Nest. 'Your mouth was twice as large as it should be. Like a jester. Now close your eyes!'

'Why?' asked Gatty.

Nest gently applied a little blacking to Gatty's eyelids and eyelashes. 'There!' she said.

'Now give me your wrist.'

'Why?' asked Gatty.

'You can't wear that tatty violet ribbon.'

As soon as Nest had finished with her, Gatty turned her back, and put her half of the violet ribbon carefully into her scrip; then she bit the hem of her gown, and worked the gold ring out of it. I can wear this, she thought.

'What are you doing?' whispered Nest.

Gatty very nearly showed her the precious ring. But then she tucked it into the little waist-pocket of her tunic. 'Nothing,' she said.

'Put on your felt shoes,' said Nest. 'The ones Mansel made. At least they'll look better than your boots.'

Gatty looked down at her, and suddenly she felt a surging fondness for this pretty, feeling, timid girl lying hot-eyed on her mattress so very far from Ewloe. She dropped onto her knees, and put her arms round Nest, and hugged her.

'Don't,' wailed a muffled voice. 'Oh! I wish I were more like you, Gatty.'

Gatty scaled the hatchway ladder, ran across the deck, and climbed the forecastle steps to Gobbo's cabin two at a time.

Signor Umberto was waiting for her. He bowed to Gatty and then she saw his slave was rocking a bundle in his arms.

'Babolo,' Signor Umberto said.

Gatty yelped. Only now did she begin to grasp the enormity of what she had agreed to do. On tiptoe, almost, she crossed the cabin and peeked at the baby. 'God's bones!' she whispered, and she shivered.

'Signora Gatti,' said the Venetian, 'where is Nest?'

'She's sick,' Gatty replied. 'Too sick to come.'

Signor Umberto frowned. 'A lady!' he said. 'My wife! Without one servant?'

'We'll say she's ill,' Gatty said brightly. 'Like she is.'

'*Si*,' shrugged the Venetian, and he pointed to the inner room. 'Please dress now. Your clothes are waiting.'

Spread out on Gobbo's bed was the most beautiful silk dress. It was yellowy-green, the colour of oak leaves when they're still silly and tender. It had almost no shoulders!

Gatty stared at it in excitement and dismay.

I can't wear this, she thought. I've worn a kirtle, but I've never worn a proper dress before.

Gatty swung off her grey cloak. She paced round the room and eyed the dress and then, very quickly, she pulled off her tunic. She put the dress over her head and slipped her arms into the sleeves.

The silk came right down to her feet, it grazed the ground, but her shoulders were nearly naked and the front of the dress was scooped.

Gatty covered herself with her hands. I can't let anyone see me like this, she thought. I can't! Anyhow, the biting flies will eat me.

241

Gatty clasped the big square buckle on the front of her grey-green sash; she inspected the little dragons with pearl eyes sewn all over her beautiful sleeves, and saw how the sleeves could be detached, exposing the full length of her arms from her rounded shoulders to her fingertips. Gatty trembled. She listened to the music of her rustling dress.

Then, out of her tunic pocket, Gatty took her gold ring. She rolled it between her palms. She eased it onto the middle finger of her right hand.

'Gatti!' called a voice. 'Gatti!'

'Yes,' Gatty replied. 'I know. I'm coming.' Then she swallowed, lowered her eyes, and walked out.

'Ah!' exclaimed Signor Umberto. 'Si! Signora Gatti. *Bella! Bellissima!*'

Gatty tucked her chin against her chest.

'You like?' the Venetian asked her.

'I don't know,' said Gatty in a small voice.

'You are Venetian lady.'

Gatty felt apprehensive. She didn't feel like herself at all.

Signor Umberto spied Gatty's ring and smiled.

'Good!' he said.

'I found it,' Gatty told him, truthful as always.

The Venetian gave Gatty an amused, knowing smile. '*Si, si,*' he said. Then he snapped his fingers, and at once his slave held out the bundle.

So Gatty took the baby into her arms.

'Babolo,' Signor Umberto said tenderly. 'You say Babolo.'

'Babolo,' mouthed Gatty. 'Babolo.'

Gatty well knew how bizarre her situation was – she, the unofficial wife of a Venetian nobleman, wearing a low-cut silk dress, mothering the child of some Cypriot woman – but it didn't feel at all unnatural to be holding a baby. She was indignant at the unjust way Signor Umberto had been treated and wanted to help him as much as she could.

'*Si*, Signora Gatti,' said Signor Umberto. 'Now when Babolo was born, you told me, "A lord is born into the world".'

'I did?' replied Gatty, wide-eyed.

'You did,' said Signor Umberto with a wink.

Gatty smiled and looked at him under her eyelashes. 'I remember now,' she said.

Signor Umberto took an amber necklace from an inside pocket. He opened it, put it round Gatty's neck and fixed the clasp.

'Amber from the Baltic,' the Venetian told her. 'For you, Gatti, to keep always,' and then he reached over Babolo and gave Gatty a lingering kiss on her pomaded right cheek.

Balancing the baby precariously in the crook of one arm, Gatty fingered the smooth beads.

'Last thing,' said Signor Umberto, snapping his fingers.

At once Mansur held up a small pot.

'Another pot!' said Gatty.

'Unguent,' the Venetian told her. 'You say unguent?'

'I don't know,' Gatty replied.

'Purple oil and mint juice and vinegar and wax,' said the Venetian. 'And rosewater. For your breasts. To make milk.'

'Never!' Gatty exclaimed.

'*Si*. When you smear it over them.'

'I told you,' said Gatty. 'You can't until you've had a baby.'

'Babolo,' said the Venetian. 'He is your baby!'

'Oh, I see,' said Gatty. 'You mean if anyone sees I'm carrying it, they'll believe I'm his mother.'

'And last last,' Signor Umberto said, 'Signora Gatti's hair.'

The Venetian nodded and Mansur stepped up to Gatty not with a linen cap but a net made of fine gold thread. He fixed it on with pretty hair-pins in such a way that it imprisoned altogether fewer of Gatty's golden curls than escaped it.

So, wearing her low-cut dress and her hair-net, and carrying her baby, Gatty walked with Signor Umberto through the streets of Kyrenia. Her heart was pounding. She wasn't so much afraid of what might happen in the court as of running into her companions. But unless they'd stopped and looked very closely, they would never have known that Signora Gatti del Malaxa was, also, Gatty.

38

From the moment Gatty and Babolo stepped into the little stone courthouse, Signor Umberto's plans started to go wrong.

'The justice is not here,' said a woman whose face looked like a shrivelled leather purse. She waved a huge key. 'I'm the only one. Me and two prisoners.'

'Where in God's name is he?' Signor Umberto demanded. And then he told Gatty, 'I can scarcely understand her. She speaks abominable Greek.'

The woman shrugged. 'He rode over to Larnaca yesterday.'

Late that afternoon, the justice returned – a man with a slight squint, a no-nonsense manner and a bull neck.

'You should have arranged beforehand,' he told Signor Umberto in good Italian. 'Then you and your wife wouldn't have had to wait.' He looked down his nose at the sleeping baby, and just touched the tip of its nose.

'Her name?' he asked.

'His,' said Signor Umberto. 'He's a boy.' He nodded at Gatty.

'Babolo,' said Gatty. She could hear her heart hammering.

'Tell the justice how old he is,' the Venetian instructed her.

'Four months,' said Gatty. 'And five days.'

'What language is she speaking?' asked the justice.

'English,' Signor Umberto replied.

'Your wife is English?'

'*Si.*'

After this, Signor Umberto told the justice the purpose of their visit, to claim land in Cyprus now lawfully his. 'I have the necessary papers,' he said. 'I have my father's will, and I have a testimonial to Babolo's birth.'

'Please,' said Gatty, 'explain what you're saying.'

'It's all right,' Signor Umberto told her. 'Leave it to me.'

'Babolo,' said the justice. 'Not Babola? Not a girl?'

'No, I told you. You want to see?'

The justice waved his right hand. 'Where was he born?'

'In Crete,' Signor Umberto replied. 'In Malaxa. Four months ago.'

'And five days,' the justice said carefully. He shook his head as if he were weighing it. 'I cannot confirm your father's land now belongs to you. You pay me and I appoint three men to witness your papers, and ask you questions.'

'What's he saying?' asked Gatty, bewildered.

The Venetian made a fist of his right hand and thumped his forehead. 'There's no time for all this,' he said, 'and there's no need.'

The justice was not used to being hectored. His red bull-neck turned redder and the blue veins swelled.

'My wife!' the Venetian said very loudly, throwing a protective arm round Gatty's waist. 'You can't keep her waiting. Her boat sails for Crete this evening.'

Signor Umberto's voice woke Babolo and the baby began to grouse and then to wail, and Gatty wasn't able to soothe him.

'Now look what you've done,' the Venetian said.

'He's hungry, isn't he?' the justice asked Gatty. He gestured to her to sit down and nurse her baby.

'You can't keep Signora Gatti waiting,' Signor Umberto repeated, more coolly now. 'Her boat sails this evening.'

'So you've said,' the justice replied.

The Venetian delved into his gown, pulled out a fistful of silver coins, and one by one dropped five of them into the palm of his left hand. He gave the justice a sly smile.

'Since when was it lawful to hurry the law?' the Cypriot asked.

'What did he say?' asked Gatty.

'Please wait here,' the justice told them. Then he walked out of the courthouse and the shrivelled old woman turned her huge key in the lock.

'Why have they locked us in?' Gatty demanded.

'Idiot!' the Venetian exclaimed.

'What did he say to you?'

Signor Umberto saw how anxious Gatty looked. 'It's all right,' he reassured her. 'He'll come back soon.'

'And Gobbo does know. I mean . . .'

'*Si, si*. He'll wait.'

But the justice did not return that evening, and he did not return during the watches of the night.

Those were the strangest hours for Gatty. She fed Babolo from the flask of his mother's milk, drop by drop, and it was comforting to feel him pulling so strongly on her little finger. She rocked him and crooned to him, and he slept. But Gatty couldn't quieten the tides of her anxieties.

When the justice returned an hour after sunrise, Signor Umberto del Malaxa greeted him with cold fury.

'Where,' he asked menacingly, 'in the name of God, have you been? How dare you leave a lord and his lady all night in this stinking little room?'

The justice pointed at Gatty and said one word.

'What did he say?' asked Gatty.

'Translate!' said Signor Umberto. 'He says I am to translate.'

'As to whether this baby is your baby, Signor Umberto, I have great doubt,' the justice began.

247

'How dare you?' shouted Signor Umberto.

'And as to whether this lady is his mother, I have great doubt also.'

'Idiot!' shouted the Venetian.

'Translate!' the justice reminded Signor Umberto. 'Signora Gatti does not hold him as a mother holds her baby. She did not know how to quieten him. She does not speak to him like a mother.'

'She does!' retorted Signor Umberto. 'In the English way. They live in a cool climate. They're not the same as us.'

The justice was wholly unperturbed. 'So why did you try to bribe me?' he enquired.

'What did he say?' asked Gatty.

Signor Umberto translated.

'The Saracens may say that the greater the bribe, the lesser the problem,' the justice observed. 'I do not.'

'Damn you!' exclaimed the Venetian.

'Signor Umberto,' said the justice in his level voice, 'you lied to me. There was no boat leaving for Crete last night.'

The Venetian lowered his eyes.

'What's he saying?' Gatty asked.

Signor Umberto translated.

'But there was a boat leaving for Jaffa,' the justice continued.

Gatty almost understood. 'Did he say Jaffa?' she asked, her voice rising. 'They haven't gone, have they?'

'I thought as much,' said the justice. 'Signora Gatti, you're not Signor Umberto's wife, are you? I think you must be a pilgrim, and that is your only reason for coming here to Cyprus.'

Signor Umberto translated and Gatty nodded. 'Yes, sir,' she whispered.

'Tell her exactly what I say,' the justice instructed Signor Umberto in a stone-cold voice.

'He says,' the Venetian translated unhappily, 'you have been punished too much already. The door is open, he says. You are free to leave.'

'What about you?' asked Gatty.

The justice understood and at once jabbed his blunt forefinger into the Venetian's chest, and said something.

'Prison,' Signor Umberto said calmly. 'Leave Babolo here. He will be safe with me.'

The justice squinted at Gatty. Then he rubbed his right thumb and forefinger.

'Oh!' cried Gatty. 'Yes! My reward.'

'Yes,' said the Venetian. He dipped into his cloak and counted five silver groats for Gatty.

'Ten,' Gatty said at once.

'No,' said Signor Umberto.

'Ten!' repeated Gatty loudly, shaking her curls and almost forgetting she was still carrying Babolo. 'You're cheating me! You promised us ten each!'

The Venetian sighed loudly and counted out five more coins, a transaction watched by the justice with grim understanding.

'What about Nest?' asked Gatty.

'No!' Signor Umberto said. 'No!' Then he reached out with both arms. 'My dress,' he said.

'How can I?' exclaimed Gatty. 'My clothes are on the ship.'

The Venetian pushed out his lower lip. He shrugged, and then gave Gatty the most charming smile.

'Oh, Umberto!' she said, shaking her golden head. First she gave him Babolo, and then she stretched out over the baby, put both arms round Signor Umberto's neck, and firmly planted a warm kiss on his right cheek.

Gatty raced down to the harbour, full pelt. Her finery swished and danced around her.

But the moment she reached the cobbled quay, she could see Gobbo's ship was not there. Where her three masts had pierced heaven, where her rigging had rapped and whipped and her sails ballooned and flapped, where her decks had creaked and her high castle stood, where her great bulk had rested almost weightless on the water, there was a white space.

Gatty's breathing was jagged. Still she ran, unable to believe her eyes. Reaching out with her hands towards what was no longer there.

Along the quay, there were iron bollards, anchors, hawsers, coils of rope, barrels, wooden boxes, grappling hooks. In front of Gatty, the empty, pearly, early-morning ocean stretched to eternity.

All at once, Gatty's legs gave way beneath her. She reeled towards a barrel, subsided against it with a moan and began to sob.

Gone! They've gone. Gone! At first, that was her only thought.

Why did I trust Gobbo?

Gatty couldn't stop sobbing. Her whole body was trembling.

Why did I trust Umberto, with all his pomades and perfumes and compliments? I'm a fool. A complete fool. Look at me! Half-naked. I'm not Gatty.

Gatty still couldn't stop sobbing.

Gone! They've gone!

Tilda's right, thought Gatty. We're pilgrims not playthings. And Emrys is right, about Lady Gwyneth turning in her grave . . .

'I need you, Gatty . . . Gatty, I am so proud of you . . .' Gatty remembered Lady Gwyneth's words and stinging tears flooded her eyes. How can I get to Jerusalem? How can I save Lady Gwyneth's soul? I promised her, I did; I promised her she could trust me. Nothing never mattered as much.

Gatty's whole body was racked with pain. Slumped there beside the barrel, dressed like a Venetian lady, she had never felt so desolate in her life.

39

A large man with a mop of copper hair tacked up to the lump wrapped in yellow-green silk. He bent over it. He inspected it.

Little pearly-eyed dragons, blowing flames. A broad sash, grey-green as a finch's chin. A hair-mesh of fine gold thread, fixed with butterfly hairpins.

'Gatty?' said the man in a cautious voice.

The lump did not move.

The man eyed the storm of golden curls half-checked by the hair-mesh.

'Gatty. Is it you?'

Slowly, very slowly, the heap shifted. One red eye looked out.

'Gatty?'

All at once, the heap shuddered.

That was enough for Snout. He dropped onto his haunches and drew Gatty to her feet. He held her shaking in his arms with the same quiet devotion with which, five years before, he had held his newborn son.

Two squabbling gulls mewed like hoarse wildcats; saltwater sucked stone. Gatty was so exhausted that she felt light-headed.

'God's bread!' said Snout in a husky voice. 'I wasn't even sure it was you.'

Gatty closed her aching eyes. In her finery, she didn't feel like herself either.

'I saw you running, I did. I thought you were one of them dancing girls, you know, from Nakin's den.'

Gatty snuffled.

'Nest told us everything. We searched for you, we kept running through the streets, shouting out your name.'

Gatty squashed her face against Snout's shoulder.

'That swine, Gobbo! He wouldn't wait. He wouldn't! He insisted on leaving for Jaffa. Nakin offered to pay him extra but Gobbo said he couldn't let down his other passengers and the weather would turn against us.'

Snout eased Gatty away from him and ran his rough hands up to the top of her sleeves, taking good care not to touch her bare shoulders. 'Look at you!' he marvelled. 'Lady Gatty! Well, I've got your cloak and your other clothes, and your boots. And your staff and scrip and your leather bottle. And the carving of Syndod, the one Emrys cut for you. Nakin's given me coins. I don't know what they're worth, mind. Now, girl, stop shivering!'

Gatty drew in both her lips.

'We're to catch them up,' Snout told her. 'We're to find a fishing boat and pay the fishermen to sail us over – Gobbo says it's only a day across to Jaffa. If they can, Emrys and everyone will wait for us there. And if they can't, they'll leave a message with the harbourmaster, and we'll have to ride after them.'

Gatty raised her puffy face. Her dark lip-cream was smeared over her chin, and her left cheek was smutted with her eye-blacking. She gazed at Snout.

'You waited?' she whispered.

Snout stood very firm and still. The only thing that moved was the light in his eyes.

'For me?'

The corners of Snout's mouth twitched. 'God's lid! I couldn't leave you behind, could I?'

'You waited,' Gatty said again. 'No one's never done nothing like this before. Not for me.'

'You wouldn't last a day,' said the cook. 'Not in that dress! Look at you! You'd be gobbled up.'

'Oh Snout!' exclaimed Gatty. She stared at Snout in complete wonder. 'Snout! You're so . . . so staunch. So faithful. I don't know what the word is. And I'm a fool. I trusted Gobbo. I trusted Signor Umberto. What if . . . I mean, what if you'd never found me?'

'I know you,' Snout said. 'You float like cork floats. You're a survivor.'

Gatty slowly shook her head and gazed at Snout with her river eyes. 'What about Nest? We got to catch them up as soon as we can.'

After this, Gatty put on her grey pilgrim's cloak over her dress and, hot as the July morning already was, she kept it well drawn around her. Then she and Snout hurried to the market in search of food. Sitting in the shade of a palm tree, they ate crusty bread, cheese, olives, black grapes, a small sweet melon.

Snout smacked his lips. 'Melon!' he said. 'I'd never even heard of it before Venice.'

Now Gatty and Snout talked, and how they talked! Gatty told the cook what had happened after she'd climbed up to Gobbo's cabin, and put on her silk dress. Snout told Gatty how Tilda kept badgering Nest until she got the truth. Gatty told Snout about mothering Babolo, and Snout said he had already run up to half the mothers and babies in Kyrenia, searching for her, and never wanted to see another baby in his life. Snout told Gatty that Nest had bravely wanted to stay behind in Kyrenia, but the others wouldn't let her, and Gatty said she'd made the most terrible mistake in her whole life, and let Lady Gwyneth and everyone else down, and Snout told her that everyone makes mistakes, terrible ones even.

Then Gatty showed Snout the ten silver coins she had wrested from Signor Umberto, and Snout was able to double that with the money Nakin had given him.

Snout pointed at Gatty's hand. 'Is that your marriage ring?'

Gatty quickly put her left hand over the ring.

'Let's have a look.'

'No,' said Gatty, but she allowed the cook to examine it.

'Not another baby!' he exclaimed. 'Twenty coins and this ring, then! We've got plenty.'

'I'm not selling this ring,' Gatty told him.

Snout sank his buck teeth into another juicy wedge of melon.

'We can't even speak their language,' said Gatty.

Not far away, two women wearing black headscarves shook out a rainbow shawl and laid it on the ground. Then one of the women started to play a reed-flute and a man sauntered up, carrying two small drums. He sat down, cross-legged, and began to tap the heart's beat, the sun's pulse, the heat and mystery of the growing day.

'Nest!' said Gatty. 'She needs me. And Everard, what can I do without him?'

'What can you do with him!' Snout replied.

'We have to catch them up,' Gatty said. 'My singing lessons. And my reading and writing.'

Snout attacked the last wedge of melon. Then he sucked his cheeks and his teeth. 'God help us if we don't,' he said quietly.

'These musicians,' said Gatty, 'they must be the ones Everard told us about. Oh! Look over there!'

'What?' said Snout.

'That monk! It's Brother Antony – the one we met at the abbey the other day, the one who spoke English. Snout! Are you blind?'

'Not so blind I couldn't find you.'

'Oh Snout! I'm sorry. It's just . . .' Gatty scrambled to her feet and pulled Snout up. 'God is with us, He must be.'

As soon as the monk heard that Gatty's and Snout's ship had sailed without them, he led them back to the high monastery. And there, his fellow-monks recognised Gatty and Snout from their visit only three days before.

Brother Antony knelt and washed their feet with cool, clean spring water, and then the guestmaster dried their feet with a shaggy towel.

The abbot himself welcomed them to Saint Mary of the Mountain. First he poured water over their hands and wrists, and then he knelt with them, and said something in French.

'Here, we honour Jesus and the Virgin Mary in each stranger,' Brother Antony translated.

The abbot smiled and inclined his head, and gave each of them the kiss of peace.

'The abbot wishes you to know you are the first English pilgrims to stay here,' Brother Antony told them, 'and you're welcome to remain as long as you have need.'

'It won't be long,' said Gatty, shaking her golden curls.

'But we need your help,' Snout added.

'We got to catch up,' said Gatty.

'I understand,' said Brother Antony. 'But you can't catch up without a boat.'

Snout held up his right thumb. 'It's only one day,' he said, 'only one across to Jaffa.'

Brother Antony gave Snout a mild look. 'Who told you that?'

'Gobbo. Our captain.'

Brother Antony translated this for the abbot and his fellow-monks, and they tutted and knowingly shook their heads.

'It's only one day if you have wings or a magic carpet,'

Brother Antony said. 'No, it's three days at least.'

'No,' gasped Snout.

'Three days and three nights with the wind behind you.'

'How do you know?' cried Gatty.

'We lived in Jaffa,' Brother Antony replied. 'All the monks here come from Jaffa. We were driven out by the Saracens.'

Gatty stared at Snout, crestfallen, and Snout stared at the ground.

'Gobbo lied to you too,' said Gatty in a low voice.

'Don't despair,' Brother Antony told them. 'God throws these challenges in our path like great boulders. Somehow we must welcome them.'

'Lady Gwyneth said that,' Gatty replied, and her eyes began to smart.

'And because of these boulders,' continued Brother Antony, 'our achievement is all the greater.'

'I got to get to Jerusalem,' Gatty informed the monk. 'We both have.'

'Of course,' said Brother Antony. 'We'll talk to the harbourmaster and as soon he finds a fisherman prepared to sail you across, he will let us know.'

'How long will that be?' Gatty asked.

'We can pay,' said Snout.

The monk smiled gently. 'We are all in the hands of God,' he said.

'How long?' Gatty demanded.

'Be patient!' Brother Antony told them. 'You're not the first to be stranded here. Pilgrims have been travelling from Cyprus to the Holy Land for more than one hundred years.'

'But unless we catch them up . . .'

Brother Antony raised his right hand. 'I will do my utmost,' he said, and he made the sign of the cross.

Then the abbot put his fingers to his lips and murmured something, and Brother Antony explained, 'The abbot says we observe the rule of silence here, but in the guesthouse you're welcome to talk.'

'But you been talking to us,' said Gatty.

'We talk when there's a need,' Brother Antony replied. 'To buy food, to offer help, to welcome stranded pilgrims . . .' He smiled gently. 'But most often, there's no need. Talk gets in the way of prayer and study.'

Gatty and Snout were the only guests in the hospice, and the guestmaster, a monk with a limp and skin like a baby, made them most welcome with big smiles and small signs. The hospice had its own kitchen and cook, its own wash-room and latrines, and Gatty was astonished when the guestmaster conducted her to her own separate room.

I'm like a lady, she thought. Like Lady Gwyneth. She stood alone in the quiet of the room. She walked around it. She laid her forehead against the cool stone walls.

That first night, Gatty didn't lie down for a long time. She folded and refolded her silk dress, with the hair-mesh and the butterfly pins and her amber necklace inside it, and was amazed to discover the material was so fine she could hold it inside her cupped hands. Then she rolled up the dress inside her spare tunic, and pushed it into her scrip.

After this, Gatty counted and recounted her gold coins and drove them, and her ring too, to the very bottom of her scrip. Then she drew out her precious violet ribbon again – her half of it – and carefully secured it round her right wrist. After this, she squeezed the hem of her cloak to check that the little almond-shaped silver seal, wrapped in a lock of Lady Gwyneth's hair, was still safely sewn into it.

'Keep it safe and secret until you get back to Ewloe.' She could hear Lady Gwyneth's voice. 'Then show it to Austin.'

Why, thought Gatty. Why does it matter so much?

Gatty got down on her knee-bones.

To begin with, she closed her eyes and made pictures in her

mind. She saw Lady Gwyneth standing in front of the rood-screen in Ewloe church, facing her people, and then rebuking Gatty in London for her disobedience, and telling her she had put the entire pilgrimage at risk, and then sitting proud on her Arab stallion, and then lying in that hospice in Venice, with a little bubble between her lips.

Gatty opened her eyes. 'My lady,' she whispered, 'I know you're near. It's like you're in this room. What? Wilful and stubborn! Like a bull glued to mud! I knew you'd say that. But you said you were proud of me too. You did.' Gatty rubbed her sore red eyes. 'My lady, forgive me for being so foolish. I almost wrecked our pilgrimage. My lady, please keep your warm eye on Nest, and her baby. She's so . . . unable. And Snout, my lady. Brave Snout waited for me. Of your mercy, please ask God to reward him. We'll catch up with the others. We will.'

After this, Gatty began to sing:

> 'Oh, little waves of Kyrenia!
> Have you seen our five companions?
> Please God, let us catch them up soon.
>
> Great waves, wild waves of the ocean,
> Have you seen our five companions?
> Please God, let us catch them up soon.
>
> Waves, have you seen our companions?
> Like a breaking wave, I raise this cry:
> Please God, let us catch them up soon.'

Gatty made up the tune as she went along, and her song was full of love and longing. She sang for herself; for Lady Gwyneth; for God. What she didn't know was that the guest-master's right ear was pressed against the other side of the door. He was entranced by Gatty's pure voice, the way she plumbed dark depths and scaled thrilling heights:

'Have you not seen our five companions?
I'm adrift. I'll drown without them.
Please God, let us catch them up soon.'

Smiling to himself, the guestmaster limped away from the door, and Gatty lay down. But dog-tired as she was she still couldn't sleep, and – quite why, she had no idea – she started to think about the wall-painting in Oliver's vestry at Caldicot.

A boat with three fishermen in it, and a shining lamp in the bow. A fourth man standing on the iris-blue water, yes, standing on the water, waving a shoal of fish into the net.

You can't walk on water unless it's well frozen, Gatty thought. Then she remembered the day when Sian had gone right though the ice on the fish-pond, and she and Arthur had bellied out, clawing and toe-pushing themselves across the ice, and saved her from drowning.

There was one gold word painted between each of the fishermen, and a line of words under the waves. If I saw them now, Gatty thought, I could read them, I could.

Early next morning, Gatty and Snout hurried down to the harbour with Brother Antony, but there was no boat in dock large enough to sail the pilgrims across to Jaffa. All the harbourmaster could do was tell them to come back the next day.

'God will answer your prayers,' Brother Antony said, 'but not, maybe, in the way you asked.'

When Gatty walked past the courthouse, she wondered whether Signor Umberto was still imprisoned there, and whether Mansur had taken Babolo safely back to his mother.

He was only interested in himself, she thought. He just used me, and Nest. He didn't care about wrecking our pilgrimage. Why was I so blind?

Early each day after that, Gatty and Snout and the monk

walked down to the harbour, and the harbourmaster shook his head. Then the three of them went through the market, buying tiles of white salt crystals, honey, sultanas, carob beans, spices and the other supplies the monks couldn't provide for themselves, and Snout asked Brother Antony more and more about how they were all used in the monastery kitchen. After this, they slowly made their way back up to the waiting abbey, heavy-laden and hot. Their early optimism at being able to catch up with their companions began to falter and founder.

Not until the thirteenth day after Gobbo had sailed for the Holy Land without Gatty and Snout did their luck change. As it happened, Brother Antony had gone down alone to the harbour and he hurried back with the good news.

'There's a Saracen fishing-boat ready to take you across,' he said.

'Saracen!' exclaimed Snout. He screwed up his face as if he were sucking a lemon.

'Tomorrow. To Acre.'

'Where?' chimed Gatty and Snout.

'Acre. It's nearer than Jaffa. It's not the answer you wanted, but I think it's the best you'll get. Acre's Christian. And all the fishermen are saying that Jaffa's too far for them.'

'Acre,' said Gatty, sounding completely lost. 'But the others were going to wait in Jaffa.'

'Or leave us a message,' said Snout.

'Oh, Snout! It's all my fault.'

'Sometimes,' said Brother Antony, 'our problems have unexpected solutions. I've been troubled about your safety in the Holy Land. The whole place is seething with brigands, Assassins, tricksters, Saracens, and there are only two of you, one a pretty young woman. But at least Acre's still Christian, and the Knights of Saint John have a house there. So you'll be able to stay with them, and they will be able to help you. You see?'

Snout nodded. Unconsoled. And Gatty's grey-green eyes were wide and troubled.

'Fear not,' said Brother Antony gently. 'God is with you.' He took off the little crucifix hanging round his neck. 'Hold this,' he told Gatty. 'Hold it firmly, and upright. Remember who died on the cross for you.'

'Amen,' Gatty murmured.

'Whoever wishes to travel to Jerusalem must bear the same cross,' Brother Antony told her.

'Amen,' Gatty said again, and she politely gave the crucifix back to the monk.

'Thirteen days have passed since I brought you back here,' Brother Antony said. 'Thirteen long days. Now then! It's three days' sailing from here to Jaffa, then your companions would have had a day of rest, and then a day's ride to Jerusalem. Seven days in Jerusalem . . . that's normal.' The monk ticked off the days on his fingers as if he were telling his rosary. 'And one day's ride back to Jaffa again. So that's . . . thirteen days.'

Gatty shivered.

'You do see, do you?' Brother Antony asked them gently. 'I very much fear that, early tomorrow morning, Gobbo and your five friends will be setting sail from Jaffa for Venice.'

40

That evening, her last at Saint Mary of the Mountain, Gatty felt almost merry. She knew she and Snout would have to find their own way to the Holy City; and beyond that, she could scarcely imagine. But at least the waiting was almost over, and she walked around with a spring in her step.

'Before our guests leave us,' Brother Antony told Gatty and Snout, 'it's customary for them to sing for their supper.'

'What do you mean?' asked Gatty.

Brother Antony smiled. 'We've sheltered and fed you here, and you can be sure we'll say prayers each day for you. In return, we ask you to give whatever you can.'

'Money, you mean?' Snout asked.

'Not in your case,' the monk replied. 'You'll need whatever you have if you're to reach Jerusalem. And as for getting home . . .' Brother Antony put his hands together in prayer. 'For a start, you must pay the fisherman.'

'How much?' Snout asked.

'Eight silver groats. Four to him, and four to me.' The monk lifted the hem of his habit, tore off a little strip with his teeth, and gave it to Gatty. 'There!' he said. 'When you reach Acre, give this to the fisherman. He'll bring it back to me; and when he does, I will know you've reached Acre safely. Then I will pay him.'

'I will!' said Gatty.

'Some guests give us coins,' Brother Antony told them, 'some give candles, and last week a pilgrim on her way to see the True Cross gave us a hen. One rich man gave us a gold ring.'

Snout glanced at Gatty, but Gatty stuck out her chin. 'It's not mine to give, anyway,' she muttered.

'I'll cook for you and your brothers,' Snout announced.

'Excellent!' said the monk. 'An English dinner on this joyous day.'

'Joyous?' said Gatty.

'Mary of Magdala. It's her feast-day.'

'But my Gatty,' Snout said proudly, 'she really can sing for her supper.'

The monk gave a small, sly smile. 'So I've heard,' he murmured.

That evening, in the monks' kitchen, Snout plucked and cleaned five chickens, and Gatty helped him. He smeared them with honey and trussed them in linen cloths and boiled them.

'Just the same as I do at Ewloe,' Snout said. 'This will please the monks.'

As was their custom, the monks began to eat in silence, but before very long the abbot broke the rule and asked the monastery cooks to bring cinnamon and nutmeg and black pepper.

'This chicken is very tender,' he told Snout, and Brother Antony translated, 'but we monks are partial to subtle spices.' He patted his stomach. 'As you know, we eat well here.'

Snout sniffed and tried not to feel offended.

'Nothing matters more than food,' the abbot went on. 'Don't you agree?'

Snout nodded glumly.

'The moment we are born, we cry out for a good meal,' Brother Antony translated, 'and when we lie dying, our last pleasure is cool water.'

Then, uninvited, Gatty stood up. 'I don't know no song about Mary Magdalen,' she called out, 'but I know that one about all the saints, flourishing like the lilies, hidden in the clouds.

'*Alleluia*,' Gatty began to sing. '*Alleluia. Alleluia.*'

In the refectory, there was a great stillness. Gatty's voice was like a scalpel, cutting away the monks' sins, and it was a balm, healing their wounds.

Time passed outside the door.

Gatty looked around her. She could tell the monks all wanted her to sing more.

'*Audi filia*,' she sang, as Everard had taught her. 'Listen, my daughter, look . . .'

The holy men listened, and they looked. One remembered his mother and one fingered his rosary; one thought of the girl he had kissed from top to toe under an olive tree, and one tried to think about God.

The abbot rose to his feet. 'You have given us fine gifts,' he said. 'You, Snout, you've given us full stomachs so we can talk to God. In your voice, Gatty, we hear the grace of God. Never in my life have I heard a voice as beautiful as yours. I only wish you could stay here. It's a pity you're not a boy!'

Gatty and Snout had never put to sea in a small boat before, and the Saracen fishing smack was really not a great deal larger than the landing-boat strapped to the side of Gobbo's ship.

It was manned by three fishermen – two boys a couple of years younger than Gatty, and their father. At first sight they looked like ruffians who wouldn't think twice about slipping a fish-knife between human ribs. The whites of their eyes were so clear Gatty could almost see through them, like the white of an uncooked egg, and their pupils were large and dark and intent. But when they smiled, as they often did! Ah, then they showed their white teeth, and their eyes shone with the light of the sea. Gatty felt at ease with them.

When she surveyed the wild waves and tangles of their dark hair, Gatty thought of Nest. No, she said to herself, not even Nest would be able to tease it and straighten it. I reckon she'd cut it all off and tell them to begin again.

There was nowhere comfortable in the boat. In the bow, the anchor and the fishboxes were under Gatty's and Snout's feet, and their knees were under their chins. Sticky fishing-nets were heaped in the boat's waist and when Gatty and Snout perched on them, they risked being whacked on the head by the low, swinging boom. As for the stern: the fisher-men sat there, forever busy, restraining the juddering tiller, trimming the sails, mending nets, turning towards Mecca and praying, and now and then slipping Gatty sideways glances.

The only shade was behind the sail and in the claustropho-bic little space under the bow. Worse, Gatty realised there was nowhere private where she could relieve herself. She had to sit on a bucket while Snout and the three Saracens turned their backs.

All morning, the short sea smacked into them broadside, and jolted the boat, and now and then showered them with spray.

'Your hair!' said Snout. 'It's shining like it did when you wore that gold mesh.'

For a long time Gatty looked out over the waves and they were all kinds of blue. Bluebell and periwinkle and thistle blue. Violet and indigo. Lapis, like Lady Gwyneth's ring. They're like blue ice as well, Gatty thought, but it's so hot here there can't never be no ice. I've never seen nothing with so many blues in it.

At first, Gatty thought each wave had a different shape, a different colour and meaning. But after a while, they all seemed much the same and quite meaningless. They all rolled through her aching head.

'This sea,' she told Snout. 'Austin told me its names.'

Snout yawned.

'Don't you want to know?'

'Go on, then.'

'The Jews call it the Great Sea and the Romans call it the Inner Sea.'

Snout yawned again.

'That's what Mediterranean means. In the middle of the world. Where we are is surrounded by the whole world: Europe and Asia and Africa.'

'Is that right?'

'This Inner Sea . . .' Gatty began, 'well, it's like the heart of the world, and yet it's so heartless. It's just beating emptiness.'

Waves smacked the boat; they thrashed it; they nuzzled and caressed it.

Gatty slept and woke and ate and slept. She felt caught in some seamless, waking dream.

Very early on the third morning, something roused her. Snout was asleep but he wasn't snoring, the two lads were both stretched out and their father was slumped over the lashed tiller; the wind was crooning in the sails.

Gatty peered ahead into the grey-green gloom: day breaking.

At once, on her bed of fishing-nets, she got onto her knees. She crossed herself, and raised her eyes.

'Behold!' she whispered.

A little wind stirred behind the boat, and the sails rustled.

'The Holy Land,' whispered Gatty. 'It must be.'

Now the west wind nudged the boat a little more insistently, and her curved timbers creaked.

'My lady,' whispered Gatty. Her heart pounded, it surged,

as if it were the ocean and she were sailing on it. 'My lady! I promised you!'

One of the boys stirred and rubbed his eyes. 'Akko!' he called out, pointing way down the coast. 'Akko!'

'Acre,' Gatty said to herself. 'I think he's saying Acre.'

Late that afternoon, the little smack slipped into the harbour at Acre, capital of the Kingdom of Jerusalem, and by then Gatty and Snout were ankle-deep in squirming fish. Fish with wall-eyes and goggle-eyes, gaping and pouting and dribbling and flapping, fish with ears, fish with whiskers, small as little fingers and large as shins. The air in the boat was thick with their dying.

And all without anyone walking on the water, Gatty thought, remembering the Caldicot wall-painting again. This sea-harvest, silver and green and black and gold; and all that food in the market at Kyrenia – honey and sultanas and chickens and geese and melons and grapes and tiles of salt and that. They can't never go hungry here.

Gatty and Snout were exhausted, salt-sticky, fish-slimy, covered in bumps and bruises. The Saracen fisherman gave them a grim nod. Then he rubbed his right thumb and fore-finger.

'He wants that strip of cloth,' Snout said. 'The one Brother Antony gave you.'

Gatty took the strip out of the inside pocket of her cloak.

Then the fisherman gestured that Gatty and Snout were to disembark and wade ashore.

'Where are we meant to go?' Snout asked.

'They're not just leaving us here, are they?' said Gatty.

But that's exactly what the fishermen did. One boy slipped over the stern and held the boat steady; and no sooner had Gatty and Snout gathered up their belongings and awk-wardly scrambled over the side, bruising their knees again on the gunwales and splashing down into the water, than the boy swung the boat around, pushed off, and hoisted himself back in. With no more than a perfunctory wave, the three of them turned away and set sail for the fish-dock. Gatty and Snout were left standing up to their hips in the warm water amongst a herd of mild-mannered buffalo, no longer surprised by humans and their strange behaviour.

The two pilgrims didn't know where to go, or what to expect. It didn't take them long to find out. Across the beach, a man shouted at them, and as Gatty and Snout staggered through the water towards him, he beckoned them. This man led them up to a large square stone building, and showed them through a barred iron gate. But the moment they were inside, he bolted it.

'No!' Gatty shouted. 'We're pilgrims! We're Christians!'

'We're English!' yelled Snout. 'Come back!'

'Pilgrims!' Gatty bawled again.

Like the fisherman and his sons, the man didn't even give them a backward glance.

Gatty stared at Snout, appalled. 'What is this? A prison?'

41

The prison or pound, or whatever it was, was surrounded by high, windowless walls and stretched about one hundred paces in each direction. On the far side was a row of columns and a covered arcade.

Two small huddles of people were sitting in this large enclosure, and a dozen or so were walking around on their own. The light was so bright that Gatty had to screw up her eyes to look at them.

A puff of wind vaulted the walls, and stirred up the fine sand and grit underfoot. The whole enclosure was a swirling bowl of dust, thick and turbulent as smoke from unseasoned wood. It got into Gatty's mouth and nose. Then slowly it began to settle again, and all the people around her reappeared, shimmering.

'What is this place?' asked Gatty. 'What are we going to do?'

'Find someone to talk to,' said Snout, 'and get out of here. Brother Antony said Acre's Christian.'

Gatty pulled back her arms until they tugged at her shoulderblades. 'I'm the wrong shape,' she grumbled, 'cooped up on that boat.'

'Me too,' said Snout.

'Come on! We can ask that man. The one on his own.'

The high walls blunted the world's sharp noises. Street cries and shouts and songs, barking and braying, grating and grinding and cracking: they became one thick underhum.

Gatty and Snout walked towards the little figure sitting cross-legged. Then they saw he was alone but not alone. He was playing his reed-flute to a snake!

The snake was as thick as Snout's forearm; it had hooded eyes and glistening scales, black-and-white, just like the little tiles in Saint Mark's in Venice. For as long as the man played, the snake reached up out of the mouth of a wicker basket, it stretched and sidled and dipped; but the moment he stopped, the snake stopped too, in mid-air, and looked straight at Gatty.

Gatty gripped Snout's right elbow.

But then the man played a soothing tune, and the snake somehow tightened into itself. It oozed back down into its basket.

'God's guts!' gasped Gatty. 'It's a good thing he knows how to play it back in.'

'Excuse me!' Snout said politely to the man. 'Do you speak English?'

The man went on playing his flute.

'English,' Gatty repeated.

The snake-charmer shrugged. Then he put his hand on his heart and smiled at Gatty, and she smiled back.

'Come on!' said Snout. 'We got to find someone in charge.'

In the gloom of the arcade, the pilgrims were astonished to find dozens and dozens more people, some standing, some leaning against the wall, some sitting or stretched out and sleeping.

'It's so bright out there and so dark in here we couldn't even see them,' Snout observed.

'They're lost people,' said Gatty, shaking her head.

One man, bald and grey-bearded, was singing quietly to himself. When Gatty tried to speak to him, he completely ignored her.

'He looks like Abraham,' she told Snout. 'In our painting

at Caldicot. Snout, I don't like this.'

Further down the arcade, a dark-skinned man with a turban and a black beard was sitting in the middle of a small circle of children.

'Children!' exclaimed Gatty. 'What's going on? What have they done wrong?'

Snout looked at Gatty with a Sunday face. 'You don't have to do wrong to do wrong,' he said.

'What does that mean?'

'Or be grown-up either. Sometimes people just say you're wrong – when you're not.'

The circle of children gasped. In his right hand, the man was holding up the most beautiful transparent red stone as big as a front tooth.

The man closed his hand, waved his fist, and opened it. The stone had disappeared!

'Come on, Snout,' said Gatty. 'We've got to find someone.'

'I've done that with Hew,' said Snout, smiling.

The children pointed to the conjuror's baggy sleeves, and began to shout. But when the man stretched out his arms, and two children searched them, the stone was not there.

The conjuror covered his moustache and his nose with both hands, and stared at the children over his fingertips. Then he took away his hands, and his beard had changed colour. It was dark red.

All the children cried out in wonder and laughed.

'Come on!' said Gatty, pulling at Snout's arm.

But then the conjuror pointed at Gatty, and with his little finger, he beckoned her to come closer . . . yes, closer . . . He reached up and pulled out of Gatty's right ear a hunk of wax as big as a gourd-stopper.

All the children hugged themselves with delight. The conjuror stared intently at the wax. Then he squelched it, and out of it he squeezed – the red stone!

Further down the arcade, Gatty and Snout saw a woman moulding a large lump of clay into a monster, and another trying to nurse her howling baby, a boy pulling the wings off a butterfly, a black man who glared angrily at them and spat at their feet.

'It's not safe here,' said Gatty.

'It's all right, girl,' Snout said warily. 'Let's go back to the gate.'

'Where is this place?' demanded Gatty. She gripped the iron bars and yelled. 'Help!' she shouted. 'Pilgrims! English!'

For an hour at least, Gatty and Snout tried to attract attention.

'We haven't done nothing wrong,' Gatty said hoarsely. 'What are they doing, locking us up?'

At last two men came out of the stone building and walked up to the gate. One of them was the guard who had let them in.

Gatty angrily rattled the bars.

'English!' said Snout loudly. 'Do you speak English?'

The men looked at Gatty and Snout through the bars.

Gatty grabbed her cloak and pointed to the scarlet cross. 'Pilgrims!' she insisted. 'We're Christians!'

One of the men sniffed and said something to the other. Then the two of them turned away and disappeared into the building again.

Gatty was so vexed that she was trembling.

'We don't know why we're here,' she said. 'We don't know how to get out. No one can understand us.'

'English?' said a voice behind her.

Gatty whirled round. Standing there was a very old man stripped to the waist. His skin was more grey than olive, and only loosely attached to the flesh beneath. It hung in two small bags under his nipples.

The old man smiled cheerfully. 'English?' he asked again.

'Yes!' said Gatty.

The old man raised his left hand, and Gatty saw the withered underside of his arm. 'You want to know why we're here.'

'Yes,' said Gatty. 'Yes, we do.'

'So do I,' he said, smiling. 'So do we all.'

'We're pilgrims, sir,' said Snout.

'In here,' said the old man, 'we're all pilgrims.'

'Are you Christian, then?' asked Snout.

'Pilgrims between life and death.' The old man sat down against the wall and gestured to Gatty and Snout to sit down beside him. 'We're all Saracens and we're all under suspicion.'

'What for?' asked Gatty.

'Just being different,' said the old man. 'Our beliefs. Our customs. The colour of our skins.'

'But those children . . .' Snout began.

'Difference,' the old man told them, 'it can be a threat and it can be a wonder. We Saracens say, how far is it from the tip of your nose to paradise?'

'How far?' asked Gatty.

'Lift your head and see!' the old man replied.

'Oh!' said Gatty. 'You mean, paradise is all around us. Each different thing. I see!'

The old man smiled. 'You do see,' he said contentedly.

'But how are we going to get out of here?' Gatty asked him. 'We got to go to Jerusalem.'

'Another Saracen saying,' the old man replied. 'Patience can move mountains.' He fiddled for a while with a little leather pouch.

'What's that?' asked Gatty.

'Put out your tongue,' the old man said. 'And you,' he told Snout. He pinched a little powder out of the pouch and touched it to Gatty's and Snout's tongues.

'What is it?' asked Gatty.

'Sleeping-salts,' the old man said. 'Dream-salts. When you wake, you'll be able to continue your journey.'

To begin with, the salts made Gatty feel calm. Her anxiety somehow dissolved. Then she could hear herself – her shallow breathing – and, hot as the day was, she started to feel cold. She rolled over and, with a sweet sigh, fell asleep.

Gatty didn't wake until dawn the next day. In her vivid dreams, she was living inside the pound. Puffs of coloured smoke came wafting over the walls. At times all the people confined with her shone through this smoke like bars of bright light, but then the wind got up and laughed and turned them into amber circles and ruby triangles and sapphire rectangles and emerald squares.

'Wake up!' said a strange man, shaking Gatty's right shoulder. 'Wake up!'

Gatty snorted.

'Wake up!' the man urged her. 'You're the English girl?'

'Yes!' exclaimed Gatty.

'You were snoring.'

'I wasn't!' Gatty pointed to the inert figure jammed against the wall. 'It's Snout who snores. Because of his nostrils. Who are you?'

'A pound-guard came and told us about you,' the man replied.

Gatty had a strange taste in her mouth. She rubbed her eyes. She looked around for the withered old man – but he had disappeared.

'Snout!' said Gatty. 'Wake up! Wake up!'

Snout groaned, and yawned.

'The guards should never have imprisoned you,' the man told them. 'Christian pilgrims!'

42

'Are you a knight or a brother?' asked Gatty.

'Both,' said the man.

Gatty wrinkled her forehead. 'You can't be both.'

Brother Gabriel offered Gatty the sweet smile of one who has seen much suffering.

'That's what we are, though,' he said. ' Now come with me.'

Brother Gabriel led Gatty and Snout out of the compound and north across the city to a handsome new stone building. The three of them sat down in a shady corner of the courtyard.

'Yes,' said Brother Gabriel. 'We're Hospitallers. Knights of the Hospital of Saint John of Jerusalem, and this is our compound here in Acre. We take the three vows of poverty, chastity and obedience, like the monks of Saint Augustine . . .'

'They looked after us in Cyprus,' Snout said.

'. . . but we're military men, and our duty is to protect and care for pilgrims visiting the Holy Land.'

'God be praised!' exclaimed Snout.

'Why can you speak English?' Gatty asked him.

'My uncle taught me,' said Brother Gabriel. 'Now tell me who you are. What is your story?'

The knight-brother's courteous attention and patience were such that Gatty told him a good deal more than he needed to know, beginning with Lady Gwyneth's death in Venice.

'Ga-tty!' interrupted Snout in an exasperated voice, and he smiled at Brother Gabriel. 'She does go on, sometimes.'

'Sometimes we need to,' the knight-brother replied.

Gatty noticed how still he sat; how he wasted no words.

'Well, you're in luck,' he said. 'I've just been summoned to Jerusalem.'

'Oh!' cried Gatty. 'You mean we can come with you?' she leaped up and grabbed Snout's right arm.

Brother Gabriel held up a forefinger. 'It may not be very far . . .'

'How far?' interrupted Gatty.

'Three days.'

'You been there before?'

'Oh yes!' the knight-brother replied. 'Many times.'

Gatty looked at Brother Gabriel in awe. 'Three days. Riding?'

'Mules,' said Brother Gabriel with a smile.

'We got horses,' Gatty told him. 'Waiting for us near Venice. Mine's a Welsh cob. She's called Syndod.' She delved into her cloak pocket. 'Look!' she said. 'Emrys the stableman carved her for me.'

The knight-brother nodded and smiled. 'I was going to say, it may not be far but it's certainly very dangerous.'

'Why?' asked Snout.

'Brigands,' said Brother Gabriel. 'Bedouin nomads. Gatty, you must disguise yourself.'

Gatty clicked her teeth. 'I'm tired of not being myself!'

Brother Gabriel smiled. 'As a pretty boy!'

'I already met Saracens,' Gatty said. 'Traders in Venice, and Osman, and that old man last night.'

'Of course there are peaceable Saracens,' Brother Gabriel acknowledged. 'Plenty of them. But there are also ruffians, armed soldiers, Bedouin tribesmen, Assassins.'

'Assassins?' asked Snout.

Brother Gabriel nodded. 'I'm afraid so. Slices of white moon between their teeth.'

'What white moon?' asked Gatty.

'The scimitar,' said the knight-brother and he slowly drew his left forefinger across his throat.

Gatty caught her breath.

Brother Gabriel just smiled. 'God willing, you'll get there,' he told them.

'I have to,' Gatty informed him in a matter-of-fact voice.

'It's the whole reason for our journey,' said Snout, 'getting to Jerusalem.'

'No,' said Brother Gabriel. 'The point of a pilgrimage is the journey, not the destination.'

'An old man in the pound said we're all pilgrims, between life and death,' Gatty told him. 'What was that place, anyway?'

'It's where the authorities hold anyone they suspect, and the truth is they suspect too many Saracens and Jews. There are people in there for very little reason and people there for no reason at all. It's unjust. But as I said,' Brother Gabriel continued, 'our mission is to protect and care for pilgrims. Some arrive and never leave.'

'What do you mean?' asked Snout.

'I don't mean they die,' Brother Gabriel said, ' though I've seen as many as ten carried out of our infirmary on a single day.'

Gatty and Snout lowered their eyes.

'No, they choose to stay and work with us. We have more than one thousand beds in our hospital.'

'One thousand!' Gatty exclaimed.

'I can help you get to Jerusalem,' Brother Gabriel said, 'and my brothers may even be able to get you back here again. But Venice? England?' The knight-brother blew out his cheeks.

*

The sleeping-salts had not finished with Gatty. In the cool of the Hospitallers' compound, she dozed, she daydreamed. Something about Saladin, the Saracen leader, visiting this very hospice, here in Acre. Something about the Hospitallers fighting shoulder to shoulder with the crusaders . . . no, she couldn't remember.

Next morning, early, Gatty woke keen as a newly-sharpened scythe, eager to resume their journey.

'And so we will,' Brother Gabriel told her. 'Tomorrow, God willing.'

'Tomorrow,' said Gatty, disappointed.

'Today I have business here in the hospital, and down in the town; and I must hire mules for you and Snout.'

'I'll come with you,' said Gatty.

The knight-brother shook his head. 'My uncle wishes to meet you.'

Gatty gave a small sigh.

'The one who taught me English,' Brother Gabriel told her.

'You didn't say he was here,' Gatty said. 'Is he a hosp . . . a whatever you are?'

The knight-brother fingered his white cross. 'No, no, not at all. He was a crusader.'

'An English one?'

'No, Norman – like I am. But he was brought up in England,' Brother Gabriel said. 'In the east. Lynn, or something.'

'What's his name?' asked Gatty. 'Why didn't he go home?'

The knight-brother smiled. 'You and your questions!' he said. 'Sir Faramond. Let me explain.'

At this moment, Snout stepped into the cloister.

'You're up early,' he called out.

'God go with you!' said the knight-brother.

Snout crossed himself. 'And with you,' he said.

'We're going to meet Sir Faramond,' Gatty told him.

'My uncle,' Brother Gabriel explained. 'He fought under Coeur-de-Lion. He was here when we besieged Acre, twelve years ago, and the Saracens surrendered . . .' The knight-brother explored Gatty's and Snout's faces.

'What?' asked Gatty.

'Saladin was unwilling – unwilling or unable to pay the ransom for them, and so the crusaders put the whole lot to the sword.'

'Killed them, you mean?'

'Massacred them,' Snout added.

'Three thousand Saracens. Not only the men. Women and children as well.'

Gatty shook her head angrily. 'Cruel!' she cried.

'Cruel, yes,' Brother Gabriel said.

'Why?' demanded Gatty.

The knight-brother shook his head and sighed. 'This is a just war,' he said. 'At all events, Sir Faramond was here, and he was badly wounded.'

'But you said the Saracens surrendered,' said Gatty, frowning.

'They did. He was wounded by his own companions.'

'Why?' demanded Gatty, much more loudly than she meant to. Her voice ricocheted round the cloister.

'He was trying to protect a Saracen girl. She was just nine, curled up like a woodlouse. Sir Faramond stood over her and his companions hacked at him until he fell over her. Then they all ran off.'

Gatty's breathing quickened. 'Did he save her?'

Brother Gabriel gave Gatty a tender smile. 'Oh yes!' he said. 'Here in this hospice Sir Faramond was nursed back to health – and we took the girl in too.'

'A Saracen,' said Snout.

'Most of our patients are pilgrims,' said Brother Gabriel,

'but we have no rule against admitting infidels.'

Gatty frowned. 'You said it's just to kill them.'

'I said our cause is just. We must recover Jerusalem for Christendom.' Brother Gabriel crossed himself.

'Why is your uncle still here, then?' Gatty asked.

'He married Saffiya.'

'Who?'

'The Saracen girl.'

Gatty put her hand over her mouth and looked at Brother Gabriel in joyous disbelief.

'Her parents were killed in the massacre, and so we looked after her and she worked here as a servant. Sir Faramond married her when she was sixteen.' Brother Gabriel smiled. 'I came out to Acre ten years ago to bring my uncle home, but instead I joined the Order and stayed.' He shook his head at the unpredictability of it all.

'Saffiya,' said Gatty, exploring the name.

'A marriage of this kind is unusual,' Brother Gabriel said. 'Most unusual. Saffiya is a very clever young woman. She taught me and some of the other brothers here to speak Arabic. You'll see.'

43

'That's the slaughterhouse,' said Brother Gabriel, pointing to a long, low building.

'Where they were massacred?' Gatty asked.

'What?'

'Where the women and children were massacred?'

'Dear Lord, no!' the knight-brother replied. 'Where the pigs and cattle are butchered, and prepared for the kitchen.'

'Oh!' said Gatty, rather breathlessly.

'The Venetians have set them themselves up very nicely here,' Brother Gabriel told her, 'as they usually do. This whole quarter of town is theirs. They have their own bathhouse, their own water mill, their own *fonduk*.'

'What's that?' asked Snout.

'A warehouse: *fonduk* in Arabic.' The Hospitaller strode through the narrow streets, with Gatty and Snout on either side of him. 'Yes,' he went on, 'their own church and bakehouse and vegetable plots and I don't know what else. So Sir Faramond is very well placed.'

'But he's not Venetian,' said Gatty.

'No,' said the knight-brother, 'but he's rich, and this quarter has the best buildings. In any case, there's no Norman quarter here.'

The outside walls of Sir Faramond's and Lady Saffiya's house – their 'little palace', Brother Gabriel called it – were muscular and gritty and gave no idea of the wonders inside.

As soon as one Saracen servant had admitted them, two

more courteously helped them to take off their battered boots.

Just look at them, thought Gatty. They're in even worse shape than I am.

Gatty stared around her. She was in some kind of hall, but there was no fire in the middle of it, and the walls were smooth white marble. The ceiling was vaulted, like the apse in Caldicot church, and although there were only three high slit-windows, the room was quite light.

'This is where Sir Faramond sees people on business,' Brother Gabriel told her. 'You know, traders and bankers and so on.'

Just as the outside of the little palace gave the pilgrims no sense of the antechamber's cool, shiny grace, the antechamber offered them no more than a hint of what lay beyond.

Two more servants were standing on either side of the massive oak doors, and when they swung them open Gatty drew in her breath. In front of her was the most beautiful courtyard, its covered arcades supported by little avenues of slender, glassy columns. The entire floor of the courtyard was paved in white marble, and in the middle was a plashing fountain.

Beside this fountain Gatty saw two people, laughing: a young woman wearing a sparkling veil, hazel-skinned, slender as a willow wand; and a handsome man, neither large nor small, with merry eyes and a nicely-trimmed grey beard.

'Sir Faramond!' Brother Gabriel greeted them. 'Lady Saffiya! Your visitors.'

Lady Saffiya inclined her head slightly towards Snout, and then she lifted her veil and gathered both Gatty's hands between her own. 'Well come,' she said. Her voice was singed and husky.

Then it was Sir Faramond's turn. He stared Snout in the

eye and warmly embraced him. Then he bowed slightly to Gatty, and kissed her on each cheek.

'Pilgrims!' he exclaimed. 'Speakers of English! An English man and English woman. What wealth my nephew has brought to our door.'

Wealth! Snout felt slightly dazed – by the diamonds sparkling in Lady Saffiya's veil. By her beauty. Her fleeting smile.

Hearing Sir Faramond to be so warm and so plainspoken, Gatty spoke plainly herself.

'I'm only a chamber-servant, sir,' she said. 'Snout's a cook.'

Sir Faramond smiled and led his guests round the fountain, and Gatty noticed he had a limp.

'Saffiya was just telling me about her uncle,' he said. 'He was a magician.'

'There was a conjuror in the pound,' Gatty told him. 'He took a red jewel out of my ear.'

'This man wasn't a conjuror,' Sir Faramond said. 'He was a magician. An impatient magician! When his barber had a queue of customers, Saffiya's uncle told him, "I can't wait. I'll have to leave my head here and collect it later." Then her uncle took his head off! And after the barber had given it a haircut, he collected it!'

Gatty and Snout looked startled; Sir Faramond laughed. 'That's why we were laughing as you walked in.'

'I met an astronomer, sir,' Gatty said, 'and he told me to be careful about laughing with Saracens. In case it offends them.'

Sir Faramond nodded. 'No one likes being laughed at,' he replied, 'but everyone likes laughing together.' He smiled at his wife. 'Well, I wish I'd met this magician. Poor Gabriel! I fear I'm nothing like such an exotic uncle.'

'Oh, I don't know,' Brother Gabriel said. 'Hacked-and-broken, Anglo-Norman, Saracen-marrying, sherbet-sipping . . .'

Sir Faramond and his wife burst out laughing.

'Thank you,' Lady Saffiya said in her husky voice, 'for such a graceful reminder.' And away she glided on her quiet feet. Snout gazed after her as if she were an angel who had bestowed a brief visit on them and was now returning to heaven.

'I have business in town to attend to, and mules to hire,' Brother Gabriel told his uncle. 'Please excuse me. I'll collect your visitors later!'

Exotic! Everything in the 'little palace' seemed exotic to Gatty.

She sipped refreshing sherbet, marvelling at the way it fizzed slightly on her tongue, like overdue apple juice. Sharp-eyed, she watched the silver fish darting around the fountain pool, and then she sank with the cumbersome red and gold fish, dreaming under the lily pads. When Sir Faramond and Lady Saffiya conducted the pilgrims into one of the smaller rooms looking onto the courtyard, Gatty kept twisting her head round and round.

'Careful,' Sir Faramond said, 'or it'll come off!'

'Like the magician's head!' Gatty replied, grinning. 'I didn't know there was no place like this.'

As with the antechamber and courtyard, the floor was marble, but the side walls were covered with turquoise and ochre tiles patterned with circles, triangles and squares. The far wall consisted almost entirely of a large double-arched window covered with a perforated stone screen, so that light streamed through it and fell on the floor and walls in dashes and splashes and elongated diamonds. The room was made as much of light as stone.

Gatty examined a strange band of squiggles inscribed on the wall beside her – just above the patterned tiles.

'It looks like writing,' she announced. 'Like the alphabet did before I learned it.'

'You know your alphabet?' Sir Faramond asked her.

'Backwards!' laughed Gatty. ' Z-y-x and w-v, u-t-s and r-q-p.' And then she said, rather proudly, 'I can read, slowly.'

'And she can write,' added Snout. 'Can't you?'

'Very slowly!' Gatty said.

'You hear that, Saffiya?' asked Sir Faramond. 'Most remarkable!'

'Lady Gwyneth,' Gatty said. 'She wanted me to learn so I could read to her. She said it's one of the greatest pleasures to listen to someone telling or reading a story.'

'It is indeed,' said Sir Faramond.

Lady Saffiya reached up and touched the squiggles, which looked like knots, or flowers, or leaves, yet somehow more organised and rhythmical.

'You're right, Gatty,' she said. 'This is writing. It's *thuluth*. A kind of Arabic scripture.'

'You mean script,' Sir Faramond corrected her. 'But yes, scripture too.'

'What does it say?' Gatty asked.

'It is the *bismallah*,' Lady Saffiya replied. 'It reads, "In the name of Allah, the Merciful, the Compassionate."'

'In other words,' said Sir Faramond, '*in nomine patris* . . . in the name of the Father, and the Son, and the Holy Ghost.'

All her life, it seemed, Gatty had listened to people denouncing Saracens. Oliver saying they had horns and tails. The friar who had come to Caldicot to proclaim the crusade, hammering the pulpit with his fists and yelling, 'Jerusalem is still in the grip of the vile Saracens. Drive them out! Kill them!'

Yet here she was, in the Holy Land, in this peaceful airy room, talking with a Christian married to a Saracen. It scarcely made sense.

'Perhaps I know what you're thinking,' Sir Faramond told her. 'I follow my faith and Saffiya follows hers. But we learn from each other. We believe one and one add up to three.'

'Eh?' exclaimed Snout.

'You got children then?' Gatty asked.

Lady Saffiya shook her head, and lowered her eyes. 'As Allah wills,' she said throatily. Gatty could feel her sadness.

So could Snout. Uncomfortably, he shifted his weight from one foot to the other.

'I'll sing over you,' said Gatty.

'What was that?' asked Sir Faramond.

'I'll sing a spell over her,' Gatty repeated. 'If you want, I mean.'

'So you can sing, too.'

'You should hear her,' Snout said. 'The abbot in Kyrenia said he'd never heard such a voice.'

'It might help,' said Gatty. 'It won't do no harm.'

Sir Faramond and his wife caught one another's eye. Neither of them said anything.

Glass windows, mosaics, fountains! Silken sheets and woven carpets! Weekly baths! Scented soap! That afternoon the pilgrims found out how Sir Faramond and his wife lived.

'It's like the Promised Land,' Gatty said.

'This is the Promised Land!' Sir Faramond replied, smiling.

For their part, Gatty and Snout told their hosts about Lady Gwyneth, and how she had died in Venice; how, in Kyrenia, Gobbo had refused to wait; how their companions were most likely on their way home.

'And you've been left behind,' mused Sir Faramond.

'We'll catch them up,' Gatty told him. 'In Venice or some-where.'

'In our coffins, we will,' Snout said in a dour voice.

'Not many pilgrims make the long journey here from

England,' Sir Faramond told them. 'Anyhow, they almost always sail down to Jaffa, because it's closer to Jerusalem. It's very pleasant to have a chance to speak English again.'

'You grew up in England, sir?' asked Snout.

'I did. Near Lynn in Norfolk. My father owned lands there. I ceded them to my brother.'

'Unto Allah,' said Saffiya, 'belong the easts and the wests.'

Sir Faramond smiled at his wife. 'Over my dead body,' he said. And at once Gatty saw this little girl, eyes screwed up, terrified, and the Norman knight standing over her.

'Now,' said Sir Faramond, 'You both long to reach Jerusalem, and we well know how dangerous it can be. Snout, Lady Saffiya will help to dress you.'

Snout gave Sir Faramond a strange look, and then guffawed.

'Not Snout, sir!' said Gatty. 'Brother Gabriel said I got to disguise myself as a boy.'

Sir Faramond shook his head. 'We've discussed this further with Brother Gabriel. If he travels as a Hospitaller, he's bound to attract attention.'

'Far better all three of you dress as Saracens,' Lady Saffiya told them. 'A nobleman with his two wives. If you're challenged, Brother Gabriel can speak Arabic.'

'You taught him!' Gatty said. 'But what if they speak to me?'

'They won't,' said Sir Faramond. 'No Saracen would speak to another man's wife. Not without her husband's permission.'

'Your faces and your hair will be covered by your *burqas*,' Lady Saffiya told them. 'Whatever you do, you mustn't say a word.'

'All right, Lady Snout?' Gatty asked, smiling.

The cook grunted.

'Now,' said Sir Faramond, 'we can help you to reach

Jerusalem . . . and maybe while you're in Jerusalem.' He glanced at his wife and Lady Saffiya gave him a firm nod.

'Yes, we'll help you. As I said, it's very pleasing to be able to speak English. You see how we live here?'

Gatty knew he was girding himself up.

'What have you to go back to?' Sir Faramond asked. 'In England? With Lady Gwyneth dead?'

Arthur, Gatty thought at once.

I've got Hew, thought Snout.

Caldicot, thought Gatty. Sian and everyone. Hopeless. My chickens.

Ewloe, thought Snout.

And Ewloe too, thought Gatty. Nest – unless she stays in Venice. Everyone. Griffith's grave. The Marches, green and blue and grey, and cool and damp, and fair and dear . . .

'What we would like,' Gatty heard Sir Faramond saying, 'is for both of you to come and live here.'

'Here!' Gatty and Snout exclaimed.

'You, Snout, you can work in the kitchen, instructing, learning. And Gatty, you and I will speak English.'

'But why?' asked Gatty, mystified.

'As we get older,' Sir Faramond said, 'we value our skills; we like to use them. Yes, we can speak English, and you can read to us, and write. And sing.'

Lady Saffiya gazed at Gatty. Her long dark eyelashes trembled.

And Snout gazed at Lady Saffiya, open-mouthed!

'To begin with, you'll say you must get back to England,' Sir Faramond told them. 'But think about it on your way to Jerusalem. Talk to my nephew. You would be happy here – as I am.' Sir Faramond smiled. 'God willing, Allah willing, Brother Gabriel will bring you back with him.'

44

Gatty rubbed Snout's hands between her own for a third time and then just tipped his nose.

'There!' she said approvingly. 'A real woman!'

'Never lost for something to say, are you?' grumbled Snout.

'I never thought the oils and creams Nest left would come in so handy. What about me? How do I look?'

Snout considered Gatty, and the expression that came over his face was like sunlight sweeping over shadowed land.

'Like a second wife,' he said with a smile.

'Have I put on too much?' Gatty asked. Gingerly, she dabbed her face on the back of her hand. 'It feels so strange, wearing this *abaya* – is that what it's called? It's so . . . floating. And so dark.'

Brother Gabriel appeared at the door. 'Beautiful!' he exclaimed. 'Especially you, Snout!'

Snout curtsied. 'Thank you, husband,' he said in a charming, light voice. 'You do look very handsome yourself.'

Gatty considered the Hospitaller. 'Like a ruffian,' she said. 'Very fiery.'

'Are you ready?' Brother Gabriel asked. 'It's almost sunrise and the mules are at the gate. We should celebrate Mass and be on our way.'

The last piece of clothing Gatty put on was her *burqa*, and she didn't like it at all. It imprisoned her. She couldn't feel the wind and sunlight on her freckled cheeks.

'Why do we have to wear it?' she asked.

'So you won't be recognised,' Brother Gabriel replied.

'No, I mean why do Saracen women have to wear it?'

'Ah!' said the knight-brother. 'To conceal their hair. A woman's hair is the most attractive thing about her, and she should save it for her husband. It may give other men impure thoughts.'

'Is that why Lady Gwyneth wore a wimple?' Snout asked.

'You may be right, Snout,' Brother Gabriel replied. 'That may be why ladies in England and Normandy wear wimples.'

Gatty and Snout were pleased to be in the saddle again, even if their mounts were only two scabby mules. But on their way out of the town they had a shock. Advancing down the street towards them was a monster with a long neck, a small head, eyes like a goat, and a huge hump on its back. It was sandy-coloured and twice as tall as a tall horse.

'Stone a crow!' said Snout.

'What is it?' demanded Gatty.

This monster's mouth was puckered, as if it had just swallowed a whole mouthful of sloes.

'Foul-tempered,' said Gatty. 'You can tell.'

The animal swished its tail and began to roar. Then, as it passed Gatty, it swung its long neck and tried to take a bite out of her. Its driver shouted at it, and it swayed past them.

Gatty's heart was pumping. 'Ugly beast!' she exclaimed. 'What's it called?'

'Man's best friend in the desert,' the knight-brother replied. 'A camel. They can travel for days without needing water. And they can carry loads over great distances. Quiet now! No one must hear you speaking English.'

Gatty took no notice. 'How far is it, did you say?'

'Ninety miles,' the Hospitaller replied, 'and an Arabic mile is much further than a Roman mile.'

'I don't know how far a Roman mile is,' Snout grumbled.

'How many days, then?' Gatty asked.

'Three.'

'Where will we sleep?'

'In caves.'

Snout struggled inside his black clothing. 'I look like a fat raven!' he complained.

'Not another word until we're out of Acre,' said Brother Gabriel.

As soon as this Saracen and his two wives left the town, they entered dry, unforgiving country. It rose up in front of them, it stood between them and the Holy City. It was the last week of July and the short grass was baked and fried. The few trees were gnarled and stunted by their exhausting fight with the sun. The hills were pale as straw, littered with grey boulders and crags.

Riding between Snout and Brother Gabriel, Gatty began to think of green Caldicot. The dark pools under the elms and oaks on the manor land. The green naves in Pike Forest where she went to snare rabbits and collect firewood. The willows weeping into the Little Lark . . .

As the sun rose, the light began to shimmer. Gatty narrowed her eyes. Whatever she looked at trembled.

'What's that?' she asked, pointing up the track. 'That black thing.'

As the three of them approached it, Brother Gabriel said, 'I wouldn't look too closely.'

Gatty did.

The black thing was a pilgrim cloak, and inside the cloak was a grinning skeleton. It was propped up against a rock, picked clean by vultures.

Gatty's mouth went dry. Then her stomach quaked and she felt sick.

'I'm afraid so,' Brother Gabriel said.

Gatty stared out of her *burqa*, confused and alarmed.

'Why didn't his companions bury him?' asked Snout.

The Hospitaller shook his head. 'Too dangerous,' he said. 'It would take too long. The Bedouin killed him, and they left him here as a warning.'

Sombre and silent, the three travellers rode through the wilderness. Now there were no trees; no piping birds, only from time to time a bird of prey, wheeling; lizards basking; the throbbing sun.

In this wilderness, Gatty began to doubt. Can we rely on Brother Gabriel, she thought? I mean, I trusted Signor Umberto, and I was wrong. And what about Snout? Will he be strong enough if the Bedouin come?

'My lady,' she said silently to herself. 'Give me strength. Give me courage, so I don't fail you. I pray you, keep the Bedouin away.' Gatty wept dry tears.

Brother Gabriel turned to her. 'Are you all right?' he asked. 'Second wife?'

Gatty couldn't reply. Inside her dark clothing, she was feeling so weak and uncertain. Have I been tricking myself all this time, she thought. Getting into deeper, always deeper water. Am I drowning? It's my own fault. How will Snout and I ever get to Jerusalem?

Brother Gabriel could sense Gatty's turmoil. 'God sees you for who you are and loves you for who you are,' he said gently. 'Not only for your strengths, Gatty. He loves you for your weaknesses.'

Gatty swallowed. Her throat was so dry.

That night and the next, the three of them slept in caves, somehow airless, stale with animal droppings. They ate their food cold.

'No fire,' Brother Gabriel told them. 'Smoke's a sure way of attracting attention.'

On the third afternoon, though, the three travellers did

attract attention. Seven horsemen suddenly appeared on the white skyline ahead of them.

'Bedouin!' Brother Gabriel warned them. 'Keep moving! Not a word! Not one word!'

The horsemen swept down off the hilltop in a glowing cloud of dust. The hooves of their horses thudded. They shouted to each other. They surrounded Brother Gabriel and Gatty and Snout.

Gatty's heart was beating so loudly she thought the horsemen might hear it. She was trembling and sweating. Afraid her *burqa* might slip down to her chin. Afraid her fear might give her away. Afraid! For the first time on the entire pilgrimage, she could smell her own rancid fear.

Now the Bedouin leader was staring straight at her with his burning eyes, pulling at his black moustache. He jabbed the air with his knife and asked her something.

Gatty lowered her eyes.

Brother Gabriel waved at the Bedouin impatiently. He barked in Arabic.

Still, the leader persisted. He asked Brother Gabriel question after question, and tersely Brother Gabriel answered him.

Gatty dared not raise her eyes again. She knew that if she were to make one false move, just one, they too would be food for vultures. She was terrified.

Then, as abruptly as they had appeared, the seven horsemen wheeled round. They shouted. They cantered away.

'Where are they going?' asked Gatty, alarmed.

'With the winds!' said Brother Gabriel.

'Are they coming back?'

'No, no.'

'I've wet myself!' said Snout. 'Why did I ever leave Ewloe?'

Then Gatty began to tremble.

'I told him we'd come from Acre,' Brother Gabriel said. 'I said we're on our way to Jerusalem. Nothing strange about that. But then he asked me about you. You, Gatty. Your grey-green eyes. He said you had the eyes of a young woman but rode like a man! My second wife, I told him. Born a long way north from here. He asked me your name. Ayesha, I said.'

'Is that when he spoke to me?' Gatty asked shakily.

Brother Gabriel nodded. 'He should never have done so without my permission. And then, if you please, he asked me whether we'd seen any pilgrims.'

'God's guts!' said Snout in a gravelly voice.

'So I told him I'd seen two,' the knight-brother went on cheerfully. 'Two pilgrims, travelling with one guide!'

Gatty still couldn't stop shaking.

That night, the three travellers slept in a cave again. They shared it with several rats and mice.

'Tomorrow?' asked Gatty.

'Tomorrow,' Brother Gabriel replied.

When she lay down with her head on her scrip, grateful at last for her voluminous clothing, Gatty wanted to prepare herself. She wanted to pray with Snout.

'Snout,' she whispered, and she yawned.

'What is it, girl?' asked Snout. And then, after a little while, 'Gatty! What is it?'

But Gatty was already asleep. Cool and easy she slept until, like a ghost, dawn assembled herself, pale at the entrance to the cave. Then Gatty woke as she had on the first day of their pilgrimage: instantly awake.

Today, she thought. Today!

45

Brother Gabriel said not a word.

Three abreast they plodded towards the crest of the hill. The sky began to open around them like a pale violet flower, a periwinkle, say, healing and infinite.

As they reached the top, a light, scented wind from the south dabbed their cheeks. The dry, scruffy ground levelled, then it began to give way in front of them.

There it was!

Jerusalem!

At once Gatty reined in.

There it was. Waiting for her.

No need to ask. She recognised it like a home from which, long ago, she had strayed. Its contours were her own heart's and mind's contours. She felt like a little girl again. No need to say anything.

The Holy City, golden, grew out of the gentle slopes on which it sat. Or was it the other way round? Did the Holy City, Gatty wondered, come down from God, out of heaven? And did the hillslopes and the valleys and everything else on earth grow out of it?

All that stood between the pilgrims and the golden domes, the clustered towers and columns and walls was one last shallow valley, dark with olive groves.

Gatty swung down from her mule. She lifted her flowing *abaya* above her knees; then she knelt on the dusty track, and bowed down so that her forehead touched the ground.

She kissed the earth.

Snout did as Gatty did, and then she grasped his hand, pulled him up and embraced him.

'The city of the living God,' Brother Gabriel said reverently.

'Amen!' shouted Gatty and Snout, reaching towards it. 'Amen! Amen!'

Then the three of them joyfully sang the *Te Deum*: 'We praise Thee, O God, we acknowledge Thee to be the Lord.'

'Today is the first day of August,' the Hospitaller told them. 'The feast day of the three sisters and martyrs, Faith and Hope and Charity.'

'Ohh!' cried Gatty, wild at last, and shining. 'It's like the Bible says: I see a new heaven and new earth. Nothing can't never be the same again!'

46

Absolving and blessing, caterwauling, dancing, elbowing, fiddling, gawping, haggling, insisting, jeering, kissing, limping, mourning, neighing, ogling, pickpocketing, questioning, rosary-telling, sweating, taunting, ululating, vowing, wailing, exclaiming, yelling, zither-plucking; zit-picking, yawning, explaining, whistling, vandalising, uttering, tale-telling, shoving, rabbiting, quaffing, pleading, oat-eating, nagging, money-changing, laughing, kneeling, jostling, hugging, gossiping, flagellating, entreating, doddering, chanting, breast-beating and arguing: from the moment Gatty passed under the Fish Gate, side by side with Snout, she was caught up in a bubbling tide of people such as she had never experienced before, not even in London or Venice. She and her mule were carried almost bodily along the seething streets and swept into the courtyard of the Hospital of Saint John.

Gatty was panting. She dismounted, and pulled off her *burqa*. She unwound her *hijab*. She filled her lungs with air, and then let it all out again, noisily.

'Snout!' she yelled, and she seized and hugged him. 'I knew we would! I knew it!' Still holding the cook, she tried to dance, but all she succeeded in doing was taking him off-balance so that they both staggered sideways, and fell over.

Laughing, Gatty helped Snout up. 'I didn't, though,' she said. 'Not all the time. Not in Kyrenia, for a start. Not when those Bedouin surrounded us.'

The Hospitaller stretched out his hands, palms upward, as if he were begging, and Gatty grew quiet.

'Jerusalem,' he said. 'The centre of the world.'

'It feels like it,' said Snout. 'At least it did out there in the street.'

'The outer world and the inner world,' the knight-brother continued. 'As maps show us, Jerusalem is the hub of the wheel.'

'The world's not like a wheel,' Gatty objected. 'It's like an egg or a pig's bladder.'

Brother Gabriel ignored this. 'The inner world,' he repeated. 'The world of the spirit. Jesus lived and died here, He rose from the dead here, but this city is also sacred to the Saracens – and the Jews. That's why we fight over it.'

'Why is it sacred to them?' Gatty asked.

'That's a short question with many long answers,' the Hospitaller replied. 'Within these walls the Temple of Solomon once stood, and this is where King David brought the Ark of the Covenant. From this city the Prophet Muhammad ascended to heaven on a winged horse while he was still alive, and glimpsed paradise. Ah! Here comes Gregory.'

Gatty and Snout watched a man crossing the courtyard: he was slight, with thin, receding dark hair and beady eyes.

'One of our helpers,' the Hospitaller explained. 'He's English.'

'Brother Gabriel!' said the man, smiling only with his mouth, not his eyes. He gave the knight-brother a perfunctory embrace, and then surveyed Gatty and Snout without enthusiasm.

'My companions!' said Brother Gabriel. 'My two wives, actually! My English wives!'

'Gatty and Snout,' Gregory said.

Gatty's mouth fell open. Snout hastily crossed himself.

'Who told you?' Gatty demanded.

The guide sighed. 'City of miracles,' he said in a world-weary voice.

'I know,' said Gatty. 'You talked to our companions.' She didn't like Gregory's waxen skin. She didn't like the way he watched her under his heavy eyelids.

'Are they still here?' asked Snout.

Gregory shook his head. 'They left you messages. Ask Janet.'

'Gregory's wife,' Brother Gabriel explained. 'Gregory and Janet came here as pilgrims five years ago, and chose to stay. I don't know what we'd do without them.'

At this moment, something near them whirred; then dust spurted, as if the courtyard had sprung a leak.

'A snake!' said Snout, tensing his shoulders.

Another whirr; another spurt; something jumped and hopscotched towards them.

A jagged stone!

'Quick!' said Brother Gabriel.

Gatty and Snout and Brother Gabriel and Gregory ran across the courtyard, holding their arms over their heads.

Twenty paces, and they were out of harm's way. But Gatty was shocked and Snout was panting.

'Saracens,' Brother Gabriel told them. 'Young boys, probably. We get used to it.'

'Why don't you stop them?' Gatty asked.

'Because we'd soon have a fight on our hands. And, as you know, in this Holy City, the Saracens are many and Christians few.'

'They do not love us,' Gregory said. 'But for the most part, they tolerate us.'

'And make money out of us,' the Hospitaller added. 'Our most sacred shrines are in their hands, and we have to pay the Saracens to see them. The cross-legged devils!'

'The crusaders will pay them and all!' Gatty declared.

300

'We've fought over this city for one thousand years!' Brother Gabriel said. 'Sometimes I think this conflict between Christians and Saracens and Jews will never end.'

Snout cleared his throat. 'Excuse me, sir,' he said. 'I'm famished.'

'So am I,' agreed Gatty. 'We haven't had a mouthful all day.'

'True,' said Brother Gabriel, 'and I'm sure Gregory will want to take you over to Holy Sepulchre before supper. What do you think, Gregory? Could Janet perhaps . . .'

'And she can tell us our messages,' said Gatty eagerly.

Janet was as warm and bustling as her husband was cool and removed. Not only that: she was half as large again.

'Yes,' she said, patting herself, 'God was feeling generous on the day He created me.'

Sitting in the little parlour the guide and his wife had for themselves, Gatty and Snout devoured bread dripping with honey and, like dry sponges, they soaked up Janet's comfortable words.

'Emrys,' said Janet. 'Was that his name?'

'The stableman,' Snout said.

'Yes,' Janet said. She fished into her apron pocket, and gave the cook a tiny horseshoe. 'Emrys said that for all God's goodness, we need luck as well. This horseshoe is to bring you luck.'

'He said all that?' Gatty exclaimed.

'And he asked me to remind you the livery stable is at Treviso,' Janet went on.

'As if I'd forget!' Gatty said.

'Naked!' said Janet. 'No, what was it?'

'Nakin,' Gatty corrected her.

'Yes, Nakin said he'll pay the feeding and stabling dues on your horse, Gatty.'

'Syndod!' Gatty told her.

301

'Yes, and pay the hiring fee for a horse for Snout.'

'God be praised!' said Snout.

'As for the stableman's wife,' said Janet, 'to be honest, I couldn't get much sense out of her. She was always weeping.'

Gatty pursed her lips and smiled.

'And then there was the clerk,' Janet went on. 'A funny little man, with his pink, pixie ears. And his high-pitched laugh! He told me you know his message, Gatty. He says it's within you.'

'He wants me to think about my own voice and everything he's taught me,' Gatty said. 'I will and all! What about Nest?'

By way of reply, the guide's wife dipped into her apron pocket again, and pulled out a little scroll.

'Nest didn't write to me!' Gatty exclaimed. She unrolled the letter and held it up. 'It's so thin you can almost see through it.'

'All the brothers use it,' Janet told her. 'Paper.'

'Paper,' Gatty repeated.

'Made from water-reeds,' said Janet. 'Papyrus reeds.'

'To my sister Gatty,' Gatty slowly spelled out.

'I should have come with you to Umberto, I know I should. I wanted to wait with Snout he was so brave but they wouldn't agree. Oh, Gatty! My baby is growing I can feel it. They all say I should stay with Sei in Venice what with nothing to go back to. Gatty, what will happen to me? I will wait for you there. May God guide you to Jerusalem. Without you is much worse.

By your loving Nest.'

Gatty's eyes were brimming with tears. 'No one's never wrote me a letter before,' she said, and she gave a single, loud sob. Then there was a knock at the door, and Brother Gabriel came in.

302

The Hospitaller gave her the sweetest smile. 'Yes,' he said. 'A letter! Janet told me.'

'She's so close,' sniffed Gatty. 'So far away.'

'Fill yourselves up,' Brother Gabriel told them. 'Bread! Honey! Janet's tender mercies!'

So Snout helped himself to another slice and ladled honey onto it.

'Manna,' said Gatty. 'And it was like coriander seed, white; and the taste of it was like wafers with honey.'

'Very good, Gatty,' Brother Gabriel declared. 'Now then, I've something to tell you that should lift your spirits. Before we left Acre, Sir Faramond gave me a fistful of gold. He told me he will pay for your keep at this Hospital and pay all your admission fees, flasks of water from the River Jordan, palm badges . . . He insists on paying for you both for as long as you're here in Jerusalem.'

'May God reward him!' Gatty said, shaking her head in wonder.

'And Lady Saffiya, too,' added Snout.

After this, Gatty and Snout went to see their dormitories. They emptied their scrips, and washed away the worst of their dusty three-day journey, and put on their crumpled pilgrim clothing. So it was already midway between noon and sundown by the time they were ready to leave the Hospital with Gregory.

Cautiously, the two pilgrims peered through the gateway, but the stone-throwers had long since gone. There was simply a stream of shuffling people.

Right outside the gate, a man was singing. He was wearing a small black cap covering the crown of his head, and his eyeballs were white.

'Samuel's a regular,' Gregory told them, 'and a rare beast. There aren't many Jews in Jerusalem.'

'But Jesus was a Jew,' Gatty said.

'And He was betrayed and crucified by Jews,' Gregory said sharply. 'The crusaders drove them all out – and quite right too. But then Saladin invited them back. Not many have returned, though.'

'What's he singing about?' Gatty asked.

Gregory listened for a while. 'Some old Hebrew song,' he said. He stared at Gatty, his beady dark eyes shining.

'Go on, then,' said Gatty.

'Your mouth is as round . . . as a golden ring,' the guide translated. 'Your teeth are like white hailstones. Your neck's like . . . the neck of a gazelle when she's thirsty and raises her eyes to heaven. Your breasts . . .'

'I get the idea,' Gatty interrupted, brushing away the words with the back of her hand.

'Where are we going?' Snout asked.

'Where each pilgrim goes first and last,' Gregory replied. 'The most holy place in holy Jerusalem.'

'Holy Sepulchre!' Gatty and Snout cried. 'God be praised!'

'Your hips,' translated Gregory, 'your hips are as narrow as the hips of a bee weaving through the orchard.'

Gatty clicked her tongue noisily. 'They're not, anyhow.'

It wasn't at all far from the Hospital of Saint John to the Church of the Holy Sepulchre, but the nearer they got, the more of a scrum there was.

'Same as usual!' Gregory called out. 'A purgatory of pilgrims! They're all going home tomorrow, and can scarcely bear to leave.'

Gatty looked around her, amazed and then troubled. Some people were wailing; some waving their staffs; some tearing their clothing. She knew all these pilgrims had been journeying to Jerusalem for weeks or months, or even years maybe, but she was dismayed at the way in which they caught emotion from each other as if it were raging fever.

They're like a huge crowd of Tildas, she thought. I don't

want to be swamped. I want to pray for Lady Gwyneth on my own.

Gregory shouldered his way through the mob, followed by Gatty and Snout, until they reached a space cordoned off around the entrance to the church. Two Saracens were sitting cross-legged on small carpets on either side of the door, and each had a metal box in front of him, with a slit in the lid.

Snout grasped Gatty's arm. He gave a huge gulp, and then began to sob.

'Snout!' said Gatty fondly, putting an arm around his shoulder. 'Snout!'

'I c . . . c . . . can't help it.'

'Wash away your sins, man,' Gregory said coolly. 'Now! Brother Gabriel's given me the money to pay for your admission.'

One of the cross-legged men took the coins and posted them into his metal box. Then he wagged both his forefingers and said something.

'Today's the first day of August,' Gregory translated. 'The end of the pilgrim season.'

'How can it be?' exclaimed Gatty, waving at the sea of people around her.

'I told you: all these people are leaving tomorrow.'

Gatty frowned. 'But if it's the end . . .' she said, hesitantly.

'You can still enter Holy Sepulchre,' Gregory told them. 'But from today on, the Church will close at sundown.'

47

Clutching Snout's damp left hand, Gatty gazed around her in awe.

It's like a huge hall full of night-sky, she thought.

Slowly her eyes grew used to the blue gloom, thick with burning incense, littered with shining, soft-edged moons and stars – candles in bloom.

Then Gatty saw the church was built on many different levels, and there were little chapels all around her, balconies, passages.

A hall full of night-sky, she thought, and a warren too. An enormous warren. I'm going to burrow into every corner.

Then Gatty removed her hand from Snout's, blew on her fingertips and took a candle from the large rack beside the door.

Around her, she could see swarms of pilgrims, upright and misshapen. She watched a procession of ten people slowly crossing the hall, each with their hands on the shoulders of the person in front of them. She heard people calling out 'Gott sei Dank!' and 'Dieu nous aide!' and 'Dios! Dios!' and listened to the undertow of people sobbing.

'You,' said a voice in the gloom. 'Girl!'

The voice belonged to a young Saracen man, sitting cross-legged on a low marble table.

'You German?'

'English,' Gatty replied.

The young man produced a little box. 'Toe,' he said.

'Look, Snout!' said Gatty.

'Toe Saint Digita,' the young man told them, gently shaking his head as if he could scarcely believe it.

Gatty reached out, wide-eyed.

'No touch!' said the man. 'Three gold.'

Snout had a careful look at the relic. 'That's not a toe,' he said. 'It's part of a trotter. I've cooked hundreds.'

'How can he!' exclaimed Gatty in disgust. 'In this holy place.'

'There'll be plenty more like him,' Snout warned her.

'Selling hope,' said Gatty.

'Charlatans! Lining their own pockets. Spend your prayers and save your money.'

The young man pouted. 'Two gold,' he said.

'No gold!' said Snout.

Gatty looked eagerly around her. She took an enormous breath and flung her arms wide. 'Oh Snout! We done it!'

At first, Gatty and Snout stayed together. Side by side, and silent, they climbed up the stone steps to Golgotha, the rock where Adam died, and Abraham almost sacrificed his son Isaac, and Jesus was stripped by Roman soldiers. Like the pilgrims in front of them, they threw themselves on their backs and spread out their arms where the soldiers nailed His hands and feet. They jammed their heads into the rock fissure right next to the socket-hole of the Cross.

Then, after waiting their turn for a long time, Gatty and Snout filed into a little rock tomb: they gazed at the stone shelf where Jesus's dead body had lain, wrapped in linen – the very place from which He had risen again.

After this, Gatty wanted to be on her own. She knew the time had come to pray for Lady Gwyneth.

'I got some praying of my own to do,' Snout told her. 'We can meet at the great door when the Saracens shout everyone out.'

Gatty took a few steps in one direction and then hesitated; she set off in another direction, then paused again. I don't know where to pray, she thought. She turned back towards the outside wall of Jesus's tomb and launched herself onto her knees. She pressed her forehead against the cool rock.

Gatty closed her eyes. She could see Lady Gwyneth in her dying-room. She could hear her confessing how she'd lain on her sleeping baby without realising it, and her whisper, feverish: 'I cannot, I cannot reach Jerusalem to do penance for my soul.'

Gatty chafed her forehead against the rock. The wall began to glisten with her tears.

'If you fail, Gatty, I will never rise to paradise. I will never see Griffith again.'

'Jesus,' said Gatty in a low voice. 'Please listen now!'

Gatty felt a hand on her left shoulder. It was a Saracen holding a large tray, piled with fresh fruit.

Gatty shook her head. But when she tried to pray again, the man just stood there, waiting. Gatty clicked her tongue and waved him away.

This is a church, not a market, she said to herself. It's the most holy place in the most holy city in the world.

No sooner had Gatty turned to Jesus again than she heard two men speaking English. They stopped right next to her.

'Wine and oil, yes . . .'

'Cumin, coriander.'

'Yes, and pepper and all the other spices. But for real profit . . .'

'Salt.'

'Exactly! We must try to pick some up in Alexandria. Failing that, we'll have to stop in Cyprus.'

Gatty looked up at the two men, but their backs were turned, and almost at once they strolled off.

Dear God, she thought. Buying and selling! Is that all that

interests them? How can I pray for Lady Gwyneth here?

When Gatty stood up her candle went out, so she stopped the nearest person, a young Saracen boy supporting a wizened old pilgrim, and touched her candle to his. The boy smiled, pursed his lips, and blew lightly over her face.

Why did he do that, Gatty wondered. His breath was so sweet.

Then Gatty went on her way like a wandering star and came to the mouth of a winding passage.

This is better, she said to herself. I'll pray for Lady Gwyneth in here. And then say all my other prayers. For Arthur and everyone.

This passage led nowhere. Or, rather, it twisted and tightened and led to a brick wall. When Gatty held up her candle, she saw the wall was completely covered with words and drawings and so were the rocks on either side of her. Not only *Yahweh* and JHVH and Ghost and *Dieu* and *Spiritus* and *Gott* and *Dominus* and Bread of Life and Lamb and True Light and *Dios* and all the other thousand names of the Holy Trinity (some of them Gatty puzzled out and recognised, some she had never heard of before), but scratched initials, rough drawings of women, men, children, dogs, boats, horses.

For a while, Gatty examined them, all these signs people had left behind them.

I wish you'd got here, Arthur. I keep thinking about how you set off for Jerusalem but had to return home, and I stayed home but had to set off for Jerusalem. You remember when I asked you about walking here?

Gatty stared at the brick wall. 'I know!' she exclaimed.

She pulled her little knife from its sheath. She scratched a line on the brick, and another one beneath it. Then a head and ears; four legs; a tail. Now Gatty cut two mounted figures. A boy in front, holding reins; a girl behind, with her arms round the boy's waist, her head resting on his back.

'Remember?' she asked. 'Me and you and Pip. So you're here now, you and me, and this is where we'll stay.' Carefully, she carved A and then G under the horse's belly and girth.

At this moment, Gatty heard the sound of tapping coming from back along the passageway. Irregular; insistent. It got louder.

I can't pray for Lady Gwyneth in here either, she said to herself. I'll have to find somewhere else.

With one last look at her carving, Gatty turned and walked back along the passage – and what she saw was a man with his back to her, chipping away pieces of holy rock with a chisel and a small hammer.

He can't do that, thought Gatty. This is Holy Sepulchre! He's robbing Jesus! It's sackliridge – or whatever the word is!

Then the man sensed someone was standing behind him. But seeing only Gatty, he just grinned.

Gatty lowered her eyes.

The man opened his right hand and showed Gatty three nuggets of rock. '*Ken?*' he said. '*Ken?*'

Gatty frowned. '*Ken?*' she repeated.

The man rubbed his left thumb and forefinger so close to her nose that it made her cross-eyed.

'No!' said Gatty. 'You're a thief! If we all do that, there soon won't be any church left.'

All afternoon, it seemed, Gatty searched for somewhere quiet to pray for Lady Gwyneth's soul, as she had vowed to do. She climbed creaking steps to balconies, she tucked herself into corners of chapels, she explored passageways.

Hall of night-sky; warren; chamber of echoes . . . Shuffles and murmurs and sobs, conversation, bursts of laughter, shouts and wails and songs: they all circled Gatty's head, indistinct and blurred.

Down one passage, she found three hook-nosed pilgrims –

two men and an old woman – facing the rock wall. The old woman cut off a white curl and tapped her forehead and, while the three of them chanted, she forefingered the curl into a crack in the wall. Then one of the men shaved off part of his moustache with a cut-throat and, baring his black teeth, he stuffed that into the wall. After them, the other man ripped open his tunic, as if he were a fieldworker on a hot day. He tore out a fistful of his chest-hair and jammed that into a fissure! Then the three of them chanted while he patted his heart.

I got the lock of Lady Gwyneth's hair, thought Gatty. She told me to leave half in Jerusalem and bury half in Griffith's grave.

Quickly, Gatty raised her gown, gnawed at the hem and drew out a few strands of Lady Gwyneth's hair. Watched by the three pilgrims, she wound them loosely round her little finger.

What shall I say, wondered Gatty. I'm not asking for a cure, like they are. I'm singing for a soul:

> 'You were a baby, you were a girl,
> Your father called you his pearl, his shining pearl.
>> Aiee! Aiee!
>
> You were the pilgrim Death took down for his wife,
> And you were a pilgrim all your life.
>> Aiee! Aiee!'

As Gatty cried 'Aiee!' for the second time, the three pilgrims joined in. 'I sing for your soul,' Gatty sang out, and then she hesitated. 'Yes, I know:

> I sing for your soul, not your flesh or bone.
> Jesus, I beg you, bring my Lady Gwyneth home.
>> Aiee! Aiee!'

Then Gatty pushed her fingertip as far as she could into a little hole in the wall and pulled it out again, leaving Lady Gwyneth's hair embedded deep inside the rock.

There, she thought. Part of you will be here for ever now.

No sooner had the three pilgrims bowed and gone on their way than the Saracens began to shout everyone out.

'No!' Gatty protested.

Brandishing clubs as large as marrows, the Saracens strode into each chapel and up to each balcony and along each passage, bawling and barking.

No! I can't go! I haven't prayed yet.

Gatty heard light steps. She screwed up her eyes and in frustration shook her head from side to side until her hair was a ball of twisting gold.

When she opened her eyes again, she saw the young Saracen boy, the one with the candle who had smiled at her and pursed his lips and blown over her.

Gatty looked at him, sharp-eyed. She shook her head.

Very seriously, the boy nodded.

'No,' said Gatty. And then, in a low, urgent voice. 'I got to stay. I got to.'

Perhaps the boy understood. He could hear Gatty's determination. He narrowed his dark eyes and opened his right hand. '*Bakchies*,' he said.

'What?'

'*Bakchies*.'

'What's *bakchies*?'

The boy fished in his pocket.

'Money!' said Gatty in disgust. 'All everyone wants is money. Don't you understand? I got to stay and pray for Lady Gwyneth.'

'*Bakchies*,' the boy said again.

'I haven't got none.'

Now, another wave of shouting boomed down the passage-

312

way, and the Saracen boy looked uneasily over his shoulder.

This time it was Gatty who understood – understood that the boy's sweet nature and his fear were in the balance. Gently, she nodded. And then, quite why she couldn't have said, she did exactly what the boy had done earlier: she pursed her lips and blew very softly into the boy's face.

The boy closed his eyes and opened them again. He smiled like a seraph. Then he reached up and gently, very gently, touched his right forefinger to Gatty's lips.

For a long time Gatty stayed in the rock passage, alone. The shouting became more distant, more occasional. Then she heard a thud as the great doors were closed; she could even hear the crunch-and-scrape of the key in the lock.

After this, there was nothing but the sound of silence: that, and the rock's husky voice when Gatty rubbed a shoulder against it, or wiggled the heel of her boot against it. The double-thump of her heartbeat. A slight whistling in her right ear.

Poor Snout, she thought. He's lost me again! He'll guess, won't he? He'll understand.

Still Gatty bided her time, brave and cautious as a hare. Then at last she tiptoed down the twisting passage and a few steps out into the hall of night-sky, heart of the warren, chamber of echoes.

Around her head, the massive building soared and stood like plates of armour, grand and unshakable. Gatty craned her neck and looked upwards and sideways; she looked all around her; and after a while this church, Holy Sepulchre, began to seem more like a mantle than armour. A strong cloak to shelter and protect her.

And yet, she thought, it's all incense smoke, all candlelight. Shimmering and trembling. As though it scarcely exists.

Then Gatty had an idea. She delved into her scrip and

triumphantly drew out the felt shoes, grubby now but still soft, still yellow, that Mansel had given her. She pulled off her boots and slipped them on.

I'll tell Mansel, she thought. I never knew I'd be so glad of them.

Gatty advanced slowly towards the very centre of the hall: like a child stepping from the safety of the beach into dark, deep water. She could hear she was quite breathless. She dropped onto her knees.

First, Gatty prayed for Snout. She told Jesus how bravely he had waited for her in Kyrenia, and asked Him to heal Snout's nose. 'It won't be too difficult,' she said. 'Anyhow, you can do everything. His lip's split halfway up to his nose, and his nostrils are too wide.'

Gatty thought of each of the pilgrims, but especially Nest. 'You got to be a father and a mother to her,' she told Jesus, 'especially if the others leave her behind in Venice. She's like a babe-in-arms.'

Then Gatty prayed for her mother. 'She used to sing to me,' she said, 'but that's all I can remember. If you can forgive me all my sins, can I see her again? My lady said I should ask you that.'

Gatty gulped. She prayed for little Dusty and for her grandmother who lay in their cottage for so many seasons, stiff and silent as a plank of wood; she prayed for her father. And after that she named each person she knew. At Caldicot. Then at Ewloe. It didn't take very long.

All right then, thought Gatty. All right! Her heart began to thump; she was shivering.

'Jesus,' she said out loud. 'Please listen now. Nothing's never mattered so much.' Her voice was jerky, and she took deep breaths and tried to steady it. 'Lady Gwyneth was coming to you here. She was, and her stomach burst inside her. You know about Griffith? Lady Gwyneth told me every-

314

thing, how she lay on him while he was asleep, and how terrible it was. She loved him. She did! She was always praying at his tiny grave and tending it.

'Jesus, I'm her messenger. Lady Gwyneth de Ewloe. It's near Chester. She was on her way to do penance for her soul, and I promised I'd come for her. Because of her, I'm learning to read and write and sing. She's changed my life, you know. Please, Jesus, please! Open your arms. Welcome her now to paradise.'

Gatty had started to sob. And each time she sniffed and almost stopped, she started again. For a long time, she remained kneeling at the heart of Holy Sepulchre.

Who am I, she thought. To be here alone in this most holy place in holy Jerusalem? I don't deserve this. I done nothing in my life. I'll make it different because of this, all my life, each day of it.

Through her tears, Gatty thanked Jesus for His grace. She asked Him to smile on the Saracen boy who let her stay in Holy Sepulchre.

'Breathe on him!' she whispered.

Then, Gatty began to sing. She sang and she sang. But when, next day, Snout asked her what she had sung, she couldn't really say.

'I sang psalms and that,' she told him. 'And songs without words. And a new song.'

'New?'

'I can't explain. A sort of song of everything. I mean, I made rock solid and gritty.'

'Rock is!' said Snout.

'I know, but it might not be, if I hadn't sung it so.'

Snout frowned.

'I made steps climb and passages twist, I made darkness blind, and candles waxen. I made light shine. In my song, I created them.'

Snout shook his head.

'With my head and heart, my flesh and blood, I made air breathe. I made air sing.'

'You and your notions,' Snout said fondly. 'You are a one.'

In the church, Gatty got to her feet. She took a deep breath and opened her arms wide.

She knew she had done what she had come to do, and honoured her solemn promise to Lady Gwyneth. And in her heart of hearts, she knew the truth of it. Jesus had heard her prayer.

Silent now and content, Gatty wandered for a long while around the hall of night-sky. And then, at some time during that August night, after dark, before dawn, she crept back down the narrow passage that led nowhere to check that she and Arthur and Pip were still there.

Gatty lay down on the naked rock. Blessed, she curled up like an unborn baby.

48

Brother Gabriel greeted Gatty and Snout warmly, and gave Gatty an amused look. 'I hear you got yourself locked in for the night.'

'And I waited outside all night,' said Snout. 'First I was cross, then I got worried.'

'So far as I know, it's the first time that's happened,' Brother Gabriel went on. 'You must have heard the Saracens' shouting.'

'Oh yes!' said Gatty in a matter-of-fact voice.

'And you ignored them?'

'Not exactly,' said Gatty. She told Brother Gabriel about the young Saracen boy, and how he'd blown in her face and she had blown in his.

The knight-brother smiled. 'You know what that means?' he asked.

Gatty shook her head. 'It was strange,' she said. 'I liked it.'

'He was blowing verses from the Koran over you,' the Hospitaller told her. 'To protect you and bless you.'

Gatty smiled broadly. 'They did and all,' she said.

'Now! I've some news for you,' said Brother Gabriel. 'Didn't you tell Sir Faramond how much you longed to see where Jesus was born?'

'Bethlehem!' Gatty and Snout exclaimed together.

Brother Gabriel smiled. 'As you know, Sir Faramond gave me money to pay for you here. But even more than that! He gave me extra so you could both go to Bethlehem!'

Gatty slowly shook her head.

'God bring him to paradise!' said Snout.

'I've arranged for Gregory and Janet to ride there with you,' Brother Gabriel told them.

Gatty clapped her hands.

'Bethlehem!' she cried.

Riding on donkeys, Gregory and Janet led Gatty and Snout through Dung Gate, and away from Jerusalem.

'How far is it?' Gatty asked. 'How many miles, did you say?'

'Five,' said Janet. 'God willing, we'll be there before noon.'

'I been there all my life,' Gatty told her. 'That's what it feels like. All the times I've heard about Mary and Jesus.'

The sky was forget-me-not, almost; the sun was hot but not scorching; an easy wind from the south, scented with thyme and rosemary, freshened their faces. Gatty and Snout were happy to be out of the city's swelter and sweat. And after visiting so many places where Jesus had suffered, they were joyous at the prospect of seeing the place where He had been born.

On their way, they rode through groves of orange trees, pomegranates and figs; and not far short of the village of Bethlehem, they stopped near a farmhouse to eat the unleavened bread, cheese and olives they had brought with them. Sheep and hens and goats strayed around them.

'I'm thirsty!' said Snout.

'That's why we've stopped here,' Janet said. 'The farmer lets us use his well.'

'At a price,' added Gregory.

'A young woman drowned here last year,' Janet told them. 'Not a pilgrim, I'm glad to say.'

'What happened?' asked Gatty.

'She toppled in while she was drawing water. Her friends could hear her, but they couldn't do anything.'

'They could have thrown down a rope,' Gatty said. 'Or tied ladders together.'

'The farmer told me it took more than a week to pull her out,' Gregory said.

'Never mind!' sighed Snout. 'Never mind! The water won't taste any different.'

Gatty screwed up her face. 'I'm not going to touch it,' she said.

'Water is water,' Snout replied.

On their way to the Church of the Nativity, the four of them rode up to a hillside cave.

'Then Herod the King slew all the children in Bethlehem and for miles around,' Gregory called out. 'All the children less than two years old. The Gospel of Saint Matthew.'

'And they threw their little bodies into this cave,' Janet went on. 'The holy bones of more than ten thousand children.'

Gatty and Snout made their way into the gloomy cave, and looked for bones. But they couldn't find any, not even a little finger or a toe.

'Not even a trotter!' Snout said. 'The Saracens got here first.'

Then Gregory and Janet led them into a second cave where a Saracen with a flaming brand was awaiting them. He showed them a rock wall shining with white ooze.

'Mary, mother of us all,' Janet called out, 'came up here and fed her baby in the cool of this cave. A drop of milk fell from her breast onto the rock, and from that day this cave has oozed.'

At last, Gatty and Snout reached the Church of the Nativity, built over the manger where Jesus was born. It was quite small compared to the Church of the Holy Sepulchre, and its thicket of shining marble pillars were as slender and beautiful as a forest of birch-trees. The roof was supported by cedar beams.

On the tips of her toes, Gatty crept down sixteen rock steps into the manger. She stared at a large silver star lying on the ground. She knelt and closed her eyes.

Before long, Gatty heard all around her a rushing sound. Like frothing water in a mountain stream. And then a distant whistling, as if one of her ears were blocked. Her breathing lengthened. She felt warm. Utterly at ease.

After a while, Gatty opened her eyes and blinked, and the rushing and whistling faded. She smiled an inward smile. It felt like I was unborn, she thought. In my mother's womb, beginning again. Before I knew anything about the world.

I can't remember my mother. Not properly. She hummed like a bee, she did, hummed and rocked me and sang softly:

How many miles to Bethlehem?

Bethlehem, was it? Or Beverleyham? Or was it Babylon?

How many miles to Bethlehem?
Not very far.
Shall we find the stable room
Lit by a star?

How many miles to Bethlehem?
Three score and ten.
Can I get there by candle-light?
Yes, and back again.

For a while, Gatty watched other pilgrims to the church laying objects on the marble floor around the silver star. Bones and coins and keys and palm-badges, phials and flasks and crucifixes: they begged Jesus and His mother Mary to bless them, and then they picked them up again and put them away in their pockets and scrips.

Gatty had an idea. She delved to the bottom of her scrip and fished out the gold ring – a woman with a baby in her arms, holding out something to his mother.

It's an apple, thought Gatty. It must be! The apple of all our sins. It's Jesus and He's promising Mary He will redeem us.

Gatty inspected the inside of the ring. A DE C! Lovingly, she squeezed it, and then she laid it beside the manger – and she didn't take her eyes off it for one moment until she had put it back into her scrip.

Saracens were selling bones and badges and other mementoes in the church cloister.

'I know you,' said Snout, 'you'll want to buy something.'

'I just want to look.'

'No,' said Snout firmly. 'We still need to pay for our passage to Venice. We'll need every coin we have.'

All the same, Gatty went off on her own and looked at the Saracens' stalls. Round and round she walked, and round again; and then, biting her lower lip in excitement, for the first time in her life she did buy something! She hid it in her scrip, and almost ran back to Snout.

'Well?' he asked.

'I bought something!' she said. Her eyes were shining. 'I did!'

'Gatty!'

'I can't tell you! Not now! It's for Oliver.'

'Who?'

'Our priest. He wrote to Austin about teaching me to read and write.'

Despite himself, Snout couldn't help smiling.

'It's all right,' said Gatty. 'It didn't cost much at all. And I'm as rich as three kings now!'

Before they left the Church of the Nativity, Gatty and Snout celebrated Mass, and on their slow way back, they visited another well – not to draw water but to see where the Star in the East had fallen to earth.

Gatty peered in and right down. Taking great care not to topple over, she marvelled at the silver fragments still dancing and leaping in the dark water.

The day's light began to drain out of the sky. As they rode back to Jerusalem, Gatty and Snout noisily sucked blood oranges and began to talk about Sir Faramond's and Lady Saffiya's invitation.

49

'I can hear him saying it,' Snout told Gatty.

'Who?'

'Sir Faramond. About me working in the kitchen, and you speaking English and reading to him and Lady Saffiya. "To begin with," he told us, "you'll say you must get back to England . . ."'

'Are you telling me you want to stay?' Gatty asked Snout.

'No, I'm going home. I've got to for Hew and, besides, I'm longing to see him. The things he says! You should hear him. But you, Gatty . . .'

'Haven't got anyone,' Gatty said in a flat voice. 'I know.'

'You could be happy with Sir Faramond and Lady Saffiya,' said Snout. 'I think they'd value you, and look after you, and you'd be living in a palace. Don't get me wrong. I'd miss you all the way back. I'd think of you every day of my life.'

'I got to go home, Snout,' said Gatty. 'Even if I don't know where home is. When I think about it, you know, the green hills and the way the air is, fresh and damp on my face, and the smell of the earth after it's rained, it makes me feel sick, almost.'

Snout smiled.

'And I got to see Nest in Venice,' Gatty went on. 'And I got duties at Ewloe. I got to dig some of Lady Gwyneth's hair into Griffith's grave, and give something to Austin.'

'What?' asked Snout.

'And then there's everyone at Caldicot,' Gatty hurried on.

'Beginning with Arthur,' said Snout.

Gatty looked at him under her eyelashes. She spread out her arms. 'I know this is the Holy Land,' she said, 'but it's all so sandy and so thirsty. So hot! All these palm-trees! I can't explain it exactly, but this isn't my air.'

'That does explain it,' said Snout. 'Well, we had better tell Brother Gabriel.'

'Sir Faramond and Lady Saffiya will be very disappointed,' Brother Gabriel told them with a gentle smile.

'It's so difficult,' said Gatty.

'When they paid for us here,' added Snout.

'No one's never asked me to choose,' Gatty said. 'Not like this.'

'They'll understand,' the knight-brother told them. 'To be honest . . . I'd go back. That's what I'd do, in your position.'

'Thank you, sir,' said Snout, sounding relieved.

'Yes, of course you must go home,' Brother Gabriel assured them. 'Snout, your son is waiting for you.'

'I know!' said Snout, bright-eyed.

'And you, Gatty, you're so young.'

'Sixteen,' said Gatty.

'When is your birthday?'

'About now. After the harvest, that's what my father told me.'

'Sixteen and lovely,' said the Hospitaller.

Gatty lowered her eyes and smiled.

'Your husband . . .'

'Husband!'

'. . . and your children.'

'I haven't got none!'

'I know,' said Brother Gabriel. 'Not yet. But they're waiting for you.'

'They can wait, then,' said Gatty, smiling.

'All the same,' the Hospitaller said, 'you'll have to be patient until we find a ship to take you home. It may take weeks, months even.'

Gatty sighed.

Snout looked quite pained, quite troubled.

'There are many sights here you haven't seen yet,' the knight-brother told them. 'Anyhow, patience is a virtue.'

But now that Gatty and Snout had made up their minds to go home, they found it difficult to be much interested in anything else.

The next morning, Snout failed to come to the refectory to break his fast. Gatty waited until she was sure all the other male pilgrims had gone out for the day and then, breaking the Hospital's strict rules, she entered the male dormitory.

The cook was lying on his mattress, staring wide-eyed at the ceiling.

'Snout! What are you doing?'

Snout didn't reply.

'Snout, you're worrying me. Please get up now.'

'What's the point?' Snout replied.

'Snout!' said Gatty. 'Heaven helps those who help themselves. Come on! I'm not leaving this dormitory until you get up.'

But Snout completely refused to get up, and so Gatty had to go out on her own for the day. She went to see the kitchen where the Paschal lamb was cooked for Jesus' Last Supper with His disciples, but her heart wasn't in it. She kept thinking about Snout; and she had nothing like enough money to buy an Indulgence, forgiving her for her past sins, or even to buy a pair of the light cork shoes everyone in Jerusalem was wearing.

What with my sins, thought Gatty, and my callouses and warts and all, I'd never get halfway up to paradise, not even in those shoes. Not in Mansel's shoes, neither. Mind you, if

Snout goes on like this, we won't even get back to England.

The next morning was no better. When Gatty went to see Snout, he just shook his head and sighed deeply.

'What's wrong?' Gatty asked him. 'Snout! What's wrong? Brother Gabriel's trying to find a ship for us. Hew's waiting for you in Ewloe.'

Snout's eyes filled with tears.

'Shall I bring you some food? You must eat.'

Snout shook his head again. 'I'm all right,' he said. 'You go out, girl. See what you can.'

Unhappily, Gatty went off on her own for a second day. She spat on the threshold of Pontius Pilate's house. She walked up to the Garden of Gethsemane. She walked down to the Golden Gate that will open only when Jesus enters Jerusalem again, and there she said prayers for everyone at Caldicot, as Oliver the priest had asked her to do, but all the time she kept worrying about Snout.

Brother Gabriel advised Gatty that she could do nothing about Snout's deep melancholy but watch and pray. So she went back to the dormitory, and sat silently beside Snout, and prayed. And later in the day, she joined company with other groups of pilgrims who still kept arriving at the Hospital of Saint John: stately black-skinned monks from Ethiopia, men and women from Armenia wearing coats of many colours; and a very rich family from Byzantium, almond-eyed, with their two priests, and two cooks, their stableman and at least a dozen servants – a whole retinue.

Reluctantly, Gatty went with them to see the grave where Lazarus lay dead before Jesus lifted him back to life again.

I wish Jesus would bring Snout properly back to life again, she thought.

After this, Gatty and the other pilgrims trooped up to the mosque the Saracens had built right over the tombs of King Solomon and King David, and she listened to the muezzin high in the minaret summoning people to prayer. But she kept talking to herself about Nest and Venice, and catching up with the others, about Syndod, and above all about Snout's melancholy. After the fifth day without him, Gatty came back to the Hospital thoroughly dispirited, thinking she had seen quite enough of Jerusalem.

Brother Gabriel was standing in the courtyard.

'I've got something to tell you,' he said. 'Where's Snout?'

Gatty shook her head in desperation.

'Not still!'

'Five days,' said Gatty. 'He hasn't eaten a thing. He's asleep for most of the time.'

'I'll go and get him up myself,' Brother Gabriel said. 'You wait here.'

Before long, Brother Gabriel brought Snout out of the dormitory. He was very pale – and he wouldn't even look Gatty in the eye.

'Now, then!' said the Hospitaller. 'Jesus must be watching over you.'

'What do you mean?' asked Gatty.

'There are two English traders here in Jerusalem.'

For the first time, Snout raised his eyes. Gatty saw how red and heavy-lidded they were.

'Yes,' said Brother Gabriel. 'They've been here for a week, and they're staying at a hostel outside Fish Gate. They came here this afternoon to ask us for help. They want an escort to Jaffa.'

Gatty stared at Brother Gabriel, made a fist of her right hand and banged her forehead.

'I know who they are,' she said. 'I do! I overheard them talking about profit and stopping in Cyprus to buy salt. Inside Holy Sepulchre.'

'They're the ones,' Brother Gabriel said. 'They're depend-able men. Honourable men. And they're prepared to sail you

327

all the way – the whole way to England!'

'You can't sail over mountains,' said Gatty. 'Not unless you're a cloud.'

Snout murmured something.

'What's that, Snout?' Brother Gabriel asked. 'Isn't this the news you've been waiting for?'

'We can't, though,' said Snout. 'We haven't got enough money.'

'Listen!' said the knight-brother. 'I've already paid for your passage out of our funds. These two traders have their own galley and they're sailing to Alexandria.'

'Where's Alexandria?' asked Gatty.

'In Egypt. And then on west through the Mediterranean.'

'West,' Snout repeated. 'Not to Venice?'

The Hospitaller shook his head.

'Not to Venice!' Gatty said very loudly. 'We can't, then.'

'Why not?' Brother Gabriel asked.

'Nest!' exclaimed Gatty. 'And Simona. And Lady Gwyneth's grave. Everything!'

Brother Gabriel lowered his eyes.

'Syndod!' Gatty cried. 'I can't leave her behind.'

For a moment the three of them were silent.

'It's the only way, girl,' Snout mumbled.

The knight-brother slowly nodded. 'I believe it is,' he said. 'No ships are sailing between here and Venice this side of Christmas, not that I know of. And even if they do, it'll be too late for you to cross the mountains before winter comes.'

Gatty frowned and shook her head. She put her hand into her cloak pocket, and closed it round her little carving of Syndod.

'They're leaving in the morning,' Brother Gabriel said.

'Tomorrow?' cried Gatty.

There were lights in Snout's eyes. He began to smile.

'A passage all the way to England!' the Hospitaller said. 'To my mind, this is a little miracle.'

That night, Brother Gabriel sat with Gatty and Snout at supper and Gatty was much relieved to see Snout eating again. But her heart ached at not being able to see Nest in Venice, and lay flowers on Lady Gwyneth's grave, and collect Syndod from the livery stables.

The Hospitaller pinned palm badges onto each of them.

'You are palmers now,' he told them. 'Wear these palms of Jericho and everyone will know you've been to Jerusalem.'

'Amen,' said Gatty.

'Amen,' said Snout.

'In making this pilgrimage, you have given other people a grave and beautiful example,' Brother Gabriel told them. 'I will escort you myself to Jaffa, and I will pray for you. God will guide you safely home.'

With tears in his kind eyes, the knight-brother embraced each of them.

Before she went to her dormitory, Gatty hugged Snout.

'I been so worried,' she said in a small voice. And then, louder: 'I been sick for days, I have.'

Snout held Gatty tight. 'You're doing this for me,' he said. 'I know you are. Not going to Venice.'

Gatty sniffed.

Without letting go of her, Snout eased Gatty away from him. 'I'm sorry, girl,' he said, and Gatty saw that his eyes were moist. 'Something got in my head,' he said. 'It stopped me from hoping and doing and everything.'

'You saved me,' said Gatty. 'You were so . . . constant. You stayed in Kyrenia and saved me, so I'm standing by you.'

'I'm sorry, girl,' Snout said again.

'Tomorrow!' said Gatty, half-eager, half-fearful. 'Tomorrow!'

Snout nodded.

'Well! We done everything. Almost everything. Oh, Snout! Your nose!'

Snout shook his head gloomily. 'I didn't think it would,' he said. 'Not really. I did try to hope, though.'

'It's quite all right as it is,' Gatty told him. She picked up her candle and held it between her hands. 'That song keeps going round in my head:

> How many miles to Bethlehem?
> Three score miles and ten.

Come on! You sing it too.'

Then Snout quietly joined in, out of tune:

> 'Can we get there by candle-light?
> Yes, and back again.'

'I wish we could!' Gatty exclaimed.

'What?'

'Get back by candle-light. It took so long, so long to get here.' Gatty stared into the flame of her candle. 'I know,' she said.

'What?' asked Snout, and he yawned.

'I'm going to pray for Nest and Syndod, and I'll say one more prayer for Lady Gwyneth, just to make sure. Then, before I go to sleep, I'll pray for us, Snout. I'll pray we get home before this candle burns out.'

50

'Some people say the whole point of a journey is to reach your destination.'

Kit the Trader looked round his cabin, blue eyes sparkling, white eyebrows twitching with a life of their own.

'But some clever people,' added his brother Raven, 'say the whole point of a journey is the journey.'

'Our lady did,' Gatty replied. 'Lady Gwyneth. She said you're reborn each day on a pilgrimage.'

'Well!' said Kit the Trader. 'You know what Saracens say?'

'What?' asked Snout.

Kit the Trader looked enquiringly at Gatty and Raven, and then at the quartermaster and the ship's two cooks.

'Travellers are blessed, even infidels! Five times blessed! They leave their worries at home; they learn about foreign people and foreign lands; they enjoy new company; they may trade and make a profit; and when they get back home, everyone's glad to see them.'

'But isn't there a saying,' Gatty asked, 'about how getting back home is never as good as thinking about it?'

'What I say,' asserted Kit the Trader, 'is the whole point of a journey is exactly that: getting back home. Here's a story to prove it.'

Gatty sighed with pleasure; she leaned back against the cabin wall and inched her buttocks forward.

'Long ago,' began Kit the Trader, 'and not so long, there was a pedlar . . .'

Like that man who stole Sian's cat and turned her into white mittens, thought Gatty.

'. . . and this pedlar had a dream that he must walk to London. London Bridge!'

Gatty and Snout caught each other's eyes, and gave each other a knowing smile.

'London Bridge!' exclaimed Kit the Trader. 'He'd never been a tenth as far before. But he couldn't get this dream out of his head, and the next night he had the same dream again: a man was standing over him, dressed in a surcoat as red as blood, and urging him, "Go to London Bridge! Go, good will come of it."'

'So that's what the pedlar did. He walked with his mastiff all the way to London Bridge. But when he got there, he didn't know why he'd come, or who to talk to. He felt completely lost.'

'Gatty got lost in London,' Snout remarked. 'Didn't you, girl?'

'Sshh!' said Gatty.

'That night,' said Kit the Trader, 'the pedlar stayed in a tavern.'

'The Three Archers?' enquired Snout.

'It was!' said Kit the Trader. 'How did you know?' But he put his finger up to stop Snout from explaining. 'Well! Three days went by. The pedlar admired a dancing bear. He saw a band of pilgrims set off for Walsingham, singing. But he was beginning to feel rather stupid.

'"Why did we bother to come?" he asked his mastiff. "You tell me that."'

'This was when a shopkeeper waddled up to him. She looked more like a hen than a woman, she did.

'"What are you up to?" she demanded. "Are you waiting for me to turn my back? I've been watching you loitering around for the past three days."'

332

'When the shopkeeper heard why the pedlar had walked all the way to London Bridge, she cackled with laughter. She nearly laid an egg!

'"Only fools follow their dreams!" she exclaimed.

'The pedlar looked at her so dismally. He was almost penniless, and very tired, and more than one hundred miles from home.

'"We all have dreams," the shopkeeper told him. "Only last night I dreamed about a pedlar with a pot of gold at the bottom of his garden. I ask you! Nonsense!" She patted the pedlar on the shoulder and tutted. "Take my advice and go back home."'

Kit the Trader looked round his cabin. Slowly he raised his left knee, his right knee, left, right; he reached out, he hugged himself; then he began to dig.

'He dug and he dug,' said the captain, 'and right next to his gnarled hawthorn, the pedlar prised out of the clammy earth a very large metal pot.'

Everyone in the cabin held their breath.

'Yes,' said Kit the Trader, 'and it was packed with gold coins.'

'What did he do with them?' asked Gatty.

Somewhere down on deck, two musicians began to play a pipe and fiddle. Then a third joined in, lightly tapping a tambourine. And a woman with a dark voice started to sing.

In the middle of Kit the Trader's cabin, a dozen little flies gyrated and twisted, as if they were tying complicated knots.

'Do with them?' Kit the Trader repeated. 'Kept some, gave some away, paid for the church to be rebuilt.'

'All because he followed his dream,' Snout added.

'You see?' said Kit the Trader. 'The whole point of the pedlar's journey was to get back home again.'

'We were in a tavern,' Gatty told Kit the Trader, 'and a French nun told us a story about a Saracen who walked all the way from Baghdad to Cairo because he had a dream he'd find his fortune there.'

'And did he?' asked Kit the Trader.

'Only when he got home again,' said Gatty. 'Under a fountain. It's very strange. Your story and that one, they're the same but not the same.'

Down on deck, the tambourine trembled and the woman's dark voice became more wild and insistent; in the cabin, the insects whirled and giddied.

'They're Saracens from Algiers,' Kit the Trader said. 'We're sailing them home.'

'Their dream-songs are sailing them home,' Gatty said, without thinking.

Kit the Trader clapped his hands. 'Exactly!' he exclaimed. 'Songs! Stories! They help us on our way.'

Getting home is not the point of my journey though, thought Gatty. The point was to go to Jerusalem for Lady Gwyneth, and pray for her soul. Gatty crossed herself and shook her head. Anyhow, where is my home? With Lady Gwyneth dead, what am I going to do?

For many days, Gatty thought about the Holy Land and her six-month pilgrimage. She thought about cradling Babolo in her arms, and Mansel so shyly giving her those soft yellow shoes, about listening to Aenor, the novice at Vézelay, telling her how she had to escape, about unbuckling Saviour's bridle on the precipice, and finding the gold ring on the beach of Saint Nicholas, and what Arthur would say when she gave it back to him.

One morning, sitting cross-legged on deck and listening to the Saracen musicians, Gatty thought to herself: I can't work it out! Oliver says hell's mouth is wide and waiting for Saracens. He told Arthur some of them have tails. And I know the Pope says they're God's enemies and we must kill them. Kill them or drive them out of Jerusalem, every single one.

Gatty frowned. They do look different, I know. Their clothes and that. But the Saracens I've met . . . Gatty began to tick them off on her fingers: those three traders in Venice; Osman, the astronomer; Signor Umberto's slave, Mansur; the musicians in Kyrenia; all the people in the pound at Acre – the snake-charmer, the conjuror and the crowd of laughing children, the wise old man; then Lady Saffiya; and that young boy in Holy Sepulchre . . .

Gatty shook her head, thoughtfully. I know some Saracens are evil, like those Bedouin who murder pilgrims, but that doesn't mean they all are. Anyhow, some Christians are evil, too. The doctor's apprentices in the mountains. Those two boys who attacked me in Candia. And what about Gobbo? What about him? He didn't care at all about his passengers – he only cared for money. Maybe Saracens and Christians are the same: good and bad, all mixed up.

While Gatty was still thinking, Snout came and squatted down beside her.

'Horrible!' he said, with a cheerful smile.

'What?'

'The wild way she sings.'

'No, it's not.'

'So's her head-dress.'

'Snout!' protested Gatty.

'A box with a frill on top, and white towels hanging down on each side and at the back.' Snout flapped his hands and grinned. 'And a black veil over her face. I don't know!'

Days passed. Gatty watched seawater so broken it chuckled and laughed; she marvelled at fish leaping and flying; she was silenced by a starburst; she squinted at the ruined tower of a lighthouse so tall it climbed right into the sky.

'Before winds from heaven blew the top off,' Kit the Trader told her, 'it was four hundred and fifty feet high. You could see it blinking from more than forty miles away. People call it one of the seven wonders of the world.'

'What are the others?' asked Gatty.

'That depends on who you listen to. The three huge pyramids – they're only a day's ride from here. The hanging gardens of Babylon. And then the Colossus, an enormous bronze man . . . he was toppled by an earthquake.' Kit the Trader rubbed his chin. 'Me,' he said, 'I think the greatest wonder is my children running out, calling and crying, and my wife waiting for me when I get home.'

Gatty shook her head, and sniffed.

'Your mother? Your father? They'll be glad to see you.'

'Dead,' said Gatty.

'Brothers, then. Sisters.'

'No,' said Gatty.

Kit the Trader looked at her kindly. 'Journeys change us,' he told her. 'They enable us. They make things possible.'

Sailing west through the Inner Sea, the sea in the middle of the world, the galley always had the morning sun at her back, driving her on, and the softer evening sun – on its bed of pink and rose – calmly awaiting her. For days on end the etesian wind waffled from the north-west, good-natured and gentle; then somewhere far south, over the desert, it caught fire and came rushing out of Africa again, breathing flames.

'When you're on deck,' Raven told Gatty, 'you must keep your head and face covered. This wind carries sand and eats people alive.'

But even when she wound her pilgrim's scarf around her face and neck, Gatty couldn't prevent dust and sandgrains from getting into her ears and nostrils and between her teeth.

The merchant galley zig-zagged between dry islands and scruffy ports on the African coast. Sicily and Malta, Sousse and Tunis, Bune, Sardinia, Algiers: a litany of names, a salt-spray of syllables.

The crew unloaded bars of smelted iron, anchors, locks,

brass cauldrons and pewter plates, bulky rolls of cloth, boxes full of hides, goatskins and fox-pelts, a few sacks of beeswax, barrels of saffron, walrus tusks, tapestries, baskets piled with amber. In gloomy warehouses and fonduks, noisy souks and bazaars, and sitting on bollards and upturned boats, Kit the Trader and Raven bargained and exchanged them for casks of olive oil, barrels of red wine and sweet white wine, sacks of sugar, glittering blocks of salt, hard white soap, layers of linen, silks and samite and brocades, costly spices and perfumes. They measured with rods and weighed with scales; they haggled and argued; they laughed and wagged forefingers; then they clasped hands, and paid the balance with pieces of silver.

As soon as the galley had passed between the Pillars of Hercules into the Atlantic Ocean, the sea somehow became much bigger, with huge swells and deep troughs. Sailing north along the coast of Portugal, Gatty began to wonder more often what her life would be like when she got back to the Marches.

When you're a pilgrim, she thought, people honour you, they do. They welcome you and feed you and help you on your way. Brother Antony at Saint Mary of the Mountain. Brother Gabriel. We'd never be here now except for them.

And when you're on a pilgrimage, you're free to choose. You can choose when to set off in the morning and when to rest, and sometimes you can choose what you want to eat. I never chose nothing in my life before.

Being a pilgrim is a kind of escape, it is, but in the end you got to go back, don't you? What if I have to work on the land again? Will I wish I was sitting by that fountain and watching Sir Faramond's fish?

I know what I thought in Holy Sepulchre about my whole life being different now, but how can it be? I can read and write, but without Lady Gwyneth . . .

'What will happen?' Gatty asked Snout. 'Without Lady Gwyneth.'

Snout scratched the back of his neck. 'Too many bugs on this boat!' he complained.

'And all!' agreed Gatty. 'My arms are all swollen.'

'Well,' said Snout, 'it's different for me, girl. I got Hew. He'll be six very soon.'

'Dusty's ten,' said Gatty. 'Except he died.'

'None of us knows what's going to happen,' said Snout, and he wiped his nose with the back of his hand. 'That's the truth of it.'

'Maybe it's best if Nest stayed behind in Venice,' Gatty said. 'It is if Sei loves her and marries her. She'll be showing by now.'

'She'll be scared to death,' said Snout. 'What I want to know is, who will be our new lord? Will the Earl of Chester appoint someone? Will young Llewelyn see his chance and try to seize the castle?'

'When I think about home,' Gatty said, 'I think about Caldicot. It's where I was before I knew it. Where me and Dusty picked up mast for the pigs, and me and Arthur got them bulls apart, and my mother sang me stories. I wish I could remember them. It's where I was going to be betrothed to Jankin, and where Arthur . . .'

'This Arthur!' said Snout, smiling. 'What is he to you?'

Gatty stared at Snout, wide-eyed. 'Oh Snout!' she cried. 'He's the person – the one person – I can always tell everything to. I tell my heart to Arthur. But now! Now he's a knight and he's going to marry Winnie.'

'You can still talk to him,' Snout said.

Gatty shook her head slowly. 'Winnie will stop him.' She gave a heartfelt sigh. 'She makes me feel so worthless.'

'That you're not!' said Snout loudly.

'Will the others be home by now?' Gatty asked.

'Not for several weeks yet,' Snout told her. 'Not by my reckoning.'

'I want to hear about everything! And I got to talk to Austin.'

'And give him something,' said Snout.

'How do you know?'

'You said so, in Jerusalem. What is it?'

Gatty almost told Snout about her silver seal, but she heard Lady Gwyneth's voice, warning her, and thought better of it.

'Go on!' Snout urged her.

'Nothing,' said Gatty. 'A dragon.'

'You've got to talk to Austin about a dragon?'

Gatty nodded.

'I keep thinking,' Snout said slowly, 'how you're, well, you're . . .'

'Betwixt and between,' said Gatty.

'You are,' said Snout. 'You're not a field-girl. Not no more. And not a chamber-servant.'

'I know,' said Gatty in a low voice.

'But you're not . . . well-born.'

'What am I, then?'

'I keep thinking,' said Snout, 'you could be a nun.'

Gatty yelped.

'I mean, what with your singing and reading and writing.'

'Oliver thought that,' Gatty told him. 'So did Sir John until he found out how much it cost.'

'You see?' said Snout.

'No,' said Gatty. 'I want to be in this world, not out of it.'

'And marry, you mean?'

Gatty gave Snout the ghost of a smile. 'I don't know.'

'I'll tell you what,' said Snout. 'You can come and live with us, girl. Hew and me. We'll rub along together until we all know what's what.'

Keeping within sight of the coast of Spain, Kit and Raven sailed their galley east into the Bay of Biscay.

'A ship full of pilgrims sank here two years ago,' Raven informed Gatty and Snout cheerfully.

Gatty looked across the heaving grey water and imagined. She thought of Simona telling her how her father had been drowned, and more than one thousand Venetians with him.

'They were on their way to Saint James of Compostela,' Raven said.

'I heard of that,' Gatty replied. 'You remember, Snout? In France? We crossed the road to Compostela.'

'Yes,' said Raven, 'the Bay of Biscay is the home of storms.'

Before long the little galley began to call in at a string of little and larger ports.

At Bordeaux, Kit and Raven rolled aboard casks of claret; at La Rochelle they treated Gatty and Snout to delicious little tarts flavoured with cowslips and gooseberries, and beakers of sweet white wine; and at Nantes, the rogue of a harbourmaster spoke reasonably good English.

'I know you come from England before you open your lips,' he told Gatty.

'How?'

'Sunburn, yes, but peaches. Pale pink roses.'

'What do you mean?' asked Gatty.

'The English complexion.'

'What's complexion?'

The harbourmaster smiled and rubbed his right thumb and forefinger. '*Le teint* . . . the colour of your face.'

'Freckles and all!' said Gatty gaily.

And then, before she realised what he was doing, the harbourmaster stepped forward, grasped her shoulders and boldly kissed Gatty on the cheek!

Gascony, Poitou, Anjou . . . At last, with a song in her sails, Kit and Raven's galley rounded Cape Finisterre in

Brittany and passed Mont Saint Michel. She headed straight for Normandy and Flanders . . .

Very early on the nineteenth morning of November, the galley weighed anchor for the last time and eased out of the port of Damme.

Almost all day, Gatty stood by the bowsprit, gazing ahead, as the boat bumped and bored through the iron-clad ocean. She stared at the great unhurried galleons of fleecy cloud and, beneath them, hastening, the muddy tails and tatters. She watched the diving terns, the skuas and black cormorants and all the swirling, screaming seabirds she had no names for. She remembered how – it seemed so long before – Snout had dropped his precious flower-stone overboard, the one Hew had given him.

It was just after noon.

And it was unmistakable: the long line, low and misty-blue, darker than the falling sky, lighter than the leaping sea, growing along the western horizon.

Gatty's heart leaped too.

'Snout!' she yelled. 'Snout!'

'What?' called Snout, as he trundled along the deck. 'What is it, girl?'

Gatty pulled back her shoulders; she pointed. 'Look!' she cried. 'Our England!'

Time is such a trickster!

It actually took Kit the Trader's snub-nosed boat ninety-nine days to sail from Jaffa to the port of Lynn in England. But to Gatty, then and later, it seemed like one sea-dream, a waking dream punctuated by great wonders and small mercies, horseshoe harbours, charmed hours ashore, faces, glimpses, storms and sunsets, songs, stories, parts of stories. It seemed like a journey that took as long as it takes for a candle to burn down.

51

Rain-ghosts arching their backs and long-legging it across pearly fields; sopping, green fog; pale, cool sunlight, telling it slant. No two days were the same. No two hours. The weather was more like early April than late November.

For six days Gatty and Snout made their way across the flat chest of England, and everyone they met told them the same story. The weather had been like this for month after month. Topsy-turvy. Arsy-versy. Everywhere the harvest had failed. Come January, February, famine would open his mouth and howl. Nursing mothers would be unable to feed their babies. Children would starve. The funeral bell would be busy.

As they walked west, Gatty and Snout kept asking the way to the Marches, Chester, Ewloe. But no one knew; no one had even heard of them.

'Wales, then,' said Gatty. 'What about Wales?'

Some people shrugged; some reassured them they were on the right road without knowing; and some waved vaguely to the west.

On the seventh afternoon, a messenger trotted up behind them. He wouldn't have bothered to stop, but Gatty grabbed the end of his horse's tail.

'The Marches!' she demanded. 'Which way for the Marches?'

The messenger winced at being asked something so

342

painfully obvious. 'These are the Marches,' he told them, waving straight ahead. 'You're on the doorstep.'

'Chester?' asked Snout.

The messenger screwed up his eyes. 'I certainly hope not,' he said. 'This is the Middle March. The way to Shrewsbury.'

'Shrewsbury,' said Gatty. 'I heard of that.'

'You'll get there tonight,' the messenger added. 'Since you're on foot, it's three days north from there to Chester – one day south to Ludlow.'

'Ludlow!' cried Gatty. 'God bless you! And keep you!'

The messenger peered down his nose. 'And save you!' he said with a meagre smile. 'If He can. Now, if you don't mind . . .'

'Snout!' exclaimed Gatty as soon as they were alone. 'Oh, Snout! We're so near to Caldicot.'

'We are?' Snout said carefully.

'We can go there on our way to Ewloe! We can, can't we?'

Snout knew he had no choice.

'We'll see everyone!' Gatty cried. 'Everything! You'll be glad.'

Next morning, the two pilgrims walked through the Middle March, rejoicing in its sloping fields and secret hollows, its clothing of oakwoods and beechwoods, still ochre and copper and rust.

At noon, they had to climb a rise so steep they had no idea what they would see over the top. And then they saw! Half the coloured world, and Wales blue-grey and trembling, as if it were still taking shape.

Quite late that afternoon, their track led them along a hissing stream, and through a widening valley. The hills stood back on either side.

'I don't know where we are,' Gatty told Snout, 'yet I know we're almost there. I know it.'

Above the manor house, the scarlet flag was fluttering. The

great copper beech was still in leaf, whispering.

Gatty felt for Snout's left forearm through his cloak; she linked both her hands around it, and squeezed it.

Snout made the sign of the cross. 'Amen,' he said. 'Amen, girl.'

And Gatty? She was like that strange, end-of-November weather: one moment alight, radiant; the next, shuddering, her eyes brimming with bright tears.

52

Gatty gave Snout a shy smile.

'Ready?' she asked. Her voice was husky.

But they'd only taken a few steps when she grabbed Snout's forearm again. 'Not so fast! I got to see everything.'

To Gatty, it all looked just the same and yet different. As if it had shrunk, or she had grown much taller.

And no, not just the same. Not entirely.

'Look!' said Gatty. 'That's Grunter.'

On the other side of the sty, Grunter pricked both ears. Then he came lumbering towards them.

'No!' Gatty exclaimed. 'He's lost an eye, he has.'

After this, Gatty began to notice one thing after another: an extra beehive; wooden tiles missing from Merlin's cottage or, at least, the cottage where he used to live before he disappeared; the elm fallen right across the Little Lark; the drooping, spotted leaves on the walnut-tree.

'Not so fast!' Gatty instructed Snout. 'I got to think.'

But how can you think clearly when each thing you see reminds you of something else?

Anyhow, the sounds of bright voices calling out to one another interrupted Gatty.

It was Sian de Caldicot with Tanwen and Joan, the village-woman, waving their shining saw-tooth knives, cutting branches of spiky red-eyed holly and yellow-eyed mistletoe, pulling dusty ropes of ivy away from the trunks of oaks, severing green tendons of stubborn, gristly yew. They were so busy that they didn't see the two pilgrims in their dark cloaks and sombre hats, standing under the walnut-tree.

Gatty watched them. It's like they're living in another life of mine, she thought. I know them but I don't.

'Sshh!' she whispered, not that Snout had said anything or even made a sound. 'Nain's Footsteps! You know, Snout. Let's creep up on them.'

Sian and Tanwen and Joan didn't notice the two pilgrims until they were only twenty paces or so away, and when they did they froze. They gripped their knives, as if Gatty and Snout were woodwoses, Welsh robbers, or even worse.

But then Gatty raised her left arm and swept off her broad-brimmed hat, and all her golden curls bubbled and boiled, and Sian yelled with excitement and ran straight at her and launched herself into Gatty's arms.

When Gatty had extricated herself, she embraced Tanwen and Joan too, and then Snout locked hands with all three of them. To begin with, they all just looked at one another, smiling but speechless; then they all tried to talk at the same time.

'God's gift!' exclaimed Tanwen in her sing-song voice. 'On this first day of Advent!'

'I know!' Gatty cried, opening her arms to the pile of holly and ivy and mistletoe and yew. 'I mean, I didn't, but I do now.'

'You're talking different,' Joan said tartly.

'I'm not!' protested Gatty.

'Gatty!' yelped Sian. 'I thought you'd never come back.'

'Who are you, then?' Joan asked Snout.

'Snout,' said Snout.

'Aha!' said Joan, and she sucked her cheeks. 'Snout. You're not Gatty's . . .'

'No, no!' said Gatty, grinning. 'Snout's my friend, and he's the bravest man in the world. Aren't you, Snout!'

'Why?' asked Sian. And then, without waiting for an answer, 'What are you wearing? What's this red cross? Look at your boots! You're so muddy!' She kept poking and stroking Gatty as if she needed to make absolutely sure that she was real.

'You heard about the harvest failing?' Tanwen asked.

'Two more mouths!' said Joan. 'Sir John won't thank you.'

'You look like scarecrows,' Sian told them. 'Christian scarecrows. And you stink!'

'Where have you come from?' Tanwen asked.

'Shrewsbury,' said Snout.

'Shrewsbury!' exclaimed Sian. 'You walked all that way?'

'Sian!' said Gatty, smiling and sighing at the same time. 'If only you knew.' But even as she said it, she realised no one is really quite as interested in us as we are in ourselves.

'If only you knew,' Joan repeated, mimicking Gatty's voice. 'Oh! Ooh!'

'Stop it, Joan!' said Gatty.

'You're not the same, you're not.'

'I am, though,' said Gatty.

Sian grabbed Gatty again. 'Gatty! You're best! You're best, after Arthur.'

Gatty's heart somersaulted in her breast. She swallowed noisily. 'He got back then,' she said.

'Yes,' said Tanwen. 'You went away and he came back.'

'Here?'

'No . . . no. He went to Verdon first.'

'When?'

'At Easter. Thereabouts.'

'Sir Arthur! Sir Arthur!' grumbled Joan. 'Whoever he is, he'll always be plain Arthur to me.'

'I got a thousand questions!' Gatty said eagerly. 'What and who and how and why and where and when.'

'When!' cried Sian. 'When! Gatty, I wish you'd come home

347

before last Thursday.'

'Why then?' asked Gatty.

'It was the wedding day!'

Gatty felt as if she had been stabbed in the heart. Her legs buckled.

'You should have seen Winnie,' Sian told her. 'All her white silk and pearls, and her flame hair in loops and ringlets. She was the most beautiful girl in the whole world.'

'We only rode back from Verdon the day before yesterday,' Tanwen went on.

'There was feasting and music and dancing for a whole week,' Sian added.

Gatty felt sick. Her head ached. Her eyes ached. Her bones ached.

'And Sir John says next year we can talk about my betrothal,' Sian said excitedly.

Neither Tanwen nor Sian understood quite what Arthur meant to Gatty, or knew how often her thoughts about him and her feelings for him had given her strength during her long pilgrimage. They were both so caught up in their account of the wedding that they didn't notice Gatty's demeanour. So sober; so downcast; even defeated. But Joan thought she understood; she narrowed her eyes. And Snout knew. He put a firm arm around Gatty's waist.

'You all right?' he asked.

Gatty screwed her right foot into the ground.

I knew they were betrothed, she thought. I knew they were going to marry. But why now? Why this soon?

How can we ever be friends?

Gatty was weeping silently. She wanted to crumple up and die. She wanted to go away. To Ewloe. Anywhere. She wanted to be anywhere but here.

'You all right, girl?' Snout asked again.

'What is it?' Tanwen asked gently. 'Gatty?'

Gatty mumbled something, and then she sighed. 'Tired,' she said in a faraway voice.

'They came back here with us,' Sian went on, 'so everyone could see them and wish them joy. They've gone to Catmole now.'

Snout nodded kindly. 'Later, girl,' he said. 'We're done in. Both of us.'

Tanwen put her left arm lightly round Gatty's shoulders. 'You're so tired,' she said. 'Come to the hall.'

53

There was no one in the great hall except for the two hounds, stretched out by the fire. Tempest opened one eye; then Storm began to rap the marl with his tail. The moment Gatty gave a little cry and sang out their names, they leaped up and mobbed her.

The small fire licked and spat. It twisted its orange fingers.

'Sir John and Lady Helen will be in the solar,' Tanwen said.

'We can go up,' declared Sian.

'I must tell them first.'

'It doesn't matter,' said Sian. 'Come on! No, Tempest, not you!'

So Sian led the way up to the small solar, two steps at a time.

Gatty felt unprepared to meet Sir John and Lady Helen. Almost unable. She just wanted to be on her own.

Sian swung open the oak door without even knocking. 'Father!' she said loudly. 'Mother! Guests!'

Sir John stood up, irritably waving his right arm. 'Sian! How many times do I have to tell you?'

Then Gatty appeared in the dark frame of the door.

'Dear God!' exclaimed Sir John. 'Our pilgrim!'

Lady Helen jumped up. '*Gogoniant*!' she cried. She hurried across the solar and swept Gatty into her arms. 'Oh, Gatty! What a sight!'

'We thought they were raiders,' Sian said accusingly. 'They stole up on us.'

'So who is this?' Sir John enquired.

'Oh!' said Gatty. 'Snout. One of us pilgrims.'

'So I see,' Sir John replied.

'God go with you, sir,' said Snout.

'Well!' asked Lady Helen. 'Where are all the others? Lady Gwyneth. Is she here?'

Gatty drew in her breath. 'No,' she said slowly. She looked at Snout.

Snout nodded. 'We'll tell you everything,' he said.

Seeing Gatty and Snout so exhausted and mud-stained, smelling their sour sweat, and learning they'd walked all the way from Shrewsbury and not eaten since breaking their fast, Sir John observed, 'All right! We've been waiting for news of you for almost ten months, so we can certainly wait a little longer.'

'No!' cried Sian, hopping around.

'Sian!'

'I told them about the wedding.'

'There's much to tell and much to ask,' said Sir John. 'And of course Oliver will want to hear every word.'

'Twice!' said Sian.

Sir John's expression softened. 'Gatty! Get Slim to give you both something to eat. Wash yourselves.'

'In the moat,' added Sian.

'No, not in the moat,' said Sir John, flapping Sian away with his right hand. 'Ask Slim to warm a pan of water, and give you a pot of soap. Wash away all the aching miles. Tanwen will find you clean clothes.'

Gatty couldn't wash away her heartache, though.

Arthur! She shaped his name with her lips without voicing it. Arthur, you know me. You know me like I know myself. You always did. What am I to do without you?

Then Gatty remembered the saying, the one Brother Gabriel had told her, about how God never asks us to suffer more than we can bear.

That's not true, she thought. He does ask us to. He takes away the people we love.

Gatty swirled the dirty water in her washing-pan and tossed it out of the kitchen door. Miserable and dry-eyed, she began to draw lines with her forefinger on the inside of the bowl.

Four legs. And a belly. A back. Two mounted figures.

A winding track. A stream larking beside it.

Five parallel lines. The notes of a song dancing along them.

Gatty stared into the bowl, trembling, and, once again, tears sprang into her eyes. They dropped into the bowl. Gatty's sigh was as deep as a dark well of lost dreams. Angrily, she wiped all the lines out.

What now, she kept asking herself. What am I to do?

Gatty put the bowl over her head like a cowl. A shield.

You and me, she thought, I know we're not close like we used to be. I mean, before you went away to be a squire. It's just that when we did meet. When we did . . . Please, little Jesus. Help me to understand. Help me to bear this.

That evening, Sir John himself made up the fire, as if it were Christmas Day, and everyone ranged themselves around it. Gatty and Snout sat side by side facing Sir John and Lady Helen. Oliver and Slim were on their left, and Sian sat next to her mother's chamber-servant, Tanwen.

'Now then!' said Sir John with no small satisfaction, stretching out his long legs. 'Where do we begin?'

Oliver cleared his throat. 'By thanking God for guarding Gatty and Snout, and guiding them home. By thanking God.'

'Very true,' said Sir John. 'And after that?'

'At the beginning,' said Sian.

Lady Helen shook her head. 'That way we'll be here all night. Gatty and Snout must tell us what matters most.'

'That's right,' said Sir John. 'Tomorrow we'll talk again, and ask and tell much more.'

'About the wedding,' said Sian.

'And the harvest,' said Sir John. 'Ghastly! The worst in my lifetime. We'll have to slaughter half our cattle before winter's over – there's nothing to feed them on. Oh, Gatty! I should tell you. A couple of things.'

'What, sir?'

'Your cow, Hopeless. She died on me this autumn.'

'Oh no!' cried Gatty. Her eyes filled with tears.

'I'm afraid so.'

'Not Hopeless.'

'Also,' said Sir John, 'I've put Ruth and Howell into your old cottage.'

Gatty lowered her eyes. She felt like the ghost of herself.

'Don't look so doleful!' She could hear Sir John's voice. 'Time waits for no one.'

'Ruth's got a baby,' chirruped Sian. 'Guess what she's called it.'

Gatty sighed. I always slept with Hopeless, she thought. She kept me company.

'Ruth!' announced Sian. 'Gatty, are you listening?'

'All the women in that family are called Ruth,' Lady Helen said.

'It's Jewish,' said Gatty.

'What is?' Sian asked.

'Ruth.'

'How do you know?'

'Now!' said Sir John. 'The two of you must have been travelling for weeks and months.'

'One hundred and seven days, sir,' Snout told him.

'Dear God! No wonder you're worn out.'

'Arthur did for even longer,' said Sian. 'He told me about it at the wedding. And about coming home and seeing Winnie for the first time.'

'One hundred and seven days,' Sir John repeated. 'You must be glad to be home.'

'But where's Lady Gwyneth?' asked Lady Helen. 'Is she all right? Has she gone straight to Ewloe?'

Gatty and Snout leaned a little towards one another; they pressed shoulders. Gatty drew a deep breath and puffed out her cheeks, and then very slowly she let all her breath out again.

'What is it?' asked Lady Helen

Gatty stood up and walked round the fire behind Tanwen. 'Change places with me,' she instructed her.

'What is it?' Lady Helen asked again.

Gatty sat down and took her left hand. 'What you fear,' she said, in a steady, tender voice. 'My lady.'

Lady Helen turned to her. 'No! No, it's not true. Tell me it's not.'

'My lady,' Gatty said again.

'Oh! Poor soul!' Lady Helen cried. 'Poor, poor soul! What happened?'

So then Snout gently explained how, in Venice, Lady Gwyneth's stomach had burst inside her.

'I sat with her when she died,' Gatty said, 'and I promised to get to Jerusalem, no matter what! To get to Jerusalem and pray for her soul.'

'Austin couldn't, though,' Snout told them. 'Gatty saved his life on the edge of a precipice but his hand was mangled.'

'Black and green,' said Gatty.

'Who is Austin?' asked Oliver.

'Austin?' said Gatty. 'Oh! Lady Gwyneth's priest.'

Oliver puffed up his chest like an offended hen. 'Her

354

priest! Are you saying her priest didn't reach Jerusalem?'

'The doctor told him he had to stay in Venice or he'd lose his hand,' Snout explained.

'And maybe he did anyway,' Gatty said sadly. 'Maybe he lost it.'

'Arthur lost his gold ring,' said Sian. 'He told me he did. That was in Venice.'

Gatty's heart lurched.

'Lost!' said Tanwen. 'Is that what he told you?'

'Where?' asked Gatty.

'On the beach near his camp. You ask him, Gatty. He'll tell you what happened.'

Gatty felt breathless. I will, she thought. I will, anyhow.

Oliver tutted and shook his head. 'So the priest had to stay in Venice.'

'And then I got left behind in Cyprus,' Gatty told them. 'Because I had a baby.'

'A baby!' Lady Helen and Tanwen exclaimed, and Oliver sat right forward on his bench.

'You had a baby?' gasped Sian.

Gatty smiled. 'Not my own! I'll explain later. I got left behind and the ship's captain wouldn't wait and the others had to go on but Snout, my brave Snout, you stayed behind and waited for me. Otherwise . . . I don't know what.'

Now Oliver was utterly dismayed. 'So . . . so you . . . you didn't . . .' His voice rose and broke, and ended in a squeak. 'You couldn't get to Jerusalem?'

Gatty gazed at Snout. Then she stared into the fire. Sir John noticed how calmly she listened and how still she sat. She always used to be so restless, he thought. The Gatty who left Caldicot was a girl; the Gatty who has come back is a young woman.

'We did,' Gatty said in a low voice.

'You did!' Sir John exclaimed. 'You did reach Jerusalem?'

Gatty nodded.

'Glory be!' cried Lady Helen.

'Why didn't you say so before?' Oliver demanded.

What was it? Everyone's excitement? The gold ring? Snout beside her? Her own achievement. When Gatty raised her river eyes, hot from the fire, they were filled with light. Not dancing but not drowning.

'We could have stayed in the Holy Land,' said Snout. 'With Sir Faramond.'

'Who?' asked Sir John.

'He was a crusader, sir. A Norman, but he spoke English.'

'He's married to a Saracen,' Gatty added.

Oliver opened and shut his mouth. He turned pink. 'A Christian!' he said. 'Married to a Saracen.'

'Yes, sir,' said Snout. 'Brother Gabriel told us it does happen sometimes.'

'Hundreds of times in Spain,' added Gatty. 'Kit the Trader told me.'

Oliver was breathing heavily. He was too upset to say anything.

'Oliver,' said Gatty. 'It's not like you thought. Not like you told me. They haven't got tails, none of them.'

'They're enemies of God,' Oliver said.

'I know you think that,' said Gatty, 'and I know crusaders do, but me and Snout have met lots of them. I've worked it out, I have. They're good and bad, all mixed up, just like Christians are.'

'God in heaven!' exploded Oliver. 'You're quite wrong.'

'Anyhow,' said Gatty brightly, looking across the fire at Oliver. 'It's all because of you.'

'What is because of me?'

'Because of you, Oliver, I can read.'

Oliver blinked several times. 'You can read?'

'And write.'

'My child!'

'That letter you wrote to Austin. Remember?'

'God be praised!'

'Not perfect, mind,' said Gatty.

Oliver laced his stubby hands over his stomach. 'Well! Who is?'

'And she can sing,' added Snout.

'Everard's taught me much more,' Gatty told him. 'He's the choirmaster in Chester cathedral.'

'You should hear her,' Snout told them.

'We certainly will!' Sir John said.

'We must give thanks for Gatty's and Snout's homecoming,' said the priest.

'Quite right!' agreed Sir John. 'In church. Everyone in the manor.'

'And Christmas is coming!' Lady Helen added.

Gatty and Snout glanced at each other. Each knew what the other was thinking.

'We . . .' Snout began. 'Well . . .'

'What is it?' asked Sir John.

'We got to get back to Ewloe, sir.'

'Not before Christmas,' Sir John said.

'No,' said Sian. 'I've made a new Christmas riddle.'

'We must,' said Gatty. 'Our companions may be back by now. Austin and Everard and Emrys and Tilda and Nakin!'

'They don't even know we're alive,' Snout explained, 'and we don't know if they are either. We haven't heard anything about them – not since the messages they left in Jerusalem.'

'And I got to find out about Nest and her baby,' said Gatty, shaking her head.

Sir John smiled grimly. 'Well, then!' he said. 'We mustn't stand in your way.'

'I got to tend Griffith's grave, sir,' Gatty said, 'and dig a lock of Lady Gwyneth's hair into it. And I got to talk to

Austin, and give him something from Lady Gwyneth.'

'I understand,' said Sir John. 'Duty first. Quite right.'

'Then we must all give thanks before you go,' Oliver said. 'And you, child, will you sing for us?'

'And tell us about golden Jerusalem?' asked Lady Helen.

'And all,' said Gatty, eagerly.

Sir John considered Gatty. 'You will come back?' he said slowly.

Gatty didn't reply. She thought about Arthur, and the wedding. About Hopeless. About her cottage.

'Gatty?'

'Sir?'

'You will come back.' This time it was less of a question, more of a quiet statement – warm and firm and understanding. Sir John gave his wife a meaningful look.

'It was a bad day when I gave you away to Ewloe,' Lady Helen said. 'Gatty, I need you here.'

'We all do,' said Sir John. 'Don't we, Oliver?'

'The child can read,' said the priest. 'And write. And sing. Who else in Caldicot can do that?'

Sir John nodded thoughtfully. 'You see, Gatty,' he said.

'Now that Gwyneth has no further need of you,' Lady Helen added. 'The poor, poor soul!'

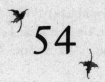

54

Gatty spread her arms and ran, yelling, into the deep bed of leaves beneath the copper beech. She staggered and fell flat on her face.

For some while, she lay there, motionless. Then she rolled over.

'What is it?' asked Snout.

'I don't know what to do.'

Snout smiled down at Gatty. 'In your coat of many colours,' he said. 'Come on!'

Gatty stood up and slapped away some of the leaves, pink and cinnamon and rust. 'When that messenger told us we were only one day's walk away, I wanted to come here so much,' she said, 'but after we got here, I wanted to go away.'

'I know.'

'Then Sir John and Lady Helen told me they wanted me to come back.'

'So did Oliver.'

'And that made me want to. But now!'

'What?'

'Everything reminds me. Everything clutches me. This fish-pond, this is where me and Arthur saved Sian when she went through the ice. Everything, Snout. The Yard and the butts and the sty and Fallowfield . . . everything clutches me. It's too late to come back. There's no hope in it.'

'But it's different now. You can read. You can write.'

'It won't be no different,' Gatty said.

Snout knew when to keep quiet. He shuffled through the crackling leaves.

'Our companions,' said Gatty. 'They're my life now. I keep wondering about Nest. Up at Ewloe, I could begin again.'

'It won't be easy,' said Snout. 'Not without Lady Gwyneth.'

'Nothing's never easy,' Gatty replied.

'Well, you're coming to begin with,' Snout observed. 'See what happens, like what we said.'

As they walked past Merlin's cottage, Gatty told Snout how some people were sure he knew magic, and how Merlin always used to argue with Oliver and how, three years before, he had simply disappeared.

Then the door of Merlin's cottage opened, almost as if he had heard Gatty and Snout talking.

Gatty stared. She took a couple of steps. 'It is!' she cried. 'Merlin!' Gatty strode towards him.

'Ah!' said Merlin, looking pleased. 'You're back.'

'Where have you been?'

Merlin considered Gatty. 'I could well ask you the same question.'

'On our pilgrimage!' Gatty told him. 'We been to Jerusalem. Here! This is Snout.'

'Good morning, Snout,' said Merlin.

'What are you doing here?' Gatty demanded.

'Doing?' Merlin repeated. 'Living.'

'You're living here?'

'Didn't I just say so?'

'But Sir John didn't tell me.'

'He didn't?'

'No.'

'Hmm! Is he beginning to take me for granted? Perhaps it's time to go away again.'

'Where have you been?' Gatty asked again.

'Oh!' said Merlin rather off-handedly. 'Where I was needed.'

'Arthur will be glad,' Gatty exclaimed.

'Isn't he already?'

'What?'

'Glad.'

'I don't know. I haven't seen him.' And then, 'Did you go to the wedding?'

Merlin closed his eyes. 'I certainly did. Wonderful! The very thing I hoped would happen.'

Gatty flinched. Then she took a deep breath. 'Merlin, if I come to live here, if I do, will you help me?'

'Help you? How?'

'I don't know. Talk to me and teach me. Like you helped Arthur.'

Merlin blew on the back of his spotty right hand. 'Will you help yourself?' he asked. 'Isn't that the question?'

Gatty smiled. 'Arthur told me you always asked him questions.'

'Did he now?'

'I can read! I can write!'

'*Mirabile dictu*!' Merlin exclaimed, spreading his cloak. 'Sir John's manor will become a court of love and learning.'

'And I got three questions for you,' Gatty said. 'That night when the old century died, and we saw nine fires burning, and Oliver rang the bell.'

'Is that a question?' Merlin asked.

'Did you fly down from Tumber Hill?'

'Ah!' said Merlin, closing his eyes again.

'And that leaping contest! We saw you, I know, but how can you have jumped forty-seven feet?'

'And the third question?' asked Merlin.

'Is it true what Arthur said? Can you be in two places at the same time?'

Merlin's eyes stayed closed. 'I cannot tell,' he said. And after a while, 'Do you believe such wonders are possible?'

'I do!' cried Gatty. 'Me and Snout, we've seen wonders. One Saracen, he told me that what we don't understand always seems like a wonder.'

Merlin opened his slate-blue eyes and smiled gently at Gatty. 'Well, then,' he said. Then he raised both arms in a kind of benediction, and went back into his cottage.

Merlin looks like that old Saracen, the one in the pound, Gatty thought. They both got the same eyes. And they both like answering questions with questions.

Before returning to the manor house, Gatty and Snout retraced their steps along the bank of the Little Lark, and they came to the place where the track divided: one way led west to Holt and Offa's Dyke, one wound upstream to Wistanstow.

Gatty remembered how Arthur had promised her that one day, one day, they would go upstream.

I told him I hadn't forgot when I wrote him that letter, Gatty thought. I'll hold him to it. Even now, I will!

And then there was a marvel.

Gatty and Snout heard the sound of hooves and saw a horseman advancing through the trees towards them. A riderless cob cantered beside him.

Almost at once, they were all upon each other.

The horseman was Austin.

The riderless cob was Syndod.

Gatty's heart began to thud and bang in her chest, as if it were a songbird imprisoned in a little cage.

'God in heaven!' the priest shouted. 'God in heaven!'

Austin dismounted, and Syndod stared at Gatty as if she could scarcely believe her slightly bloodshot eyes. Then she sort-of barged her with her muzzle, and whinnied.

362

Gatty and Snout and Austin embraced, and even then Syndod was not going to be left out. It seemed nothing short of a miracle that God should have brought them all together, in a damp wood, in the Middle March, on that first day of December.

Streaming with tears, Gatty clung to Austin. Then she buried her face in Syndod's muddy bay coat and, as she'd done very early one morning nine months before, she caught her pony's delicate breath. Sweet April grass. Violets.

'God gives us marvels and moments such as these,' said Austin. 'They're consolations. Light in the darkness.'

'Amen,' chimed Gatty and Snout.

Now came all the words – a stream, then a torrent. Austin told Gatty and Snout he was utterly amazed to see them and they said they'd arrived at Caldicot only the previous evening, and were on their way to Ewloe; Austin said in that case they could all go back together, and that he and the others had reached Ewloe just fourteen days before. Then he showed them how his right hand had completely healed, leaving only a jagged scar.

'But what are you doing here?' Gatty asked.

'As you can imagine,' Austin replied, 'I scarcely wanted to set off on another journey. But it's my duty to tell Lady Helen about Lady Gwyneth.'

'We've told her,' said Gatty.

Austin nodded. 'I suppose you have,' he said in a resigned voice. 'And then, I knew I must tell Lady Helen and Sir John about how we'd . . . mislaid you.' The priest gave Gatty a keen look. His bushy eyebrows kept twitching.

Together they walked back towards the manor house, Gatty leading Syndod, her bright voice rising, dipping and rising.

She and Snout told Austin how they had reached Jerusalem, but not before having to wait in Cyprus for three weeks, and bouncing across the Inland Sea in a tiny fishing-boat, and being held overnight in a pound and rescued by a knight-monk, and surrounded by Bedouin murderers.

'And in Jerusalem,' Austin asked, 'you prayed for Lady Gwyneth's soul?'

'I did!' said Gatty jubilantly. 'In Holy Sepulchre, and everywhere!'

'Meanwhile,' said Austin, 'I waited in Venice, and began to doubt whether the others were going to come back. They were more than two weeks late.'

'What happened?' asked Snout.

'Gobbo's ship was battered by storms. He had to put in at Ragusa for repairs.'

'Nest!' said Gatty. 'Is she all right?'

'She is,' Austin replied, lifting his eyes to heaven.

'She found Sei?'

'Oh yes.'

'What?'

'He didn't want her to stay in Venice.'

'No!' cried Gatty.

Austin nodded thoughtfully. 'So she came back with us – crying most of the way.'

'Nest!' said Gatty sadly. 'Poor Nest! What about her baby?'

'Safe inside,' Austin reassured her.

'God be praised!'

Austin read Snout's thoughts. 'And Hew's all right too,' he told him.

Snout gave the priest a huge, grateful smile and, after that, his face was wreathed in smiles all day.

'He'll make a good altar-boy, your son will,' Austin said. 'In fact, everyone's all right. We've all got aches and cuts and bruises, of course. And Tilda's hands . . . they're no better, for all her prayers.'

Snout gave a prodigious sniff. 'Like my nose,' he said.

'In fact,' Austin went on, 'Tilda says they're worse than before. As you can imagine, everyone at Ewloe is distressed about Lady Gwyneth. Everyone's grieving for her and very anxious.'

'What will happen to Nest?' asked Gatty.

'It's not only Nest,' the priest replied. 'What will happen to us all? Who's going to be the next Lord of the Manor? Will the Earl of Chester and the Welsh lords fight over Ewloe? They've done so before. We began to talk about all this in Venice, after Lady Gwyneth died, and the nearer we got to home, the more often we thought about it.'

'It was the same with us,' said Snout.

'But Nest can stay at Ewloe, can she?' Gatty persisted.

'Nest's not the first girl to have a baby out of wedlock,' Austin replied. 'We'll look after her, if that's what you mean.'

'I'll be there to help her,' Gatty said. 'I promised her I would. The end of February.'

'But as to what will happen after that,' Austin went on, 'none of us knows. As if things aren't bad enough, with the harvest failing.'

'Here too,' Gatty told him.

'I suppose the Earl of Chester may summon me to talk to him,' the priest said, 'but I fear we can do little or nothing. English or Welsh, the lords of the land make their choices and decisions without taking much notice of their priests or people.'

'And Syndod?' said Gatty. 'My Syndod! You brought her all that way? Over the mountains and all.'

'Don't thank me,' Austin said.

'What do you mean?'

Austin rubbed his dark chin. 'When I spoke to Lady Gwyneth before she died, she told me she was proud of you.'

'Did she?' said Gatty in a small voice.

'She said she wanted you to have Syndod. She said that when we all got back to the stables in London . . .'

'Like we didn't!' interrupted Gatty.

'. . . I was to keep her for you.'

'Keep Syndod for me?' Gatty said wonderingly.

'And astonish you!' added Austin, with a sharp smile.

'But what if we'd gone back to the livery stables?' Gatty asked. 'What if we'd done that and Syndod wasn't there?'

'We had no way of knowing whether you'd come back to Venice, but it didn't seem very likely,' Austin replied. 'To tell you the truth, it didn't seem likely you'd come home at all.'

'That's what we thought sometimes,' Gatty said.

'But in case you did . . .' Austin said, 'Nakin made arrangements with the stablemaster in Treviso, and Nest rode Syndod back to London.'

'Nest!'

'And when the time came to sell our horses back to Sayer . . . you remember him?'

'Sayer and Solomon!' said Gatty with a smile.

'I kept Syndod.'

'Oh, Austin!' exclaimed Gatty, shaking her golden head in amazement.

Still talking and talking, Gatty and Snout and Austin crossed the stone bridge, and tied up the two horses.

Then Gatty led the way in and walked straight up to Sir John and Lady Helen, who were standing beside the fire with Oliver.

'Another pilgrim!' said Sir John.

Flushed and eager, Gatty introduced Austin, and told them he had come all the way from Ewloe.

'So who should we expect next?' Sir John asked, giving Austin a little sideways smile.

'Sir John de Caldicot!' said Austin in his strong, deep voice. 'Lady Helen. I've made this long journey in vain.'

'No journey's in vain,' Oliver interrupted. 'No journey. I'll give you chapter and verse.'

Sir John held up one hand. 'Later, Oliver, if you will.'

'My duty, my sad duty . . .' Austin began.

'We know,' said Lady Helen. 'Poor soul! She had the dragon's blood in her veins.'

Austin slowly and gravely made the sign of the cross. 'Before she died, she spoke lovingly of you,' he said.

Lady Helen lowered her eyes and gently shook her head.

'And then,' Austin continued, 'the second purpose of my journey! It was to tell you that this sweet . . . Gatty . . . had been left behind in Cyprus and was unlikely, most unlikely ever to find her way back home.' Austin paused and looked warmly at Gatty and Snout. 'Never in my life have I made a journey for so little reason. And never, I may add, have I been so happy to do so.'

'Indeed!' said Lady Helen, clapping her hands.

'Austin's brought Syndod!' Gatty told them joyfully.

'Who?' asked Sir John.

'My cob! My Welsh cob!'

'There's a good name!' Lady Helen said. 'Syndod.'

'He brought her back from Venice,' Gatty said. 'And you know I told you about Austin's hand,' Gatty went on, 'all black and green. Look at it now!'

Austin held up his right hand. 'It was mangled,' he said. 'And but for our Gatty, I'd have been mangled all over. Like a rabbit after a kite's finished with it.'

'Can you write with it?' Oliver enquired.

Austin smiled. 'I'm left-handed,' he replied.

'But you don't use it, I hope,' Oliver said darkly. 'Your left hand.'

'I found a Saracen doctor in Venice,' Austin told them, 'and he had a cure. All kinds of herbs I'd never even heard of before.'

'You see,' said Gatty. 'It's like I said. They've got medicines and know about the stars and singing and snake-charming. They haven't got tails.'

'But they are not Christian,' said Oliver, between his teeth.

'The Saracens are certainly infidels,' Austin said, 'but a fair number of them live in Venice and they do have great skills. They're good, kind people. I've seen them with my own eyes. Your Gatty, she's an eager student!'

Oliver sniffed. 'I dare say,' he said. And then he relented. 'You taught her to read? And write?'

'As you asked me to do,' Austin replied.

Oliver puffed himself up a little and beamed. 'To the best of my knowledge,' he declared, 'Gatty is one of a kind.'

'One Gatty is quite enough!' said Sir John.

'Outside the monasteries,' Oliver went on, 'is there any other Marcher woman, any at all, young or old, who can read and write?'

'I just remembered something,' said Gatty.

'I have just remembered something,' Oliver corrected her.

'Yes.' Gatty scooped up the gown of her cloak, still spotted with mud and dung; she thumbed-and-forefingered the hem, and then began to tear at it with her teeth.

The others watched her without saying a word.

'That's it!' Gatty exclaimed triumphantly, ripping the hem and secreting something in the palm of her hand. 'Poor old cloak!'

'What is it, Gatty?' Sir John asked.

'I forgot and I just . . . I have just remembered. Before Lady Gwyneth died, she gave me something and said I mustn't tell no one about it. No one at all.' Gatty smiled ruefully at Snout. 'Not until I got home.' Gatty turned to Austin. 'And then, Lady Gwyneth said, I must be certain to give it to you.'

Gatty opened the palm of her right hand. On it lay the little, almond-shaped silver seal. The dragon, winking.

Austin's white face flushed. 'You know what this is?'

'No,' said Gatty. 'Must be important, though.'

The priest's breath was quite jerky. 'Oh yes!' he said. 'In her will, Lady Gwyneth speaks of this seal. Y *ddraig*. The dragon.'

'What is it, then?' Lady Helen asked.

'Lady Gwyneth says that if she falls mortally ill while she's on pilgrimage, she will entrust this seal to another person, and tell that person to give it to me – to give it to me once we're back home.'

'Like I have,' said Gatty.

'Like I have done,' said Oliver under his breath.

'In her will,' Austin continued, 'Lady Gwyneth says that if anyone should give me this seal within twelve months of her death . . .'

'What?' asked Sir John.

'. . . that person would in return be entitled to a parcel of Lady Gwyneth's own land.'

Lady Helen clapped her hands over her mouth.

'Land?' Sir John repeated, looking very serious.

'Her own acres,' said Austin, 'close to Ewloe Castle.'

Sir John looked at Gatty, and frowned. 'Are you sure?' he said.

'Quite sure,' said Austin.

'But she's . . . well, a chamber-servant.'

'Quite sure,' Austin repeated firmly. 'I know, if anyone does, how very greatly Lady Gwyneth esteemed Gatty.'

Sir John looked at Gatty, this girl he had known since the day she was born. 'I've never heard of such a thing,' he said. 'It won't be easy for you to claim it.'

'You understand?' Austin told Gatty. 'Your own land.'

'Me?' said Gatty.

'Oh Gatty!' cried Lady Helen. 'This will change your life.'

'It certainly will,' said Sir John. 'With land comes responsibility. You'll have duties to the people who work your land, just as they will have duties to you. With land comes position and respect.'

'Your own chamber-servant!' Lady Helen exclaimed. 'What you wear and what you eat and what you eat off and what you drink and who you know and . . .'

'Yes,' said Sir John. 'This will change everything.'

55

'Go up to Arthur's old room, then,' Lady Helen said. 'That's empty.'

'Thank you, my lady.'

'I can't think why, though,' she added. 'The hall's warmer.' And then, as Gatty bounded up the fourteen wooden steps to the gallery, carrying her cloak and saddle-bag, 'Don't take long now! Gatty!'

Arthur's old room wasn't empty, though.

Gatty inspected the slice of apple-tree trunk – the one she had helped to haul up from the Yard and Arthur used as a perch for his inkwell. She sat in the short window-seat, and put up her knees, and pressed her back against one side of the alcove and her feet against the other. She felt the late afternoon wind, chill on her cheek as it funnelled though the wind-eye, slightly hissing. She ran her hand over the ramping dragon Arthur had cut into the stone on the left side of the alcove. She listened to something or other scritching in the thatch.

The small stone room was charged with memories.

Gatty began to peel off her clothes, and as she did she remembered snatches of the song she had sung inside her head almost twelve months before:

> Will I be standing in the manger?
> Will I be kneeling at His crib?
> I got no gift I can bring,
> But I can sing . . . I'll bring songs!

The church bell began to ring: first two jerky croaks, somehow caught in the bell's bronze throat, but then a clear, lovely, rhythmical pealing.

A church service, thought Gatty. For me? Well, me and Snout.

Gatty drew her beautiful yellowy-green silk dress from her saddle-bag, and carefully spread it out on the flagstones.

No, she thought. I can't! I can't wear it. Who does she think she is? That's what they'll say. Everyone will.

Gatty stared down at the dress.

Maybe Joan's right. I'm not the same. Not the same as I was.

I am, though. I'm the same but not the same because I seen so much and learned so much. But being different isn't wrong, is it? That old man in the pound, he said difference can be a threat but it can be a wonder.

Gatty inched her tongue through her lips. I am who I am, she thought, and I can't do nothing about it. They'll get used to it. They'll have to.

I know! I'll cover my dress up in church. I won't let no one see it, not until after.

Gatty pulled off her tunic. Then she raised the dress over her head, and she slid her freckled arms into its airy, gorgeous sleeves.

It's strange, she thought. These sleeve-dragons with their pearl eyes, and Arthur's alcove-dragon; my silver seal-dragon; and Lady Gwyneth with dragon's blood in her veins. Dragons everywhere!

Gatty's dress rustled and settled around her. When she pinched the silk, it stayed pinched – and she almost had to pinch herself to believe it was really hers. She placed the grey-green sash around her slim waist, and clasped the square, silver buckle.

Before she had time to find and put on the amber necklace

Signor Umberto had given her, Gatty heard steps galloping up the staircase. Very quickly she gathered her cloak around her.

The door burst open.

'Gatty!' exclaimed Sian. 'Are you ready?'

'No!' said Gatty.

'You've got to be. Everyone's waiting.'

Gatty pulled her violet ribbon out of her bag. 'Here,' she said, 'tie this round my wrist.'

'Why?'

'Because I say so.'

'Cert-ain-ly, my la-dy!' Sian replied, exaggerating each syllable. 'Come on! Everyone's here!'

'What do you mean?'

'Lord Stephen. Lady Judith.'

'Lord Stephen!'

'Sir Walter de Verdon and Lady Anne.'

'Them!' exclaimed Gatty.

'Sian!' called a voice from far below. 'Gatty!' It was Lady Helen.

'I didn't know they were coming,' Gatty said.

'Much better than that!' said Sian, her eyes flashing.

'Oh no!' cried Gatty, alarmed.

'What's wrong?'

'I didn't know! I didn't know they were. I just wish . . .'

'What, Gatty?'

'I just wish, well, it was everyone at Caldicot. I wish Nest were here.'

'Who?'

'She's good at all this. Better than I'll ever be. I haven't even run a comb through my hair.'

'You never did before,' said Sian in a surprised voice.

'Here! Help me with this hair-net.'

'It's gold thread!' breathed Sian.

'Just fix it with these pins. Now! My perfume.'

'Perfume!'

Gatty rummaged in her saddle-bag and uncorked a small pot. Then she dipped her little finger-tip into it, and dabbed it behind Sian's left ear.

'Eek!' exclaimed Sian. 'It smells like Christmas!'

'Cinnamon and sandalwood and musk,' Gatty told her, dabbing some onto herself. 'Now this.'

'What is it?'

'For your lips. Brazil-wood cream.'

'You're different, Gatty,' said Sian enthusiastically. 'What else have you got?'

'Gatty! Sian!' It was Lady Helen's disembodied voice again. 'Hurry up!'

Gatty smeared some cream on her own lips. Then she scooped up her pilgrim's hat, jammed it on, and tied the scarf under her chin.

'Here's your staff,' said Sian. 'Come on!'

Gatty could hear all the chatter and laughter coming from inside the church. But when Sian unlatched the heavy oak door and swung it open, everyone turned round to look at her. And except for one low whistle and a snigger, and a behind-the-hand, stifled 'Wooh!' they all went quiet. Oliver was waiting in front of the rood-screen, with Austin and Snout on either side of him.

'A time to be born and a time to die,' he said, grimacing, 'and a time to wait, and wait, and wait.'

'I know,' said Gatty. She looked at Oliver, abashed, and her long, golden eyelashes flickered.

'Yes,' said Oliver. 'Well!'

Snout took Gatty's right hand. 'My fair pilgrim,' he said.

'My only Snout,' replied Gatty.

'Sian,' said Oliver, 'you may go and tell Sir John and Lady

Helen that we're ready to receive them and all their guests. You may tell them we're at last ready to receive them.'

'Shall I tell them twice then?' asked Sian, wide-eyed.

'Go on with you,' said the priest. 'And don't trip over your long tongue.'

Sian hurried out, leaving the church door wide open, and the villagers began to murmur and then to chatter again. Gatty inspected the wall-painting of Jesus sitting on a rainbow, and that miserable huddle of men and women standing outside the gates of Hell, and the glaring monster with the half-naked woman between his teeth. As soon as I can, she thought, I want to look at that painting in the vestry. The one of the fishermen. I want to read its gold words.

Then Gatty heard a noise in the porch, and Sir John with Lady Helen on his arm stepped into the church.

Gatty stared at the door into the dark. Next, Lord Stephen limped in, leaning heavily on a stick; Lady Judith's right hand was clamped under his other elbow. Then came Lady Alice de Gortanore, so light on her feet she looked as if she had been blown in by the wind. And she was followed by Sir Walter and Lady Anne de Verdon, smiling and sprightly as lambs.

Still Gatty stared, fearful. Her heart! It throbbed in her chest, her temples, her wrists.

And then, spring-heeling, bold, and one step ahead as usual, came flame-haired Winnie.

Gatty's breath. She didn't have any!

Still she stared.

Spring-heeling, bold, and one step ahead – of Tom de Gortanore.

Tom de Gortanore! Funny, ambling, kind, blue-eyed Tom, Arthur's cousin, who never hurt a fly if he could help it.

Gatty gazed at them as they followed the others up the nave to the benches. She stared at them, uncomprehending.

While Sir John's guests were taking their places, Sian advanced on Gatty. 'I'm your chamber-servant!' she said in a hoarse whisper.

'What's happened?' Gatty asked at once.

'What do you mean?'

'What are they doing?'

'Who?' asked Sian.

'Winnie and Tom. Where's Arthur?'

'Arthur?'

'You told me. You told me. Their wedding, Arthur, Winnie . . .'

Sian's face lit up. 'Not Arthur!' she exclaimed loudly, and then she put her hand over her mouth.

'Not?' gasped Gatty.

'Of course not! While Arthur was on crusade, Winnie fell in love with Tom.'

Oliver cleared his throat and clucked twice. 'May our thoughts and feelings and the words of our mouths please you, O God,' he began.

Gatty didn't know whether she was boiling or freezing; dressed or naked; whether she was standing downside up on the floor or upside down on the roof-beam. You could have bounced her floating heart from side to side of the church.

But as Oliver assured everyone that, despite the failure of their harvest, they were twice blessed in one season, first by Winnie's and Tom's marriage and then by Gatty's return, she knew she was laughing out loud, laughing and sobbing. Both.

'I told you all,' Oliver called out, 'that, God willing, one of our own lambs would reach Jerusalem. Do you remember? I asked her to pray for each one of us at the Golden Gate and each of the holy places.'

'You did too,' Snout said to Gatty under his breath.

Oliver beamed. 'And now Gatty has come back to us,' he

said. 'The same but changed. She can sing, you all know that. But because of Austin here, the priest at Ewloe, she can read! She can write!'

Austin's bushy eyebrows twitched. 'The truth is,' he said in his powerful, dark voice, 'Gatty all but taught herself.'

Oliver locked his hands over his portly stomach in almost complete satisfaction. 'Not perfectly, mind. But then, who can?'

In the inviting pause that followed, a voice called out loudly from the back of the church, 'You, Oliver!'

Everyone laughed.

'I suppose that was Macsen,' Oliver said.

Another pause, and then the same voice drawled, 'I suppose it was,' and everyone laughed a little bit more.

'Gatty and Snout are our lifeline to Bethlehem,' Oliver continued. 'Each one of you, high-born or low-born, healthy or hungry, old or young, man or woman, is joined through them to the birthplace of our Saviour, just as each baby is joined – joined by its *umbilicus* – to its mother. Draw near with faith.'

Oliver gave the pilgrims an expansive wave and stepped aside.

Gatty loosed her scarf, swept off her hat, and at once remembered she was wearing her golden hairnet! There was nothing she could do about it.

She looked around at the people who had known her all her life, all gathered now under one roof, and smiled calmly. Then she turned her gaze to Sir John's noble guests. Proudly, she looked at Winnie.

Winnie observed the golden ring on the middle finger of Gatty's right hand, and the rash of green silk below the hem of her thick grey cloak. She took note of her golden hairnet. Winnie returned Gatty's long gaze, and then she lowered her eyes just a little; very slightly, she inclined her head.

Gatty took a deep breath. 'When we rode through Dung Gate on our donkeys,' she began, 'out of Jerusalem, you know what I thought? I've been riding to Bethlehem all my life! Listening to Oliver and the Bible and that. Looking up at this wall-painting here – the star, the shepherds, the manger . . .

'There's so much! Well, I got to begin somewhere. We rode through groves of orange trees, and pomegranates, and figs. And me and Snout, we saw the well, the one the Star in the East fell right into.'

'And the cave,' added Snout. 'We saw the cave where Herod the King threw the corpses of all the little children, ten thousand of them.'

'And another cave,' said Gatty, 'glistening and white, where Mary fed Jesus.'

It was so quiet you could hear the sound of the candles burning. And in this stillness hushed and deep as midnight, the latch of the church door lifted.

Everyone started and caught their breath!

Through the door and straight into the shadowy gloom at the back of the church stepped a small woman, wearing a white cloth cap. A man followed her, not smiling but almost smiling – it was Merlin!

Gatty knew Arthur was there. She knew he was standing in the porch. She knew it before he stepped in and closed the door, lightly and fiercely.

For just one startled moment, Gatty and Arthur caught one another's eye.

Oliver cleared his throat. 'The cave where Mary fed Jesus,' he prompted Gatty. 'You saw the cave.'

'Yes,' said Gatty. 'One drop fell from Mary's breast onto the rock, and ever since then that cave has oozed milk.'

'The Church of the Nativity looks like a copse,' Snout told everyone.

'Inside it does,' Gatty agreed. 'A copse of shining birch trees, only all the columns are marble. Silvery-white marble. You go down sixteen steps into the manger. Rock steps. There's a large silver star lying on the ground.'

Gatty closed her eyes. 'I felt like I was unborn,' she said. 'Like I was still in my mother's womb, beginning again.'

'All the pilgrims were laying things on the ground,' Snout went on. 'Bones and badges and stuff. They were asking Jesus and Mary to bless them.'

'I got one thing blessed,' Gatty said, holding up her right hand. 'This ring here! This most beautiful ring, with Mary on it, and Jesus in her arms.'

Gatty didn't look at Arthur. Not quite. But she knew Arthur was looking intently at her.

'Badges and bones,' said Snout. 'Saracens were selling them at their stalls up in the cloister. I told Gatty we'd need every penny we had and she wasn't to buy anything, but she did anyhow! I still don't know what.'

Gatty smiled. Unhurried, she opened her scrip, and burrowed into it.

'You know who it's for, though,' Gatty said.

'Oliver,' Snout replied.

Oliver puffed himself up. He blinked several times.

'When I left Caldicot,' Gatty told him in a low voice, 'I think you were ringing that bell for me. And you wrote to Austin.' She turned back to face everyone. 'It's because of Oliver,' she called out, her voice rising, 'because of Oliver as well as Austin that I can read! I can write!'

Still, Gatty did not look directly at Arthur.

She took out of her scrip a palm-leaf, rolled and secured with thread.

'It looks like a scroll,' Gatty said. 'You can't read it, though.'

Oliver tried to undo the thread, and turned even more pink

than he was before. He began to puff.

'Here!' said Gatty. She put it between her teeth and nipped it. Then she shook her head and smiled sweetly at everyone.

Oliver carefully unrolled the leaf. On the palm lay three royal gifts. The priest examined them so closely his nose almost grazed them; he sniffed them; he just touched them with the tip of his forefinger.

'Gold!' announced Oliver.

The congregation gasped, and everyone who was able to got to their knees, even Lord Stephen and Lady Judith.

'Gold dust!' Oliver called out. 'Frankincense. Myrrh. From Bethlehem.'

At once Oliver turned to face the east, and processed through the choir, followed by Austin. He raised Gatty's gifts in front of the shining cross and then, reverently, he laid them on the altar. The gifts of the three wise men from Arabia.

'Soon as we got to Bethlehem,' Gatty went on, 'Snout and me longed to come home again.' She paused for a moment, going on some inward journey. So many tides and blessings and sorrows. So much she could not tell.

'Yes,' said Gatty, 'home again. We couldn't think of nothing else.' She stared straight into the gloom at the back of the church. 'Once upon a time,' she confided, 'I thought I could walk to Jerusalem instead of going to Ludlow Fair.' Gatty's smile broadened into a grin. 'Where I didn't ought to have gone anyway. Hum beat me for that! And I remember, I asked Arthur, "Where is Jerusalem, anyhow? Is it further than Chester?"'

At the back of the church, in the gloom, a young man called out, 'Gatty! You can't walk to Jerusalem!'

Gatty closed her eyes. She could feel tears springing in them, hot and quick. 'I can and all!' she called out. She was choking.

'You can't,' said the voice at the back of the church, firm and warm, almost teasing. 'Only a magician could. It's across the sea.'

Gatty blinked away her tears. She looked into the gloom where Arthur was. She looked lovingly at the people of Caldicot. She looked into her own heart, and in her beautiful, red-gold voice, steadily she sang:

> 'How many miles to Bethlehem?
> Not very far.
> Will we find the manger
> Lit by a star?
>
> How many miles to Bethlehem?
> Three score miles and ten.
> Can I get there by candle-light?
> Yes, and back again.'

Perched on window-ledges, round-shouldered, and high on the pulpit, arching their necks like swans, squat in their sockets on the bench-ends, all the candles in the church trembled. Everyone in the manor of Caldicot was visited and touched by their light.

Gatty sang again, opening her arms, and everyone sang with her, some of them in tune:

> 'How many miles to Bethlehem?
> Three score miles and ten.'

Gatty's voice got up and danced high over the tune.

> 'Can I get there by candle-light?'

Higher and higher it soared, before coming to rest with peace on its outstretched wings:

> 'Yes, and back again.'

For a moment, so short and forever, there was no sound in the church at Caldicot.

'With our children here,' Oliver called out, 'with our lambs, each of us has been to Bethlehem and back again. When the north wind whistles, when our stomachs knot and cramp, when bony starvation stands at each door, let us remember this. Let us feed on this in our hearts with thanksgiving, as now, Lord, we give thanks that Gatty has come back to us.'

'Amen,' said Sir John.

'Amen,' said his people, almost with one voice.

Sir John stood up and turned round to face everyone. 'In this church,' he said, 'we have heard great wonders. We have seen great wonders. And now, in my hall, you'll find wassail. Two casks of it! Yes, and Slim has made a shredded pie for each man and woman and child in this church. Come, now, and greet our fine pilgrims.'

With this, Sir John gave Lady Helen his arm, and the two of them led the way out of the church, followed by their guests and by Oliver, Austin and Snout.

After this, all the villagers made a rush for the door, gossiping, laughing.

Then Merlin stepped out of the gloom. With his slateshine eyes he gazed at Gatty, unblinking, and she knew he could see all her thoughts, all her feelings; he could see right through her.

Merlin offered his arm to the small woman wearing the white cloth cap, a woman with eyes deep as little wood-violets, and ears that stuck out like Arthur's. Then they too left the silent shell, the almost empty church.

56

So it was.
   Not by chance.

But not as Gatty in daylight or dream had once imagined it.

Perhaps as God ordained it.

Gatty started to walk slowly down the nave from the rood-screen, and out of the blue shade Arthur walked towards her. What? Twenty steps or so. Later, each told the other it seemed like the longest walk in their lives. Over the mind's mountains and across the heart's oceans. Despite, and because, and after, and only when.

Gatty and Arthur met within a field of fallen stars. Right in the middle of the wheel of candlelight, not so much shimmering now as misty and glowing.

Then Gatty shrugged off her dark, heavy cloak. It dropped and subsided at her feet. And there she stood in front of Arthur in her winking silk dress, almost shoulderless, dragon-sleeved.

Arthur bit his lower lip.

Gatty pulled off the gold ring. She had to tug at it a bit. Mary holding Jesus in her arms so safe that black storms could shout and the earth itself could shake and He would still be all right. She took Arthur's strong, warm right hand and slipped the ring on to his fourth finger. It was a perfect fit.

Arthur looked at the ring. He looked at Gatty.

'You found it?'

Gatty nodded.

'On Saint Nicholas?'

She nodded again.

'Oh!' exclaimed Arthur. 'You're wearing your ribbon!'

Gatty inspected it, so tatty and stained, so precious. 'My half,' she said in a husky voice.

'Let me see,' said Arthur.

'Arthur, in my will, I granted you Hopeless. Hopeless, my cow.'

'I know Hopeless.'

'I granted her to you if I didn't come back. But she died this autumn.'

Arthur winced. Then he carefully turned back his left sleeve, exposing his half of the violet ribbon.

Gatty drew in her breath sharply.

'When I came back from the crusade,' Arthur said, 'and you weren't here and I read your letter . . . I should have been happy for you. Escaping from fieldwork. Hunger. Going on your great pilgrimage.'

'And when you told me you were leaving on crusade, and going to Jerusalem . . .' Gatty faltered. 'For two years and maybe three.'

Arthur shook his head. He shook away the hurt. 'You can sing,' he said, almost reverently. 'As angels sing.'

Gatty pushed out her lower lip. 'Oh yes? How do they sing, then, Arthur?'

'You can read.'

'And you're a knight?'

'And write.'

'And Catmole? Your own manor?'

'You too, Gatty! Your own land.'

Gatty shook her head. 'I haven't claimed it yet.'

'Sir John told me. I'll help you. I'll help you claim it.'

'It's up at Ewloe.'

'I know that. I was going to find you there when I got home . . .'

'At Ewloe?'

'. . . and then Sir John said you'd already set out for Jerusalem.'

'We're both there!' Gatty exclaimed. 'Both of us.'

'Where?'

'In Jerusalem.'

'What do you mean?'

'I carved us on the wall, didn't I. The wall in Holy Sepulchre. You and me, riding Pip. We're there, Arthur, now and always!'

'Oh Gatty!'

Gatty, she pulled off her golden hair-net, with the pins still in it. Her silver-gold curls laughed and they danced.

'Now,' repeated Arthur, 'now and always,'

Stars and flames. Gatty's river eyes.

'And all!' she said.

WORDLIST

abaya (Arabic) a black cloak-like dress, covering the whole body, worn by Muslim women

Armenian mouse (in Latin, *Armenius mus*) another name for the stoat or ermine

bakchies (Arabic) a tip

bismallah (Arabic) an Islamic invocation or exclamation, used especially before each chapter of the Koran: 'In the name of Allah, the Merciful, the Compassionate'

braies baggy linen drawers

brazil-wood the red wood of an East Indian tree (imported by the Arabs to Europe) that produces a rosy pigment

burqa (Arabic) a piece of black cloth worn by a Muslim woman to cover her face. Some styles leave the eyes uncovered

buss a two or three-masted ship, sometimes called the *navis* or *bucius*, used for trading

cefn (Welsh) ridge

cantred (in Welsh *cantref*) a district containing one hundred townships

etesian a mild northwest Mediterranean wind that blows in July and the first half of August

fonduk or **funduk** (Arabic) a warehouse

galiote a small long ship with two banks of oars

galley a class of ship equipped with two (bireme) or three (trireme) banks of oars, and one or two masts carrying lateen sails

gambeson a cloth or leather tunic, worn for protection or for padding under armour

groat a silver coin used throughout Europe. It was equal to four pence

hijab (Arabic) a scarf or veil worn by Muslim women

ken (Hebrew) yes

kirtle a loose gown combining a bodice or blouse and a skirt

Knights Hospitaller members of the Sovereign Military and Hospitaller Order of Saint John of Jerusalem, Rhodes and Malta, which was founded during the 11th century as a hospice for pilgrims to the Holy Land

the land oversea the name for the territory, including Palestine and the Nile Delta, over which Christians and Muslims fought during the Crusades

lateen sail a triangular sail suspended at 45° to the mast

marl clay

merchet a sum of money paid to a lord for permission for a daughter to marry

minaret a tall and slender tower connected to a mosque, from the top of which a crier (known as the *muezzin*) calls the people to prayer

mirabile dictu (Latin) amazing to say!

mort d'ancestor a writ served by a man complaining that he had been deprived of an inheritance from his father

morterel pieces of bread or cake boiled in milk

muezzin (Arabic) a public crier who from a minaret calls people to prayer five times each day; a prayer leader

nain (Welsh) grandmother

nef a bulky round ship, raised at the ends to form towers

novice in religious orders, a person (often a child) under probation prior to taking monastic vows

pandy (Welsh) mill

People of the Book Jews and Christians (Islamic law decreed tolerance for them)

the Pillars of Hercules the huge rocks standing at the entrance to the Mediterranean, one in Spain (the Rock of Gibraltar), the other in Morocco

ramping rearing up (a threatening posture)

raston a small, round loaf

reckling the smallest or weakest animal in a litter

rhyd (Welsh) ford

rood-screen a screen (most often made of wood) across the nave of a church, separating the nave from the choir and altar

saetta (Italian) a kind of galley or long ship

samite heavy silk, sometimes threaded with gold

shawm a kind of oboe, with a double reed in the mouth-piece

syndod (Welsh) a marvel, a wonder

twitchel a fork in the road; also a narrow passage between hedges

thuluth (Arabic) an Arabic script used for ornamental inscriptions

umbilicus (Latin) the navel

vellum the best kind of parchment, made from the skin of a calf, lamb or kid

wassail spiced ale

woodwose or **wodwo** a wildman, covered in hair or leaves